V. _ _ _ _

by
Linzi Carlisle

*For my mum and dad, who raised me with an enduring love
for the written word*

Table of Contents

PROLOGUE

The little boy tip-toed into the kitchen, his bare feet cold on the linoleum. He gently stroked the woman's hair from her face, frowning at the fresh bruise revealed. When she didn't stir he took the glass, wiping his thumb over the lipstick smear before touching it to his own lips. With the glass rinsed he lifted her hand and removed the envelope, damp from both the whisky and her tears, and crept up the stairs to the attic room, settling himself at the typewriter. Once he'd done his best to decipher the drunken, smudged scrawls, he began to type, anger coursing through his young veins at the man who caused this much pain to the love of his life.

THE STRUMPET AND THE BROWN PACKET

I knew that little strumpet was up to something as soon as I saw her watching for the postman yesterday.

She thought I wouldn't notice her peering through a crack in her net curtains each time she heard footsteps passing on the pavement, but I did, of course. It was so obvious. She couldn't open the door fast enough when the postman finally walked up her path, later than usual due to Rosemary Spindlebury running after him waving a letter at him and going on about him keep delivering letters for Wisteria Terrace to her by mistake. He'd actually walked back down the road with her, even put a hand on her arm! Then that snobby cow had started giggling with him and coming over all coy, made me sick to be honest. He'd stood there chatting with her for all of five minutes, having his time wasted by some woman with ideas above her station, poor man and him with a job to do too.

Anyway, as I was saying, that little strumpet, Maureen, was very anxious for her delivery. It wasn't very big, a small brown packet. I would've missed it if she hadn't drawn my attention to it by her ridiculously desperate behaviour. She'd grabbed that little packet out of his hands and shut the door before he'd even turned round to go back down the path.

I could just make out through her net curtains that she was going upstairs with it.

The sun was at the wrong angle which meant that even by trying to look from my bathroom window I still couldn't quite see what she was doing up in her bedroom. It really annoyed me, and when Mr Alison, the butcher, phoned about my joint of beef, I was quite short with him, as a result, I'm afraid.

When it got to six o'clock and her poor husband hadn't got in from work last night it got me wondering... he sometimes has to travel for business. I usually know when, as he takes an overnight bag with him in the boot of his car, maybe I'd missed it. I must pay more attention in future...

I made a point of watching her front door closely then, even went without my cup of tea, as I was so sure something was going to happen. Sure enough, I saw that gangly young man who rents rooms above the pub, sloping down the road looking shifty. Calls himself an artist... I just call him a long-haired layabout. Artist, my foot! I haven't seen any paintings being sold. Most he's done is paint Mrs Mark's spare room for her, and charged her an arm and a leg for it no doubt.

Bold as brass he walked up to Maureen's door and didn't even have to knock! She must have left the door on the latch. Once that door closed I could only imagine what was going on in there, I bet she was all over him. Disgusting!

They'd closed the curtains, which was proof they were up to adulterous acts. They didn't go upstairs, that was something, at least she spared her poor husband the indignity of having their marital bed defiled by their fornicating.

I felt very disturbed through dinner (cold ham salad due to the fact that I hadn't had time to cook anything), George looked at me a bit strangely and even asked me if I was okay a couple of times. I managed to find a few excuses to pop upstairs and have a look through the curtains but it was dark by then and I couldn't see anything. When I looked for the last time as I went to bed, her lights were off.

It took me ages to get to sleep, my mind wouldn't switch off from what they'd been up to, filthy pair. I felt quite hot and bothered by it and even had to turn the bedcovers down a bit to cool down.

As soon as George was gone this morning I was back at my window and there it was! Screaming out for the whole world to see! Some tarty little wisp of red satin with black lace, hanging on the line.

My mind went back over her usual laundry offerings... white cotton knickers, the odd beige pair too... these were new. She certainly didn't buy them at Madam Couture in the village, or in Beedham's department store in the next town.

I came over quite odd and shaky at the thought of her cavorting around in them with that so called artist... I must have jogged the curtain a bit too much because the next thing I knew she was looking right up at me as she took them off the washing line. I dropped the curtain back straightaway but I could have sworn she gave me a smug smile...

Right there and then I knew they must have been in the packet she was waiting for so impatiently. Bought from some sex catalogue specially for her dirty little tryst with lover boy.

Now here's her husband arriving home... her looking all sweet and innocent giving him a kiss on the cheek... He has no idea...

It's not right... someone should tell him what a little tart she is...

Of course, I won't be able to sign my name... just a short note perhaps... unsigned... like the other ones...

A DUTIFUL SON

'Here we are, George, it came in this morning. And how is your dear mother?' Mrs Pringle smiled as she popped the bottle of Lavender Dreams into a bag and handed it to him over the counter. 'Is she keeping well? We haven't seen her out and about for, well, it must be months now, close to a year, even.'

'George took the bag with a smile. 'Thank you, Mrs Pringle, Mother is very well, nice of you to ask. But since her fall...'

Mrs Pringle and her assistant nodded and made clucking noises of sympathy.

'He's a good son,' Mrs Pringle chattered away as she bustled around behind her counter, after George had left. 'Fancy, still buying her favourite perfume, regular as clockwork, every month! Two this month, said he misplaced the first one. I practically have it on standing order for him. Pity there's not more like him in this world, caring for an elderly parent, and her out at that lonely cottage all on her own too.'

The subject was forgotten as the bell above the door rang and Britney and Chantelle entered the shop, making a bee-line for the cosmetics displays. Mrs Pringle arched an eyebrow at Sheila, the two women nodding at each other knowingly, as they watched the girls closely.

Sheila picked up the feather duster and headed towards them, making a show of flicking imaginary dust from the bottles of shampoo, close to where the two girls giggled and nudged each other as they examined the mascaras.

With no purchase made, the two girls left the shop, and Sheila tutted as she straightened the display. 'Those new estate girls will be the death of me,' she sighed.

'Let's have some tea,' suggested Mrs Pringle.

~

Sasha opened a bleary eye, grimacing as bright sunlight hit her face. Groping for her watch, she knocked the wine glass from her bedside table, its remaining drops splashing onto the rug. The sound of it rolling across her wood floor hurt her head, and she groaned.

Eleven o'clock. Crap, how did it get so late? Forcing herself into an upright position, she grimaced again, this time at the red wine decorating the cream-coloured rug. The smell of congealed pizza hit her nostrils and bile rose in her throat. Wrinkling her nose in disgust at the half-eaten pizza in its box on the end of her bed, she stood up.

It was Eric's fault. She'd been fine, her screw him attitude having stopped her from feeling hurt at his neglect. The last time she'd seen him had been three weeks ago. Out for drinks at their local pub, they'd ended up overdoing it a bit, Eric especially, and it wasn't until the barman had come over to inform her that they were closing that she'd realised he'd gone. The idiot had gone to the loo half an hour earlier and forgotten that she was even with him. He'd gone home without her, and after that she'd been determined to expunge him from her life, once and for all.

It hadn't seemed to bother him for he'd made no effort to contact her and, if the photo Mandy had sent her from the pub last night was anything to go by, he certainly wasn't missing her. She brought the photo up on her phone, reading the accompanying caption, *Don't shoot the messenger*. Don't worry Mandy, I don't have a gun. There was Eric, grinning like an idiot, red-faced, a beer in one hand, a redhead in the other. Or, to be more specific, a certain body part of the redhead in another.

Get a grip, Sasha, why d'you even let it get to you? He's treated you like crap from the beginning. The trouble was, they'd had fun together, were even good together, at times. It was just that she never knew where she stood with him. Eric, the good times guy, the let's get hammered guy, the I'll see you when I see you guy.

She'd been fine last night, sipping her glass of wine like an adult, only smoking two or three cigarettes as she'd worked on her latest case. And then the photo had arrived and all bets were off. She'd opened another bottle, drunk its contents far too quickly, while smoking the rest of the packet of ciggies, and then she'd ordered her go-to comfort food, pizza with chicken, onion, and green peppers. That had necessitated the opening of another bottle, and well, the rest was history.

Her phone rang. It was Mrs Wendham-Smythe. Oh hell, she'll be wanting to know if I've found Fifi, *her extremely valuable Pomeranian*, yet. Something glimmered in the back of her mind, as she answered the phone, trying to sound efficient, and she rummaged around for her notes. She'd solved it last night, hadn't she, when she'd been studying the photos she'd taken while out on surveillance?

'I have a very good lead that I'm busy following up right now, Mrs Wendham-Smythe. If I'm right I hope to be returning Fifi to you later today.'

Pulling off her tee shirt, she stepped into the shower. It was time to set a trap for the dognappers.

~

'It's only me, Mother!' George hung his jacket on the hook in the hallway, popping his head around the door of the front room.

Mrs Newton smiled at him from her chair and George felt a rush of tenderness. Poor Mother, she'd been through so much, it was a shame she struggled to talk now, but they managed, the two of them. 'I'll make some tea, be with you in a jiffy.'

George hummed as he put the kettle on, laying out a tray with cups and saucers. He placed the bottle of Lavender Dreams on the tray, Mother's favourite, she'd worn it for as long as he could remember.

Bluebottles buzzed at the kitchen window and George sprayed them angrily with the fly spray, waiting for them to die before collecting them up and placing them in the kitchen bin.

'There we are, a nice cup of tea! And I've got a surprise for you, your favourite, Lavender Dreams, for my favourite girl!' Placing the tray down, he opened the bottle of perfume and liberally sprayed some on Mrs Newton's neck. Smiling, she allowed him to lift her arms and spray her wrists too.

'There, that's better! And just for good measure,' George sprayed the perfume around the room. 'Such a beautiful smell, Mother!'

'Well now, I expect you want all the latest news! All is well at home, Dorothy was a little off colour yesterday, but she seemed fine this morning. Mrs Pringle asked after you, you know, Mrs Pringle, from Pringle's Chemist?'

Standing up, George held his mother's tea cup to her lips. 'Not too hot is it? There we are, nothing like a nice cup of tea.' He sat back down and picked up his own cup, sipping it between his chattering.

A buzzing sound distracted him and, frowning, he jumped up. 'Blasted flies! I'll get the spray, must be the weather.'

With the flies dispatched, George resumed his chatting. 'Work's okay, you'll be pleased to hear. Old Mr Ramsbottom's retiring at the end of this month. Of course, by rights I should be in line for his job, but you know what it's like these days, all youngsters and computers and the like. Although why they think we need computers, when I know everything there is to know about paper, I really couldn't say.'

'Well,' George collected up the tea tray a little later, 'I really must be off soon, Mother. Let's get you sorted out and ready for the night.'

He frowned, looking around, as he closed the front door behind him. No sign of anything, must be a fox. Stopping at the gate, he looked around again, but there was nothing there.

~

She'd known they wouldn't be able to resist the lure of a French Bulldog. Parked along the street, Sasha watched as the mobile dog grooming vehicle pulled out into the London traffic, after their unsuccessful visit to a mystified Mrs Trenton at sixty-four Parkview Terrace. Keeping a safe distance, she followed them, until, forty-five minutes later, they pulled up at a locked gate leading to an old warehouse. Twenty minutes later, she watched the couple leave on foot, and, satisfied that they'd gone for the day, left her car and went to investigate.

The warehouse backed onto a canal, and she was able to gain access by walking along the old towpath and squeezing through a gap in the wall. The building itself wasn't even locked, and as soon as she entered the sound of dogs barking filled the air. With her torch on Sasha walked along peering into the cages, looking for Fifi. Excited dogs jumped up hopefully, and she comforted them, promising they'd be back with their owners soon.

Poor little Fifi cowered at the back of her cage, as Sasha's torch shone on her. 'It's alright, baby, I'm taking you home to your mummy.' She picked up the bundle of fluff, cuddling her, and, with a last look at the other dogs, left the warehouse. With Fifi safely in her car, Sasha called the police, giving them the address, and informing them that she'd heard dogs barking and noticed suspicious activity.

An hour later, she smiled, as the police, dog units, and the RSPCA, began to remove the poor hounds from their place of captivity. Hopefully they'd all be reunited with their families soon. She started her car and headed for Mrs Wendham-Smythe, a relieved Fifi curled up in her lap.

TIRED TESS

'Is that you, Chantelle?' Tessa Watson sighed, brushing her hair from her face, as she put the iron down, and walked into the hallway.

The sound of giggling, and a door slamming, signalled the presence of her daughter and, presumably, her friend. Too tired to walk upstairs she returned to her ironing, calculating that she needed about another hour to finish Mrs Spindlebury's pile. Then she'd start on the dinner.

With Dave working extra shifts at the paper plant it meant that she was often alone in the evenings, when she got in from work. But it also meant that she had more to do on her own, and between the two of them, their daughter was making the most of her freedom.

With the ironing finished, Tess packed up and dragged herself up the stairs, tiredness washing over her. 'Chantelle?' she knocked on the door, opening it at the same time, and walked in as the two girls hurriedly pushed their bags aside and smiled at her.

'Oh, hi, Britney, are you staying for something to eat? What about homework, girls, make sure you get it done before dinner, Chants.'

'We're doing it now, Mum,' Chantelle made a point of pulling books from her bag, Britney picking up a small object as it fell on the floor, and quickly shoving it in her pocket.

'Thanks, Tess, but Mum wants me home tonight, babysitting my little brother.' Britney grimaced.

Tess smiled distractedly as she left the room, her mind on what to do for dinner.

THE ART OF LETTER WRITING

I'd just got back from posting my letter, and let myself in the back door, when I heard George's key turning in the lock. No doubt he'd been to visit his mother again, that old monster, she never liked me. Of course, since her fall she never went out, which was fine by me. George thought the sun shone, of course, would never hear a word against dearest Mother. Now he was up there every day, checking on her, calling in after work, making her cups of tea. If he made me half as many cups of tea as he made that woman wouldn't I be the lucky one.

He'd be wanting his dinner, but he'd have to wait. I needed time to collect myself. It was always the same after one of my letters. They were works of art, though I do say so myself.

Once I'd tidied away my cuttings and replaced the scissors in the drawer, I took a moment to indulge in the pleasure of a job well done. I mean, someone had to do it. Someone had to tell people of their failings, didn't they? It was my duty. I crossed off poor Peter's name in my book, noting with satisfaction how many letters I'd sent now. But my list was growing, this village was a cesspit of lust and evil.

George surprised me suggesting that we go out to the club for a bite to eat. He was in high spirits, come to think of it he'd been in a good mood for months, it wasn't like him at all. Probably all that time he was spending with his perfect mummy. I swear he loves her more than he loves me.

So, my whole routine had to change on George's whim, just like that, and I felt quite annoyed. Did he think I could just drop everything whenever it suited him? He'd looked at me strangely when I'd said I was busy this evening. Did the fool think I just sat around doing nothing?

I made a point of putting the two potatoes back in the vegetable rack, and slamming the kitchen drawer after I'd put the potato peeler away. The pies, from Mr Alison, were still in the fridge so I couldn't really make a point about them.

I felt all flustered, my evening was ruined now. How was I going to keep checking on things if I wasn't there? I needed to get into the bathroom to see what that strumpet was up to, but George was in there. I could feel my chest getting tight, this was what he did to me, made up his own mind about things without a care about me.

I still needed to check on Barbara Fenton, so I went into the spare room quickly and, sure enough, there she was out in her back garden. I knew it. Bottle of wine out on the table for the whole world to see. The woman had no shame, not even after my letter.

I was about to go into George's study (study, as if he thinks he's important), when he came out of the bathroom and headed in there himself. He had the nerve to ask me if I was ready. Did I look like I was ready?

I took a deep breath. I really, really, needed to see what was happening in the Burton household. Something wasn't right, there, I'd bet my life on it. Now it would have to wait. I was so worked up, I tugged my comb through my hair, sprayed on some of the perfume I'd found in George's briefcase the other day, and stomped downstairs.

It was when we'd got in the car that George started acting strangely, sniffing the air, looking at me like I'd done something terrible. It was only a bottle of perfume, what did it matter? He bought her bottles and bottles of the stuff, what was wrong with me helping myself to one? It's not like he ever bought me any. Maybe he should then I wouldn't have to steal his dear mother's precious Lavender Dreams. He said some things I won't repeat, it's not decent. So I ignored him, gave him the cold shoulder all the way to the club.

And there she was. Holding forth like she thought she was the wretched Queen of England. Rosemary mutton-dressed-as-lamb Spindlebury. That woman's voice alone was enough to drive me mad. Waving her hands around, dripping with rings, expecting everyone to hang on her every word.

I was trying to see who else was at her table. Her husband, Reg, of course, wearing that cap and ridiculous yellow cravat he always wore, and that couple from Towerby Crescent. But who were the other two? George pulled me by my arm, making it look as if I was staring at them. The nerve of the man. He chose a table in the corner, the worst table in the club, couldn't see a thing on account of the plant blocking the view. I think he chose it deliberately.

I was so at sixes and sevens that I agreed to a small sherry. I needed something to calm me down with the evening I was having.

With George at the bar I was left alone, with nothing to look at, drumming my fingernails on the table and looking like a fool. The noise they were making, all that laughing, as if they were having a wonderful time. I could hear her above all of them. That Reg wasn't much better though, growling away in that common voice he had. Did he think money made him better? You only had to listen to him.

I knew where he was from, even if he thought no-one did. I could spot a disguised Dartford accent a mile off. How my sister Sylvia suffered that place I do not know. I vowed I'd never go back, the last time we visited her in her squat little terraced house on East Hill, with all those lorry fumes blowing dirt on her net curtains.

And now here he was with all his airs and graces, his wife acting like lady muck. And where did their money come from? That got me. It buzzed through me, that first thrill. I'd have to do some investigating.

George was taking a long time to get a half shandy and a sherry. What was wrong with him? Could he not manage a simple task like that without it taking half an hour? And now there he was greeting Reg, I could hear him, all simpering and sucking up, as if money made them special.

Oh, George, when will you learn? Those types will always make someone like you the butt of their jokes. Reg Spindlebury's right, of course, you probably do hold the record for longest serving employee at the paper plant without a promotion, but there's no need to let him see how upset you are, even if everyone is laughing.

I told him I was going to the ladies, all that waiting around had played havoc with my bladder. Maybe by the time I came back his face wouldn't be such a bright shade of red. I slammed my handbag down on the counter, huffing to make my point. These wretched mobile phones, was nowhere sacred anymore? You couldn't even go to the ladies without being disturbed by someone chattering away. I strained to recognise the voice. It was familiar. Now she was whispering and giggling. I had to spend ages pretending to wash my hands, waiting to see who she was.

I gave Lilith Morton a cool smile when she finally emerged from the toilet cubicle, still on her phone. She hurriedly finished her conversation, didn't want me hearing her dirty talk, no doubt. The woman really ought to know better. She was forty, if she was a day, and her behaving like some teenager, when she had a teenager of her own, and a young boy. The way she dressed these days was downright disgusting. No wonder her husband divorced her. She deserved her downfall, having to move onto that new estate.

But who was she talking to? And why in the ladies? Maybe it wasn't such a bad thing that George made me come out to the club tonight. There were vile things going on everywhere. I waited for her to leave, then, and this was the highlight of my evening, just as I opened the door I caught Reg with his hand on a woman's bottom. They were whispering and giggling in the passageway by the bathrooms. Her cheap blonde hair was the giveaway, she worked here, oh, this was good.

They didn't see me and I joined George at our table, my head swimming with so much information. George was pleased that I'd perked up. I even told him it had been a good idea to come out.

POISONOUS WORDS

Tess tried to stifle a yawn, with difficulty, groaning inwardly as she saw the two women approach, their loud voices carrying across the shop floor.

'Tessa, dear, you look tired, I hope you managed to finish my ironing?'

Tess fumed quietly and fixed a smile on her face. 'All done, Mrs Spindlebury, Chantelle will drop it off with you after school this afternoon.' She noticed the sympathetic expression on Barbara's face and smiled at her in greeting, receiving a warm smile in response.

'Make sure it's before five, won't you?' Rosemary Spindlebury took her companion's arm and guided her away, murmuring something to her as they walked off.

Her smile now a grimace, Tess shrugged helplessly as she turned to her supervisor and friend, Von. 'I can't stand the way she talks to me, Von, like I'm her servant.'

'I know, love,' Von put her arm around the woman's thin shoulders in sympathy, 'Do you absolutely have to do her ironing? Isn't Dave taking extra shifts at work, what with the big paper order?'

Tess nodded miserably. 'He is. I just don't know where the money goes though. He gets mad with me if I ask him about it.

Von sighed, Tess was a good woman. She deserved an easier life. Perhaps she could speak to Mr Ford, see if Tess couldn't get a raise, she was an asset to the store.

The two women folded scarves in companionable silence.

~

Rosemary Spindlebury looked warily at her friend Barbara, as she ordered a glass of white wine in the store's restaurant. 'Isn't it a little early for that, dear?'

'It's three o'clock in the afternoon, Rosemary, why don't you join me?' Really, Rosemary had become such a bore, a little drink might lighten her up a little, goodness knows she could do with it.

But Rosemary stuck to her mineral water. Let Barbara drink if she wanted to. Couldn't the woman see what it was doing to her waistline? She looked down, pleased at her own flat stomach. Cutting back on the drinking had been wise, and worth it to keep one's shape, as well as one's husband.

~

Tess's phone pinged with a message from Dave. *Working late babes, don't wait up.*

So that was that then, another night on her own. At least she didn't have any ironing work tonight, maybe she could relax, take a long bath, read some of her new book. She'd pick up something nice for her and Chantelle's dinner on her way home, it would be a treat to spend a little time with her daughter.

~

'Mr Ford, do you have a minute?' Von tapped on the office door as she walked in, smiling. Peter was a kind man, she was sure he'd be open to the idea of a raise for Tess.

'Not now, Von!' Mr Ford looked up agitatedly from the paper he was holding, covering it with a file.

He looked exhausted, circles under his eyes, and he never snapped. 'Is everything okay, Peter?' Von's eyes clocked the sheet of paper with a single typed line on it, before he covered it.

'I'm just busy, lots going on. Sorry I snapped.' Peter smiled wearily at Von, 'Can we talk tomorrow?'

'Sure we can, no problem, sorry I bothered you.' Von left the office a little intrigued. She'd have to bat on Tess's behalf another day.

Peter uncovered the sheet of paper again and picked it up with a trembling hand.

YOUR SLUT OF A WIFE IS HAVING AN AFFAIR WITH THE ARTIST

Who would say something like this? Maureen would never cheat on him, would she? But why say it then? And with the artist? So specific, so sure of the facts. There was only one artist in their village, what was his name now? But he couldn't remember. He did however recall that he rented rooms upstairs at The Spotted Dog.

Peter felt finished. To have his wife called a slut was so offensive, especially when she was no such thing. She couldn't be. They were happily married, had been for almost ten years now. But still, the doubt niggled in the back of his mind and wouldn't go away...

~

Barbara Fenton poured herself another glass of wine, looking around her garden contentedly. She loved summer, it was so nice to be able to sit outdoors. It would be nicer if she had someone to enjoy it with though. Even Lilith seemed to be busy these days, she hadn't seen her for a week or more. They weren't exactly best friends, didn't share confidences, but they enjoyed each other's company over a bottle of wine. Which was more than she could say about Rosemary.

In the early days she and Rosemary had enjoyed a few drinks together quite often. She'd actually had the impression that Rosemary was a seasoned drinker. It was in the way she'd held her wine glass, leaning back in her chair with her legs crossed, the tilt of her head.

Barbara drank her wine, enjoying the hazy feeling washing over her as she reminisced. She must be on her fourth glass, fifth, if she counted the one she'd had at Beedham's, under Rosemary's disapproving gaze. Why had Rosemary become so boring, scared to have a drink? Maybe she was worried about what she'd say under the influence...

A vague memory came into Barbara's mind of Rosemary suddenly clamming up. What was it? They'd been slowly getting sloshed, watching some awful reality show on TV, some town in the South, a bunch of truly astonishing young people, false tans, false boobs and the like. Rosemary had said something...

A movement out of the corner of her eye made her look up and she lifted her glass defiantly. Mad bloody Dorothy was at it again. It was a wonder she didn't wear her curtains out with all that twitching. Had the poor cow nothing better to do? And don't think she hadn't seen her at Beedham's, lurking around in the restaurant.

'Cheers!' she called out, grinning in the direction of the window overlooking her back garden. The sudden stillness of the curtain pleased her. There, that had spoiled her fun.

DOROTHY NEEDS SOME NEW HANDKERCHIEFS

I don't often go to Beedham's on account of it being in the next town and having to take the bus, but I needed some new handkerchiefs, and Beedham's was one of the few places that still stocked them. Tissues. Disgusting. Everyone used tissues these days. Little crumpled up pieces of dirty paper left lying around, or in pockets. Filthy unhygienic habit.

George had gone off to work in a good mood, even whistling as he unlocked the car door. What was he so happy about? Of course, he'd left a mess in the kitchen for me to clean up. Didn't he know I had a busy day?

He'd locked his study as well, which was most inconvenient, as I'd hoped to check on activities over at the Burtons. I couldn't put my finger on it, but I knew something was going on there. The house was always shut up, curtains closed, lights on half the night. I was hoping to catch some movement during the day, but dear George had put a stop to that.

Nonetheless, I was in a wonderful mood. Peter Ford should have received his letter. The excitement was excruciating and, as a result, I couldn't settle to anything. I hoped I might catch sight of him at the store, but I didn't have any luck there. I'd planned my day carefully so that I'd be back in time to see him arrive home to face his strumpet of a wife, who deserved everything that was coming to her. I'd done him a favour.

It was a pleasant surprise to see that the cow, Rosemary Spindlebury, was in Beedham's with her little drunk lapdog, Barbara Fenton. I managed to manoeuvre myself so that they didn't see me, and took a table behind them. I had to stifle my laughter when Rosemary ticked Barbara off about her drinking. Oh, if she only knew.

I didn't overhear anything interesting, more's the pity. But I've decided to find out exactly how those Spindleburys got their money. There's more to it than just a good pay check, I'd warrant, what with him being from Dartford, and all.

The handkerchiefs are displayed alongside the scarves, overseen by two dreary looking women who looked like they had the world on their shoulders. I caught a word or two about the younger woman's husband, working late, not enough money, the usual stuff that if people only paid attention, meant trouble. I've been around a long time, long enough to know that when a husband works late too often, and money's still tight, he's spending it on someone else.

I made a big to do of going through all the hankies, examining them for flaws, until the younger woman got bored and carried on chatting with the older one. People don't really notice me you see, they think I'm unimportant. That's their biggest mistake.

Once I'd made myself a cup of tea back at home, I jotted down some notes in my book. *Tess. Husband Dave. Works at paper plant? Living on new estate – poor people. Daughter Chantelle* – ridiculous, what happened to proper names like Vera and Brenda? The world's gone mad if you ask me. I blame all this reality television from the Americans.

I was excited to have another new project to add to my list. This village never disappointed. Was there a big sign somewhere, that I'd missed? *Welcome to Parva Crossing, the village of adulterers, thieves, and sinners.*

I'm going to destroy that Barbara Fenton. How dare she look up at my window and raise her glass like some kind of drunken creature? And she grinned! The gall of the woman. I couldn't stay there watching, she'd taken the enjoyment out of it.

Of course, George came in reeking of that wretched lavender, as usual. If I didn't know better I'd say he had a woman on the side. The idea amused me, he did have, if you counted that hag of a mother of his.

I made scrambled eggs for dinner. It was quick and easy and wouldn't take long to eat. I made so many trips to the bathroom during the evening that George asked me if I had a funny tummy. It was the perfect excuse and I played it up, managing to spend a total of two hours checking the strumpet's front door, from the bathroom and bedroom windows.

Why didn't he come home? This was the worst part of it all, missing out on the results from my letters. I had to give up in the end, George needed the bathroom and I must admit that I felt quite tired from all the excitement of the day. I went to bed disappointed.

THE SPOTTED DOG

He couldn't help himself. He'd been on the way home when he'd turned the car around and headed for the pub. Just to see who the guy was, he told himself. He wasn't going to say anything, just watch.

If Peter was honest, the very act of going to The Spotted Dog, to have a look at the artist, felt like a betrayal of Maureen. And what did he hope to achieve? Did he think he'd be able to discern, just from observing the guy, if he was having an affair with his wife?

'What can I get you, darling?' The blonde behind the bar smiled at Peter as she leant on the counter.

Peter took his pint and turned to face the room, wondering where to sit for the best vantage point. It was a quiet night it seemed, quite a few tables were empty, and he sat down with his back to the wall. He had a good view of the door, the pool table in the adjoining room, as well as the door that led upstairs to the accommodation. He took a mouthful of lager and scanned the ten or fifteen faces scattered around.

Surprised to see that he'd finished his pint already, he got himself another drink. Turning to sit back at his table he was distracted by cheers from the pool table. Someone had won, someone had lost, he supposed. A door opened behind the pool table and, just for a second, he glimpsed men sitting around a table. The door swung closed, the sign 'no admittance' clearly fixed to it.

This was stupid. What was he doing here? Maybe he should just go home and tell Maureen about the letter? But then he'd have to laugh it off. And what if it was true? But what if it wasn't? Thoughts raced through his head as he drank steadily, another three beers following the first two, in quick succession, until he was feeling nicely numb. The offensive letter was burning a hole in his pocket. Standing up, he visited the bathroom and flushed it down the toilet, not wanting it in his possession a moment longer.

His phone buzzed but he ignored it. He knew it would be Maureen, worried about him, but he just needed some time to think. He ordered a double whisky, downing it quickly before getting the same again. The blonde raised an eyebrow, questioningly, but said nothing.

~

Cal finished cleaning up, showered, and decided to pop downstairs for a pint and a pie from Jules. Tying his hair back, he entered the pub through the residents' door. Handy that, life couldn't be more convenient than to live above a pub. It was temporary, or so he'd been telling himself for the last six months or so, but he'd probably move on eventually. Although, he quite liked the village life, and Parva Crossing was as good as any other village he'd ever spent time in, better probably. Nice enough people, picturesque place, slow pace of life where nothing much ever happened. He could do worse, especially after the crap he'd escaped from previously.

Jules handed Cal his pint and he hungrily ate his pie as he looked around, nodding at a couple of guys he recognised. Wiping his mouth, with the paper serviette, he froze. Crap. That was Maureen's husband. What was he doing in here? Having one too many by the looks of it.

Cal watched Peter, intrigued. It always interested him, seeing what the husbands were like. They had no idea what their wives were doing behind their backs. Of course, they always found out eventually, but he and Maureen had a way to go yet, it was still in the early stages...

~

Sensing eyes on him, Peter looked up, hazily, from his drink, and straight into the eyes of his quarry. The two men locked eyes for a moment, before Cal looked away. He knows I know, Peter thought, why else would he be watching me and then look away so quickly? His head felt muddled, his thoughts confused. It must be true. That one cruel line on the sheet of paper was true. He felt sick.

~

Why was he looking at him so strangely? Cal looked back over at Peter, to find him still staring, and half-raised his glass to him, in greeting. But Peter stood up unsteadily, pushing his chair back with a screech, and left the pub. Cal shrugged, maybe the guy was just having a bad day.

~

He shouldn't be driving, he thought drunkenly, as he bumped the car down the track to the river, bouncing against a tree and lurching to a halt dangerously close to the bank. He needed to think, couldn't go home right now. But he couldn't straighten out the thoughts in his head, everything was swimming around in there. Maureen. His beautiful wife. They'd been happy, hadn't they?

An image came blurrily into his mind. This morning, as he'd been getting dressed for work, Maureen had dropped something on the floor. She'd hurriedly picked it up and stuffed it back in the drawer. But the way she'd done it, almost guiltily, with a quick glance in his direction to see if he'd noticed, now raised a red flag. Red. That was it, it had been red. Something small and red. Maureen never wore red underwear, or any bold colour, come to think of it.

He was going to throw up. *She was having an affair*. He fumbled for the door handle, opening it and stumbling away from the car. The vomit spilled from his mouth in hot, angry, spurts as he doubled over in agony, tears welling up in his eyes. Reaching out a hand to steady himself against a tree, his hand touched only thin air and he tumbled over, tripping on a tree root before falling into the icy oblivion of the fast-moving, dark waters of the Black River.

OLD NEWSPAPERS

I wet myself. Just a little bit, mind. It can happen when you get older, not that I like to talk about that. It was the sudden excitement, you see. I didn't know what to do first, clean myself up and change my undergarments, or smooth out the newspaper and carry on reading.

It was a sign that I'd been chosen. I was the messenger for a higher power. It was my duty to cleanse the village for the innocent, from all the evil going on around them. I could hear the angels singing as I realised that I was the chosen one to cleanse Parva Crossing. I felt giddy with excitement. And that's when I wet myself.

I decided to wash and change first. Cleanliness is next to Godliness, after all.

We don't get a lot of post, so it was unusual to have the postman ring our doorbell with a parcel for me.

My sister, Sylvia, had been having a clear out. She thought I might like the shell owl our mother had kept, from a holiday in Eastbourne, many years ago. It had been in an old box, filled with Mother's pointless items, and, for some reason, my sister had thought of me.

I dropped the owl in the bin, I didn't want the stupid thing, it was missing one of its plastic eyes anyway. I was still holding the decades old, yellowed newspaper it had been wrapped in, and thinking that it might be useful for my cuttings, when my eyes fell on the photo.

I knew straightaway that it was him, even without the beard. The eyes don't change. And there she was, hanging on his arm, grinning at the camera. I read the caption underneath the photo, "Mr Turner and club employee." More like filthy animal with cheap prostitute, I spluttered.

I soaked up the words, *cash-in-transit heist, Essex, case dropped due to lack of evidence, getaway driver, Dartford, Bangles, strip joint.* Strip joint, I knew it! *Two million pounds, cash never recovered, where are the couple now?* You're wrong! I shrieked triumphantly at the yellowing piece of paper, they're not on a beach in Costa Brava, they're right here!

I sat in the kitchen for the whole morning, just staring at the piece of old newspaper. My stomach felt full of butterflies and my heart was beating so fast I thought I might faint if I stood up. My useless sister had just sent me, unwittingly, the best gift I could ever receive. But I had to decide what to do with it. When I felt able to stand, I went upstairs, got out my notebook and made some notes.

Reginald Turner, cash heist getaway driver from Dartford.

Rochelle, stripper from Bangles strip club in Essex.

I laughed so hard I had to put my notebook down. Tears ran down my face. That snobby, affected, dripping in gold, cow, was a stripper! She used to take her clothes off in front of men! I howled and shook, and still the laughter kept coming. I hadn't had so much fun in ages.

I tried to decide if I should send out letters to the whole village, after all, they should know what vile people were living among us. Or would it be more fun to send a letter to her first? Just giving her a little clue perhaps? That reminded me that I needed to buy more glue.

I clean forgot about the strumpet and her poor husband amidst all the excitement.

A YEAR EARLIER

'Well, that's it, babes, ready to go?'

Tess looked over at her husband and forced a smile onto her face. He looked haggard and anxious, the grey circles under his eyes more pronounced in the sunlight. 'Sure,' she said. 'Let's go. Chantelle, ready?'

Chantelle appeared, her red eyes and sulky expression evidence of how much damage Dave's gambling had done to their lives.

Tess locked the front door to their house, correction, what had been their house, their beautiful home, with its pretty garden, lovingly tended by her, and handed the key to the bank's agent.

'Thanks, Mrs Watson, and good luck.' The agent smiled sympathetically at Tess, as he walked off and got into his car, as if he was about to leave, wanting to give them the dignity of at least saying goodbye to their old home without him watching them.

'I hate you!' Chantelle cried as she got in the car. 'How could you do this to us, Dad? I'm leaving all my friends to go and live in some dump of a village in the middle of nowhere. I won't have any friends and life will just be shit.'

'Chantelle, please, enough.' Tess reached out to stroke her daughter's hair, looking at Dave with a raised eyebrow. 'Dad knows what he's done and he's sorry. He's trying to make things right. This will be exciting! A new place, new home, we'll work it out together, it'll be fun.'

They drove away silently, each with their own thoughts.

Tess's mind drifted as Dave drove them on the journey to their new home. There was no going back now, but it was hard to stop the 'what ifs'. What if she'd noticed Dave was gambling earlier? What if she'd noticed he'd stopped paying the mortgage? But Dave had always dealt with the money, call them old-fashioned, but she'd been happy to be a stay-at-home mum to Chantelle.

She'd watched the other mums in the neighbourhood, with sympathy, always rushing, juggling kids, husbands, jobs, after school clubs, etc. She was so lucky to have Dave, with his good job at Mason's Materials. His middle management salary afforded them a comfortable lifestyle and an overseas holiday each year. Chantelle attended a decent school and had good friends. Sure, they'd made sacrifices, had gone without a few of the luxuries only affordable for a double income family, but they'd felt it was worth it. Yes, life had been good.

What if they hadn't carried out retrenchments? Would Dave have come right? Got a hold on his gambling debts and made up the difference on the mortgage? Stop it, Tess, she spoke to herself sternly. It's over. She leant back in her seat and closed her eyes.

Dave's hand on hers stirred her. 'You alright, babes?' He smiled tiredly. 'It'll be okay. This new job is alright, not quite the same level as before, I'll have to work shifts, and I know it's a lot less money, but we'll get there. You'll get a little job for a while, help us along, just for a bit.' He squeezed her hand and turned his attention back to the road.

Panic hit the pit of her stomach. She'd have to get a job. Not that she minded working but it had been a long time since she'd worked in the offices at Mason's, where she'd met Dave. She felt so out of touch now, not sure what she'd be any good at. And what job would she find, where they were moving to, anyway? Chantelle was right about one thing, it certainly was in the middle of nowhere.

Chantelle's phone pinged constantly, in the back of the car, with messages from her friends, her rapidly typed replies audible by the tap tap on the screen of her phone.

Eventually they stopped at a service station for refreshments and a toilet break. Tess's phone was showing a missed call when she got out of the car. She'd had it on silent in her bag, not wanting to talk to anyone. It was her sister. Her heart warmed, and she smiled as she called her back. 'Hi, Sash, it's me, sorry I missed you.'

'That's okay, sis, didn't feel like talking to anyone, huh?' Sasha smiled sympathetically into the phone as she walked towards the coffee shop to meet her new client.

The two sisters talked companionably for a few minutes, with Sasha promising to come and visit them once they were settled. 'Call me, Tess, if you need anything, promise me?'

Hamburgers and fries devoured, cokes drunk thirstily, and they were back on the road for the final part of their journey.

As they drove through Parva Crossing, they looked with interest from the car windows. Small lanes led off from the main high street, the village's many cute stone cottages' front gardens filled with colourful blooms. Cutting the village in half, as it rushed on its way under the bridge, was the river. It truly was the quintessential English village.

Dave drove on, heading for the new estate, and Tess drew a deep breath. This was it then. And there was the removal truck, waiting patiently in front of their new home, number 9, Riverside Gardens.

It wasn't so bad really, quite a cute little house, in a row of matching cute houses. For a rental they could have done a lot worse. The developers of the estate had, at least, constructed them in a style sympathetic to the houses within the village, of which the estate, formerly a farmer's fields, was now a part of.

The rental agent, Barbara Fenton, welcomed them with hugs and smiles, a faint whiff of alcohol and peppermint on her breath. She opened up for Tess, taking her by the arm and leading her inside, chattering away, before finally leaving them to settle in, having gushingly urged Tess to call her for anything, anything at all.

As the men bustled in and out, heaving their furniture in, Tess looked around, pleased to find a small garden at the back. Her heart lifted slightly, she'd explore later but it looked like the garden had a small gate, leading to the river perhaps? For now, it was time to sort out the furniture and unpack the boxes in their new home.

STILL A YEAR EARLIER

Trying to drag her eyes away from the patchy, burnt, and tufted hair of the woman opposite her, Sasha picked up her tea cup, while her new client, Hazel, replaced the scarf around her head.

'So, what is it that you want me to do for you exactly, Hazel? You say the salon reimbursed you, and have offered you a complimentary haircut and colour, once your, er, hair grows back?' *She'd be waiting a hell of a long time by the looks of it.*

Hazel nodded, wiping her eyes. 'As if I'd ever set foot in that place again,' she said bitterly. 'I want you to find out why it happened. I've been going to Scissors Sisters for years, and I've never had a problem. No, someone did this deliberately and you have to find out who.'

'Okay,' Sasha nodded, making notes. 'And, if you don't mind my asking what do you intend to do with the information I uncover? You do realise that I can't be involved in anything that may result in you taking harmful action against someone else, don't you?'

'I don't see what it's got to do with you. I'm paying you to do a job. I want something to be done. Someone did this to me and I want to make them pay. I want them to regret it. Oh no, I don't mean-' She stopped speaking at Sasha's alarmed expression, before sobbing in anguish. 'Martin will probably dump me now, I'm no good to him like this. I can't even face him.'

'Martin? Is he your, er, husband? Boyfriend?'

'Well, he'd hardly be my husband would he?' Hazel snapped. 'I can't hide this abortion from my husband can I, what's wrong with you? No, Martin's my boyfriend, obviously, well, he was, I don't suppose he will be for much longer.'

'Okay...' *She was finding it hard to warm to this woman.* 'But you do have a husband?'

'What's that got to do with it, and what business is it of yours? Yes, Douglas, but he's got nothing to do with this.'

Definitely feeling chilly towards her now. But a job was a job. 'Right, well the thing is, Hazel, if I'm going to take this case, I do need to know everything, so why don't you start at the beginning?'

Half an hour later and Sasha was fully appraised of Hazel's dead loss of a husband, her affair with Martin, and their romantic nights away at various hotels. 'And there's no-one at the salon who might have a grudge against you?'

Hazel looked incredulously at Sasha. 'Well, I wouldn't need you if I knew that would I? But no, there's no-one. Marlene's been doing my hair for years, she's like a friend to me. Like a, well, like a counsellor, friend, and sister, all rolled into one. Well, she was, obviously she won't be anymore, I'd never let her near my hair again after this. Anyway, she was devastated about my hair, totally devastated, quite rightly. She couldn't stop crying. Not that it was my place to comfort her, after all, she was responsible for my hair, she should have taken better care of me. No, someone else did this. One of the other girls must have meddled with my hair colour, and at the very least I want them fired.'

Trying not to let her growing dislike of this woman show, Sasha wrapped things up. 'Right, we're almost done, what can you tell me about the other girls at the salon? Have you had a problem with any of them? Even just a small disagreement?'

'I don't speak to them. There are the other stylists, but I don't even know their names, and the girls who assist but they're not important, they just do the grunt work don't they, sweeping and making tea? I make it a point to never speak to those types, you don't know where they're from after all, they're just as likely to steal from your handbag when you're not looking.' *Really, this woman was incorrigible.*

'I see. And what about Martin? Is he married?'

Hazel waved her hand dismissively. 'Some dowdy wife I believe, lurking in the background. He never speaks about her, obviously.'

It was a relief to get away from the woman. With an attitude like that it was no surprise that someone had sabotaged her hair. Whoever it was deserved a medal.

Sasha appraised her reflection in the bathroom mirror. Maybe it was time for a haircut. She picked up the phone and called Scissors Sisters.

'You're in luck, Marlene's had a cancellation for tomorrow morning. *Perfect, the same day and time as Hazel's appointment was*. Will that be for a colour too?' *Probably not a good idea, not until she'd found out who the perpetrator was*.

Arriving at the salon at nine o'clock sharp, Sasha was whisked through, seated, gowned, and holding a cup of tea, before she'd even met her stylist. A moment later she found herself smiling at an attractive middle-aged woman who introduced herself as Marlene. 'Everything alright, my darling? Give me two minutes and I'll be with you. Sasha isn't it? Back in just a tick.'

Sasha sipped her tea, observing the activities around her and listening to the salon chatter. Girls in chic black uniforms, and heavily made-up faces, appeared to move in synchronicity, sweeping the slightest scrap of hair from the floor, carrying cups of tea and coffee to clients, and wheeling trolleys filled with hairdressing paraphernalia between styling stations, as she'd been told they were called. *You're at styling station three, Sasha*.

'So, I walked out on him, right there and then.' 'A bit more off the length I think.' 'The wedding's in two months, I'm so excited.' 'He just suddenly announced it over dinner, I want to be a woman.' 'Shirley starts big school, as she calls it, in September.' 'So, what can we do for you today?'

Sasha started, realising that Marlene was back and talking to her. 'Oh, er, just a trim please, tidy up the split ends and stuff.'

Marlene looked disappointed. 'You're sure I can't tempt you with a restyle? A few layers popped in would lift your hair beautifully, give it more body, Sasha. And if we added a few platinum highlights here, and here,' her hands moved rapidly around Sasha's head, lifting hair and plumping it. 'That would bring out your blonde colouring fabulously.' She stepped back, looking at Sasha questioningly.

Faced with the awkward difficulty of disagreeing with a hair stylist, Sasha went for diplomacy. 'It sounds wonderful, but I'm a little short on time today. Perhaps the layers? That sounds good.' *Why not, she could do with a new look.*

Back rolled her chair, and a hand gently lifted her arm. 'Come with me,' a girl who could have stepped straight out of the Robert Plant music video escorted her to what was no doubt the *hair washing station.* I could get used to this she thought, as fingers massaged her scalp and neck, easing out tension knots she hadn't even known were there. More chatter filtered through to her as she relaxed, secrets confessed, gossip shared, good news imparted. This place was one big confessional.

Marlene was certainly skilled at extracting information, as well as cutting hair. Before Sasha knew it, she'd told Marlene all about her issues with Eric - she'd also, she realised, told a number of other people nearby. Her eyes flicked surreptitiously to the girl sweeping in the vicinity, before moving to the styling stations either side of her. Both the stylists and their clients, would have heard every word Sasha had spoken. As she had, of course, heard theirs.

For instance, she knew that Jennifer, at styling station two, was off on holiday tomorrow, and that her stylist, Roxanne, hadn't had a proper holiday for a year, and that she'd always dreamed of going to the Maldives. She also knew that Delia, at styling station four, was about to serve divorce papers to her cheating husband, something her stylist, Nicola, agreed vociferously with, having done the same thing a year earlier, and never been happier.

That familiar little spark of excitement shot through her suddenly. She glanced at Delia in the mirror, wondering what was behind the decision to divorce her husband. As she watched her, the woman's phone rang, and her stylist, Nicola, stepped away discreetly while her client spoke into her phone.

'No, my mind's made up, no, I'm not interested. Well, you should have thought about that before you cheated on me, shouldn't you? No, of course you can't move back in, Martin, it's over. Don't you get it? Why don't you move in with your little whore girlfriend?' She snapped her phone closed, closing her eyes, and leant back in her chair, sighing.

Martin! That was the name of Hazel's boyfriend. The one with the so-called dowdy wife. The one who took Hazel away for romantic nights in hotels. Well, Delia certainly wasn't dowdy, she was actually very attractive, so, if she was who Sasha thought she was, then Martin hadn't been strictly honest with Hazel.

Unable to hear anything further while her hair was being blow dried, Sasha played out a scenario in her mind. Hazel had told Marlene about Martin, had even told her about their nights away, and Delia had heard everything. Delia had then doctored the hair colourant in revenge. It was a good plot, but how could Delia have been sure that Hazel was talking about her own husband? Only Delia would be able to tell her that, but Delia was leaving and Sasha was still trapped in her seat.

'Wow, it looks stunning, Marlene! Thank you!' Her hair really did look amazing. 'Maybe I'll take you up on that highlight suggestion next time.' She carefully slipped off her bracelet, letting it drop to the floor, as she picked up her bag and left her styling station.

Taking her receipt from the receptionist, Sasha looked at her wrist in surprise. 'Oh, my bracelet, it must have fallen off!' The receptionist was off to styling station three in an instant, and Sasha quickly leant over the appointments book, taking photos with her phone. Thanking the receptionist for finding her bracelet, and promising to get the clasp checked, Sasha left Scissors Sisters, her hair swinging and shining in the sunshine, and a photo containing Delia's phone number, in her phone's gallery.

Finding that the direct approach was always best, she phoned Delia. After an explanation, and assurances that she wasn't out to cause trouble, the woman agreed to meet with her.

'I just want to know how you did it,' Sasha said. 'If I'm honest, I'm kind of in admiration at what you achieved, not many women get to take such satisfying revenge on their husband's mistress.'

Delia laughed. 'Mistress, hardly that, one of many, only she doesn't know that. Anyway it happened like this. Last week I happened to find a hotel receipt in Martin's suit pocket for the Oliver Plaza. It was for the Tuesday night, a double room, and a night when he was supposed to be away in Nottingham on business.'

Sasha nodded, when would men learn that their carelessness was their worst enemy?

'So,' Delia continued, 'I knew he'd spent the night with a woman, but I had no way of knowing who, of course. And then, like a gift, I was having my hair done by Nicola, as I do most weeks, and seated at the station next to me was a woman I recognised as a regular client of Marlene's. I'd always found her quite unpleasant, far too much to say about other people, and a rather arrogant attitude in general. Anyway, she happened to mention, in her loud voice, that she'd spent the Tuesday night with her boyfriend at the Oliver Plaza. My ears pricked up, I knew it must be her, but as if she knew I needed final confirmation, she carried on twittering away, Martin this, and Martin that, and poor Martin's dowdy wife. I saw red, Sasha, I don't mind telling you.' She paused, sipping her coffee, before continuing.

'Marlene had just dispatched her assistant to mix up the colourant for her client's hair, and I'd already got my foils in, so I pretended to go to the bathroom, which was just past the colour station. I waited for the girl to begin mixing the colourant, and then I told her that I thought someone had just called her at the front desk. I simply picked up the bottle of ammonia and squirted loads of it into the bowl. And then I sat back down and waited.' Delia smiled at Sasha, looking a bit sheepish. 'I know, I'm awful, aren't I?'

'Not at all,' Sasha grinned. 'I'd say she asked for it. And I suppose the rest is history?'

'I had to try not to stare as she started to complain about her scalp burning, and then panic ensued, they washed out the colourant, everyone was running around. I did feel bad, I was worried that someone would get into trouble, but the girl was adamant that she'd mixed the correct quantities, and as luck would have it, it appears there'd been a problem with rogue colourants lately, so they put it down to that. I'm only sorry that I didn't see the final results before I had to leave. Was it terrible?'

'Really terrible, I don't even know how to describe it to do your work justice. She's just got tufts of hair, and the odd bald patch. One thing is, she'll never know it was you, I think this will be one case that Sasha was unable to solve.'

Sasha put the phone down to her client, Hazel, breathing a sigh of relief. *Utterly useless, don't know why I bothered asking for your help; totally incompetent; waste of my time; you can't expect me to pay you; you needn't think I'll recommend you to anyone else.*

She glanced up at her reflection in the lounge mirror. Marlene had done a fabulous job, she'd definitely have the highlights put in next time. She'd just have to be careful not to say too much, after all, you never knew who might be listening...

SPECULATION IS RIFE

'I dunno, Brit, I don't really need any more make-up, you know?' Chantelle felt awkward, she liked Britney but nicking stuff from the shops was something she'd never considered before she'd met her new friend. If her mum found out she'd kill her.

'Oh, come on!' Britney tried to cajole her. 'Well, what else are we going to do? I'm bored. Nothing ever happens round here. Check, there's that mad woman.'

The two girls watched Dorothy as she walked along the street, muttering to herself. They nudged each other and giggled, falling into step behind her.

Dorothy entered the stationer's, followed by the two girls, and stopped in front of a display of staplers, Sellotape, and glue. She didn't appear to notice that Britney had moved next to her, picking items up to examine them.

'Take it!' hissed Britney, sliding the glue stick into Chantelle's bag.

'I don't need it.' Chantelle moved away, not sure whether to try and put the item back, or whether that might draw more attention to herself. 'Britney, let's go,' she headed for the door, beckoning her friend.

The girls wandered along the high street, bored.

Suddenly a police car drove past, its light flashing, an unusual sight in the small village. Something must have happened. Finally, some excitement! By common, unspoken, agreement, both girls turned and headed in the direction of the flashing light. They stopped on the bridge, where it crossed over the Black River, straining their necks to try and make out what was going on further along the river bank.

~

It wasn't like Peter not to come into work, and especially not to phone in, Von thought worriedly. He'd certainly seemed distracted yesterday when she'd tried to talk to him about Tess. But there was no more time to think about it, the store was busy and she and Tess had piles of new stock to unpack in between customers.

~

Barbara closed up the rental office for the day, well it was just a little early, but who was watching? She had a slight headache which required the attention of two complementary treatments. One would require a quick visit to Pringle's Chemist for some aspirin, the other could be achieved by popping into the supermarket where she could pick up something for her dinner, as well as the liquid refreshment to accompany it.

Leaving her car in the small parking lot next to the office, Barbara walked along towards Pringle's Chemist, surprised to see a small gathering of people on the bridge. Mrs Pringle would know what that was all about, the woman knew everything that went on in their village.

But Mrs Pringle didn't know, and neither did Sheila, her assistant, both women's enquiring faces, and surprised expressions, conveying the fact quite clearly. Mr Newton, in the chemist at the time, professed to have no idea either and a few minutes of pleasant speculation passed, before Sheila finally attended to Barbara's needs in the headache department.

Mrs Pringle made a note in her order book to increase George's order of Lavender Dreams from one bottle a month to two. What on earth was his mother doing with the stuff? Drinking it?

~

Cal thought back to his call from Maureen, earlier. 'I'm sorry, Cal, I can't today, Peter didn't come home last night and I'm worried sick, it's not like him at all.'

He wondered if he should have mentioned that he'd seen Peter in The Spotted Dog the night before, but decided it had been best to keep silent. He just hoped that whatever was going on between them got sorted out. The last thing he needed was trouble between the husband and wife. That wouldn't end well for him.

With his afternoon unexpectedly free he took a stroll along the High Street, picking up the newspaper, and taking a seat outside the coffee shop. A large cappuccino and a muffin perfectly accompanied his leisurely observation of local comings and goings.

~

Barbara picked up a pasta meal for one from the refrigerator and headed for the wine aisle. White wine, she decided, to accompany her chicken carbonara. She checked for today's deals, finding a cheap Australian wine, and added three bottles to her basket. Hearing a sniggering sound, she looked round to find Mad Dorothy giving her a knowing look.

'Hi, Dorothy, looking for some wine? Planning a romantic evening with George, are you?' Barbara held up a bottle, 'How about this one?' She laughed to herself, as the muttering woman's face flushed red before she turned abruptly and walked in the opposite direction.

With her shopping placed in the car, Barbara decided to walk along and join the growing crowd on the bridge. A policeman was fixing up blue and white tape from tree to tree further along the river bank, and as they watched a van joined the other vehicles. Figures in white overalls descended from the van and the onlookers watched with rapt interest as a white tent was erected, obscuring most of their view.

Barbara felt filled with foreboding. This couldn't be good, not good at all. She wondered who it was and whether it was someone she knew, after all she was familiar with many of the residents in the village, including on the new estate. A hand touched her arm, causing her to turn.

'Oh, Cal, it's you, hi. Any idea what's going on?'

Cal shook his head, 'No idea, Barbara, I was having a coffee when I noticed the police car shoot past.' He looked worried, biting his lip and anxiously looking towards the white tent. 'D'you think someone's drowned? Have they said who it is?'

'Cal, are you okay? What's worrying you?' Barbara steered him away from the two school girls who were listening in on their conversation. 'What is it?'

~

Britney nudged Chantelle, with a glint in her eye. 'Look who's over there. Let's follow him again.'

~

Barbara drove home, pulling her car into her driveway, and quickly deposited her meagre shopping in the kitchen. Surely Cal was just putting two and two together and making five. Perhaps she should pop round, but she didn't want to worry Maureen. Maybe they'd just had a fight, and Peter had stormed off to a hotel for a night or two, without telling her. But Peter and Maureen virtually never fought, they were one of the lucky ones, a happily married couple.

No, she'd leave it for now, have a glass of wine out in the garden.

MOTHER'S TRAY CLOTH

George tucked his mother's perfume away safely in his briefcase, before leaving the chemist's. How intriguing it all was. He'd stroll along to the bridge and have a look before heading out to Mother's. He had a few minutes to spare.

The crowd had grown quite large, and George hung back, not wanting to become involved. Crowds made him uncomfortable, people started talking to you. He preferred to be on the outside looking in, he was a periphery person, the sort of person people's gaze wandered over with no interest. Remaining at the end of the bridge, George could still make out the white tent and the white-clothed figures moving around on the river bank, further down.

The flashing lights of the police cars added a sense of drama to the whole spectacle, as George listened to the speculation around him. Talk of murder and drowning was rampant, as the onlookers got carried away in the excitement of it all.

Well, it would certainly be something to tell Mother about, he thought happily. She loved a good gossip and they would enjoy a good guessing game this evening about who it might be.

He walked away, heading back to his car, and made his way out to his mother's cottage. He could have walked, it was such a nice evening, and it wasn't far, but he'd have a few extra minutes with her this way.

'Oh have I got a story for you tonight, Mother!' Hanging up his jacket, George entered Mrs Newton's front room, where she sat, patiently awaiting his arrival. He leant down and kissed her forehead gently, as she looked up at him. 'Let's keep the curtains open, it's still lovely and light. I'll go and put the kettle on and make us our tea, then I'll tell you all about it!'

There, Mother's hand-embroidered tray cloth looked so pretty on the tray with the cups and saucers. Opening up the packet of fig rolls he added two to the arrangement, one on each saucer. Looking around for a Tupperware container to put the rest of the packet in, he frowned at the flies buzzing at the window. Poor Mother, it wasn't her fault she couldn't get up to open a window during the day.

The flies having been dealt with, George carried the tray through. 'Tada! Tea and fig rolls, your favourites!' His mother's smile was reward enough, and he placed the tray down, before opening up his briefcase to retrieve the Lavender Dreams.

'This is the most beautiful scent in the world, Mother, it reminds me of you whenever I smell it. Here, let's lift your arm, a little spray on your wrist, that's it, beautiful.' A sound distracted him, and he stood up to look out of the window. No-one there, of course there wouldn't be, Mother's cottage was at the end of a tree-lined lane, her nearest neighbours a mile back, or more.

'There, Mother, so what do you make of all that then?' George sat back in his chair, beaming proudly at his mother. 'I told you I had a story for you, didn't I? I wonder who's body they've found, I mean to say, it must have been a body, what with the white tent and everything. Mr Ramsbottom wasn't at work today, his wife phoned in, said he was sick. Maybe she murdered him and threw his body in the river.' George giggled happily, he loved these times with Mother.

'Oh, you don't think so? No, you're probably right, Mrs Ramsbottom can hardly lift a tea cup, I should say, so I doubt she could throw her husband's body in the river! Pity though, maybe I'd get that promotion if he'd been murdered. I know, I know, naughty George, I'm only kidding Mother.

No, don't say that, Mother, it's not true, I'm cleverer than you think, I make things happen. I've *made* things happen. You said I'd never amount to anything, but just you wait and see, I've got lots of surprises for you. No, you'll have to be patient, trust your little Georgie.'

The time had flown past, it had been a very pleasant visit, well, apart from their tiny squabble, thought George, as he switched on the little table lamp next to Mother. Rising to take the tray out to the kitchen, a sound distracted him again, and he frowned as he looked out of the window, seeing nothing but his own reflection.

'I'll close up the curtains now then and get you ready for the night, Mother. I'd better not be late home, I'll be in trouble with Dorothy. Yes, I know, she's a stickler is Dorothy.'

'Goodnight then, Mother, see you tomorrow!' With the front door securely locked, George made his way down the garden path, locking the garden gate behind him. You couldn't be too careful these days, even in Parva Crossing. He peered into the dusk as he unlocked his car, sure he'd heard a noise again. Was that movement behind the bushes? A flash of white caught his eye and then it was gone.

DOROTHY FULFILS HER WIFELY DUTIES

I was so disgusted I left the supermarket in a rage, forgetting to buy George's cereal. Too bad, he'd have to have toast for breakfast, wouldn't kill him. Who did he think I was anyway, his slave? Did he think I had all this time every day, just to run around for him?

I stormed into the house, my head filled with her dirty talk. How dare she? Her! That drunken slut. How dare she talk to me like that? Dirty, filthy, woman. Implying things about me and George. I'd show her. I'd make sure she felt the shame she deserved.

I was shaking so much, I had to sit down and take a few moments before I could even put the kettle on for a cup of tea. This is what these people do to me. It was while I was sitting there with my tea that I realised I hadn't checked on the strumpet across the road. You see? It was a conspiracy. A conspiracy of the vile creatures in this village. They were trying to confuse me, stop me doing my good work.

I gave myself a talking to, calmed myself down, tried to gather my thoughts. I had so much to attend to. The stripper whore and her common criminal of a husband, if he even was her husband, no doubt they were living in sin, well, they'd have to wait. Let me think, let me think.

I paced up and down in the kitchen, trying to think clearly. What first? She needed a letter, yes, it was time. But the strumpet, I needed to check, I'd forgotten, might have missed something. I'd never forgive her for that. I was at sixes and sevens, George would be in soon and I hadn't made dinner.

My head felt foggy, I needed my notebook, that would be best. There, that was better. I read through my notes, nodding, feeling more in control as I made my lists. But there was no time to get my cuttings out now. I usually take my bath before George arrives home, I like my privacy, but there's no time.

The house is quiet. No movement, no sign of life. No sign of her husband's car either. The curtains are all closed at the Burton house, nothing to see there. She, that vile cow, was already outside, drinking the devil's poison. Hope it kills her.

'Dorothy, are you alright? What are you doing up here, who are you talking to?'

I hadn't even heard George come in, got quite a shock to find him standing right behind me. I should have smelt that cloying lavender, it was even more sickly smelling than usual. Maybe George was wearing it. That made me giggle.

George made me stay at the table during dinner. He seemed very fidgety himself, pleased about something. He kept asking me all sorts of questions. How had my day been? Had I done anything else, written letters, or gone shopping? What business of his was it anyway? I'd made his dinner. I'd fulfilled my wifely duties, hadn't I? That thought made me feel sick, the things it implied. It reminded me of what she'd said in the supermarket, as she'd waved the sinful bottle under my nose.

I couldn't tell George about it obviously, there are some things we don't talk about. So, I told him I'd had a busy day, that I'd popped to the shops, that I'd needed some glue. Glue! Now I remembered about the girls. Those two, common as you like, thieving bits of trash. I needed to think, needed my notebook.

'Did you see the police cars today in town, Dorothy?' he asked, just as I was standing up to excuse myself to go and make notes about their stealing. I stopped dead, sitting back down. 'It seems they found a body in the river. Dangerous that river, I've always said so. Wonder who it is?'

Well, bodies in the river are one thing, but I didn't see what it had to do with me, right at this minute. I really needed to get up to my windows. My windows on the world, I thought, with a laugh.

I know, let me think, I know I have to write the letters. But there are so many, don't you see? I can't rush them, you do see that? Can I just pick one for tonight? The voices quietened down and I let go of my head. I pointed to a name on my list, 'This one?'

Well, I'll have to wait for George to go to bed. I was feeling a little unclean, not having had my bath. It wasn't my fault, they told me. They understand everything, which makes me feel better. They're right, duty comes first. My bath is not important when I have sinners to expose. It's the only way to keep our village clean and pure. And that cleanliness will wash off onto me, it was perfect.

She's still out there drinking her poison. Perhaps I should- but no, the girl was the chosen one, it was agreed. Stealing was a sin. I nodded, as I crept downstairs and got my cuttings out. These parents of today, no control over their children. I'd teach them a lesson, bringing shame on our law-abiding community, allowing their devil spawn to carry on like she did.

BARBARA BRINGS MUFFINS

Maureen's eyes were sore as she opened them and she rubbed them, lifting herself wearily from the couch. What day was it? Was it last night that the police had come? Or the night before? She felt disconnected, confused, couldn't collect her thoughts.

The pain returned, tearing through her body, and, slumping back onto the couch, she doubled over, clutching her belly, trying to fend off the awful truth that threatened to push its way into her head again. He was dead! Peter was dead! She couldn't bear it. Tears seeped out of her swollen eyes as she groaned, rocking back and forth, her arms trying to squeeze the pain away.

Finally her crying eased, more from the absence of any tears left to cry than from any lessening of her pain. She stood slowly, feeling dizzy, and made her way to the kitchen. Coffee was needed, she thought, her gaze falling sadly on Peter's coffee mug, sitting alongside hers on the counter. 'The Boss' proclaimed his, while hers bore the words 'My husband has a sexy wife', gifts they'd bought each other at Christmas.

She couldn't bring herself to use the mug, choosing a plain one from the cupboard instead, and made a strong coffee, drinking the scalding liquid down and feeling a little energy creep back into her body. The energy boost was enough to see her through a shower and, dressed in clean clothes, she returned to the lounge, tidying the room on autopilot, as her thoughts whirled around in her head.

None of it made any sense. Why would the police say Peter had been drinking heavily? Peter hardly drank and never went to the pub straight from work. He also never ignored her calls. What had happened to make him behave so out of character? The ring of the doorbell pulled her from her musings. She didn't feel like talking to anyone, especially not the police, not again.

But a careful look from the lounge window revealed that it was Barbara, that was okay, she could talk to Barbara, just about.

'Oh, Maureen, I'm so sorry, my darling.' Barbara enveloped her in a hug, faint traces of alcohol evident beneath the peppermints. 'I've brought muffins, I know, you're not hungry, but I bet you haven't eaten a thing!' Barbara bustled about, leading Maureen back to the lounge and settling them both on the couch.

'I'm making us some tea and we're going to have muffins. You can't refuse me, I made them this morning and I'm going in late to work, so you're stuck with me.' The sounds of the kettle being filled and mugs taken from the cupboard reached Maureen's ears as she leant back on the couch. Barbara really was a kind person.

Surprised to find that she did, in fact, have a slight appetite, Maureen broke off pieces of the cheese muffin and ate them, watched approvingly by her friend. The tea was hot and strong, just what she needed, she thought gratefully.

'Did the police have any answers for you?' Barbara looked at her friend anxiously. 'Anything they could tell you at all, about what they think happened?'

Maureen filled her in as best she could, voicing her confusion over Peter's behaviour. 'He's not a big drinker and never goes to the pub after work, Barbs. We might go together, or I might meet him there occasionally, but he'd never go on his own like that. He wasn't answering my calls, that's not like him either. It's like something happened, something that made him act so out of character, but I don't know what.'

'We're going to get to the bottom of it, hun, I promise you. Are they sure, now don't get upset with me, we must consider all possibilities, are they sure that it was an accident? They don't think someone did this to him? Or,' softening her voice even more, as she spoke the next words, 'that he did it to himself? Maybe he was depressed?'

But no, as the two women talked, they agreed, no-one could possibly have done this to Peter. He was the nice guy, the guy everybody liked. He didn't have a bad bone in his body. And he was happy, he was always happy, that was his nature. Something must have happened to make him act the way he did that night. And he definitely didn't end his own life, not Peter.

'What about at work? Maybe something happened there to upset him? Are the police going to check?'

But again, no. The police had nothing to check, it was an accident as far as they were concerned, caused by his own misuse of alcohol.

'Well,' said Barbara. 'We don't have to leave it at that, I'll speak to Von, if anyone knows it'll be her.

TREATED LIKE A QUEEN

It's almost painful to watch one of my creations disappear into the post box. I don't really want to let go, I want to keep it. But my life's duty has become clearer over these past few weeks and I must do the work the voices tell me.

They're speaking to me more often now, even when I don't want them to. Sometimes it's nice to chat with them, they are so full of praise for my skills. It fills me with pride to hear the things they say.

Putting together the cuttings for the thieving devil child was a great pleasure. She must be stopped and if the parents are too useless to do their job then I must do it for them. It was quite a party, I don't mind telling you. We played music and sang all my favourite songs, while that fat, lazy, husband of mine snored his way through the dark hours.

I don't really need my scissors, it feels more creative to tear the paper now. I can feel tears in my eyes as I gently place each letter on the paper and stick it down. The letters feel like my children.

I am becoming a creature of the night, this is when I find my strength. I will write all my letters at night I decide, as I dance around the kitchen in my nightdress and dressing gown.

I say goodbye to my child in the morning, after an early visit to the letter box. It's not far, a short walk from our back door, and I'm heading back up the garden path when I notice the curtain twitching upstairs. For some reason this makes me giggle, George is using my windows on the world. He doesn't have permission, it's wrong. But I smile up at him and wave happily. It's a beautiful day, the sun is shining and I've sent my child out to right a wrong.

George walks into the kitchen, as I enter through the back door, and I wonder what's wrong with him. He seems to have a confused look on his face a lot these days. Maybe he's losing it.

He wants to know what all the mess is. Can't he see I've been busy with my duties? He shouldn't be downstairs yet. I haven't had time to clear my cuttings away. I have every right to get angry with him. I'm not screaming at him, that's the voices, I tell him. But he looks more confused, poor man.

I agree to a lie down, yes, I am feeling a little tired. It's handy that I'm still wearing my nightclothes, I just have to take my dressing gown off and get into bed. I must have slept for quite a few hours because it's lunchtime when I wake up.

I wonder when the mother will receive my letter. She will want to know who I am, so that she can thank me, I'm sure. But my modesty is my burden and I must bear it bravely. Not for me the praise for my good works. It is enough to know that I am following the path set out for me by the powers above. Their words of praise and encouragement are all I need.

I decide that a visit to Beedham's is in order. I want to see her evil face, the face of a bad mother, not caring how she raises her daughter. While she stands there, idling her time selling the disgusting paints and devices that whores use, her daughter is behaving like a common criminal.

The bus is late, which makes me really angry. This driver should be reported, he's not up to his job. Doesn't he know that good timekeeping is the measure of a good man? Did I read that somewhere or did I just make that up? Yes you're right, I nod in agreement, smiling, Dorothy is a clever girl.

I think people know that I have been chosen for a special duty in our village. I can feel them looking at me as I walk to my seat on the bus. I'm trying to talk to my friends, but they're all talking at once. Slow down I tell them, one at a time.

The bus is quite full but, when I take my seat, the person next to me gets up and chooses to stand by the door. It's a mark of respect, we agree, laughing happily. I feel like the Queen, with my courtiers accompanying me, advising me, and we discuss what I should say to the bad mother.

But I can't get close to the bad mother, everyone is in a cluster. They're all talking at once, looking upset. What is wrong with these people? It's such a beautiful day. They should be happy. But my friends and advisors are looking after me, and they are quite right, I shouldn't make contact with the evildoers.

I must let my work send its message, let it be the cure for all the sin creeping into our village. She looks up and sees me looking at her and I think she's going to tell me she's sorry. I smile, filled with warmth, as happiness bubbles up inside me. Playfully, I let my hands drift through the scarves on the counter, humming a tune.

I catch a few words here and there, but they are whispering, they don't want me to hear. They're talking about Mr Ford. Poor Peter. Tears well up in my eyes. That good man, he must be so pleased to know what his wife is doing behind his back. Now he can send her away in disgrace. He deserves better. If only he knew it was me who had sent him the letter, he could thank me.

I'm getting used to people looking at me now, and I sigh, this is what happens when your good works are recognised. I used to be ignored, overlooked, but not anymore. Even the security guards are trying to look after me. It's a beautiful day I tell them, as they take my arm. They keep their distance, as if they're afraid to come too close. They're so respectful. They're really very lovely, asking me my name, where I live, and they laugh with me as we walk along.

Of course I'm alright, I snap at a stranger outside Beedham's, not quite sure how I got there. Yes, I'm feeling a little dizzy. No, I don't want to sit down. I'm feeling irritated now, something spoiled my fun and the day seems dark. The sun has disappeared and it makes me angry.

I walk up and down the pavement, trying to remember why I'm here. Something about Peter, Mr Ford, no, it's about the mother, yes, but she was talking about Mr Ford. What were they saying? Maybe he told everyone about his whore of a wife. That must be it.

I haven't eaten, I realise, as my tummy rumbles noisily. But it's getting late and I haven't been to the butcher. I'm upset now, what am I going to do for George's dinner? I still have to take the bus back, Mr Alison will have closed up and I'll have to go to the supermarket instead.

EVERYONE'S GOT THEIR SECRETS

'This is nice!' Tess smiled around the dinner table at her husband and daughter. 'When's the last time we three ate together? We should do it more often.'

'Yeah, sure, Mum,' Chantelle squeezed her shoulder as she stood up and walked past to take her plate to the kitchen. 'What's for pudding?'

'You'll be lucky!' Dave laughed, 'Since when does Mum ever do pudding?'

'Actually, there's ice cream in the freezer.' Tess watched, amused, as Dave and Chantelle made a rush for the freezer, scuffling and laughing with each other. Just like the old days.

'So, how was your day, love?' Dave came back to the table, after taking out the dirty dishes and putting the kettle on.

'Well,' Tess sighed, 'Pretty sad, actually. Our boss, Mr Ford, died. Turns out he drowned in the river a couple of nights ago. Such a tragedy, we were all in shock when we found out.'

'So that's what the police were doing by the river! Me and Britney were there watching, we thought someone had been murdered! Was it murder? Is it in the paper?' Chantelle picked up the local paper and leafed through it, disappointed to find only a short paragraph stating the bare facts about the incident.

'That's rough, babes, did you know him well?'

But no, Tess hadn't seen a lot of Peter Ford, didn't really know much about him at all. He was a nice man, pleasant, gentle nature, that was all she could say. Von had known him better, having worked at the store a lot longer than Tess, and was very upset.

'It's quite a mystery really, like, no-one knows why he parked his car down by the river late at night. There's talk of him having got drunk at The Spotted Dog, but Von says that's not like him at all. His poor wife, she must be devastated.'

'Everyone's got their secrets, love, who knows what was going on in his life? Maybe he topped himself.' Dave got up to make the tea, as Chantelle announced that she was going to take a bath and get changed into her pyjamas.

'That reminds me of something else, we had a mad old woman in the store today, in her dressing gown! Can you believe it? Walking around, muttering and laughing to herself. The security guards had to escort her out. Shame, poor thing, she shouldn't be allowed to wander around on her own like that, should have someone looking after her.'

Chantelle giggled, 'I saw her too! She was in the stationers when me and Brit popped in after school! In a pink dressing gown, and she was wearing her slippers! We've seen her before, round the village, but she was dressed normally, although come to think of it, she was acting weird then, talking to herself and stuff.'

'Oh well, every village has to have its nutter, I suppose,' Dave grinned, 'as long as it's not either of you two!'

~

'Chants, I'm telling you, this village is packed with weirdos!' Britney was busy texting her friend, keeping one eye on her little brother as he stirred the baked beans.

'Can you believe she was in Mum's store, as well? That means she probably went on the bus like that!' Chantelle grinned as she typed.

'We should follow her!' You can put the toast on now, Shane!' The one benefit of babysitting her little brother was that at least he was happy to do what she told him, in this instance, to make beans on toast for their dinner.

'Yeah sure, what, like that other weirdo? We need to get a closer look there, see what's going on. That freak is up to something seriously sick! I mean, what is even going on in there?' They both laughed delightedly, there was nothing better than a little mystery for them to solve, it helped quell the boredom of village life.

'Gotta go, dinner!' Britney signed off and Chantelle smiled to herself. Britney was a cool friend, maybe moving here hadn't turned out so badly after all.

KNICKER THIEF AT BUBBLES LAUNDERETTE

Sasha was feeling miserable. Thirty-four years old, no 'proper' boyfriend (you couldn't count Eric), no social life and not even a cat for company. She licked her finger to pick up the last few crumbs from her plate. Really, Sasha? Is it not bad enough that you ate the cupcake, without having to finish every last crumb?

Ever since she'd found Fifi for Mrs Wendham-Smythe, a little box had arrived at her home each week, the contents of which she was utterly helpless to resist. She'd have to tell her to stop she decided ruefully, looking at, what she realised in horror could only be the beginnings of a muffin top.

Sasha's thoughts strayed to her sister. She missed her. Sure, they texted often, managed the odd quick phone call, but it wasn't the same as having her up the road. No popping in with pizzas on a Friday night, the chats over too many glasses of wine. She was lonely. Eric hardly counted as a reliable boyfriend, in fact, half her and Tess's chats over their Friday pizzas and wine had been about why she continued to let him use her the way he did.

Turning her attention to her latest case, she perused her notes again. This was different, and rather amusing, she had to admit. Someone was stealing customers' underwear. And not just any old underwear, just the really large stuff. It seems they had a very particular kind of pervert frequenting Bubbles Launderette. Well, this one shouldn't be too difficult, she should be able to spot him a mile off, an image of him already forming in her mind.

The next morning Sasha arrived at Bubbles with a bag of carefully selected underwear, bought earlier from the charity shop along the road. The cashier had raised her eyes slightly, at Sasha's purchases, but Sasha had smiled and shrugged nonchalantly. Making a point of spreading out the items on the top of the table, she slowly placed them into the washing machine, observing the reactions of the other customers.

Surprise, of course, was the main reaction, of those who bothered to look, most customers just wanting to finish their laundry and get home.

Three hours later, and she was bored stiff. She must have washed and dried her selection of underwear about three times now, and no-one had shown the slightest bit of interest. Maybe the knicker thief didn't come in until later. Sighing, she packed up her bag and went off for a walk.

After a lunch break, during which she'd consumed a burger and chips, she returned to Bubbles. *If she carried on eating like that she'd fit into these knickers.* She held up the voluminous undergarment, making a show of it, before dropping it into the top loader. Doing the same with a huge beige bra, she clocked the guy two machines along. He was definitely interested in her laundry. Glancing at him suspiciously, she watched him wink at her, a smirk on his face.

He didn't *look* like a pervert, but who knew? Slowly, and deliberately, Sasha withdrew the next pair of gigantic knickers from her bag, before accidentally dropping them onto the floor. The guy's eyes were fixated on the knickers. Slowly, she picked them up, catching his eye again, as she placed them into the machine. *Did he just lick his lips?* Tipping the rest of the items onto the sorting table, Sasha spread them around, making a big display of it, before placing them, one at a time, into the washing machine.

While the machine whirred Sasha kept her eye on her prey, leaning forward when he removed his own washing and transferred it to a tumble dryer. It looked like genuine guy stuff, shirts, tee shirts, jeans, and the like. He sat down on a seat close to hers, and she could feel him glancing her way a few times.

Pretending to need change, she left her wet underwear sitting in an open tumble dryer, and moved across the shop to the change machine. The wall mirror gave her a clear view of her suspect. But he remained seated, his eyes following her movements. Maybe he only stole dry items. She sat back down and waited.

Her suspect's tumble dryer was finished before hers, and he made a point of removing his clothing excruciatingly slowly. *He's waiting for my load to finish!* A few minutes later her tumble dryer switched off. *Here we go, time to reel him in.*

Sasha picked out a couple of pairs of the huge knickers and laid them on the sorting table. Keeping an eye on him she turned to the tumble dryer, pulling out an enormous pair of tights. These she draped alongside the knickers, before doing the same with what must be the largest bra she'd ever seen. Pretending to turn her back she fiddled with her phone, as if reading a message, all the while watching him surreptitiously.

He was definitely interested. Was that a slight sheen of sweat on his upper lip? He licked his lips. He wanted them, she was sure!

'Sorry, I've got to ask.'

Sasha swung round, startled. 'Yes?'

'This is going to sound corny,' he grinned mischievously. 'But what's a hot chick like you doing with the most enormous underwear I've ever laid eyes on?' His face crumpled with amusement. 'Sorry.' He held his hands up, as if to ward off an attack. 'You're going to say it's for your gran, and I'm going to look like a real bastard, aren't I? And then you'll refuse to go out for a drink with me.'

Staring at him, she realised that he was actually pretty cute. He was also clearly not her knicker thief. Grinning, Sasha retorted. 'Sorry, did I miss the bit where you actually *asked* me out for a drink?' *Was she flirting with him?* He did have nice brown eyes...

'Well, a guy's gotta ask, it's not often you find such an attractive woman in here. And something tells me you'd have an interesting story to tell. And I'm a good listener. *And*, can I take you out for a drink? My name's Sam, by the way.' His eyes crinkled at the corners as he smiled disarmingly at her.

About to reply, Sasha's eyes fell on her pile of underwear on the table beside them. The tights were gone!

She lunged for his bag. 'Where are they, Sam? What have you done with them?' She tipped his clean laundry out onto the table and rifled through it. *No tights*. About to apologise, and feeling embarrassed, she was stopped in her tracks as Sam put his hand out.

'I think I've just fallen in love with you. You're the most intriguing character I've met in a long time.' Laughing, he tried to be serious. 'Listen, whatever's going on, I'm sure it's going to make for an entertaining story, why don't you come for a drink, there's a pub just along the road?'

But Sasha was busy scanning the other customers in the launderette. No-one looked suspicious. She rushed to the door and looked up and down the street. Shaking her head, she returned to Sam. Whoever it was had got clean away.

Feeling that she definitely owed the poor guy an apology, *and he was cute*, Sasha smiled at him. 'Tell you what, Sam, why don't I buy *you* a drink, to apologise?'

An hour later she and Sam were still sitting in The King's Head and on their second bottle of wine. Every now and then Sam would collapse into fits of laughter. 'Sasha, you must have the weirdest job I've ever heard of. I've got to say, when I saw you waving those huge knickers around, I was pretty gobsmacked. I couldn't take my eyes off them!'

'Yeah, well thanks to you and your suspicious behaviour I didn't nab the guy. I've absolutely no idea what he looked like. I'll have to do it all again tomorrow.'

'I'm sorry I won't be here to see it.' Sam placed his hand over hers. 'I fly back to the States tomorrow morning. But I still have all night...'

Realising that he was hinting, she tried to think rapidly. Was he cute? Yes. Did she fancy him? Hell yes. Had she had too much to drink? Probably. Did she want to sleep with him? Well, she could definitely have her arm twisted... Should she sleep with him? Probably not. No, definitely not. *That too much to drink thing...* Smiling resignedly Sasha removed her hand. 'I have to go now, Sam. This has been fun, but I do have to go.'

Sam shrugged, nodding. 'No problem, it was worth a try. I'm really glad I met you though, Sasha. You've made my last evening in London one to remember.'

They left the pub together, and, realising that they were going in different directions, Sam leant in and kissed Sasha on the cheek. And then he was gone.

She headed for the pizza takeaway, further along the parade of shops. She'd had pizza on her mind since she'd thought about those Friday night's with Tess, and the smell had wafted along, as she and Sam had walked to the pub, tempting her. She'd get her favourite, chicken, onion, and green pepper.

Sam had been right, she thought later, as she munched on pizza and sipped more wine, her job was pretty bizarre at times. She started laughing again, as she thought of his expression when she'd tipped his bag of laundry out. She hadn't had a job turn into so much fun in ages. But she was no closer to finding her knicker thief, so it was back to Bubbles tomorrow afternoon. Hopefully the perpetrator would be back for more of the same.

Looking out of the window the next morning, Sasha groaned, a hangover, a rainy day, and hours to be spent at Bubbles. Her job didn't feel like so much fun at this moment. She cracked an egg in the frying pan, buttered some bread, and armed with a mug of tea and a fried egg sandwich, sat herself down at her laptop. She might as well complete another module in her private investigating course before heading to Bubbles.

Dreaming about owning her own detective agency, Sasha almost bumped into the man entering the launderette at the same time as her. She began to apologise, but he was in already, letting the door swing back into her. *Thanks a bunch.* Well, he was keen to do his laundry. Interesting...

Taking up position at the machine next to the man, she watched his reaction covertly, as she ostentatiously waved a colossal corset in the air, *she'd been thrilled with this find,* before dropping it playfully into the top loader. The man paused, glancing at the corset, before hurriedly averting his eyes. Beginning to enjoy herself, she stretched out the mammoth pair of black nylon knickers to their full extent, before consigning them to the washing machine. Draping an enormous bra over her arm, she made a show of tipping out the rest of her underwear onto the table, before dropping each item in one at a time.

While her machine hummed busily, Sasha took a seat across from him and observed the man. Black suit, worn in places to a shine, scuffed shoes, off-white shirt, and that dreaded of all things, a comb over gracing his rather sweaty looking pate. Now this was more like the image she'd had in her mind.

Playing the same game as the day before, she slowly and deliberately transferred her washing to the dryer, making sure to leave the corset hanging out of the door, noting the man's reaction. He was sweating, his eyes glued on the fabulous collection of large underwear as it made its way into the tumble dryer. His hands trembled as he placed his own washing into the dryer next to hers, and Sasha was sure she'd found her culprit. Now for her pièce de résistance. The no change act. Off she went to the change machine, all the while watching him carefully in the mirror.

In a flash the man made his move, lunging for the gigantic corset and pulling it from the dryer, then glancing round before quickly grabbing the titanic sized black nylon knickers for good measure. Hastily cramming both items into his bag, he was sitting back down watching his washing tumble, in an instant.

Sasha sent Carol, the owner, a quick message and waited for her reply. The next move was up to her. Carol replied immediately, she was ten minutes out, and wanted to go with the first option.

Waiting outside for Carol, Sasha kept the knicker thief in sight, and when the culprit left the launderette both women followed him at a distance. They didn't have far to walk, he slowed down as he passed an estate agent's, and fumbling for his key, opened the door between the agent's and a betting shop. Sasha made her move.

'Hold it right there!' She stepped in front of the man, with Carol blocking his escape from behind. 'I think you've got something belonging to me.' His eyes darted back and forth between the women, before realising he had no way out. 'Hand over the knickers, and everything else you've stolen from Bubbles and maybe we can keep the cops out of it.' *It was so hard not to laugh.*

'Please, don't call the police. I'll return it all.' The knicker thief was now sweating profusely, and both women wrinkled their noses in distaste. 'It's upstairs.'

They followed him up the stairs and into his flat, stopping in amazement at the array of underwear decorating every surface. The bed was hidden beneath a pile of ladies' oversized underwear. *This guy had a seriously weird fetish.*

'We just want the stuff you stole from Bubbles, but I suggest you return the other items to wherever you nicked them from, alright? Oh, and you're banned from Bubbles, alright? Carol, have you got your list?'

They left the man weeping softly on his bed, as he sorted out the other stolen items of underwear, and headed back to the launderette. 'Sasha, thank you, there are going to be some very happy customers at Bubbles, I'm sure they'll be hugely grateful.' Both women fell about laughing as they realised what Carol had said. 'Fancy a drink?' Carol raised an eyebrow at Sasha.

'That sounds great, let me just retrieve my laundry.' Carol raised her other eyebrow at this. With her charity shop haul bagged up, Sasha and Carol popped along to The King's Head and proceeded to make light work of two bottles of wine, with quiche and salad to soak it up, before bidding each other a rather tipsy farewell later.

Sasha had one last stop to make before heading home. She tucked the bag of large underwear into the corner of the doorway, outside the knicker thief's door, with a note attached. *Next time pay for your ladies' knickers from a charity shop. I'm sure they'll be enormously grateful for your generous custom.*

She was still sniggering at her, admittedly rather lame sense of humour, when she arrived home, but hey she was a little drunk so that was fair enough.

IT ONLY TAKES ONE SENTENCE TO SOW DOUBT

The letter stood out like a sore thumb, it's typewritten address an unusual sight in the days of computers. Tess picked it up with a frown, turning it over in her hand, before tearing it open.

What the hell? Furious, she looked at the envelope again. Well, someone knew her name and address, but what kind of sicko would do this? She re-read the typed sentence on the enclosed sheet of paper, with a trembling hand, her heart racing with anxiety.

YOUR TRASHY DAUGHTER IS A THIEVING LITTLE COW
AND YOUR HUSBAND IS A CHEATING BASTARD

Tess gasped as she put her hand out to steady herself against the small table in the hallway. She felt sick. Turning, she stumbled to the kitchen where she filled a glass from the tap, drinking the water in messy gulps.

It was lies, of course it was. Chantelle would never steal, she was a good girl. Wasn't she? Doubts began to swim in her mind. Stop it Tess, that's what they want whoever they are, it's not true. And Dave? Her mind enquired quietly, would he cheat on her? Was he cheating on her? No way, I don't believe this, it's just vindictive lies. But who would do this?

And now she was going to be late for work. As she waited for the next bus, Tess mulled over the cruel words in the letter. Maybe Chantelle had fallen out with someone at school? Girls could be super bitchy, that was for sure, and if that was the case, the extra cruelty about Dave was just to cause as much hurt as possible.

~

'Don't worry, Tess, it's quiet, I'll be fine 'til you get here. Are you sure you're okay?' Von put her phone back under the counter, worried about her friend and colleague. A customer walked over and Von switched on a smile, she'd check with Tess once she got to work.

Her phone rang again and, worried that it was still Tess, she answered without checking who the caller was. 'Oh, Barbara, hi how are you? What? Oh yes, poor Maureen, how is she? An accident? Yes, that's what we all heard. No, I can't think of anything, the poor woman, it's natural to want answers of course. Well, I'll certainly give it some thought and I'll look around in his office, but I can't honestly think what I'd find to help you. Yes, of course.' Replacing her phone, she hurriedly attended to the two women waiting rather impatiently for her attention.

Tess's white face confirmed that something was wrong, as soon as she joined Von behind the counter. 'I'm sorry I'm late, Von, I missed the bus and the next one was delayed.' Tears welled up in Tess's eyes and Von hurriedly put her arm around her, steering her away from nearby customers.

'Go to the staff room, my love, put the kettle on, I'll find someone to cover.' Von scanned the shop floor, looking for a free member of staff, and having sorted things went off to join Tess.

Rage bubbled up inside her as Von read the single typed line. What kind of person would say such things? 'Oh, Tess, you poor thing. It's lies of course it is, your Chantelle's a good girl, I know that and so do you. And Dave? He's a good husband, you know he'd never cheat on you. It's probably a girl from school, jealous over something maybe? You should throw it away, forget about it.'

Tess nodded miserably, 'I know it's lies, all of it, of course it is. But I can't help wondering, that's the trouble. Should I tell Dave? Should I tell Chantelle? No I don't think so, it'll upset her and it's the last thing she needs, she's just settling down at her new school. She's making friends, seems happy.' Tess's voice trailed off.

'Tess? What is it? You're unsure about something. You know that's what whoever did this wants.'

'I know, it's just, her friend, Britney, she is kind of, I don't know, she could be trouble I think, possibly. But she's a nice girl, Chantelle really likes her, no, I'm sure she's fine. But Dave, well, he has been working late a lot recently...'

'Oh, Tess, come on, you're letting your imagination run away with you. You know he's been taking extra shifts, you even told me.'

'But money still seems so tight, it doesn't make sense. Oh Von, what if it's true? What if he's got someone else? It would explain the late nights, and why we never seem to get straight with our finances.' Tess groaned, holding her stomach as she leant over.

'No,' Von spoke determinedly, 'This letter is someone's idea of a sick joke. This is exactly what they want, you mustn't give them the satisfaction of believing their lies. Throw it away, my darling, forget all about it. That way they don't win.'

With Tess comforted and reassured, and a further cup of tea drunk, this time accompanied by a biscuit, the two women returned to their counter.

~

Barbara finished her call to Von, wondering if any good would come of it. She doubted it, but at least she could tell Maureen she'd tried. A flurry of clients kept her busy until well into the afternoon and two viewings and one signed tenant later, she finally closed up her office. She'd pop to the shops and get some gin, oh, and something to eat for her dinner.

The balmy summer days were a pleasure, she thought, as she walked along the high street. She'd make a salad, sit outside, and enjoy her solitary evening. A few gin and tonics were all the company she needed, although she could always count on the company of dotty Dorothy of course, twitching her curtains as she spied on her neighbours. That woman seriously needed to get a life, or help.

As she walked back to pick up her car from her office, Barbara noticed a familiar face, wasn't that the daughter of one of her tenants? Yes, Riverside Gardens, that was it, the name escaped her for the moment. But what were those girls doing? Were they following someone? Him? Why on earth would they be following him? She watched them, with amusement, as they trailed the man along the road and out of sight. Playing at sleuthing, she supposed, shaking her head, probably from watching one of the popular TV series, but not the worst thing they could be doing these days.

After a healthy chicken salad and a few not so healthy gin and tonics, Barbara remembered that she hadn't spoken to Maureen. It wasn't too late, she decided, and clicked on her friend's name on her cell phone. Having reassured Maureen that Von from Beedham's would do a little investigating regarding Peter, the two women chatted for a few minutes longer.

'Oh, I'll tell you something funny that I saw today,' Barbara laughed. 'Those two girls from the new estate, acting like spies or something, following him they were, he had no idea... Hang on, Maureen, that lunatic is watching me again... Oh, okay, you've got to go? No problem, chat soon.'

'What?' She yelled up at the window, the alcohol fuelling her resentment at being spied on by her irritating neighbour. 'Never seen anyone drink before?' There, that made her feel better, she'd never seen a curtain close so quickly in her life. Defiantly, she poured herself another drink, holding it up to no-one in particular. 'Cheers!' she slurred happily.

FOUR PRETTY LETTERS

She-devil! I couldn't believe it! How dare she shout at me? Was everyone going mad tonight? George even had the nerve to tell me to take a bath earlier! All because I asked him why he was so late. I knew what the time was, he couldn't fool me, saying it was only six o'clock when I knew it was past eight o'clock. Told me to lie down, laughed hysterically at me when I said he must have another woman, and him stinking of that sickly lavender again. Of course, I knew he'd been visiting his old harpy of a mother, he should have just married her. That made me giggle.

I ran the bath taps, to get away from him, but there was no time to waste with bathing we decided, as we sat in the bathroom having a talk, we needed to plan my letters. It was nice to have my friends back, made me feel all warm and happy. Tonight was the night, yes, I nodded in excitement, I would work through the night, making my beautiful letters, my children.

I waltzed back downstairs, humming, as I smiled secretively at George. The fool, of course I wasn't talking to anyone, yes, I'd had my bath, yes, I felt much better. I sang quietly as I put the kettle on, grinning at my friends when George wasn't looking. They were making me laugh so much, the things they were saying about him behind his back, oh he had no idea.

It was George's fault there was no dinner, not mine. I wasn't the one swanning in so late. My friends found it hilarious when I told him I'd thrown his dinner in the bin, especially when he checked and it wasn't there. I was laughing so much the tears were running down my face, he looked so stupid, his red face peering in the bin.

He'd drawn himself up, pompous fool, held out the newspaper at me. Did I know it was Mr Ford they'd found in the river? That stopped me in my tracks, like he was proud about it. Now my head was hurting as I tried to think, it was all wrong, she was supposed to be punished, not him.

I was all worked up, waiting with my friends, for him to fall asleep. Finally, I could hear his snoring through my bedroom wall. So many thoughts were muddling around in my head, and the voices, everyone talking at once.

I got up and checked my windows, noting the lights on at the Burton house. Lights on at the dirty strumpet's too, that was interesting. Probably her filthy lover paying her a visit I thought with disgust. She still needed teaching a lesson, carrying on and her poor husband not cold in his grave. I basked in the warmth, as the voices agreed with me, praising me for my good morals.

I hummed to myself as I worked, smiling and talking quietly to my companions. Dorothy was such a clever girl. I felt quite proud as I explained everything to my new friends. I couldn't see them, not exactly, but they were there, just out of sight, like shadows.

I lost sight of the time to be honest, I was enjoying myself so much. I didn't need sleep, that was for the weak. I didn't need anything, just my cuttings and my glue. I was an artist. A true artist, not like her lover, the fake, with hair like a woman's. I giggled happily, at the thought, as I stuck down my cuttings.

I looked proudly at my finished work. Four pretty letters. On four sheets of pretty paper. Not that plain paper from George's work that he always brought home. Oh no, mine was beautiful. I held them up to show everyone. We decided it was time to put everything away before George came down, so I cleared up and went upstairs, taking my envelopes with me.

I sat on my bed, swinging my legs happily as I looked at my neat envelopes spread out on the bed cover. I could hear beautiful music playing, it was such wonderful day I thought happily, as I stood up and twirled in front of the mirror.

Oh, I wished I could see that drunken trollop's face when my letter was opened. She thought she could get away with such brazen behaviour, offending us respectable people with her goings on. Not any more, I laughed.

Hmm, I paused over one of my envelopes, pity I didn't have more information on that one. But it was enough to spoil her fun and put a stop to it.

I hugged myself with excitement. Save the best 'til last. I started to laugh again. I was going to destroy them. This was only the beginning. I was a genius, I agreed happily, smiling around my room. I couldn't wait to get started on more letters for them, as soon as they'd received these ones. The music got louder, really, was George going deaf? Must he play the radio so loudly in the morning?

I don't usually shout, it's not becoming in a lady, but it was so inconsiderate of him after my busy night. I opened my door and shouted, as I went downstairs. But the voices were shouting as well and I felt fuzzy in my head, music, noise, shouting, all at once.

'Dorothy?' I nearly jumped out of my skin when George touched my arm, a funny look on his face. He was looking at me oddly a lot these days, don't ask me why, he was lucky to have such a good wife at home looking after him if you ask me.

He was still in his dressing gown, had only just come downstairs he said, because he heard me shouting. What music, he wanted to know? I put the kettle on, feeling confused at his lying. I watched him go back upstairs and stop at my door.

'No!' I ran up the stairs, I don't mind telling you. He has no right to go into my room. My letters! 'Get out!' I screamed at him, pushing him away from my door. I had to stay up there until I heard him leave for work after that. He'd thrown me right off. I needed to collect my thoughts and check that I had enough stamps for my envelopes.

Of course, he tapped on my door making out he was concerned about me before he left. But I ignored him. He'd caused me enough upset for one day. I waited until I heard his car drive off and then I brushed my hair, adding a pretty hairclip to match my dressing gown, and prepared to pop to the post box.

There, all my pretty letters safely posted, four more beautiful children sent out into the world, ready to do their good work. I sat down on the bench, beside the old Victorian post box, and had a rest. I was quite exhausted. I needed a cup of tea and a little nap, perhaps back indoors on the couch.

And then the sound of the kitchen door closing woke me up. I got up, feeling a little woozy, oh it was him. Said he'd forgotten something. I didn't believe him, he looked shifty, hiding things in his pocket. Go back to sleep he told me, the nerve of the man, and me with so much to do.

DÉJÀ VU

He tried to calm himself, one hand on his rapidly beating heart. Those damned bitches had no right sneaking around, sticking their noses into his and Mother's business. How dare they come into Mother's cottage? Rage coursed through him. And now look what they'd made him do. He hadn't meant for it to happen, he told her, it was an accident. Yes, he knew what he had to do, she couldn't stay here, of course. He'd attend to it as soon as he could.

What about the other one? No, he couldn't, please, did he have to? Yes, he knew there were only a few of Mother's pills left, but surely, well, he couldn't do that, not deliberately. He needed to think, needed to make a plan. He checked outside the front door for the umpteenth time, much to Mother's mockery, using his foot to nudge the old iron door stop into its familiar resting place. A wave of déjà vu washed over him, the years falling away to when he was a young boy. Strange how no-one ever looked twice at something that was in plain sight. Oh yes, he was a clever boy, and one day he'd tell her about what he'd done for her all those years ago.

He walked upstairs to the attic room where the typewriter sat in the middle of his old desk. Sitting down, he slowly fed a sheet of paper into the typewriter, as memories flooded his head.

Sitting, cowed, at the typewriter, as her shrilly voice berated him. 'Do it again, it's not good enough! You're never good enough at anything, George!'

Desperately wanting to tell her about the letters he typed for her, but instead, hanging his head. 'Yes, Mother, sorry, Mother.' Trying again, wanting to please her, the crumpled balls of paper piling up on the floor as she tore them from the typewriter. And then, heaven, typing the whole sentence with no mistakes and being rewarded with Mother's beautiful smile.

'That's my good boy', her arms around him as he breathed in her scent, 'Come now, go and put the kettle on, you can make us some tea.'

Beaming up at his mother, as he stood up, oh he loved to make her happy, she was everything to him. She was his whole world.

He shook his head, to dispel the memories, and began typing the first letter. Well, well, well, this was very interesting. He had to hand it to her, she had a way of finding things out. An idea formed in his mind, clever old George, it might just work, yes, one less dipsomaniac in society wouldn't be a bad thing. But didn't she know that letters like this were unacceptable? Mother would be proud of him, the way he turned these ridiculous missives into neatly typed letters. He hadn't told her yet, was saving it up as a surprise. It would make a wonderful story over tea and crumpets perhaps, one evening. And then finally Mother would see how clever he was, how powerful. Then maybe he could tell Mother about the letters all those years ago, and about *him*, and what he'd done for her...

Yes, yes, I know who *she* is, but who's this one? A single mother? He racked his brain, but couldn't think who she might be, the address giving nothing away. Still, he'd send it out with the others, after all, he had to say he agreed with the sentiment expressed. He checked the time, on his watch. It was quite late, but Dorothy wouldn't notice.

MISSING

'Come on, babes, let me take you out for a drink, we can get a bite to eat there, as well. You deserve a night off.'

It was nice to have Dave home at a reasonable time, Tess thought happily. But what about Chantelle? She hadn't come home, was probably at Britney's. She should have let her know though, she knew the rules. Should she tell Dave about the letter? But no, if she did, he'd know what had been said about him, and he'd lose the plot about what was said about Chantelle. No, she'd take Von's advice, ignore it, not let some sicko have the satisfaction of having caused them all upset. Try and have a nice evening together, they so rarely got the chance why spoil it?

'Send her a text, she's fine, let her be, it's good that she's made a friend.' Dave was in a great mood.

Yes, it was good to be out together, felt like the old days. Feeling nicely relaxed after their pub meal, Tess watched Dave as he headed to the bar to get them another round. He was splashing the cash around a bit though and they couldn't really spare it at the moment. She checked her phone again, still no reply from Chantelle. She'd have to speak to her about that.

She watched Dave, as he chatted to the guys at the bar. He seemed to know quite a few of them, no surprise really he probably worked with some of them. There seemed to be a lot of chat going on though, with the barmaid, and that guy with the long hair, people gesticulating, pointing at one of the tables.

'What is it, Dave? What's everyone talking about?' Tess put her phone away, she'd deal with Chantelle later. 'Really? Mr Ford was in here the night he died?'

Dave nodded. 'Apparently he was in here that night, drunk as a skunk, knocking back pints before hitting the double whiskies. Must have stopped off at the river on his way home, fallen in somehow.'

Their little house was all in darkness when they arrived back, Chantelle must have gone to bed already. Tess was about to creep upstairs to check when Dave slipped his arms around her, nuzzling her hair. 'Leave her,' he whispered into her ear, gently kissing her neck.

Tess turned to him, lifting her face to his, as the two kissed and lowered themselves to the couch. Their lovemaking had been infrequent since the stress of losing their old house and starting a new life. It was wonderful to feel desire rising inside, and to feel Dave's obvious desire pressing against her.

They pulled off their clothes and hungrily explored each other's bodies, giggling like teenagers as they shushed each other, not wanting to wake their sleeping daughter.

'That was brilliant.' Dave smiled into Tess's eyes as he stroked her hair away from her forehead. She smiled back happily, *they were going to be okay*. 'You go up, babes, I'll put the kettle on, bring us some tea.'

Tess crept upstairs and used the bathroom, before slipping into her robe in the bedroom. She'd better just check on Chantelle she thought, heading along the passage and quietly opening the door to her daughter's room.

'What is it, love?' Dave looked at his wife's worried face, with concern, a cup of tea in each hand.

'She's not here. Where is she? It's 11.30pm!' Panicked, she called her daughter's phone, looking at Dave, in anguish, as it just rang. 'I'm calling Britney. Or should I call her mother? I don't have her number though. Oh, Dave, this isn't good.' Tess's eyes welled up as she frantically scrolled through her phone to find Britney's number.

With shaking hands, she called Britney, waiting anxiously for the girl to answer. Nothing. She called again, looking desperately at Dave. 'No reply.' They looked at each other, fear mounting as they began to panic. 'What's her mother's name? I can't remember, not sure if we even know her surname.'

'Get dressed, we'll go round there, can you remember the house number?' Dave's face was grim as he pulled his jeans on, hurriedly yanking his tee shirt down over his head.

But Tess couldn't. 'I'm sure the road is Bank Crescent, or is it Bankside? All the damn street names sound the same here,' Tess wailed, as the two picked up their pace.

'Tess,' Dave stopped, taking hold of his wife's shoulders. 'Calm down, think. You dropped the girls there one afternoon, remember, when I was off sick? You said it was a nice house, pretty garden or something?'

'Yes, that's right! It's in a row of terraced houses, smaller than ours, towards the edge of the estate. Oh, and I had to turn the car round, it was a dead end. I've got it, Bankside Close, that's it! And it's Lilith. The mother's name's Lilith!' The couple started running as Tess found her bearings. 'And it wasn't a pretty garden, it was pretty window boxes, the houses are right on the pavement!'

Tess waited breathlessly, as Dave hammered on the front door. 'Lilith? You in there? Lilith, open up!' A tiny voice from the other side of the door asked who it was. 'It's Chantelle's mum and dad, is that Britney's brother? Is Britney there? Is your mum there, son?' But neither Britney nor his mum were there, he informed them, and he wasn't allowed to open the door.

'What the bloody hell's going on? Is everyone missing tonight?' Dave fumed.

'Dave, don't say that, please.' Tess was on the verge of tears. Lights played over them, coming down the road as a taxi pulled to a halt outside the house, and they turned to watch Lilith stumble from the cab and make her way unsteadily towards them.

'What sort of mother leaves her little kid on his own all night?' Dave roared angrily, at the woman.

'Dave, please,' Tess held his arm. 'Lilith, it's Tess, Chantelle's mum. We can't get hold of our daughter, and your daughter's not answering her phone. D'you know where they are? Your son says he's on his own.' Tess could feel sobs rising inside, along with her panic, and tried to hold them down. If she started crying she might not be able to stop.

'Lilith looked at them, confused. 'What are you talking about? My Britney's here, babysitting Shane. And who are you, to have a go at me?' The woman drew herself up defiantly. 'Where were you then, if you don't know where your own daughter is?'

It's true, thought Tess, she should never have gone out, not when she hadn't been able to get hold of Chantelle. 'Look, this isn't helping, can we come in? Speak to Britney? Maybe Chantelle's with her and they fell asleep or something?' Please God, she thought, let that be the case.

But a tearful Shane informed them that he was definitely alone. Britney had never come home. He'd made himself a cheese sandwich when she didn't arrive and he got hungry. The three parents looked at each other in mounting panic. Not waiting for permission, Dave ran upstairs to check the rooms, before coming slowly back downstairs, shaking his head.

Tess was filled with despair. Now she'd have to tell Dave about the letter, couldn't keep it a secret when they had no idea where Chantelle was. But not in front of Lilith, back at home she decided. They left with assurances to let each other know if they heard anything and that once home, if there was still no sign of the girls, they would let Lilith know, and both would phone the police.

With no sign of Chantelle or Britney back at home, Dave picked up the phone and called the police, his face grim.

'Dave,' Tess felt tears welling up in her eyes. 'There's something I need to tell you.'

'And that's all it said? Chantelle was a thief? You're sure? Talk to me, Tess, I know you're hiding something.' Dave was furious.

Stumbling over her words, Tess told Dave the accusation against him, his angry reaction reassuring her that there must be no truth in it.

'You didn't believe it? It's all a sick bunch of twisted lies, about Chants *and* about me, you know it is, babes. But who would do this to us? What kind of sicko does this? Where's the letter? Let me see it.' Dave paced angrily.

'I threw it away, oh, Dave, I should have kept it, but Von said to just get rid of it.'

'You told Von? You told Von but you didn't tell me?'

Their frustrated discussion was cut short by the arrival of the police, and Dave opened the door to the two officers.

RESERVATION MADE

Half-asleep, Sasha listened worriedly, as Tess cried and garbled out words about Chantelle; missing; another girl; her and Dave at the pub; her fault.

'Tess, slow down, what's happened, take a deep breath and talk to me slowly.'

With a superhuman effort, Tess forced herself to calm down and explain the situation to her sister. Leaving nothing out, she brought Sasha up to speed, ending with the question, 'She hasn't called you has she, Sash?'

But Sasha shook her head as she spoke into her phone, 'No, I wish she had, but I'll keep trying her number, and I'll send her a text. And you never told her about the letter, Tess? Sure? You didn't fight about it or anything? But you told the cops about it didn't you? Oh, Tess, of course you should have, no, I'm not saying it could be related, but you need to tell them everything. The police make a good point though, my darling, these things do happen all the time, I know it doesn't help, but it's true. Kids fight with their parents and take off thinking they'll teach them a lesson. No, I know that's not Chantelle, but she's been through a lot of changes, honey, she could be acting up over something? I'm sure the cops will be keeping an eye out for her but they're right when they say she'll probably be back home by tomorrow.'

'But what if she's not!' Tess wailed into her phone, feeling half comforted by Sasha's words but unable to bear the alternative, that her daughter wouldn't walk back in the door as if nothing had happened. That she might never walk back in the door...

Sasha made a decision. 'Tess, if she's not back by tomorrow, although I'm sure she will be, I'll come up, okay? But let the police guide you, and talk to her friend's mum again, see if she has anything else she can tell you about her daughter that might help. But I bet you anything you like you'll be phoning me in the morning to say she's back home.'

But Tessa didn't phone Sasha in the morning to tell her Chantelle was home, and by late afternoon there was still no sign of either girl. Neither Tessa nor Dave had gone to work, both spending the day in a state of high anxiety, rushing to answer phones the second they rang, to no avail. There was no word from Chantelle.

Lilith Morton, equally, had spent the day at home worried sick about her daughter. A neighbour had taken Shane to school and picked him up, enabling Lilith to remain at home in case Britney appeared. The two mothers had talked on the phone, sharing anything they could think of with each other, which was very little when all was said and done.

Tess hadn't, however, told Lilith about the poisonous letter, not seeing how it could possibly have anything to do with Chantelle being missing, as her daughter hadn't known that Tess had even received it. Neither mother could think of a single reason why their girls would suddenly disappear from their homes and both mothers were, by late afternoon, in terribly distressed states.

A sixth sense had caused Sasha to spend the day tying up loose ends and making preparations for the possibility of a trip to visit her sister. There was a pub with rooms in the village, the spotted something, she'd found out online, she could stay there if she went. Tess would want her to stay with them, but they only had the two bedrooms and she wouldn't stay in Chantelle's room, that just wouldn't feel right. Finally she thought, after almost a year I plan to visit my sister, and it takes my niece going missing to make it happen. She picked up her phone to call Tess, maybe Chantelle had walked indoors this very minute. But she'd decided already, no matter what, she was going to visit Tess.

A tearful Tessa confirmed that there was still no sign of Chantelle, and that the police had returned to request a photograph, the same being requested from Lilith, of Britney.

'Okay, I'll be on my way soon, sis, I'll give you a call when I stop on the road. No, don't make up the couch for me, no, not Chantelle's room, hun, she'll be needing that, no, I've made a plan, I'll talk to you soon.' Sasha rushed around throwing the last few items of clothing and toiletries into her bag.

Bringing the details for The Spotted Dog back up on her phone, she called the pub. A quick chat with someone called Jules and she had a room booked for the next few nights. Deliberating on whether she should make another call, as she loaded her car, Sasha wondered if Eric would even notice she'd gone away. Probably not, no, she'd leave it for now, maybe call him when she got there, maybe not, it wasn't like they were really a couple anymore.

YOU MUST BE SASHA

Tess threw the front door open before Sasha had even turned off the engine, flying out and virtually pulling her from the car. 'Oh, Sash, it's so good to see you!' She burst into tears as she hugged her sister.

Sasha held her, stroking her hair, as Tessa's sobs showed no sign of calming down. 'It's good to see you too, sis!' She allowed herself to be dragged through the front door where Dave stood waiting to envelop her in a bear hug, his sobs mingling with Tess's.

'Kettle. Tea. And where's the loo? I'm bursting!' Sasha took control. 'And then you can tell me everything.'

With the essentials taken care of, the three of them sat down in the lounge and Sasha listened carefully to everything that had happened. With no leads the police were planning to conduct interviews with the girls' classmates and following on from that a search would be organised.

'Look, Tess, the police know what they're doing of course they do, you've got to trust them. And you need to tell them about the letter.'

'But what can that have to do with anything? I never mentioned it to Chantelle, so she wasn't upset about it, she didn't even know about it! And all that crap about Dave, it's all lies, it's just some sicko.'

Dave laid a steadying hand on Tess's arm. 'Babe, if Sash thinks we should tell them then I think we should. I'm not saying it's got anything to do with it, but they need to know everything. We should have told them straightaway, now they'll probably wonder why we didn't say anything.'

Sasha nodded. 'And after all, whoever the sicko is, the cops need to find him or her, find out why they sent you the letter in the first place. Maybe they know something, maybe they-no, it doesn't matter. Let's just say we need to tell them, and soon.'

Tess groaned, 'You were going to say maybe the person who wrote the letter did something to Chantelle, weren't you?'

'Look, let's just tell the cops first thing in the morning, okay? Let them decide what's important.' Sasha yawned, 'I really need to get to the pub, have a shower and get some sleep. I'll come back tomorrow, early, and we'll go together if you want? Okay?'

With promises and agreements made, Tessa and Dave waved Sasha off, and she headed for The Spotted Dog.

The welcoming smells and sounds enveloped her as she opened the door to the pub, a heady mixture of beer, food, and the waft of fresh cigarette smoke as a smoker came in from the beer garden, all accompanied by the gentle murmur of voices.

'You must be Sasha?' A smiling blonde walked out from around the bar and welcomed her, taking her bag. 'What d'you want first? A drink? Something to eat? Or shall I show you to your room?'

'That all sounds good!' Sasha smiled, liking Jules instantly. 'My room first I think, so that I can freshen up, then a large glass of white wine will go down a treat. No food tonight thanks, I ate on the way.'

The room was up two flights of stairs, under the eaves, with its own en-suite. Nice, Sasha looked around approvingly at the clean, tasteful room, its curtains gently moving in the breeze from the open window.

After a hot shower she pulled her jeans on and threw on a fresh tee shirt, before heading downstairs. Taking the large glass of wine from Jules with a grateful smile, she perched on one of the bar stools and looked around. It was the perfect country pub, she thought happily, if only she were here for pleasure rather than under such grim circumstances.

A large male presence appeared beside her and ordered the 'same again', before turning to her with a smile. 'You must be Sasha, I'm Cal.'

Something flipped in her stomach as she looked into his twinkling eyes. *Wow*.

THE PAST CATCHES UP

'Ro? Ro, what the bloody hell is this? You and your big mouth, who have you been talking to?' Reg's red face glared angrily at Rosemary as she hurried through from the kitchen, where she'd been about to prepare breakfast.

'What is it, Reg?' She took the sheet of paper from him, reading the single typed sentence, before looking at him in horror. 'Oh God, Reg, someone knows! But how did they-' she paused, noticing an envelope with her own name on. Picking it up, she tore it open and extracted an identical sheet of paper. The typing was the same, the words, however, were different.

The couple stood as if dazed, staring at one another, before laying out the two sheets of paper and reading them again.

YOU CAN'T ESCAPE THE LAW FOREVER. I KNOW WHAT YOU DID.
LOOSE LIPS SINK SHIPS, ESPECIALLY DRUNK ONES.

The letter addressed to Reg was non-specific, but he had no doubt as to what it was referring.

Rosemary's letter, on the other hand, was very pointed.

YOU'RE NOTHING BUT A CHEAP BIT OF TRASH.
VILE STRIPPER WHORE.

We're in trouble, Ro, this is serious, who did you tell? Think, woman!' Reg paced agitatedly up and down the hallway.

'I didn't tell anyone, Reg, I swear.' Rosemary's eyes filled with tears as she frantically racked her brain to think of anything she might have let slip.

'It's been over thirty flaming years! We were home free, we got away with it, and now someone's found us, someone knows. I told you never to get close to anyone, never get too friendly, keep it casual. Who did you tell, Ro?'

'Reg, I'm telling you the truth. I don't even have any close friends, maybe Barbara, but even she's hardly a *close* friend, we've never exchanged confidences, never done the girly chat thing.' She stopped, thinking back to when she used to have a few drinks with Barbara in the early days.

'Did you tell her? Did you tell her, you stupid cow? You used to go round and drink with her before I put a stop to it, what the hell did you say to her, Ro?' Reg thumped the wall with his clenched fist. 'What did you say to your little drinking buddy, you stupid little idiot? Tell her about the money did you? Drank too much did you? Decided to confide about us being on the run?' Reg was shouting as he grasped Rosemary's shoulders, shaking her until she yelled at him to stop.

'Reg, I never told her, not one word, it's the truth! Yes, we used to get a bit tipsy together, have a few glasses of wine, but I stopped, you were right, it was safer that way. She never suspected anything, how could she? I didn't tell her anything!'

'Ro, I swear, we're not leaving this house until you've thought back over every pissed conversation you ever had with that woman. It has to be her, you gave something away you just didn't realise it.'

Rosemary blew her nose, for what felt like the hundredth time, as Reg fired more questions at her. 'Please, Reg, we've been at this for hours, there's nothing else.' She felt wrung out, this was the old Reg, she hadn't seen much of him in recent years. 'I've told you a million times, we talked about shopping, clothes, oh I don't know... gardens, holidays, that sort of thing, nothing personal, it was all just the usual crap women talk about over a glass of wine or two.'

'Did you go out anywhere? Watch any movies? Borrow a book or something? Anything that might've made you say something by mistake?'

Movies. Rosemary hesitated, a flicker of something in the back of her mind. What was it now? A TV show, that was it, she remembered now. But it was nothing, a passing comment, Barbara had been too sloshed to even notice her slip-up, she was sure.

'Ro?' Reg's voice sounded sharp and urgent. 'You've thought of something, what was it? I swear to God, woman, you tell me right now.'

'Ow, Reg, you're hurting me!' Rosemary pulled her arm away, rubbing it where Reg's fingers had gripped the skin, causing red marks to appear. 'It was nothing, a tiny thing, she didn't even notice. We were watching some show on TV, I dunno, a reality show or something, a bunch of stupid kids, fake tans, all that stuff, we weren't even watching it properly, it was just on. They were in Essex, Basildon, I recognised the street where the club used to be. It's still there, just got a different name. I think I started to say something about how I used to work there, but I stopped. I stopped, Reg, I never even finished saying it. She was half-cut, wasn't really listening to me.'

'Oh, she was listening alright. Probably did some digging, wanted to find out about your past. About *our* past. I told you people are always going to wonder where we came from, where our money came from. I'm just surprised she didn't do it sooner. Pissed her off lately have you? And now what? What's she going to do next? Ask for money that's what. She wants us to know it's her and that you're the drunk fool who told her. We're in big shit, Ro.' Reg jumped up, his angry pacing around the living room making Rosemary even more nervous.

'I'll talk to her, Reg. See what she says, I'm sure there's a simple explanation, she's not like that, I'm sure of it.' But Reg wasn't listening, his mind was working overtime, he had to come up with a solution and fast.

He was quiet while they ate their somewhat belated brunch, the TV on although neither of them could have said what the programme was. The rest of the day and evening passed in a tension-fuelled atmosphere, Reg's dark glares and furrowed brows filling Rosemary with anxiety. When she began to make moves to go to bed, asking him nervously if he wanted a cup of tea first, he finally spoke.

He was very clear, she was to go to bed, she wasn't to talk to anyone, not answer the phone, nothing. He would sort this out. She was to forget all about it, forget the letters ever existed. And she was definitely to forget all about Barbara Fenton.

'I'm going out.' Reg was grim. 'You close the curtains and go to bed, you hear me?' He slammed the door and Rosemary did as she was told, not wanting to think about where Reg was going or what he was going to do. But this was the old Reg, he was back...

AND THEN THERE WERE TWO

The three women's day had started the same, in as much as they all woke up, but from there things progressed in different directions.

Sasha opened her eyes dreamily, revelling in the comfortable bed, the soft bedding, the absolute peace and quiet. It was so different to London, she could get used to this.

She allowed herself a few moments of reflection on the evening before. Wow, that Cal was sexy... One glass of wine had turned into three, *or was it four?* as they'd chatted at the bar, popping out for the odd cigarette in the warm evening air. She felt a flutter of excitement at the thought that he was in the room across from hers, probably lying in his bed, his long hair tousled on the pillow... Stop it, Sash, you're not here for romance.

Romance. That stopped her thought process in its tracks. Eric. She hadn't told him where she was. She'd thought about it, for about one minute, but then she'd thought about the photo of him with the redhead. It wasn't as if Eric ever kept her informed of his movements. She wouldn't hear from him for a week or so then when she phoned him it would be a 'Sorry babe, I've been busy, I'll call you tomorrow we'll go out.' Always on his terms, when it suited him. No, she didn't owe him an explanation, if anything he owed her one. And probably if she was honest she and Eric were not even a couple, not anymore.

She sighed to herself, she'd better get up. Poor Tess, she'd be expecting her early and it was imperative that they tell the police about the letter as soon as possible, of that Sasha was sure. With that thought in mind she jumped out of bed and after a quick shower, dressed and headed out of her room.

Jules, the barmaid, was waiting for her as she entered the pub. 'Morning, love! Beautiful day isn't it? Got time for some breakfast? Help yourself to fruit and yoghurt and I'll get the kitchen to cook some eggs for you. Sunny side up alright?' Jules bustled off, without waiting for a reply.

Checking her watch, and realising that she was quite hungry Sasha did as she was told and served herself some fresh fruit, before taking a seat at the lone table with a breakfast setting laid out. Obviously Cal didn't have breakfast here then...

After fresh farm eggs and bacon, and strong tea, Sasha reluctantly reminded herself that she wasn't here on holiday and with a quick thanks to Jules, headed for her car, and her sister.

~

Barbara woke up with a mild hangover, nothing out of the ordinary there, and groaning, forced herself to get out of her bed and start the day. Her routine was always the same, downstairs to put some coffee on, back upstairs for a shower then check the post as she enjoyed her coffee and toast.

Taking a bite of her buttery toast, she frowned at the envelope in her hand. Something odd about it, yes, vaguely familiar, and so with slight foreboding her finger slit open the envelope. What the hell, again? This had to be some kind of joke. No, not a joke. It had to be that mad old cow. How dare she! And her as mad as a hatter. She read the spiteful words again, in disbelief.

YOU'RE NOTHING BUT A SAD OLD DRUNK.
YOU'RE AN UGLY, FAT, ALCOHOLIC,
WITH NO FRIENDS BUT THE BOTTLE.

Her eyes swam with tears. It was so cruel, even if it was from a mad woman. Why would she do this? Evil cow. She'd laughed off the first one, crumpling it and throwing it in the bin without another thought. But this one was so hurtful. She sat there for a while, her toast forgotten, coffee going cold, feeling sorry for herself. It was true that was the trouble, she was a sad old drunk.

The letter stared at her accusingly until, angrily, she snatched it up. She didn't want it in her house. Holding it over the burner on her gas stove, she watched the words disappear as the paper blackened and curled before disintegrating into tiny pieces.

Feeling slightly better although still miserable, Barbara forced herself to get ready for work and dragged herself off to the office. She'd put it out of her mind for now, try not to think about it.

~

What a beautiful day! A wondrous day! Oh, to sleep the sleep of the just! My friends are not around, they have let me sleep after all my hard work. I miss them, but know they'll be back. He's gone off to work, I heard him muttering to himself as he moved around the house. Even had the gall to knock on my door! Go away! I shouted at him. Leave me in peace! It makes me laugh to shout at him, in fact I shall shout all the time from now on, yes.

I'm floating around the house now, smiling happily at my beautiful things. I love my collection of dolls and I spend some time picking them up and talking to them. Yes, I know you've been feeling neglected but you're still my friends, you're still the keepers of my secrets. They're my new friends that's all, they understand about all the work I've had to do.

My new friends have left me notes, how nice. I must keep watch out of my windows, I must watch the drunk so that I can write another letter. I frown, the perfume bottle is almost empty, I'll have to take another one out of George's briefcase when he's not looking, I need it more than that old crone. I'm his wife, he should be buying me perfume, not her.

My dressing gown is so comfortable, my cloak, my protection against the evils of the world. I'll never take it off again. My fingers stroke it lovingly as I walk happily around my home. Where are my babies now? Have they arrived safely at their destinations?

I'm excited and I want someone to talk to. Where are my friends? Why don't they come? Maybe I need to write some more letters. Yes, I must find my notebook, there's always more work to be done.

~

'I feel so stupid now,' Tessa was crying. 'I should have told the police about the letter straightaway, maybe it would have helped. Oh, Sash, where is Chants? What's happened to her? And why don't either of the girls answer their phones?' The phone rang and Tessa ran to answer it, as Sasha stood helplessly, wishing she had some answers for her sister.

'Lilith? What? A letter? Well, what did it say? Yes, of course, I'll come round. Is it about the girls? I'm coming right now, my sister's with me.'

'Lilith's received a letter. Sash, what's happening? What are these letters about? Who's doing this? Have they taken our girls? It's all my fault, I should have said something sooner.'

'Slow down, Tess, take a breath. Is she the mother of Chantelle's friend?' Tess's nod confirmed this. 'Right, let's go! We'll go there first and then we're all going to the cops, this has gone far enough.'

The two women headed round to Lilith's with grim faces.

Sasha slipped the hateful letter into a plastic bag, well, you never know, maybe there'll be some fingerprints on it. 'Tess? Is this similar to the letter you received?'

'What?' Lilith's mouth gaped open. 'You got a letter too? Well, where is it? What did it say? Was it about the girls?'

'Oh, Lilith, no, it wasn't about the girls. Well, it was saying something awful about Chantelle and about my husband. It was spiteful. I, I threw it away. I thought maybe it was a girl from her school, or something. And then- then Chantelle didn't come home.' Tessa stopped to blow her nose before continuing. 'It arrived the day she disappeared, it was typed, like yours.'

The three women looked at the plastic shrouded letter, reading the words again.

WHO'S LOOKING AFTER YOUR CHILDREN
WHILE YOU'RE OUT SCREWING OTHER PEOPLE'S HUSBANDS
YOU DISGUSTING WHORE?

'Look, Lilith, we're going to have to go the cops, tell them about these letters. You don't have to tell us anything, you can tell the police. But if we know if the stuff in the letters is true or all lies then we can try to figure out if it's someone who knows you maybe.'

Sasha turned to Tess, 'Tess, you're sure it was all lies, the letter?'

'How can you ask that, Sash?' Tess looked at her sister, with wide eyes. 'Chantelle's not the type of girl to steal! And Dave's faithful I know he is. I don't know who wrote it but it's lies!'

'Stealing?' Lilith's voice was sharp. 'I found something in Britney's bag the other day, make-up, expensive, not the sort she can afford. I didn't know what to do, was going to ask her when the time was right. But then she was gone.'

'Lilith, this is important,' Sasha's mind was whirring, 'If Britney was shoplifting, and the girls are best friends, there's a chance they were doing it together.' No, listen to me, Tess, hear me out. This means that someone was watching them, the same person who wrote these letters. Don't you see? This could help us!'

'But Dave's not cheating on me, I know he's not.' Tess began to feel doubt, her Dave, he wouldn't, but he'd been out late so many times lately...

'Lilith, it says you're having an affair, or affairs, are you seeing anyone? Could anyone have seen you with a man?'

'What? No! No way- oh no, wait a minute, you don't think I was seeing Tessa's husband? I can't even remember his name, and I'm not! I'm not seeing anyone! It's the truth.' Lilith looked embarrassed, 'At least, I'm not seeing anyone, I, well, it gets lonely, you know? Being a single mum to two kids? I go to the odd bar, sometimes, and, well, I've been trying out online dating.' She flushed, 'I haven't even met up with anyone, just a couple of e-mails and phone calls that's all, just harmless flirting. And I don't see how anyone could even know about it!'

'So,' Sasha spoke slowly, thinking things through as she went, 'Some sicko's sending out these letters, they've got the information a bit wrong here and there, but some of it's possibly, or almost, true. Someone's been watching you all, someone knows enough about you and your families to think they know your secrets. It's time to go to the police and tell them about the letters.'

~

Driving back to the office after a property viewing, Barbara found her mind going back over the words in the letter from that morning. It was *her*, she knew it, so why did it bother her so much? Why did she care? And more to the point, what was she going to do about it? Maybe she should go to the police, tell them, that would show that crazy cow! But now she'd destroyed the letter, had nothing to show to the police. Dammit, she should have kept it.

As she paid for her shopping, that evening, Barbara felt as if all eyes were on her. Did people talk about her behind her back? *Poor Barbara, that sad, old, drunk.* Stop it, Barbara, so you like a drink, so what? Nothing wrong with it! She took the bag with the bottle of vodka in it, and left the off licence, she definitely needed a drink or two tonight.

After they'd dropped Lilith home, Sasha and Tessa stopped at the off licence. 'I think we need some wine,' announced Sasha.

'Oh, there's Barbara!' Tessa called out and waved, as the woman walked off towards her car. 'Strange, she's normally so friendly, wonder what's wrong with her?'

'Well, we've done the right thing, sis, P.C. Weaver seemed to take it all pretty seriously, said she'd pass it all on to her boss. So, the cops know everything now.' Sasha poured more wine into their glasses, as they heard Dave opening the front door. 'If there's any connection, they'll find it.'

'Any connection to what?' Dave got himself a beer and joined the two women as they began to tell him about their day.

It was a bittersweet evening for them all. Pizza and wine, like the old days, but not quite. With no Chantelle, an air of despair hung over everyone and eventually, as the sun began to drop, Sasha decided it was time to head back to the pub.

~

George is late home, very late, it's getting dark. I leave the lights off, enjoying creeping around my house in the dark. Boo! I shout at shapes in the darkness. I'll shout at him when he comes in. Maybe he'll fall down the stairs. That makes me laugh. Karma. Karma larma jarma barma karma chameleon, my singing makes us all laugh. I know what he did, he speaks in his sleep, I tell my friends. He doesn't know I know. I smile at them and they chuckle with me as we imagine him falling down the stairs in fright.

They call me to the windows, I mustn't forget to look they say. Oh yes, the notes they left me, there's still much to be done. We gather around, opening the window and peering out into the gloom. She's there! She's looking up at us all! Oh, it feels good to shout so loudly, I haven't had this much fun in ages. 'Drunken slob! Drinking the devil's poison! Disgusting boozy floozy!' We're all laughing as she shouts something back, can't quite catch the words, something about mad and old. The window blows shut as the wind picks up and once I've caught my breath, we peep quietly back out through the glass. Shh, don't let her know we're still watching...

~

Barbara pours herself another drink. She feels better having shouted back at that mad old cow. At least she's gone now, and she can enjoy her drink in peace. She looks at the bottle, surprised to see it's half empty. She needs some more ice and staggers up to fetch some, before returning to the patio and settling down with her glass of cold vodka. She's pissed, she knows it, is finding it hard to lift her glass without spilling it. Her head's swimming slightly, she should have eaten something, too late now, she should go to bed. Maybe one more drink and then, oh, was that a noise? 'Who's there?' Is someone in her garden? Her face breaks into a surprised smile. 'Oh, it's you! What are you doing here?'

As she struggles to breathe, her eyes stare up beseechingly at the window of her tormentor. She tries to wave for help, kicks out with her legs, as she gasps for air. Everything starts to go black and the last things she sees is the glint of mad Dorothy's eyes, peering out from her window at her.

~

We look around at each other and nod happily. Yes, the vengeance comes to those who sin. The shadows are my creatures I've created, they are doing the bidding of the higher powers. I brought them to life, with my letters, my babies. They are finishing the work that I started, she won't sin any more. I watch, as the shadow punishes her, the drunken whore, and leaves her to fall onto the ground. She looks disgusting, her skirt has lifted up and I can see her underwear, it's unseemly, but she asked for it. She must be left to her shame. The shadow is still moving around, it looks right up at me, why does it look like *him*, wearing his stupid cap and cravat? But we move back from the window, shh, don't let the shadow see us.

~

The pub was quite busy when Sasha walked in, trying to decide whether to have another drink or head straight up to her room. As Cal's face lit up in a smile, she made her decision, she'd have one drink.

ONE MORE DRINK

They stayed outside, by mutual consent, after popping out for a smoke. The pub garden led gently down to the river bank, wooden tables and benches scattered on the lawn, garden lights twinkling in their watery reflection.

Taking a seat at one of the tables, Sasha sighed, 'It would be so nice if I was here for a holiday, this place is so beautiful. You're really lucky to live here, Cal, you know that?'

Cal smiled, 'You could say that. I don't usually stay in one place for long, but I'm finding no desire to move on at the moment. Especially at the moment.' He looked meaningfully into Sasha's eyes. Man, this woman was hot. Hot in a mature way, *grown-up sexy hot, lived a life hot.*

'You know I'm only here for my sister, right? For Tess? I can't get distracted, Cal, not right now. Her daughter's missing and that's that, I've got to help her, support her and Dave. I've got to do whatever I can to be there for them, and to help them find her.' She stopped, as Cal placed his large hand over hers, as it lay on the table.

'Let me help you. Whatever you need. I'm here, you can bounce ideas off me. I can drive you around, show you the whole area, help you look for her. I'm not busy right now, my last commission just bummed out so I'm all yours. Say yes, Sasha.'

Why did she feel that if she said yes, it would be to more than just his offer of help? Her cautious side told her to say no, what with Chantelle missing and Eric back in London. *Don't complicate things* it said. Her reckless side had other plans though. *Say yes, he's gorgeous. He's not only gorgeous, he's steaming hot, sexy, funny, attentive...*

The frisson that ran through her, at his touch, refused to go away. 'Yes.' Dammit, where did that come from? 'I didn't mean that, I, no, I can't, Cal, thank you but no.' She picked up her wine and gulped it down, to hide her confusion.

'Sasha, I'm just offering to help that's all, no strings. Come on, I'm a local, I know everyone, well most people, I know my way around, you need me. Don't worry I'm not going to jump you in the middle of a field somewhere.'

That's a pity. His grin was infectious and she found herself responding with a giggle. 'Okay, okay, you win, I could use your help! But not tonight, it's getting late, a girl needs her sleep you know.'

'Good but not before one more, a nightcap, I'll be back in a second.' Cal was up and off into the pub before she had time to respond.

As she waited, Sasha walked to the bank and watched the dark waters flowing by. What was the river again? She'd read it in the leaflet in her room. Oh, the Black River, of course, as if the colour, especially at night, didn't give it away. It looked strangely menacing in the dark of night, a sinuous, ever-moving dark serpent, its slick surface, glinting in the lights, not as pretty as she'd thought when she'd first walked out here.

Cal placed their drinks down on the table and walked over to join her. 'Spooky looking this time of night, hey? During the day it's this beautiful river running through the village, its surface glinting in the sunlight as it moves. Well, it was...'

'What d'you mean, was?' Turning to look at him, she could see sadness in his eyes. 'What is it, Cal? What happened?'

They sat back down, sipping their whisky, as Cal told her about Peter Ford's body washing up on the riverbank. 'I didn't know him at all, only saw him once or twice, the last time was the night he must have drowned. He looked so unhappy, he was drinking heavily. None of it made sense, to be honest, they were so happily married, she never stopped talking about him.'

'Who? Who, Cal? Who never stopped talking about him?' Sasha tried to follow the story, as Cal stumbled his way through it.

'So, let me get this straight,' Sasha's inner radar was buzzing noisily, there was a connection here, had to be! 'A man who'd been happily married for nearly ten years, to his lovely wife who commissioned you to paint her for him for their ten-year anniversary, suddenly goes out drinking alone, miserable as hell, and ends up dead in the river?'

'Yep, pretty much, sad huh? Wonder what happened?'

'Cal, I'll tell you what happened, a poison pen letter, that's what! I'd put money on it!' Sasha was excited, her mind whirring frantically with ideas. 'Yes, I know what you're thinking, it sounds like an Agatha Christie story. Well guess what? It is, we're in St. Mary flaming Mead and I'm Miss flippin' Marple!'

Cal grinned suddenly, 'A bit sexier than the Miss Marple I remember... sorry, sorry!' He put his hands up in surrender. 'Tell me what you're thinking.'

'I'm not exactly sure of it all yet, Cal, but someone's sending out anonymous letters. We're talking mean spiteful stuff designed to hurt.' Sasha gabbled excitedly. 'My sister received one, and so did her friend, well, neighbour. The mother of the other missing girl! Don't you see? Peter might've got one too! Maybe that's why he was so upset! I need to find out!'

'We could ask Barbara, she knows his wife, Maureen, they're friends I think.' Then, in answer to Sasha's enquiring look, 'Barbara's the rental agent in the village, rents out most of the houses on the new estate. Maybe she'll speak to Maureen for us, or we could just go and see her ourselves?'

'No you're right, let's speak to Barbara, get her to talk to Maureen, find out if Peter received anything strange in the post. Wait a minute, so Barbara probably rented my sister's house to her, so she'll know her as well. Seems like everyone knows everyone here. Oh yeah, right, small village of course.' She smiled, as Cal shrugged and nodded, her eyes glancing round distractedly at the sound of a couple leaving one of the nearby tables. *Blast, they probably heard everything, it would be all round the village next.*

'Should we phone Barbara now? Is it too late? But this is important, do you have her number?' Sasha was so worked up with all her theories, she wanted action, regardless of the time.

Cal looked at his watch, 'Well, it's after ten, might be a bit late... although old Barbara does like a drink most evenings. Okay, I'll try her number, I can always leave a message.'

But Barbara's mobile phone just rang. When it went to answerphone, Cal left a message, asking if he and Sasha could pop in and see her in the morning, at her office. 'It's the best we can do,' he looked at Sasha. 'She'll probably call me back in the morning otherwise we'll just go to the office.'

She couldn't sleep, her mind was racing with ideas, she was onto something, she was sure of it. Turning the light on, beside the bed, she picked up the tourism leaflet about the village, wanting something to distract her, and flicked through it.

Drowsy finally, she dozed off, her mind swimming with missing girls, the river, historic post boxes, Cal's face, ancient bridges, old milestones in people's gardens, no wait, that wasn't right, it wasn't the milestones... anonymous letters, a drowned man...

WHAT DID THEY DO WITH THE DRUNKEN SAILOR?

I'm being a good girl for the doctor, on my best behaviour. Yes sir, no sir, three bags full sir. I can hear him and George whispering together outside my door, hurry up, hurry up, I've got things to do.

Dr Singh comes back in smiling at me, he smells of cigarettes and his turban is lopsided, he must have bumped his head. He went to bed and bumped his head and couldn't get up in the morning. I want to laugh at my cleverness. Don't light your devil's sticks with a match Doctor you might singe your turban. I'm going to call him Dr Singe. Tears run down my face as I try not to laugh out loud. I'm having such fun.

He wants to know when I last slept. George has been telling tales. Georgie Porgie, pudding and pie, kissed the girls and told a lie. I smile slyly, you won't trick me that easily. 'I sleep eight hours every night, Dr Singe.' I'm spluttering with laughter, I can't help it, the doctor looks so surprised.

I do as I'm told and lie down on my bed, I'm being such a good girl. I peep out from under one of my eyelids, Dr Singe is writing a letter. He's giving it to George. More whispering, more secrets. George wants to kill me. He wants to murder me and the doctor is helping him. 'Yes, Dr Singh, one tablet at night,' George is smiling at his accomplice. One tablet of poison so that I never wake up. Murderers!

As soon as they've gone I get up and look out of my window. The drunken whore has gone. She's disappeared. Oh yes, I nod at my friends, my avenging creatures have taken her. What did they do with the drunken sailor? What did they do with the drunken sailor? They've put her in a boat until she's sober. Early in the morning. I do a little jig with my friends, laughing with them as they tell me how clever I am.

Shh he's coming back up the stairs, pretend you're asleep. My friends hide as I lie down on my bed and close my eyes.

~

'Tess? It's Sash, yeah fine, any news? Oh, hun, I know, I'm sure they're doing all they can. Listen I've got a few ideas, just need to find some things out and I'll come round. Yeah I'll see you later. Call me if you need me.'

'Cal, it's fine, let's take my car, you can tell me where to go. Where to first? Barbara's house or her office?'

Cal frowned, it wasn't like Barbara not to answer her phone or to respond to his message. 'Let's go to her office, she should be in by now, maybe she's just been really busy this morning.'

'Strange.' Cal walked around, peering in the windows of Barbara's rentals office. 'She should be open by now. Her car's not here though, maybe she's out with a client. We'll wait for a little while, she shouldn't be long.'

A pleasant half hour of chatting in the car later and Barbara still wasn't back. By mutual agreement they decided to go to her house just in case she was there. Sighting her car in the driveway they pulled up and walked up the little pathway to her front door.

'Am I the only one who's starting to feel a little concerned here?' Sasha looked up at Cal as he pressed his finger on the doorbell again. She tried to peer in the front window but couldn't make anything out through the lace curtains.

Wordlessly the two began to walk down the side of the house towards the gate. Sasha followed Cal into the back garden and they stopped at the sight of the patio table, complete with a half empty bottle of vodka. A glass lay broken on the ground next to a fallen chair.

'This isn't good!' exclaimed Cal. 'Maybe she went on a bender last night. Let's check the back door.' He turned around and stopped, reaching out to touch Sasha's arm. 'The door's open.' They walked in cautiously, feeling a little uncomfortable about invading Barbara's privacy but with niggling feelings of concern.

There was no doubt about it, Barbara was definitely not in her house. They'd checked every room, calling out as they went, until they returned to the kitchen, unsure of what to do next. Sasha leant against the stove, resting her hands behind her as they discussed the situation.

'So Barbara was drinking last night, that's clear. She was alone, there was only one glass. She didn't sleep in her bed and her car's still in the driveway. Where the hell is she then?' Lifting her hands up in a question as she spoke, Cal grabbed her hand, turning it over.

The black ash was all over Sasha's hands. Turning to the stove, they looked at the blackened fragments spread over the stovetop. Sasha gently picked up one of the fragments, trying to decipher the words on it. 'D. R. U. perhaps an N. I think, that's all I can make out, what about you?'

Cal picked out a few letters. 'U.G.L. that's it, I think, hard to tell. What d'you think it is?'

Sasha's eyes gleamed, her theory was right she was sure of it! 'I think Barbara received a poison pen letter as well! Cal, she did, I'm almost certain that's what this is! Probably something about 'you're a drunk or an ugly drunk, or something mean like that! She must've been upset, burned it over the gas flame. Then she went on a drinking spree, I don't blame her, poor woman.'

'That's all fine, Sasha, but then where the hell is she now? And what do we do? Do we go to the cops? What the hell's going on in this village? First Peter Ford drowns then your niece and her friend go missing and now Barbara. I'm beginning to think you're right, this is St. Mary whatever the hell it is you called it!'

'Okay let's try to stay calm, not jump to conclusions, she may be fine. Could she have walked anywhere? What about her friend Maureen, Peter's wife, who you were painting? Does she live far?'

The two of them closed the kitchen door and, leaving everything else as they'd found it, *just in case we do need to go to the police*, got back in the car and Cal directed them to Maureen's house just around the corner.

BLACK OVER WILL'S MOTHER'S

Mrs Pringle looked up at the sound of the bell, her face breaking into a welcoming smile at her regular customer. 'Good morning to you, Mr Newton, and how are you today?' Her arm was already reaching for his order, two bottles each time now, when she paused, 'Mr Newton, is everything alright?' She and Sheila glanced at each other and shrugged. She tried again, 'Morning, Mr Newton!'

'Ah good morning to you, Mrs Pringle, Sheila.' George approached the counter, smiling distractedly at the two women.

'You were away with the fairies for a minute there, Mr Newton! Everything alright with your mother? And how's your dear wife? Warm weather we're having isn't it? It must be the hottest summer on record! Who needs France, eh?' Mrs Pringle chattered away, handing the bottles of Lavender Dreams to Sheila to ring up on the till.

'Mother's very well, thank you for asking, I'll be along to see her after work today. Poor Dorothy's not so good I'm afraid, having a little trouble sleeping. Dr Singh wrote me a prescription for her.'

With the prescription being filled efficiently by Sheila, Mrs Pringle took the opportunity to engage in a little chat and a gossip. 'Oh, your poor dear wife. Nothing worse than not being able to sleep. I hope she's not been overdoing things. And you so busy with work and looking after dear old Mrs Newton! I wonder how you cope at all! You really should get some help, I'm sure you could-'

'No!' George's sharp retort stopped her in her tracks. 'No, thank you, Mrs Pringle, you're very kind, but we're doing just fine. Mother doesn't like outsiders, wouldn't tolerate that idea at all. Oh no, Mother and I are quite fine, just the two of us.'

'Well if you're sure,' Mrs Pringle sounded doubtful, 'But you just ask if you need anything, you hear? Anything at all. Now, these pills for Dorothy, one each night an hour before bedtime. Mind she doesn't take more than one they're very strong.' She placed the paper bag containing the pills on the counter beside the perfume bottles, where Sheila waited patiently.

'Terrible about those missing girls isn't it?' continued Mrs Pringle. 'Their poor mothers must be beside themselves with worry! And all this after that business with poor Mr Ford. What's the world coming to I ask myself? And here in our peaceful little village, never seen the likes of it. And what with those nasty letters doing the rounds too. Oh you hadn't heard? Sheila's nephew's friend heard something about it at the pub last night, you know how people gossip. Not that I give it any credence, mind.'

'The missing girls? Oh yes, I expect they ran away, those two looked like trouble if you ask me. The mothers these days, they don't keep control of their children, that's the problem. Off they go poking their noses in where they've no business, running wild, breaking the law. And letters you say? Well maybe it's about time, someone keeping a check on people's morals I shouldn't doubt.' George stopped, taking out his handkerchief to wipe his brow. 'Forgive me I'm not feeling quite myself. Now, I've taken up enough of your time, how much do I owe you, Mrs Pringle?'

'Poor man,' Mrs Pringle shook her head, sadly, after George left the shop. 'No wonder he's not himself. First he's taking care of his elderly mother, how he does it I don't know, and he's obviously worried sick about his wife, doesn't want to show it of course. And this heat! It'll storm later I shouldn't wonder.' She stepped around the counter, making her way between the aisles and out of the entrance door, looking up at the clouds gathering in the distance.

'Oh yes, it's looking a bit black over Will's mother's.' She walked triumphantly back into the shop and joined Sheila, as she waited for the kettle to boil. 'Yes, you mark my words, we'll have a storm later, you see if we don't!'

Sheila, finally able to get a word in, asked the question many others had asked of Mrs Pringle before. 'And who exactly is Will's mother?'

'Oh, I'm not sure to be honest, dear. It's something my mother used to say, God rest her soul, I think it was her cousin maybe, no, that's not right, her aunt was it? No, maybe it was her mother's brother's mother. No, that would be her own mother wouldn't it? Come to think of it, I believe my grandmother used to say the same thing, so that would mean... Oh, there now, you've got me all in a muddle! How's that tea coming along?'

Sheila smiled to herself as she passed the mug of tea over to Mrs Pringle. Her and her old sayings, still it was nice the way she kept the old family sayings going, even if she didn't know where they came from.

~

As Cal and Sasha stepped from the car outside Maureen Ford's house they looked up at the sky. The clouds were building ominously as the sky darkened over the village. Sasha brushed a flying ant from her arm, 'It's going to storm, can't say I'll be sorry, it's so damned hot!'

Cal leant in towards her, 'Hold still.' He reached for her face, touching her hairline gently. 'There, a flying ant got stuck in your hair.' His eyes held hers for a second longer than necessary before he pulled away.

Clearing her throat, Sasha looked away, hoping Cal hadn't noticed the sudden reddening of her cheeks. Dammit, what was it about this man? Wrong place, wrong time, she told herself sternly.

Maureen answered the door, managing a weak smile for Cal as she welcomed them in. 'Please excuse the place, I haven't felt much like, well, anything, to be honest.' She looked enquiringly at Cal, who introduced Sasha, expressed their sympathy for her loss, and explained why they were there.

'I haven't seen Barbara for a few days, I'm trying to think when it was. She came round, very kind, brought muffins with her. We were talking about Peter.' She stopped, wiping her eyes with an already damp tissue. 'She was going to talk to someone at the store, Von, as I recall, see if she'd noticed anything strange about Peter that day. Why? What's happened? Has something happened to her?' She looked at them both, wide-eyed, as they sat together on the sofa opposite her.

'Well the thing is Maureen, we think that maybe-' Cal's leg pressing hard against hers made Sasha stop.

'I'm sure it's nothing to worry about, Maureen, we were just concerned as we couldn't get hold of Barbara. I'm sure she'll call me back when she's not so busy.' Cal turned the conversation away from Barbara, gently raising the issue of the painting he'd been commissioned to do.

'Maureen, I want you to know there's no obligation on your part, I'd only begun preliminary sketches. I'm sure you'd rather forget all about it and I fully understand. I'm just so sorry for your loss and I know that the last thing you need is a painting that will remind you of all that's happened.'

Cal was really a very kind man, she thought, gentle and thoughtful. She could tell by Maureen's grateful smile how relieved she was.

Back in the car Sasha turned to Cal. 'Sorry, I wasn't thinking, the last thing that poor woman needed was me expounding my theories. I'm glad you stopped me.' *Especially by pressing your leg against mine* came the unbidden thought...

The sky was turning a menacing shade of dark grey as they wondered what to do next. Rumblings of thunder could be heard in the distance, the odd flash of lightning illuminating the clouds for a second. Sasha's phone rang. 'Tess? Any news?'

Cal looked at her expectantly as she finished the call. 'Have they found her? What is it? Both of them? Where?'

Sasha shook her head slowly. 'I'm not sure, poor Tess and Dave, they're hoping so but it doesn't sound right to me. Why would Chantelle just take off? And to Manchester of all places? There's been a sighting of two girls who match the description of Chantelle and Britney. The cops want them to go in and view some CCTV footage they've had sent down.

They're on their way there now. I guess we'll have to wait and see. Tess said there was something else, that she'd tell me later, but nothing to do with the girls.'

A flash of lightning lit up the sky, followed by a loud rumble as the thunder rolled closer. 'Look, why don't we head back to the pub for a while, have a spot of lunch, wait to hear from Tessa? We should get indoors before this storm hits anyway, I think it's going to be a big one.'

The rain started falling just as they were parking the car outside the pub, large drops splashing onto the roof with lazy thuds. 'We'd better make a run for it!' Cal grabbed Sasha's hand and they ran for the pub entrance just as the heavens opened in earnest, soaking them both instantly.

They were laughing as they entered The Spotted Dog, shaking their hair, still holding hands.

'Hello, Sash.'

Her hand dropped from Cal's as she looked at the owner of the voice, the lone customer at the quiet bar.

'Eric!'

JEALOUSIES

Cal took in the situation in one second. This wasn't just a friend of Sasha's, these two were an item or at least, noticing Sasha's troubled look, the guy thought they were... And Sasha obviously hadn't been expecting him nor was she pleased to see him.

He watched her expression change from perturbed surprise to a big smile pasted onto her face but not quite reaching her eyes, her voice sounding overly bright as she replied.

'Eric, what a surprise! What are you doing here?' Sasha's mind was racing, what to do, what to say, how to explain him to Cal. And why was she thinking about Cal? Had Eric seen them holding hands as they came in and, most importantly, *what the hell was he doing here?*

Cal was surprised at how disappointed he felt, Sasha was gorgeous, if he was honest. But this guy obviously thought he had some claim to her so maybe he should make himself scarce, give Sasha a chance to talk to the guy. 'You okay?' he murmured, taking her quick nod as confirmation but noting again her slightly bewildered look.

Eric watched the exchange, trying to gauge what was going on, and then watched as Sasha walked towards him, a smile fixed firmly on her face as the other guy crossed the pub to a door and disappeared.

Standing up he opened his arms and enveloped Sasha in a hug, kissing her slowly on the mouth before pulling away slightly. 'Hi, baby, I had a hard time tracking my girl down.'

'Your girl? Eric, I don't hear from you from one week to the next, never know where I stand with you, and don't get me started on the redhead. And then you pitch up here calling me your girl? How did you know where to find me?' The thought came into her head, Tessa had mentioned there was something else, well this was obviously it. 'Tessa!'

She watched him nod, pleased with himself, as he informed her he'd wanted to surprise her, fancied a mini-break in the countryside anyway. 'Dammit, Eric, this isn't a holiday! Her daughter's missing and I'm trying to give my support and to help find her, how dare you use her to track me down, and then come here for a flippin' mini break!'

Jules cleared her throat quietly behind the bar as she placed a large glass of white wine on the counter, with another beer for Eric. 'Thanks, Jules,' Sasha noticed her quick wink. Jules was an expert, she could read this situation of that she had no doubt. 'Jules, I'm sorry, this is Eric, a, er, a friend of mine, I had no idea he was going to turn up here.' Then a thought occurred to her. 'Eric, you hadn't planned on staying? Not here?'

'Well of course, here,' Eric was grinning. 'Where else did you think I'd stay? You've got a double bed haven't you? I'll pay any extras, I'm sure Jules here doesn't mind.' Without waiting for any acknowledgement from Jules, Eric picked their drinks up and led the way to a table in the corner of the pub. Sasha had no choice but to follow.

Jules's raised eyebrows and Sasha's shrug conveyed a much longer private conversation in the way that only women are privy to, and she helplessly sat down at the table. A bright flash of lightning lit up the gloomy room for a moment, closely followed by a deafening boom of thunder as the rain pelted down. One thing was clear, no-one was going anywhere in this weather.

'So, baby, you're playing at private detective now are you? Who are you trying to be, Miss Marple?' Eric's amused voice riled Sasha and especially his reference to Miss Marple, that had been her line. 'Surely you don't think you can help find a missing girl! Leave that stuff to the police, Sash, it's not your game. You're the problem fixer, isn't that what you call yourself? Stick to stolen handbags and missing dogs, baby, leave the other stuff to the professionals.'

She fumed silently, annoyed by his words as much as his presence. Taking a huge glug of her wine she thought frantically. She was stuck with him, at least for tonight, but he couldn't stay.

'You can't stay. Eric, I mean it, you can stay tonight but you must leave tomorrow. I'm here for Tess, in every way, and yes I am 'playing at detective', as you so nicely put it. I'm working with someone, he's got local knowledge, we're following leads.' She downed the rest of her wine, placing her glass down a little too loudly on the table.

'Working with someone? Is that how you describe it? That would be the guy you came in with, all cosy, would it?' Eric's eyes flashed with jealousy for a second.

Typical. How she had yearned for Eric to show some kind of jealous possessiveness of her in the past. Now that he was exhibiting it, it gave her no thrill at all, how ironic was that? 'Think what you like, Eric, Cal's helping me and I've got no time to sit around here, we have plans this afternoon.'

Eric's arm snaked around her shoulders, pulling her close. 'Oh no you don't, the only plans you have this afternoon are with me up in your room.' His mouth found hers again, this time his tongue making its presence known, forcing her lips apart to probe her mouth.

Her eyes caught the movement by the door to the upstairs rooms and she tried to pull away as Cal walked in and went up to the bar. But Eric pulled her closer still, murmuring in her ear. 'What do you say? You, me, and a bottle of wine up in that nice double bed of yours? It's the perfect weather for it.'

This time she did manage to pull away but had to admit that in this weather there was no way she and Cal would have been able to go anywhere. I have to call Tessa,' she blurted. 'She's expecting me. And I need to talk to Cal.'

Eric watched with slight irritation, as Sasha talked rapidly to the man at the bar. The sound of the crashing rain and rumbling thunder made it impossible to hear anything. No, there was no way Sasha would be attracted to a guy like that, what was he, some kind of ageing hippy? No, definitely not her type, maybe she was telling the truth and he was just helping her. And what had she meant about the redhead? She couldn't possibly know about that.

'I'm really sorry, Cal, I had no idea he would turn up here and now he's staying, at least for tonight. It's, well, it's complicated. But I've told him he has to leave tomorrow, I'm needed here for Tessa and I need you too. Can we talk in the morning after breakfast? Plan what we do next?'

Sasha's pleading face tugged at something inside and his soft eyes smiled gently into hers. 'It's okay, Sasha, do what you have to do, this weather's so terrible anyway, I don't think we could have achieved anything more today. I'll be here in the morning, let me know when you're free.'

He watched her walk back towards Eric, trying to quell the momentary jealousy that flared up at the thought of Sasha spending the night with that smug jerk. 'What pies do you have today, Jules? Think I'll take one upstairs, work on some painting.'

The pub started to fill up a little with the lunchtime crowd, wet umbrellas standing inside the door pooling their water onto the flagstone floor. A musty smell pervaded the bar, as damp jackets gathered on coat hooks, the noise of chattering competing unsuccessfully with the storm.

'Let's get something to eat!' She wasn't using delaying tactics, she really wasn't, she was hungry. A pub lunch would be nice then maybe, if the weather cleared, she and Eric could go round to see Tess and Dave. Although on second thoughts, they would hardly be in the mood for a social visit from her and her 'on off' boyfriend. Dammit! She still hadn't called Tess. She quickly sent a text asking Tess to let her know about the CCTV footage.

'Nothing better than a country pub!' Eric wiped his mouth with the linen napkin, leaning back in his chair with a contented sigh having enjoyed his sausages and mash. He smiled at Sasha, she was looking extremely desirable, all flushed from the wine. He felt a surge of heat run through him at the thought of what he would like to do to her. Correction, of what he was *going* to do to her.

His chair screeched on the floor as he pushed it back to stand up. 'Time for bed, baby!' Collecting his bag from where he'd left it, at the end of the bar, as well as another bottle of wine from Jules, he took Sasha's hand and they headed up to her room.

CANDLE-LIT NIGHTS

Cal heard their voices murmuring, as they came up the stairs, then Sasha's door opening and closing. Well that was that then. The rain was still pounding on the roof above him, for which he was grateful. The last thing he wanted was to hear what was going on in her room. He forced himself to focus on his painting, screwing up his eyes slightly as he gently brushed a streak of burnt sienna across the canvas.

~

Sasha looked around her room in despair. Eric had been in here for less than five minutes and already the place looked like a bomb had hit it. His bag had been tipped out onto the bed, shoes kicked off inside the door, jacket thrown over the chair, and a slight pool of wine sat beside the kettle where he'd poured them drinks.

With a flash of irritation she went into the bathroom and grabbed some tissue to wipe it up. Eric followed her in, snaking his arms around her waist. 'How about a shower together? He nuzzled her neck as his fingers began to unbutton her shirt.

'Eric, please! I need to clean up the wine you spilled.' She struggled free, turning and walking out, and as she wiped up the wine her phone rang. It was Tess.

'Tess, tell me! Oh okay, it wasn't them? You're sure?' The two sisters talked for a few minutes as Tessa filled Sasha in on her visit to the police station and then. 'Yes, he's here. He shouldn't have called you, sis, I'm sorry about that he had no right. Yes everything's fine.' The toilet flushed and she watched Eric coming through from the bathroom.

'Okay well that would be nice but are you sure you're up to it? We'll have to see how this weather is, hun, it's crashing down here at the moment. Same at yours? Alright, well if you're sure. Oh, he's working late is he? Well why don't I bring round takeaway then, for the three of us? Look, Tess, Cal and I, we've got some theories, there's been another letter, or two, possibly. No we can't prove it, but we're working on it. I'm sure I'm onto something, sis. I know, I know it isn't helping find Chants, but it might in time. Alright then, sis, around seven, see you later.'

'We're going round to Tess, my sister, this evening, okay? We'll take food. She needs me, Eric, or you can stay here, up to you. But this is why I'm here.'

Poor Tess, Sasha felt filled with frustration. She knew that somehow she was heading in the right direction. She just needed to fit all the pieces together, find out a bit more information. She must put together a timeline, a list of who'd received letters, once they'd found out a bit more about Barbara and Peter. And where was Barbara? Potentially there were now three people missing, but the police only knew about two. No-one was even looking for her, no-one but her and Cal...

'You need to chill, Sash, come here, have some wine.' Eric swiped his pile of clothes up and threw them onto the chair to join his jacket, patting the bed beside him where he'd sat down.

'Eric, I'm actually a bit knackered if you must know, I'm sorry. I don't mean to be a killjoy but I'm not here for fun, and no more wine for me, I'm driving later.' She sat down on the bed, there being nowhere else to sit.

The storm was getting worse, heavy winds whipped the rain against the windows, as lightning continued to flash rapidly followed by crashes of thunder. The room was dark even though it was only afternoon, and she switched on the little lamp beside the bed. They chatted for a while, Eric telling her stories of work (he was a property developer, buying up old buildings in inner city locations for development into mixed-use zones of living and work space, restaurants and shops), as she laid back on the pillows fighting drowsiness.

Eric had almost finished the bottle of wine when the power went out. 'Now I know why I never wanted to live in the sticks.

Babe, face it, we're not going anywhere in this weather. Phone your sister back, tell her. Then you can have some wine, but we'll need another bottle. I'm sure our lovely barmaid downstairs can whip us up a sandwich.'

She came to, sighing inwardly, he was right, rather irritatingly. It was madness to try to go out in this weather. She could see Tess tomorrow, go round there with Cal. The thought cheered her, yes, much rather Cal than Eric, the last thing her sister needed was to meet the mystery 'boyfriend' at a time like this anyway.

'Alright, Eric, you win, I'll call her. I'm going downstairs to talk to Jules, see what the story is about the power. I'll be right back.'

She paused on the landing, wondering if Cal was in his room then made her way carefully down the two flights of stairs and entered the bar, lit now by candles. It looked wonderfully cosy, and she was surprised to see a number of people in the bar. Clearly some people were not cowed by the storm.

She recognised him by his shape, his large frame illuminated by the flickering flames as he sat at the bar. 'Cal.' She tapped his shoulder.

'Nightmare with an upside to it, this,' Cal grinned. 'Nothing else to do but drink beer. Get you anything? Where's your friend?'

'He's upstairs, I can't stay but thanks. I just wanted to talk to Jules, find out what's happening. I can't believe she's got any customers tonight in this weather!'

'Poker night. The guys don't miss that, not for anything. Looks like the power will be off for a couple more hours, they're working on it. Here's Jules.'

'You alright, Sasha?' Jules's face expressed understanding at her situation. 'Sorry about the power, should be back on in an hour or two. I've got a couple of candles for you, nice and romantic, if that's what you want...'

Sasha accepted the candles, more out of the need for illumination than for the desire for romance, and arranged for some sandwiches to take up as well as more wine. She might as well have a drink while she waited too, she wasn't driving now so to hell with it.

She and Cal chatted about their ideas while Sasha waited for her order, and it was with disappointment that she saw Jules carrying through a wrapped plate of sandwiches. She bought another bottle of wine and reluctantly stood up, clutching the candles along with everything else.

'Here let me help you.' Cal leaped up, offering to take the plate, but Sasha was fine, if he could maybe just hold the door open for her she'd manage. They said goodnight at the door leading upstairs and Sasha paused for a moment, watching Cal walk back to the bar.

Wait a second. Was that Dave? She peered through the gloom as a man entered the pub making a beeline for a door in the far corner of the room. As the door opened she caught a glimpse of people sitting round a table, their faces shadowy in the light of the candles. And then the door swung shut.

Maybe it wasn't Dave. She was probably mistaken, hard to see anything in this half-darkness. But it was poker night... and Dave had had a problem before... and he was supposed to be working late... Her mind mulled over everything as she made her way carefully up the stairs.

No, she wouldn't say anything to Tess, it probably wasn't him and even if it was, Tess had more important things to worry about right now. If Dave was gambling again it was something to be dealt with once they'd found Chantelle. She'd file it away for later consideration.

Opening the door to her room, she struggled in with the sandwiches, wine, and candles. 'Eric? Can you help?' Feeling her way carefully, she placed the plate down on the table, putting the bottle of wine beside it. 'Eric?' She lit a candle and stood it, in its holder, on the table, before looking round to see why he was so quiet.

A slight feeling of relief ran through her as his gentle snores reached her ears. Moving his clothes from the chair into the cupboard, she sat down and poured herself a large glass of wine. She'd never felt more like getting drunk.

STOLEN CLOTHES AND PARTY DRESSES

I'm still alive. George can't finish me off that easily. As I fall on the ground I giggle, looking around to see if any of my friends are watching. But they're nowhere to be seen. Ah, I nod knowingly, they're hiding from *him*.

I can hear him banging and crashing around downstairs, disturbing me. Making a big mess in my kitchen no doubt. 'Shut up! Stop disturbing me!' I can hear them laughing now, in the wardrobe, so I open the door. As they help me brush my hair and fix some pretty clips in it, we discuss our plans for the day.

I'm still a bit wobbly when I go downstairs but I hum a tune and do a little dance as I enter the kitchen. I'll show him.

'Dorothy, for God's sake get some clothes on!' George wrinkled his nose as his wife's unwashed odour reached him beneath the mask of Lavender Dreams. 'Or better than that take a wretched bath first!'

I'm sure he's going mad I whisper to my friends, before George grips my arm and marches me upstairs. He's hurting me, I always forget how strong he is for such a little man. I start to laugh at that but I stop laughing when I close the wardrobe door and look in the mirror. I'm naked. Naked as the day I was born. He did this. Stripped me to look at my body. Disgusting pervert.

I'm so upset when I can't find my nightgown. Or my dressing gown. George has stolen my clothes and left me naked. But I stop crying when one of my friends passes me a dress from my wardrobe. Oh, this is perfect. I do a little twirl in front of the mirror. Yes, perfect.

His face is a picture when I go back into the kitchen. You don't have to tell me I look nice, George, my friends already did. I smile at him complacently as I pour myself a cup of tea from the pot. I smooth my fingers over the shiny fabric of my dress, pleased with how it sparkles in the sunlight.

I'm faraway, there's music and dancing, everyone's laughing. Oh, it was Christmas that's what it was, the paper plant party. I was wearing the dress, feeling like a princess, all dressed up in my full-length gown. Oh, I should be wearing the matching shoes, but no, my slippers are more comfortable. What's that?

'Dorothy? Did you hear me? Where are you, girl? You're miles away. Come on, we don't want to get the doctor in again do we?'

Oh no, we don't want Dr Singe back with more poison. I sit up straight, smile at George and shout. 'What?'

That got him. Now he's paying attention to me. What bodies? 'I didn't do it!' I shout.

'Of course you didn't do it, Dorothy, silly old girl. Peter Ford's was an accident, or so they say. But now they've found the woman, well, it makes you wonder what's going on. They don't say who she was.'

Poor, nice, Mr Ford. That poor cuckolded man with his cheating wife. It's supposed to be the bad ones who get punished. That's what my friends told me. That's why the shadows punished her the other night, her with her drunken behaviour bringing disgrace on the neighbourhood.

'I didn't mean for Mr Ford to die,' I cry. 'It's only supposed to be the bad ones who get punished. They lied to me and I thought they were my friends.'

'There, there, old girl. Blow your nose, that's it, there's a good girl. Now what's all this about your friends?'

Now they look unhappy with me, glaring at me, shaking their heads. Quiet, Dorothy, don't tell him, it's our secret. I'm all confused. Why didn't the shadows punish the strumpet wife? I want to ask them but they've gone.

The tea is all wet on my pretty dress as I get up from the table too quickly. Upstairs I get out my writing papers and start to make a new letter. I feel better once I've torn up some papers and laid the letters out on the page. I want to tell him that I'm sorry, that it should have been her. But I don't know where to send it to. Where is he now? I stick the letters down on the paper, smiling sadly at my little child, before putting it into an envelope. I'll keep it with me, maybe my friends will tell me where to send it.

PLAYING AT DETECTIVES

Sasha eased quietly out of bed, careful not to disturb Eric. Taking a quick shower, she wondered how best to deal with the situation.

The fact was she was here to help and support Tess. She wasn't here for Eric's amusement. And then there was Cal. But Cal was helping her, that was all. Wasn't it? Making a decision, she scrawled a quick note and left it on the bedside table next to Eric's phone then, feeling slightly guilty, crept from the room, closing the door gently behind her. Maybe he'd get the message now.

Crossing the landing she tapped softly on Cal's door, hoping that he was there. *And oh, he certainly was.* All his half-dressed gorgeousness was there. Trying not to stare, Sasha quickly explained that she was thinking of heading over to Tess if Cal wanted to come with her. But they'd need to leave now.

She watched as he pulled a tee shirt over his head before shrugging it down over his chest and taut stomach. Grabbing a shirt and his phone he grinned, he was ready, let's go.

As Sasha drove them out of the pub parking area, Cal turned to her. 'Sash, are you running from something? Or someone? Why all the rush?'

'Oh, Cal, I don't know what I'm doing to be honest. Am I running? Kind of. But he shouldn't have come, shouldn't have just turned up out of the blue.' She glanced at Cal's kind face, 'Eric's not my boyfriend, not in the true sense of the word. He's just, oh, he's just a guy who thinks he can come and go in my life when it suits him, and I'm tired of it. He should be gone today, it's for the best. I'm here for Tess that's what's most important.'

'Does Tess know we're coming over?' Cal enquired, gently moving the conversation away from Eric.

'Not exactly, I said we'd come over today, but I didn't say when. Poor thing, she needs answers. She needs to find her daughter. I mean, where the hell *is* she, Cal? All we've got is a tenuous link between some suspected letters. And none of it sheds any light on where Chantelle might be or even if she's alright.'

'Listen', Cal laid a hand on Sasha's. 'Let's stop for some coffee, you can text your sister and arrange a time. It'll give us a chance to go through what we know so far. The Coffee Shack's just up here on the left and they make a mean espresso.'

The tantalising aromas of fresh coffee assailed their senses as they entered the coffee shop. Cal ordered them double espressos and croissants, and they settled down at a corner table. But suddenly he jumped up, a frown appearing on his face.

Sasha watched him as he took two great strides to the table in the centre of the room, picking up the morning paper and staring at it in dismay. Slowly he made his way back to their table, his eyes still on the paper in his hands.

'Cal? What is it? What's happened?' Dread filled Sasha as she waited for his reply. 'Cal, tell me! What is it? Is it Chantelle?'

He looked up at her. 'They found a woman's body in the river last night. No identification. No other information.' He reached over and placed his hand on hers. 'Don't think the worst, not yet, it could be anyone, Sash.'

'Oh no', groaning, Sasha buried her face in her hands. 'Tess is going to lose it. Well does it say how old she was? A woman or a girl? It must say something! Let me see!'

But there was no further information. Nothing to tell them the age of the woman, or if it was an accident.

Suddenly Cal's head shot up. 'Barbara! What if it's Barbara?'

They looked at each other in horror, both aware that Barbara was missing. And both sure that she'd been the recipient of one of the letters. Cal slowly picked up his phone and scrolled down to Barbara's name, pressing call, before listening to a disembodied voice telling him that the number could not be reached. Shaking his head at Sasha he placed his phone back on the table.

They drank their coffee, the croissants having lost their appeal. Sasha crumbled a few pieces of the buttery pastry, nibbling half-heartedly as her mind whirred.

'Tess!' she suddenly exclaimed. 'We need to get to Tess before she sees this in the paper. No wait, what about the police? Would they tell us anything? Should we try them first, on the way?'

Cal paused, his hand about to break a piece from his croissant. 'I do know Nick, slightly, Nick Crossley. Had the odd beer with him at the pub, played a few games of darts, that kind of thing... He's one of our local constables, we could try him I suppose, not sure if he'll be able to tell us anything but it could be a worth a try.'

'Okay good, let's try!' Sasha was already getting up from the table, anxious now to find out about the woman found in the river as soon as possible. 'Do we just pitch up at the station?'

Nodding, Cal pushed his chair out as he stood up, following Sasha as she hurried from the coffee shop.

The local Police Station was in an old building at the end of the high street, its ancient brickwork and small windows giving it an old-fashioned charm. Were it not for the discreet sign on the wall, one could be forgiven for mistaking it for another of the village's pretty cottages, decorated as it was with flowering window boxes on the outside window ledges.

Cal and Sasha entered the small station and, finding no-one at the counter, pressed the bell. A door at the back opened and a young uniformed officer approached them, a slightly harried look on her face. 'Can I help you?' she asked, looking from one to the other of them enquiringly. Her face flashed with recognition as she looked back at Sasha, and she smiled.

Cal asked if Nick was around and then, deciding it was more appropriate, amended it to P.C. Crossley. P.C. Weaver informed them that he would be in shortly, but could she assist in the meantime? Nodding, when they said they'd wait for him, she pointed to the chairs, telling them to wait there.

The noticeboard caught Sasha's attention, devoid as it was, of anything other than a missing persons' notice. She gasped, clutching Cal's arm 'Chantelle,' she whispered. 'My niece, that's her on the left.' Chantelle's smiling face looked out at them, with Britney's laughing face next to hers.

As they were looking silently at the poster, voices could be heard in a back room, and then a door swung open as P.C Crossley appeared, walking around the counter. 'Cal isn't it? How are you? What can I do for you?'

'Nick, this is Sasha. Sister to Tessa Watson, Chantelle's mother.' His eyes glanced to the poster, 'The mother of one of the missing girls.'

With hands having been shaken, Cal explained that they were anxious to find out about the woman's body found in the river the night before. 'Can you tell us anything at all, Nick? Do you know who she is? We're on our way to see Tessa now, she's going to think it's Chantelle. Anything you can tell us, was she young? Old?'

P.C. Crossley stood silently for a moment, deliberating on how much to tell them. 'Look, I shouldn't really be telling you anything, we haven't officially identified her yet. But okay, I can tell you that it isn't Chantelle. It's not your niece, Sasha. And it's not her friend Britney either.

Relief flooded through Sasha, but at the same time anxiety about Barbara rose inside her. 'So it's an older woman's body? Could it be, I know this might sound weird but, Barbara Fenton's missing. Well we think she's missing, that something's happened to her. We can't get hold of her, you see, and she wasn't at home yesterday.'

Cal took over, explaining briefly about what they'd found at Barbara's house, and voicing their concerns. He touched on the fragments of burned paper, saying they thought that Barbara might have received a letter too.

Nick Crossley's eyes flickered with interest before becoming slightly guarded. 'Sasha, you came in with your sister, and Britney's mother, didn't you? Spoke to Jane? P.C.

Weaver? You told her about the letters they'd received? If you know anything else you really need to tell us. Look, you'd better give me some more details about your friend, let me look into it, see what I can find out. Come through, let's take down some details. And we don't want to say too much about any alleged letters, the rumour mills are already starting in the village, you know what some people are like.'

They followed P.C. Crossley behind the counter and into a small room where they took seats at a table. With Barbara's details having been given to him, they rose to leave. But Sasha stopped, looking at Cal before speaking. 'I know this sounds a bit crazy but the other body you found in the river, Maureen Ford's husband? Are you sure it was an accident? It's just, there seems to be a lot of strange things happening, and all these letters, I just wondered...' her voice trailed off as she felt embarrassment wash over her.

P.C. Crossley was smiling as he shook his head. 'Listen, leave the police work to us okay? No going playing detectives, you two. We only deal in facts here, not rumours and gossip. Let us do our job okay? Thanks for calling in, we'll check on your information about Barbara Fenton, you leave it all to us.'

They left the police station feeling a little subdued. 'Well, that was a bit embarrassing.' Cal grinned at Sasha, 'I think we've just been told off and put in our place. But at least we know it's not Chantelle, or her friend for that matter. So we can give your sister some reassurances. But I'm still concerned about Barbara whatever Nick says.'

'It's my fault, I shouldn't have said anything about Peter. It's not like we've got any reason to think he's related to all this. But it is weird all the same.'

~

Nick Crossley accepted the tea from Jane, gratefully. 'What d'you think? Think they're on to something? Could there be anything in it, that Barbara Fenton received a letter as well? If so we've got something seriously sick and twisted going on in this village of ours.'

Jane Weaver nodded, 'Well, we'll definitely bear it in mind when we go to her house. Unfortunately they've already been in there and been all over her house by the sounds of it, doesn't make our job any easier. But let's not forget we all know that Barbara liked a drink or two, it doesn't mean it's suspicious. We'd better tell the sarge, see what he thinks.'

Sergeant Denton listened to everything the two constables had to tell him, nodding here and there, before leaning back in his chair. 'Well at this moment we have an unofficially identified woman's body taken from the river, and we have our local artist and his girlfriend playing at detectives. But you did the right thing, Nick, in not telling them, the last thing we need is some kind of mass panic on our hands. You're sure the body is Barbara? Where are we with relatives we can call to officially identify her? Chase it up. In the meantime get round to her house and check it out. See if there's any substance to their story about a letter, or remains of one. I feel like pinching myself, it's turning into a bloody nightmare here! Missing girls, poison pen letters, dead bodies in the river, what the hell!'

NOT THEM

Tess opened the door, allowing herself to be enveloped in a big sisterly hug, before Cal was introduced. Her wan face and mismatched clothes bore testament to her state of mind.

'Come through, I'll put the kettle on. Dave'll be up soon, he was working an extra shift last night.'

Sasha's head jerked up briefly at the mention of Dave's late shift, but she kept quiet, time enough to find out what Dave was playing at once they'd found Chantelle. *If they found Chantelle*, said a quiet voice in her head...

With the tray of steaming mugs on the coffee table, Sasha cleared her throat. 'Tess, I don't know if you've seen the paper, darling? It's not Chantelle or Britney, we've talked to the police but...'

Tessa cut her off before she could continue. 'What is it? Did they find something? What's happened?'

At the sight of Tessa's already pale face blanching even more, Sasha moved quickly around the coffee table and sat beside her sister, taking her hand gently. 'They found a body, sis, in the river. It's not either of the girls, this was someone older, that much we know for sure. I promise you it's not Chantelle.'

'Dave!' Tessa called out, and again, 'Dave! I need Dave.' She looked imploringly at her sister, her eyes welling up with emotion. I don't know how much more of this I can take. Why can't they find my baby? What's happened to her? And who did they find in the river?' She rocked back and forth, moaning quietly, as steps hurried down the stairs.

Dave entered the lounge, a look of absolute panic on his face. 'What's happened? Is it Chantelle?'

'No, Dave, it's not Chantelle.' Sasha rushed to reassure him and after briefly introducing Cal, filled him and Tessa in on what they had learned from P.C. Crossley that morning.

'What kind of hellhole village *is* this?' Dave all but shouted. 'My beautiful daughter's missing, as well as her friend, and now there's been two dead bodies in the river! Was she murdered? Sash? Was she murdered? You've got to tell me! What about Peter, Tessa's boss? Was it an accident like they said? Are they covering something up here? Is it going to be Chantelle's body they drag out of the river next? Oh God!' He groaned, covering his face with his hands as he slumped onto the floor, his back against the sofa.

Tessa reached for him, stroking his shoulder as he wept silently, his hands hiding his tears. Her own tears were falling freely now, the collective stress becoming too much for them as they gave in to their emotions. She slid onto the floor and husband and wife held each other, rocking gently, as Sasha and Cal looked away not wanting to be witness to such raw emotion.

Suddenly Tessa looked up. 'Lilith! I need to tell her! She might think it's Britney! I need to phone her, we promised, if we knew anything. Are you sure? Sure it's not either of the girls?'

'We're sure, sis, it's an older woman. We think, well, I may as well tell you, but we're worried it might be Barbara. Barbara Fenton? Your letting agent? But it's not confirmed, we can't say anything.'

'Barbara? But why? What's Barbara got to do with this? Why would Barbara's body be in the river? I can't believe it, poor Barbara, how could that happen to her? I don't understand. Is it something to do with the girls? Is someone taking women and, no, I can't bear to say it. If it's true then where's my baby? Where are Chantelle and Britney?'

Cal spoke up, explaining about their efforts to find Barbara, their visit to her house and finding the fragments of burned paper on the stove.

But why were they looking for Barbara in the first place, Dave wanted to know, how did she fit in to the whole situation? Wasn't Sasha trying to find out about Chantelle?

This time Sasha took up the story, explaining her theory about Peter, that something might have happened to make him behave so out of character, the possibility that he may have received a letter too, and that they'd planned to ask Barbara as she was a friend of Maureen's, his wife.

'So are you saying you think someone killed Peter?' Tessa looked confused. 'I thought it was definitely an accident?'

The phone rang, stopping all the talk as Tessa ran to answer it. It was Lilith, she'd seen the paper, that much was apparent from Tessa's side of the conversation. Tessa's apologies for not phoning her earlier were followed by a garbled explanation about Barbara, more letters, and Peter. Concerned about spreading rumours, Sasha gently took the phone from Tessa, talking calmly to Lilith and making it clear that they weren't in any way sure who the woman was but that it definitely wasn't either of the girls.

With Lilith reassured, the four chatted some more before Dave reluctantly said he had to get ready for work, and Sasha and Cal made moves to leave. Tessa was due to return to work the next day she informed them, saying there was little point in her waiting at home for news, she'd be better off keeping her mind occupied.

The two sisters made plans to get together again as soon as possible and, with goodbyes said, Sasha and Cal left.

NO FLIES ON MRS PRINGLE

Rosemary Spindlebury's hands trembled as she held the newspaper, reading the small paragraph over and over again until the words were imprinted in her mind. It was Barbara, she just knew it. What had Reg done? She glanced up the stairs fearfully, knowing that he would be down soon and wondering what to do. Should she throw the paper away? But then Reg would want to know where it was. Maybe she shouldn't say anything, just put the paper on the breakfast table as usual. Or should she ask him? But if she asked him she'd be acknowledging what he'd done. What if she asked him and it turned out not to be Barbara? He'd be angry with her for accusing him. No, she should just leave it, not say anything at all. But what if she didn't ask him and he hadn't done anything and it wasn't Barbara at all? Well that would be alright then wouldn't it? Maybe she could find out about Barbara, give her a call maybe...

She was so wrapped up in her thoughts that she didn't hear Reg coming down the stairs. His voice in her ear made her jump. 'For crying out loud, Reg, you frightened the life out of me! What are you doing creeping up on me like that?' She laughed nervously, trying to fold the paper and casually place it back on the hall table.

'Not so fast, Ro, what's got you so deep in thought, eh?' Reg took the paper from her, his eyes scanning the front page, divided up as it was into various snippets of local news. 'Nothing much here, same old same old.' He dropped the paper on the table and asked what was for breakfast.

Collecting herself, and sure that she'd been overreacting, Rosemary hurried off to the kitchen, telling him his boiled eggs would be ready in about five minutes.

With breakfast over, Rosemary made a decision. 'Reg, I'm just going to pop out for a few bits at the supermarket, okay?'

'Well I'll come with you, it's a nice day, maybe we should get lunch out somewhere later. What d'you need at the shops anyway?'

'Oh no need for you to come, I just need some milk, bread, oh, and some soap, we're running low and, yes that's right, I was thinking about getting some wine in for later, I thought I'd call at the off licence as well. Let's not go out for lunch today, maybe tomorrow, I'll do us a salad, get some lettuce and tomatoes to go with that cold chicken.' She shifted nervously, wondering if he'd accept her explanation.

Reg raised his eyebrows, glancing at the full loaf of bread on the counter. He then slowly rose, opened the fridge and, taking out an unopened two litres of milk, held it up in front of Rosemary. 'Bread? Milk?' he spoke softly. 'Why d'you really want to go out, Ro? And since when did you start turning down the offer of lunch out?'

'Oh I must have missed it, not concentrating, but no, I thought a nice ciabatta to go with the salad. And I want to get some wine.' She turned away, busying herself at the sink, running the saucepan under the tap, conscious of his eyes on her back.

His hand reached across her, turning off the tap before closing around her wrist. As he turned her to face him his grip tightened. 'Ro? Not bailing on me are you? If you've got something to ask me go ahead, ask.'

'No, it's nothing, Reg, nothing at all.' She forced a laugh, 'You're right, let's go together, it'll be nice. We'll do the shopping and then have lunch, it's the perfect day for it.' She'd have to think of another way to find out about Barbara, she couldn't ask him, not now, not the way he was looking at her.

~

'Oh dear me, poor Dorothy, bless her, well these things happen don't they?' Mrs Pringle bustled around behind the counter. 'But she shouldn't really be taking her pill while she's in the bath, George, no wonder she dropped them all. What's that? Oh no, no need to bother Dr Singh, what with him being so busy. No, no need at all, I'll write it in the book, have a word with him next time he's in. But I do think you should supervise Dorothy's pills, George, I really do, make sure she doesn't have any more accidents.'

With Sheila dispatched to count out replacement pills for Dorothy, Mrs Pringle leant her elbows on the counter and brought up the subject of the body found in the river. It wasn't that she relished all these tragedies, she was quick to point out, but it did make one wonder what was going on didn't it? And what did George make of it all? Did he think it was another accident? Could it be murder? Surely not! And who was it, did he think?

George mumbled vague responses to Mrs Pringle's questions, knowing that she didn't really expect answers. And he and Mother were getting along just fine, thank you. Yes he knew she was just being a concerned friend, and he appreciated it. Of course he would ask if he ever needed any help.

He gratefully received the bottle of pills from Sheila, settling with cash before remembering that he needed some more fly spray. Hesitating, he wondered if he shouldn't just buy it at the supermarket, but there were no flies on Mrs Pringle.

'Something else was there, George? What do you need, anything, you just ask! You'd be surprised what a village pharmacy stocks these days, well we have to, so much competition. I was only saying so to Sheila the other day, wasn't I, Sheila?'

Sheila nodded, the two women looking at George expectantly.

'Fly spray? Why yes of course, my dear. Now would that be the scented one or the odourless? Sheila, be a love and fetch one of each, let George have a look. It's this heat, brings out the flies in their hoards. I was only saying to Sheila the other day, these flies are becoming a real nuisance, wasn't I, Sheila?'

With his fly spray paid for, George said his goodbyes to the two women and watched by their smiling faces, left the shop.

'Well I think we need a cup of tea after all that, don't you, Sheila? Be a love and put the kettle on, there was something I needed to do. Now what was it? My memory's not what it was that's for sure. There, it's clean gone, it'll come to me later no doubt. It's all this talk of bodies in the river, makes you forget everything else that it does.'

Sheila dutifully put the kettle on, wisely choosing not to point out that it was Mrs Pringle who had raised the subject of the bodies.

COMMUNITY CARE

Sasha browsed the selection of women's products, half an ear on the conversation at the counter. Mrs Pringle was clearly the verbal equivalent of the local paper, not much that happened in this village escaped her, she'd bet.

She popped the pads and tampons into her basket before picking up some other necessities, and was just about to look for painkillers when Mrs Pringle swooped.

'Well now I didn't hear you come in at all! Don't think we've seen you before! What can I help you with, my love? Whatever it is I'm sure we've got it! I was only saying to poor George, Mr Newton that would be, you'd be surprised what a village pharmacy stocks these days what with all the competition!

Painkillers? Yes of course, dear. Headache is it?' And then with a quick glance into Sasha's basket, 'Or is it ladies' troubles, dear? Oh yes, you poor thing you do look a little pale. I used to suffer terribly with all that. Thank the Lord those days are behind me!'

Sasha followed Mrs Pringle to the selection of painkillers, not having as yet to say one word, such was Mrs Pringle's ability to keep up an endless monologue with ease.

'There you sit down, dear, fancy a cup of tea? Sheila's just making some aren't you, Sheila? Get some colour back in those cheeks, and you can tell us all about yourself.'

'No really,' Sasha finally found her tongue, 'I must be going, you've been very kind.' Really, how did anyone get anything done if you were offered tea and a sit down in the pharmacy of all places! 'If I can just settle up?'

'Yes of course.' Mrs Pringle, not in the least offended, but with a slight air of disappointment at the lost opportunity for another chat, called Sheila to ring up Sasha's purchases.

'Well she's a dark one.' The two women sipped their tea, watching Sasha, thoughtfully, as she left the shop. 'Wonder who she is? Tourist perhaps? She looks a little familiar though...'

'I'll get the biscuit tin shall I?' asked Sheila.

'Sorry about that,' Sasha took the seat opposite Cal in the Village Patisserie. 'I got caught in the chemist, that Mrs Pringle sure knows how to talk! Did you order? Oh good, I'll just pop to the loo.'

Cal watched Sasha as she went to the ladies. She looked pale, it was probably getting to her, all the emotion with her sister and the missing girl, plus the appearance of that bloke back at the pub. He felt a stab of jealousy again at the thought of him. He hoped Sasha was right and that he'd be gone today.

She sank down on the toilet, feeling weak. Blast, it was coming back she was sure of it. The hated endometriosis. Her gynaecologist had sounded so hopeful, after her last laparoscopy, that she'd be problem free for some time, possibly a year or so at least. But now she was spotting and she wasn't due, not that that meant much. She knew her body too well, that slight clammy feel to her skin, her hair hanging lifelessly, and the beginnings of the dreaded grinding pain deep inside.

Having taken the necessary precautions against any embarrassment, she returned to Cal and their lunch.

'Everything alright, Sash?' Cal looked at her kindly as she played with her sandwich half-heartedly. 'I know it must be getting to you, all the emotion and the frustration. But we are making some kind of progress at least, we're figuring things out. It hasn't got us any closer to finding your niece, but we're on the right track don't you think? It must all be related?'

'Oh, I'm okay, Cal, it's not really all that, I've just got a bit of a stomach ache, you know, the usual...' Feeling a little embarrassed she gave him a small smile, before taking out the packet of pills and popping two out of the blister pack. They probably wouldn't be strong enough, not if it really kicked in like it usually did. Angry with herself for not bringing her strong painkillers with her, she swallowed the pills with her coke.

No, she didn't need to lie down, she assured him, she'd be fine. They should make their list of everything they knew so far, see where they were.

They looked up as the bell above the door dinged, bringing in two more customers. The woman looked nervous, a smile fixed on her face, as the man led her to a table in the back of the little restaurant. He acknowledged Cal with a nod, to which Cal responded with a 'Reg, Rosemary.'

'Now there's a little local mystery,' Cal leant closer to Sasha. 'Bags of money, those two, but no-one knows where it came from.

'Well, that sounds intriguing, tell me more...' Sasha leant forward, perhaps it would take her mind off the pain.

'Have you tried searching for him online? Or her? Most people leave some kind of trace on the internet. What's the surname?' Sasha was already typing into her phone, the hint of a mystery quickening her interest, as it always did.

'Nope, nothing! Weird, like I say you usually find something on the internet. No Facebook page even. I suppose they could be in witness protection? No, too much money for that by the sounds of it. Still, even if we knew their story I doubt it'd have anything to do with what's happening in this village.'

~

'I think I'll just pop out for a bit, dear, run some errands. It's quiet so you'll be fine on your own won't you?'

Sheila nodded, she'd be fine, Mrs Pringle should take her time, enjoy the weather. She didn't say that she'd enjoy the peace and quiet. It wasn't that she didn't love the gossip and the constant chatter, but every now and again it was nice to just *be*. Maybe she'd get to chat to some customers herself for a change.

It was only a few minutes' walk to the Newtons' residence, and she did privately admit to a slight concern at the ease with which she'd handed over more pills to Mr Newton. Not that she doubted his story, oh no, Mr Newton was a pillar of the community, a man of good standing. She'd known him and Dorothy for as far back as she could remember, his mother too of course. But she was just a little worried about Dorothy. Yes, best to put her mind at rest, just a quick visit, think of it as community care. She smiled to herself, liking the phrase. That was it, community care. As the local village pharmacist that was all part of her job.

Noticing the curtain twitch as she drew close, Mrs Pringle was pleased to know that her visit wouldn't be in vain. Dorothy was obviously at home, perhaps they'd have a cup of tea and a nice chat.

'Oh my don't you look smart! Off to a party, my dear?' Mrs Pringle tried to hide her surprise at Dorothy's attire, extremely inappropriate for the time of day, and a big stain all over the dress too, that really wasn't like Dorothy at all. 'Off out are you? Have I come at a bad time?'

Dorothy blinked, trying to clear her mind. She'd been about to do something, now what was it? And why was Mrs Pringle here? She looked down at her hand. Oh yes the letter, that was it, she'd been trying to work out where to address her letter to.

'Oh you need to post a letter! Well I can help you with that, dear! Here, you give that to me and I'll drop it into the post box for you on my way back to the chemist. Now how about a nice cup of tea? I always say there's nothing better than tea on a hot day to cool you down. Let's go into your lovely kitchen and put the kettle on.'

Well, Dorothy didn't look right, that was for sure. She'd certainly done the right thing in coming round. Poor dear thing, lack of sleep was obviously affecting her. And as for the dress well, she couldn't make sense of that, what on earth was she thinking getting all dressed up in an evening dress during the day?

With tea made and poured, Mrs Pringle tackled the subject of Dorothy's lack of sleep.

'Now, George tells me you're having trouble sleeping, dear. Of course, Dr Singh knows what he's doing, if he's told you that sleeping pills are the answer then rest assured that's what you need. But Dorothy you must be careful, no taking your pills while you're in the bath, you don't want another accident. What's that? Why yes of course you're taking baths, but be a good girl and take your pills when you get out. Less chance of an accident I always say.'

Dorothy smiled at Mrs Pringle, trying not to laugh. He'd sent her, Dr Singe, or was it George? It was a conspiracy, they were all in on it, all trying to poison her. She'd act along, be a good girl, but they wouldn't catch her out, oh no, she was too clever for them. But what was all this about pills in the bath? And what accident? But she'd play along, that was the clever thing to do her friends told her, whispering anxiously in her ear.

Well Dorothy didn't smell too fresh. Mrs Pringle surreptitiously sniffed again, yes, a definite smell of body odour, and her hair was greasy, something was amiss, but for all her talk, Mrs Pringle found some subjects rather delicate, personal hygiene being one of them. But of course it was no doubt all connected with lack of sleep. Yes that would be it, poor woman wasn't sleeping, no doubt she was just a little off balance. A few good nights' sleep would set her right.

'So George is doing the laundry is he? Oh what a good man he is, the perfect husband, and him working full time as well.' So that was it, her poor husband was trying to cope with all the washing, probably got behind and Dorothy had put on the dress, probably had nothing else clean, poor love.

Pleased with her assessment of the situation and satisfied that she'd fulfilled her community duty, Mrs Pringle took her leave of Dorothy with promises to visit again soon. No really, it was no problem about the letter, Dorothy should put her feet up or take a nap. She needed to catch up on her sleep then she'd feel better.

Odd. Mrs Pringle stopped on the pavement after closing the gate, wondering what the sound was. And then, shaking her head, she headed off along the road.

Dorothy collapsed on the floor, unable to contain herself any longer. Oh that was fun, pretending to believe all the lies that woman spewed out of her mouth. Did she think she was born yesterday? They all knew she'd been sent by George. But she'd fooled her, made her think she was going along with it. She howled with laughter as her friends did impressions of Mrs Pringle.

But what about her letter? What had she done with it? She looked around in confusion as her brain tried to make sense of what had happened. She'd been holding it when that woman came to disturb her. Mrs Pringle took it, she remembered now. She stole it! How dare she? She'd taken her baby. She'd stolen her baby! Now she wouldn't be able to tell him she was sorry. Tears welled up in her eyes.

Well really, how on earth did Dorothy think she was going to post a letter without putting an address on the envelope? Mrs Pringle tutted to herself as she looked at the envelope in her hand. Of course, the postman knew pretty much everyone in the village, but still, what would the world be coming to if we all just addressed our letters by name and no address?

Feeling a great sense of goodness, Mrs Pringle affixed a stamp from her purse, before writing in the address. She didn't even need to look it up having posted her own card only a day or two earlier. But it was rather inappropriate to address it to him. Oh of course, Dorothy had made a mistake, poor dear, it was obviously for *her*, she'd just missed the 's' off. Having added it in, she dropped the letter in the post box before returning to the pharmacy.

NO FIG ROLLS

No fig rolls. That made him pause. What now? His hand lingered over the space where the aforementioned biscuits were usually stacked, as he pondered his choices. Chocolate digestives, no, too hot, they'd melt, rich tea were a bit plain, ah, malted milks, just the ticket.

He added his choice to the contents of his basket before making his way to the bottled water. Of course he and Dorothy never bought bottled water, such a waste, and harmful to the environment if the programmes on TV were to be believed. But it was the easiest in the current circumstances so that was that.

Glancing into his basket, he moved to the jams and spreads, selecting a jam at random. It didn't really matter what he chose, she wouldn't be needing it much longer, not if he followed Mother's instructions. His hand trembled slightly as he wiped his brow with his handkerchief. This was all Mother's fault.

He stopped dead in surprise. He'd just blamed his mother, his dear mother, and her a paragon of virtue. How could he even think such a thing after all she'd done for him over the years? Get a hold of yourself George, old boy, Mother isn't to blame, they are. If they hadn't come sniffing around, well, everything could have carried on as before, but they ruined it those little bitches, sticking their noses in where it didn't concern them. No, Mother was right, he must follow her instructions, she always knew best.

Feeling better, he dropped his shopping in the boot of the car, deciding to drive rather than walk. The clock on the dashboard told him that she'd be waking soon, he'd have to hurry. There'd be no time to deal with the other one, not in his lunch hour, Ramsbottom was already starting to look at him askance as he hurried out for his lunch each day. No, that would have to be done at night. He sighed, these late night excursions would be the death of him. Dorothy shouldn't be a problem as long as she took her pills, maybe he could give her a double dose. Sweating with the tension of it all, George parked the car outside the cottage and fixed a smile on his face. It wouldn't do for Mother to see him looking worried, she liked to see her boy happy.

'Only me, Mother! There you are looking as beautiful as ever, how's my gorgeous girl today? Oh good, that's what I like to hear.' Kettle on, biscuits on a plate, tray ready, see to Mother, his mind whirred as he rushed through his routine. 'Right, let's settle you comfortably, a nice spray of your favourite fragrance? That's it, beautiful just like my girl. What's that? Oh yes the flies, not to worry, I've got some more spray, bought it from the chemist's, Mrs Pringle, you remember her? That's right, the one who never stops talking! D'you know they sell all sorts there these days, have to, competition from the supermarkets. It certainly was Mother, much better in the old days.'

He closed his mother's wardrobe and went back downstairs. That was everything put back tidily, no-one would ever know. Suddenly his ears picked up the ringing of a phone and he stopped in his tracks, glancing at Mother, terrified that she'd heard it too. She glared at him and he began to shake as she shouted in rage at him.

'I'm sorry, Mother, there's been so much to attend to. Yes, yes I realise I've been stupid, but I'm not always here, it's not my fault I haven't heard them ringing.' That had been a mistake, he should know better. 'No you're right, it *is* my fault. But I'm going to take care of it right now, I promise.'

Leaving his mother with her tea and biscuits, George unlocked the door to the basement before picking up the bag with its mix of contents. He listened at the top of the stairs, reassuring himself that all was well, before descending carefully. It wouldn't do for him to fall, he knew too well how that could turn out.

He was just in time, the girl was groaning as she came round. 'Brit? Brit, you there? Who's there?'

'Shh.' He checked her blindfold and made sure her ankles and wrists were still securely tied. Wrinkling his nose in disgust at the smell, he pushed her onto her side, removing the soiled dustbin bag and wrapping it into a small parcel. With a clean bag on the floor, he rolled her onto it before cleaning his hands with a wet wipe. She choked as he pushed the pills into her mouth, followed by water, and tried to spit them out. *Next time he'd dissolve them in the water bottle.*

She listened to the sounds, something being unwrapped, a knife spreading crackers, and her hunger hit her as the sweet smell of jam reached her nostrils. Hungrily she ate the first cracker, before he took her bound hands and placed them onto the plate in front of her, then moved them to the water bottles.

'Why are you doing this? Where's Britney? You sick freaking bastard. They'll find you, you can't get away with this.' She stopped, listening to the sound of a metal box opening, things banging against each other. He was looking for something. And then a smashing crunching sound. Their phones, he was smashing their phones.

She was aware of footsteps moving away. He was leaving, going up steps, and then the sound of a door closing firmly. Shoving another cracker in her mouth she chewed hungrily, before trying to move and feel around her. But she was stuck, he'd done a good job of restraining her, the sick creep. Her head began to swim as the pills took effect, making her feel nauseous. Reaching around blindly she found the water and drank a whole bottle before slowly falling over onto the floor.

WOMEN'S TROUBLES

Sasha excused herself again to go to the ladies. She was in trouble, she could feel it. Damn it, why did this have to happen now? She hated her useless body for what it did to her.

'Cal, sorry, I won't be a minute.' She stood up, her head suddenly swimming, and made her way to the bathroom, her ears ringing and vision narrowing. Stumbling slightly she held onto the chairs for support as heat consumed her, breathing a sigh of relief when she sank down onto the toilet without blacking out.

Cal watched Sasha with concern, something was wrong, either that or 'women's troubles' were a lot worse than he'd given them credit for.

Pull yourself together, Sash, you can't stay in here. She blew her nose, crying never helped, and doubled up on the pads for extra protection. It was no good, she was going to need stronger painkillers, she'd have to see a doctor. And she'd have to explain to Cal, couldn't just put it down to a simple 'time of the month'.

A knock on the door startled her. 'Sash? You okay? What's wrong? What can I do to help?'

She cringed, it was so embarrassing, she hardly knew him, not really, and here she was caught in such a personal situation. 'I'll be right out, Cal, just give me a minute. I'm okay, really.' She flushed the toilet, looking for an air freshener, to no avail. As if the heavy loss wasn't enough, the irritable bowel that invariably accompanied it was just too much to cope with sometimes.

She washed her hands and splashed some cold water on her face, hoping to bring a little colour back to her cheeks. But her grey face grimaced back miserably. Give it up, it is what it is, you can't change it. You'll have to tell him. But first you need to get back to the pub and lie down.

The thought of her room and her bed, filled her with resolve. Move, one foot in front of the other, slowly so you don't get too dizzy. Tell Cal you need to get back to the pub. Then tell him what's happening.

'What about Eric?' Cal voiced the thought for both of them as he helped Sasha with her seatbelt.

'D'you think he's gone? Shall I check with Jules?' He looked at her worriedly, not wanting to get in the way of anything but equally, wanting to help her in any way that he could.

Sasha leant back against the headrest, trying to think above the pain. She nodded, 'Would you? Just find out if he's still there or not?'

Their shared relief at the news that Eric had left a few hours earlier, *'Tell Sasha to call me, if she can find the time'*, caused a comfortable silence to descend over them both as Cal drove Sasha's car back to the pub.

'Sash, you poor thing, it sounds terrible.' Cal handed Sasha her tea as she positioned herself more comfortably on her pillows.' I had no idea it existed, and to suffer with it for so many years, and all those operations,' he shook his head in sympathy.

She smiled wanly, 'I know, I hate to go on about it, makes me sound like a drama queen, or a hypochondriac, but it truly is crap. Sometimes it gets really hard to try to live a normal life. That's why I started up my little business to be honest, at least I can control my work hours without worrying about a boss thinking I'm slacking off work every month. But I just can't bear the thought of any more ops, I've had so many my belly looks like a war zone.' Her eyes swam with tears and she looked away, embarrassed to appear so weak in front of him.

'It's okay, cry, I don't mind,' Cal placed his hand over hers and squeezed gently. He handed her a tissue and waited for her to blow her nose. 'What can I do? We can get the doctor, maybe he can give you some stronger pills?'

Nodding, Sasha agreed, 'That would be great, will he come here though? I don't think I can face going out at the moment.

Damn, it's so frustrating, there's so much to do, we're onto something, I know we are, and now my stupid body is ruining everything as usual.' Groaning, she doubled over, clutching her stomach as the pain ground into her.

She came to a couple of hours later, surprised to find that she'd slept after Dr Singh's visit. Cal was sitting by her bed watching her anxiously. 'I've got your pills, here, take some, here's some water. And Jules made us some sandwiches, you should probably eat something those are pretty strong according to the doc.'

More tea, sandwiches, and that wonderful feeling of pain subsiding, brought such relief that Sash felt filled with energy. She smiled at Cal, 'Thanks, Cal, you've been amazing, I'm sorry I put this on you. I'm feeling so much better, I should be able to get up soon.'

Cal grinned, 'Take it easy, we don't have to go anywhere right now, let's just talk things through okay? Let's run through the time frame, see where we are.'

They sat back a couple of hours later and looked at their list, satisfied they'd covered everything. Peter's death, still a mystery as to what happened, had he received a letter beforehand, was that why he went on his drinking binge? The letters to Tessa and Lilith, probably Barbara too; the girls' disappearance; Barbara's disappearance; and finally, the discovery of what they were sure was her body.

'That's the lot.' Sasha pulled herself up, surprised to find that she was feeling hungry, those pills had certainly done the trick, for now at least. 'I don't know where it gets us, but that's everything we know so far. I think I should take a shower, then maybe we could get a bite to eat? Well, if you're free? If you fancy it?' Embarrassed, her voice tailed off, poor Cal, she was assuming the guy had no other life, that he was at her beck and call.

'Sounds great!' Cal grinned, 'I'll go and hop in the shower too, mine, that is!' He laughed as Sasha blushed, 'Then I'll meet you downstairs, if you're sure you're up to it?'

They settled in a corner banquette, comfortable with each other, as if they'd known each other much longer than just a few days, and waited for their pizzas to arrive. It was always the same when she'd had a bad session, she craved pizza loaded with chicken, onion, and green pepper, and instead of wine, whisky and coke.

They both ate ravenously, the pizza, and the whisky and coke both working their magic on Sasha. 'I feel so much better!' she smiled at Cal as she leant back contentedly.

THE BEST SCRAMBLED EGGS

It was hard to actually leave the house that morning. Stupid as it seemed, as long as she was there she'd felt a link to Chantelle. Going out, closing the door behind her, felt as if she was deserting her daughter. Or giving up hope. The thought made her shudder, her grief and worry threatening to rise to the surface and undo her fragile control.

But needs must, she couldn't afford to lose her job, and if totally honest knew that staying in the house every day was no good for her mental state. She tried Chantelle's phone, as she always did about a hundred times a day. Nothing, it didn't even ring. Trying not to think about what that might mean, she gently placed the envelope on the floor in the entrance hall. If Chantelle came back while she was out, *when*, she corrected herself, *she must stay positive*, the first thing she would find was a letter from her mum telling her how much she loved her. And telling her to phone her right away. *Please God*, she whispered quietly, as she closed the door.

Von had prepared carefully for Tessa's return, wanting her poor friend to feel welcome, at ease, but also busy enough to keep her mind distracted from her missing daughter, at least within reason.

'Tess, my darling, it's so good to see you!' Von's arms embraced Tessa in a tight hug, before she got down to business. 'There's quite a lot to do, so we'll catch up on everything when we take our morning break. I've made you some tea, it's under the counter, but could you help me by unpacking the new stock? My knees are playing up today so, if you don't mind, I'll deal with customers while you go through the boxes. I don't think I can cope with all that bending up and down right now.'

Von's plan seemed to work. Tessa, grateful to not be pulled into a conversation about Chantelle, quietly got on with the job of opening up the boxes of stock, and the morning passed slowly along. With a fresh supply of summer scarves, (the long hot summer was showing no sign of ending), and other accessories, pretty bags, wallets, sunglasses, etc, unpacked and ready, the two women companionably discussed how to best display everything.

'We'd normally be bringing in some autumn stock by now,' Von chattered. 'But I for one am happy to keep summer going as long as possible. It's the new manager's idea, he-' she paused, worried that just the mention of a new manager would bring thoughts of Peter, and then quite possibly the woman's body also found in the river, and definitely Chantelle, to Tessa's mind. So many tragic events. But a quick check on Tessa and she resumed. 'Oh, you haven't met him yet! Mr Wilburn, Trevor, he's very nice, quite charming actually! Well anyway, he's decided to hold back on the change of season stock and keep pushing summer. Clever. Customers are keen to freshen up their accessories, have something fresh to wear to their next barbeque. We had a new batch of flipflops in and you should have seen them flocking round buying a pair or two in different colours.' She checked her watch, 'Let's take a tea break before changing the displays.'

Ten minutes later and the two women had covered the basics of the last few agonising days. The tragic death of their boss, with the same fate apparently befalling another woman as yet unidentified, had been discussed, both of them avoiding the unspoken fear that the same fate might befall Chantelle and Britney, if indeed there was any relation to the deaths and the girls' disappearance.

Tessa's eyes fell on a woman at the next table who was busy writing something on a sheet of paper.

'Von, you remember that awful letter I received? Well, just a sentence or two really, Britney's mum received one too. Hers was just as cruel, something about her leaving her children while she was out with men. She was devasted, poor woman. And then well, I may as well tell you, but it's just between us, my sister Sasha, she's trying to help it's kind of what she does, well no, she's not a detective or anything but she's good at finding out stuff. Well anyway, she's got this idea that Barbara received a letter too. They've got no real proof, she and Cal, he's the artist? Yes, he's helping her. Well they went to Barbara's house and found charred paper, they're sure Barbara burned a letter. And now she's missing. And, oh Von, they think the body might be hers. You were friendly with her? Oh no, I'm so sorry, that's awful, but it might not be her. I shouldn't have said anything. What is it? What's wrong?'

Von's hand was over her mouth, her eyes wide. 'How could I have forgotten? I was in Peter's office that day, the day he, well, the last day he came to work. He was distracted, even short with me, which wasn't like him at all. I remember glancing down at his desk, seeing a sheet of paper with typing on it, not much, maybe a sentence or two. He covered it up, hid it from me, I think, and I forgot all about it after everything that happened. And I feel so bad for Barbara, she phoned me a few days ago, last week maybe, and I never phoned her back. She was asking about Peter. Oh, poor Barbara, such a kind person.'

Tessa's excitement was short-lived as she realised the implications of what it could all mean. On the one hand, the fact that Peter may have received an anonymous letter too meant a definite link between the deaths, surely, if indeed the body was identified as Barbara. But then what did her letter, and Lilith's, have to do with their daughters' disappearance? The letters were addressed to them, the mothers, not the daughters, and both mothers were still here. What did it all mean? Neither she nor Von knew what to do with the information. 'We need Sasha.'

~

The sound of her phone ringing finally entered her consciousness bringing her fully awake. A quick glance at her watch, shock at how late it was and that she'd *slept* so well, and she answered Tess's call. 'Tess, this is huge! This is so important! We had no way of knowing if Peter had received a letter or not, we suspected but this is it, confirmation, I'm sure

149

of it! We need to meet your friend. This evening? Perfect! I'll bring Cal, we'll go through everything then.'

Fully awake now, Sasha climbed carefully out of bed, checking the towel she'd lain on the sheet for any signs of damage. Relieved that all was fine, she attended to her ablutions as quickly as possible before realising that she'd, quite obviously, missed breakfast, was hungry, and that her pain was beginning to gnaw away deep inside. She needed food, followed by more of Dr Singh's magic pills, and she also needed Cal.

His door was open, his 'Come in, Sash', heard as she was about to tap on the open door. Putting down his paintbrush, he looked up and smiled. 'How're you feeling, any better? I'm guessing you got some sleep. I'm also guessing you missed breakfast?'

Sasha excitedly updated Cal as he cleaned his brushes and laid them neatly down on his table. By mutual consent they headed down the stairs where Sasha apologised to Jules for missing breakfast.

Cal, taking a quick look at Sasha, voiced his concern. 'Are you sure you're okay to go out? You look pretty washed out, I mean, you look great, but you-' he stopped as Sasha laughed.

'Cal, it's okay, I look like crap, I know I do, you don't need to be kind. I just need some food and more pills. I'm through the worst now, it happens like this, once it breaks it settles down, well, hopefully. I can't let it control me, I'd have no life otherwise. But can we take your car, if you don't mind? I'm still a little foggy plus once I take the pills it's probably not a good idea to drive...'

Cal drove them to a little tea shop on the outskirts of the village, the old-fashioned kind popular with the many tourists visiting the area, where, according to him, they did the best scrambled eggs. He wasn't wrong. The generous helping of creamy farm eggs, buttered toast, and masses of tea, was perfect. With the pills washed down, Sasha groaned happily. 'I don't know when I last ate such delicious eggs. Oh, not that Jules's cook's aren't good, but these were just perfect.'

Swiping back and forth on her phone she finally made her choice, and with the photo posted onto Graffic, typed her caption – *Another mystery solved! I've found the best scrambled eggs EVER!* She looked up. 'Cal?'

Cal had picked up the local paper he'd bought on the way to the tea shop and had put aside until they'd eaten. He laid it down between them on the table so that they could both read the headline and paragraph informing them that the body found in the river was definitely Barbara.

'I'm sorry, Cal, you were friends,' Sasha laid her hand over his. 'All the time it wasn't confirmed there was hope, although-' A customer pushed past, bumping her chair forcefully, causing her to stop mid-sentence. She looked round in surprise, raising her eyebrows. 'An apology would have been nice,' she rolled her eyes at Cal.

'Hey!' Cal glared at the man's back as he left the shop, before turning his attention back to their conversation. 'We knew.' Cal's face was sad. 'We knew it was Barbara. What we don't know is why. And dammit, Sash, we're going to find out. We're going to find out why and we're going to find your niece. It says here the inquest is this afternoon, we should go, it's at the town hall.'

What bothered them was why the letters had resulted in two deaths. The Police were sure that Peter's death was accidental, the inquest had confirmed this, and they'd find out more at this afternoon's inquest into Barbara's death. And where did this leave Chantelle and Britney? No matter what they knew, it brought them no closer to finding the girls. And they needed to find them fast, two deaths so close together in one village were enough. They left unspoken the thought that the next death could be one of the girls.

CAT GOT YOUR TONGUE?

George tried not to yawn as he went through his paperwork at his desk. He was finding it hard to concentrate. The pills had knocked Dorothy out good and proper, she was still asleep when he'd left for work, so there was no danger that she'd woken in the night and found him missing.

It had been a waste of time though. Angry with himself for not being more prepared, he thought about what he needed. More dustbin bags that was for sure, he shuddered as he remembered what he'd found when he'd tried to move her body. *The* body. *It*. He had to think of it as an 'it', that might help. It was the heat of course, it had happened quicker than he would have thought, not that he was an expert, well, not exactly... Obviously the basement was damp as well as hot, that must be why, because it hadn't been like that before. *Stop it, George, it's ancient history.*

The thought of the maggots and the smell made him retch all over again. He'd need bleach, more fly spray, air freshener. Gloves, yes, mustn't leave any fingerprints, but what about the bags she, no, it, was already in? Wipes, baby wipes, that should do it, he'd wipe the bags over before moving it. But what if baby wipes didn't remove his prints? Bleach then, to be safe. Yes, that should do it.

He got up and made his way to the little staff room in need of a cup of tea, only to find a group of staff discussing the news of the body in the river. His hands shook as he poured milk into his mug. Barbara, they were talking about Barbara.

'She was your neighbour wasn't she, George?' One of the young computer department staff asked, grinning, 'What happened, have an argument did you? Fall out over all those wild parties you have at night? Decided to finish her off and dump her in the river?' The group in the staff room cackled and looked at George, waiting for his reply.

He looked around in a panic, spilling his tea slightly, thoughts whirring in his head. The last thing he needed was anyone even *joking* about him dumping bodies in the river. His eyes fell on the paper someone had left lying on the table. 'Show some respect! You should be ashamed of yourselves. It's time to get back to work, all of you.'

'Alright, George, we were only joking.' The group wandered off still talking about Barbara.

Picking up the paper he quickly read through the paragraph, wondering what the police had discovered. The inquest was scheduled for this afternoon. Maybe he should go, see what they said. No, he couldn't justify his presence, or maybe he could, neighbourly concern perhaps? So that was two of them now... maybe the police would think there was a serial killer out there. He shook his head, Peter Ford's death had been ruled an accident, and the woman had certainly had a drinking problem, would they think she'd fallen in as well or that she'd been murdered? He needed to attend the inquest, Ramsbottom would just have to put up with it, he'd play on his sympathy, that was it, dear neighbour, sadly missed, yes that would do it.

Ramsbottom glared at George, over his glasses. 'Your mind's not on the job, George. Rushing out here and there, you need to set an example to the youngsters or else where will we be? But go if you must, take it as a late lunch, that'll do it, hadn't realised you and the wife were so close with her. Funny state of affairs if you ask me, people dying left, right, and centre. Never used to happen, I blame the new estate, that's what it'll be, always brings trouble that sort of thing. Hmm.'

Now what was he going to do? He wiped his brow, feeling clammy as anxiety bubbled up. He couldn't fit it all in, not in his lunch hour, he'd have to try to get out a bit earlier, check on the girl then catch the end of the inquest. Yes, that was the important part, what they wrapped up with. He could read the rest in tomorrow's paper.

~

Rosemary glanced up as Reg came into the kitchen. She'd hoped she hadn't woken him, slipping out of bed quietly when she'd heard the thump of the paper landing on the doormat. Still trying to absorb the news, she slipped the paper behind her, hiding it with the cushion. 'Tea, Reg? The pot's still hot.' Her hands were shaking as she poured his tea, she felt like she was going to throw up.

'What's got you all in a tizz, eh? You've got the shakes woman.' Reg hummed as he stood looking out of the window. 'Beautiful day, we should take a drive somewhere, lunch out? How'd you like that, Ro? You look like you need cheering up.'

How could he be so calm? Well, he wouldn't be, not when he saw the paper. Would he admit it to her? Where would that leave her if he did? An accessory. She'd be an accessory to murder! What if she went to the police now? Told them what she thought he'd done? No, what she *knew* he'd done. But Reg knew her too well, he'd know she might do that. She froze, mid-thought- that was why he wanted to drive her out somewhere- he didn't trust her. But he hadn't seen the paper yet, her rational brain kicked in, he didn't know Barbara had been identified. But he must have known it would only be a matter of time. She wondered again how he could be so calm.

'Ro? What d'you say? Cat got your tongue? Where's the paper? Thought I heard the letterbox earlier. Ro?' His voice took on a menacing tone.

She looked round to see him eyeing the corner of the paper showing above the cushion where she'd tried, unsuccessfully, to hide it.

~

Sweating profusely, George slipped silently into a seat at the back of the room. He'd made it. Just. They were summing up the details and he listened carefully.

So that was that then, cause of death strangulation by person or persons unknown; investigation to continue; no suspects. Standing up, he left the room as quietly as he'd entered and hurried back to work.

~

Inspector Kavanagh cleared his throat before making his announcement. There was to be a search for the missing girls tomorrow afternoon. Anyone who wished to offer their services should be at the Police Station at 2pm. No, no indication that the two cases were related. A Police diving team had been loaned to them and would be searching the river. No they were not assuming the worst, but in the absence of any other information or sightings they felt it was the right time for a search. Yes, the parents of the girls had been informed.

Sasha looked at Cal in a panic. 'Tessa didn't tell me! My phone, where is it? I must have left it in the car. She's probably been calling me. She'll still be at work, unless she's gone home.'

'Here, borrow mine and call her.' Cal handed Sasha his phone as they left the town hall.

A tap on her shoulder made Sasha turn around. Dave was behind her, white faced, his dark eyes large as he looked at her in agony. 'Sash, what does this mean? The cops told us this morning they'd be organising a search. I mean, what the hell now? Have we got a serial killer on the loose in the village? Is that what they think? Why else would they decide to do a search straight after finding out Barbara was strangled?'

'Dave, hi, I was about to call Tess. I didn't know you'd be here? Look, I'm sure it's just timing, nothing more. There's no reason to think Barbara's death has anything to do with Chantelle or Britney. They probably just announced it now while they had a group of us together, to ask for our help.'

While Sasha spoke to her sister on the phone, she watched Dave and Cal talking. They were joined by Nick Crossley, who'd been liaising closely with Dave and Tess. Even as he chatted, his eyes were ever watchful, scanning the faces of the villagers as they milled around talking. A further glance around told her that P.C. Jane Weaver was doing the same thing, watching everyone with interest. They're looking for anyone suspicious! The thought struck Sasha like a bolt. They're looking for Barbara's murderer among us all!

Dave was frantic with worry. 'I've been out searching for my daughter every chance I've had. And now you want the whole village to look for her and Britney. Not that I don't want all the help we can get. But why now? What's changed? You said it was just the next step in the process, a precaution, to, what did you say - eliminate the possibility of foul play? But then you tell us Barbara was flaming well strangled! Tell me, Nick, honestly, d'you think there's someone going round strangling women? And what about the other body? The guy - what was his name? Ford? What about him? Two dead bodies in the river and you tell me they're not connected? And my poor daughter's still missing and you've got nothing! I swear, I can't take much more of this.' His shoulders shook as he began to weep, tears of frustration and worry running down his face.

Cal put his arm on Dave's, leading him away from curious onlookers. 'Sash? We need to get Dave home. I'll drive his car, you follow in mine?'

Sasha handed Cal his phone, nodding, as he led Dave away. 'Tessa's on her way home already, we'll meet at their house.' A movement caught her eye and she frowned. It looked like the same guy who'd rudely smashed her chair earlier, or maybe it was just similar clothes, she'd only seen him from behind after all.

'P.C. Crossley, Nick, hi, we'll see you tomorrow for the search. I think we need to get my brother-in-law home. Poor Barbara, I'm so sorry. What we were talking to you about before, did you find anything out? The letter, she got one, right? Can you tell us?'

Nick smiled gently. 'Sasha, we're still investigating so I can't really talk about it, but we did make some interesting discoveries. You'll understand that I can't discuss it and jeopardise our investigation? And before you ask, there's no reason to believe Barbara's death has anything to do with your niece's disappearance. Bad things happen. And sometimes they happen at the same time that teenage girls decide to be teenage girls. We hope our search will turn up nothing, but need more feet on the ground. P.C. Weaver and I have conducted a number of searches in the area already, but with only two of us we can't cover a wide enough area. So, we'll see you tomorrow.'

Having thanked Nick, but still with her own suspicions and concerns, Sasha retrieved Cal's car and headed to her sister's house. Her mind had been so preoccupied with everything that she'd not given her pain a thought. The pain killers had begun to wear off now though and she was aware of a heavy gnawing pain growing deep inside. She could also feel that she was losing heavily, she needed to get to a bathroom urgently. This wasn't good.

MONSTER IN MY BODY

Rosemary Spindlebury was feeling nicely sloshed, that warm fuzzy feeling that made everything feel just fine. She smiled at Reg warmly over her G&T, her second was it, or her third? She'd lost count.

How could she have honestly thought that her Reg had done anything? He'd been such a sweetie today, she thought happily. 'I love you, Reggie,' she slurred.

'That's my girl.' Reg grinned at his wife. 'I told you a nice day out would make you feel better. You get yourself all in a stew over the tiniest things. You read something in the paper and you think the worst. You forget all about that now, ah, here's our food.' It had been a good idea to keep Rosemary busy all day, she always loved being spoiled, lunch, a new bracelet and a fancy handbag, and she was a happy woman. Didn't take a lot. And plenty of drinks. Now a good meal at the club, and she'd go to bed forgetting all about that woman.

'Let's get a bottle of wine, eh, girl?' Might as well make damn sure she passed out and forgot all about Barbara pain-in-the-neck Fenton. There was no-one to connect them to their past now, how fortuitous, he thought, grinning happily, remembering the beautiful sight of Barbara's dead body sprawled on her patio.

~

'You're sure you're okay, Sash?' Tess looked at her sister worriedly. Von had just left having told them everything she could recall about the incident with Peter Ford and her suspicion that he'd received some kind of unpleasant letter, albeit only a typed sentence or two, from what she could tell. The four of them had then spent the evening together, talking over the events of the past few days. Tessa had quaveringly announced that Chantelle's phone was no longer ringing, it was just dead. Realising which word she'd used had set her off into fits of tears. Dave then ordered Chinese takeaway for them all and they'd ended up having quite a pleasant evening, surprisingly. With all the worries and fear of what might have happened to Chantelle it was nice to relax with company and feel normal for a few hours. But Tessa knew her sister and, looking at her grey face, voiced her concern.

'I'm not sure,' Sasha answered honestly, 'I can't believe it's back so soon after my last op but something's not right, and I know my body. I'll see how the night goes.' She smiled, kissing her sister on the cheek as she hugged her tightly. 'Love you, sis, see you tomorrow.'

With goodnights said all round, Cal drove them back to the pub, all the while looking anxiously at Sasha as she sat quietly beside him.

They decided to have a night cap to discuss the day's events, Sasha having assured Cal that a whisky and coke was always soothing. The food she'd eaten earlier, together with more painkillers, had calmed everything down again. She'd stay positive, maybe she'd be okay.

They took their drinks out to the garden, taking a seat on one of the benches overlooking the river. The calm of the night was peaceful, the air warm from the continuing heatwave. Cal lit them cigarettes, passing one to Sasha silently, and they sat companionably for a while before Cal spoke.

'Look how low the river is! I hadn't really noticed, we've been so busy with everything that's happening.' They stood and walked to the edge of the bank, peering down in the moonlight to see the banks exposed. 'This heat is taking its toll, even after that big storm, if it carries on this river will just be a trickle.'

Back at their table they talked about the inquest, disappointed that there hadn't been more information. 'Poor Barbara, it's so awful, to think that someone strangled her with their bare hands. She must have looked right into her killer's eyes. We don't know why, we don't know who, and we don't know if it's got anything to do with Chantelle and Britney's disappearance. I feel so helpless, Cal!'

Cal slipped his arm around Sasha's shoulders, and she leant against him, finding his touch comforting. She could feel her heart beating faster and wondered if he could tell. Was he as attracted to her as she was to him? Even if he was, and there'd definitely been some flirting here and there, the timing was so wrong. They couldn't start something all the while Chantelle was missing, and Cal had just lost a friend. No, it would be wrong, plus she was feeling like crap, her endometriosis knowing just when to rear its ugly head and destroy anything nice in her life.

As if on cue, she felt a tug, deep inside. She was still losing heavily and knew she'd need to get to the bathroom pretty urgently.

'Sash, you okay?' Cal's murmur jolted her from her thoughts, his lips gently moving against her hair. If she looked up at him now he'd kiss her, he was finding it harder and harder to resist her.

As if knowing Cal's thoughts, Sasha pulled away. 'I'm sorry Cal, I have to go to bed. I'll see you in the morning. Sorry.' She stood up and, taking her empty glass, made her way back inside.

Cal stayed at their table, smoking another cigarette, wondering if he'd given his feelings away and scared Sasha off. But then she'd seemed to enjoy their gentle flirting here and there. No, it was probably all the worry, and she was obviously suffering from something which clearly caused her embarrassment. He'd have to hold back, wait until they got through this dark time and hope that her niece was found safe and well. Maybe then...

~

George gently carried his mother's light as a feather body up the stairs and deposited her on her bed. Helping her into her nightgown he kept his eyes averted to preserve her dignity. Dignity had always been so important to Mother. And she'd been so sweet to him this evening, hadn't berated him for anything, had gently but firmly encouraged him in what he had to do now.

The girl had taken her pills in the water bottle earlier, offering no resistance, accepting of the situation it seemed, and would now be asleep with no chance of waking for hours. The idea of the rope had been confirmed to him at the inquest, it was perfect, as was the river as a final resting place. Mother agreed, telling him how proud she was of her clever son.

Saying goodnight to Mother, he descended to the basement, trying not to think of what he had to do.

~

Ha! Stupid George, he was so easy to trick! Take your pills, Dorothy. There's a good girl, Dorothy. Three little bags full, Dorothy. Well, he wasn't going to poison her that easily. And where did he think he was going at night? Sneaking out like a schoolboy. Everybody had an opinion, voices rising as they all fought for Dorothy's attention. A girlfriend? George? The thought was so funny she shrieked with laughter, holding her stomach as she rocked back and forth on her bed.

Better check he's not coming back, he mustn't catch me awake. I'll just peep out of the curtains. But now I feel sad in a funny way, she's not there anymore drinking her devil's poison. Yes I know it had to be done, but why did it have to be *him*?

Dorothy stepped back from the window, trying to think clearly amidst her confusion. She'd thought it was her friends moving silently in the dark, her shadow creatures, but now she pictured him again, wearing that stupid yellow cravat and flat cap. Was it real? Sometimes it was hard to know what was real and what wasn't, everything seemed so foggy. But no, it *was* him! He was a bad man. He'd taken her away from her. Yes she knew she wasn't her friend, but... You let him take her away, you let me think it was you, why did you lie?

Slyly she looked at her friends, you want me to tell *her* what he did. That's why. That's why you wanted me to look out of my window to the world. Clapping her hands in glee, she jumped up, gathering her papers. Happiness bubbled up inside her as she and her friends went downstairs and laid out her things. She started tearing the letters to make her next baby.

Sasha woke in agony, the pain searing through the one side of her body. The leg cramp was so bad she cried as she doubled over, feeling nauseous. A thin film of sweat coated her body and she could feel the dreaded wetness underneath her. Gathering the towel and holding it between her legs she tried to stand, steadying herself before attempting to make it to the bathroom. The ringing in her ears was so loud she could hear nothing else and she fumbled for the light switch as her vision tunnelled into darkness. With no sight and the disorientating ringing, she groped blindly for the bathroom door but blacked out before she found it, falling onto the floor.

What was that? Cal's ears pricked up as he lay in bed. Something had woken him, a thud. He waited for more sounds but all was quiet. Slipping out of bed he opened his door, noticing the light shining underneath Sasha's door. He tapped gently. 'Sash? Are you alright? Sash?' Testing the door handle he found it unlocked and, after a moment's hesitation, opened the door.

'Oh God! Sasha, what happened?' Rushing to her side, he gently turned her over, relieved to hear her groan as she opened her eyes. She started to cry as her hands automatically tried to hide the towel between her legs. Another round of pain doubled her up and she had no choice but to clutch her stomach. 'That's it, I'm taking you to hospital!'

With another towel underneath her, *thank goodness she always travelled with a couple of old towels*, Sasha sat on the bed drinking water. Cal passed her the ginger biscuits she'd asked for from her table, and she ate two before taking her pills. 'Can you help me to the bathroom?' Her voice was feeble, 'Just give me a few minutes of privacy.'

He hovered outside her room while she was in the bathroom, frantic with worry. Relieved when she called him back in, he rushed in, noting that her face at least had a little colour in it once more. 'I'm taking you to the hospital, no arguments.'

'Please, Cal, they won't be able to help me, not here. It's my endometriosis, it's back with a vengeance. Bloody evil bastard monster in my body. I need to see my doctor in London. I probably need another op. I'll call him but there's no point in going to the local hospital I promise you. I could drink some tea?' She looked at him pleadingly.

'Alright, Sash, no hospital. But I'm taking you to London first thing in the morning. No arguments. You can phone your doctor first thing and we'll go straight there. Tessa will understand.' He put the kettle on and wrapped a blanket over Sasha's shoulders as she began to shiver.

LAPAROSCOPY REQUIRED

Another pointless day. Maureen sighed. It was becoming harder and harder to get out of bed each morning. Every day the same meaningless routine, make the bed, tidy the house, wash the cups up, force herself to eat something. She should go out, but where? And what for? It was as much as she could handle to go out for fresh milk and bread.

Life without Peter was unbearable. But to then lose her friend as well... She remembered that the inquest had been held the day before. Poor Barbara, she should have gone, but it was a step too far, the memories of Peter's inquest still too fresh and painful. The findings would be in the paper, she'd see if it had been delivered yet.

With a reason to get up, she climbed out of bed and pulled on her robe. She'd leave the bed, make some coffee and read the paper.

~

Jules's face was filled with concern as she assured Sasha that she'd keep her room for her. 'Go, Sasha, you poor thing, it must be awful. Cal, let me know how you get on okay?' She waved them off and went back into the pub to begin the day's preparations.

Cal helped Sasha into her car, having acknowledged that hers was the more reliable vehicle than his old Beetle. He turned to her, 'What about Tessa? We need to let her know, and that we won't be at the search.' But Sasha was barely holding it together, all her willpower being used up in the simple act of sitting in the car and preparing for the journey back to London.

'Sit tight, I'll call her and explain. I don't think she'll be too surprised.'

He was right. Tessa knew her sister almost as well as she knew herself. 'Oh poor Sash, I'm not surprised, Cal, she looked terrible last night. Look, she mustn't worry about anything, tell her. Just get her home and to her specialist. And call me, yeah? As soon as you have news? No, don't feel bad about the search, either of you, she's been so supportive, you too, Cal. And yes, I'll let you know how we get on this afternoon. I'm dreading it, but in some ways it will feel good to be doing something physical and not just waiting for a call. Dave's been out looking whenever he can, and the police, of course, but to have extra help will be a boost. But I don't want to find anything, I just want Chantelle to walk through the door. I don't care where she's been or what she's done, I just want her back.'

~

George dragged himself out of bed. He was too old for this. Refusing to think about the night's unpleasant events, he first peered around the door to Dorothy's room. Still sleeping soundly. The pills had done the trick and she was none the wiser about his nocturnal absence. With his morning ablutions completed he went downstairs, opening curtains and putting the kettle on.

~

Closing her eyes tightly, Dorothy pretended to be asleep. She was too clever for him. She listened as he made his way back upstairs, heard his wardrobe open, the rattle of coat hangers as he selected his shirt for work. She sniggered quietly, nudging her friends to keep quiet, as his grunts reached her ears. His shoes were on, he'd be coming to wake her.

I should have been an actress! I'm so good at this! Big yawn, open my eyes a little, stretch my arms. 'What time is it? I slept so well. Dr Singe's tablets are wonderful! And how did you sleep, George, my darling?' The shouting had become an enjoyable habit, she loved seeing George recoil slightly, a look of confusion on his face. Darling! She hadn't called him that for years, stupid word, especially for him. That's what made it so funny. She'd have to think of some more words like that.

165

Blinking in surprise, George tried to fix a smile on his face. Pulling her curtains open, he commented brightly, 'Lovely day! Oh, you had a good sleep, that's wonderful, er, my love, me too, yes, me too.' He'd have to try to get Dorothy to have her hearing checked, all this shouting, it gave him a headache. And now why was she laughing? Like a mad woman. He hadn't got the energy to deal with her, not this morning. And, oh God in Heaven, she was still wearing that blessed dress, did she sleep in it? Realising that he was holding his breath, he sniffed the air tentatively. She hadn't bathed, he was sure of it, the whole room had an unpleasant odour to it, sour, a mix of unwashed clothing and, well, it smelled like onions, yes, that was it. His face creased in disgust, body odour, his dear mad wife stank of body odour.

~

They were making good time, the roads quiet with very little traffic. Sasha had slept a little and woke up as Cal pulled into a service station. 'I thought we'd stop for the loo and get a drink. Maybe a bite to eat too if you're up to it?'

'Great, and I need to check my mail, Mr Bailey's secretary said she'd e-mail me once she'd talked to him but she was very doubtful that it could be back so soon. I know my body though, I know it's back.' Breakfast smells reached their nostrils as they entered the service station, making them both feel hungry, and they met back in the cafeteria a few minutes later.

'Okay, so he's in surgery this morning but will see me as soon as I can get there. If I'm right, and it's back, he'll admit me today. We'll go to my place first, drop our stuff, you'll need the key if I'm in hospital.'

~

Maureen read the newspaper's account of the inquest into Barbara's death for a second time. Someone had strangled her friend. It was unbelievable. Poor, dear, Barbara. Friendly helpful Barbara. She was a good, kind, person, with no enemies, who on earth could have done that to her? And why? And what about Peter? The thought played in the back of her mind. They'd said Peter died from drowning, no-one else involved, but were they sure? Maybe they'd missed something. No, don't think about it, it makes it worse. Better her beloved husband died naturally, if you could call it that, than at someone else's hand. Which took her mind back to Barbara. She'd honestly thought that Barbara had somehow ended up on a bender, *yes, she knew Barbara's weakness for the bottle*, and had somehow slipped and fallen into the river. Awful as that was, it was preferable to the thought of a cold-blooded killer strangling her with his own bare hands. Shuddering at the thought of what her friend's last moments must have been like, she put the paper down on the coffee table.

The sound of the letterbox opening and the thud of her post landing on the doormat distracted her from her miserable thoughts.

Bills, circulars, and what looked like more condolence cards. Her eyes glanced at the mantelpiece, overflowing as it was with cards from their many friends and neighbours. She'd open them later. Picking up the paper again, she decided to catch up on the local news.

~

The office was abuzz with chatter when George arrived, a little late and hoping that Ramsbottom wouldn't notice his tardiness. He still felt half asleep, but his senses soon quickened as snippets of conversation reached his ears, *the missing girls, search planned for that afternoon*. Hovering in the staff kitchenette he listened to the various conversations and took his time making a coffee.

'Ah, George, there you are!' Ramsbottom's voice boomed out as he was making his way back to his desk, worrying thoughts rushing through his mind. 'Staff are all disturbed about these blessed missing girls. One of our own, of course, makes it a tad difficult. One of 'em's young Watson's girl, poor fellow. Anyway, it's at 2pm, I'll make an announcement, right thing to do, let those that want to help go and do their bit. We'll hold the fort, eh? Not like we can't manage it? I knew I could count on you, there's a good chap. Got a fellow coming in about some new dye, young Dave informs me, very worried he is, doesn't want to let us down. But he must be at the search

I told him. Your daughter's missing, I said, nothing more important. George will handle the meeting, he knows his dyes. Two-thirty, don't forget now. Yes.'

~

Sasha's flat felt stale and unloved as she opened the door, pushing it slightly to shift the pile of letters on the doormat. It felt kind of weird, Cal being here with her, like they'd crossed some kind of unspoken boundary. It also felt quite nice. But there was no time to explore those feelings, they needed to hurry.

Malcolm Bailey's face was serious when he finished examining Sasha. I won't know for sure without a laparoscopy, Sasha, but from what you've told me and from what I can deduce, I'd say we've definitely got some adhesions in there, some quite large. Something's definitely causing all that blood loss and pain.' He checked his file again, 'We cleaned you out six months ago, you should have been clear for a year or more, it's a bugger that's for sure. We'll get you checked in now and schedule you for surgery first thing.'

IT SHOULD HAVE BEEN HER. NOT YOU

The morphine drip took her pain away and she slipped in and out of sleep, conscious of Cal's presence beside her bed. 'What time is it?'

Checking his watch, Cal informed her that it was after one. He'd better call Tessa and update her before she left for the search.

~

She'd join the search. It was at 2pm she noted, having read the announcement in the paper. Surprised at her decision, but pleased with it, Maureen headed upstairs to dress. It would feel good to be helping and it would take her mind off everything else at least. She'd see Cal, and that nice girl Sasha, the mother's sister, perhaps she could partner with them.

Realising that she hadn't opened the cards, and with a few minutes to spare before she had to leave, Maureen quickly tore open the envelopes, reading yet more kind words, before placing the cards with the others. The last one was flimsy, crackly, and didn't feel like it contained a card.

She looked in confusion at the haphazard arrangement of letters affixed to the paper. It was hard to even make sense of it, the cuttings, well, torn pieces of paper, being of differing sizes and placed in no particular alignment.

I'm sorry. Was that right? *It should have been her. Not you.* What? Who? What shouldn't have been me? What *was* this? She turned the paper over in her hand, examining it. Floral stationery, who even used that these days? It looked like something a child would make, streaks of glue smearing some of the printed letters where they'd been stuck down. Glitter had been sprinkled onto the glue and heart stickers had been placed in various places on the paper. Mystified and disturbed, Maureen picked up the envelope to examine it. It was definitely addressed to her. Wait though, the address was in a different handwriting. It was definitely her name though, Mrs Ford.

She needed to leave now or she'd be late. Maybe a child of a neighbour had wanted to send a letter to say they were sorry. Yes, that would be it, and maybe they just didn't get the words right. But then- no, the tone was a little sinister- *it should have been her not you*- and it really didn't make any sense. She must go. She'd talk to Cal, ask him what he thought, he and Sasha. There was no-one else she could ask really, now that Barbara was gone.

~

George watched the bulk of the staff depart, frustrated and agitated that he had to stay at the office. But then again it might have looked strange for him to join in the search for the girls, and better he kept away from it all anyway. It's not like they were going to find anything. Well, surely not yet. And not around here, if he'd done it right. What were they going to do? Comb the fields around the village, walking in lines? He'd seen the TV shows.

The rep arrived for his meeting and George joined him in the small conference room. Talk of paper dyes took over the next hour or so and, when the secretary brought in a tray of drinks, the two men sat back, satisfied with how things had gone.

'So, big search going on in the village, George? Missing girls, I hear. Probably done a runner, be in London, something like that, teenage girls being what they are, although you never know, could've been murdered by some sicko. Rough on the parents, poor Dave, nice chap, bet he never thought this would happen when he moved to your peaceful little village. You always think London's the problem, but evil's everywhere I always say. Got a whole diving team too. Saw them setting up as I drove along by the river.'

George sat up a little straighter in his chair. 'Diving team, you say? Wonder what they've got that for?'

'Oh, come on, George, you've had two bodies turn up in your river already, cops obviously think you've got a serial killer on the loose in the village. They're not going to broadcast it, but that's what they'll be thinking.' He nodded knowingly, he was an avid watcher of crime series on TV, he knew what he was talking about.

~

Maureen looked around for Cal, not seeing him among the throngs of villagers gathered outside the police station. The turnout was huge, the village and surrounding areas had clearly taken the plight of the missing girls to heart. Her eyes fell on a pale-faced woman holding the arm of a man, presumably her husband. She looked familiar and Maureen realised she must be Sasha's sister, the mother of one of the missing girls. They were talking to another woman who looked equally pale. The other mother probably.

Not wanting to disturb them, and with no sign of Cal, Maureen stayed on the sidelines, waiting for instructions from the police. A hand gently touched her arm. 'Mrs Ford? Maureen? I'm Von. I worked for your husband. I'm so sorry. He was such a kind man. I'm sorry I didn't speak to you at the funeral. But we were all there from the store, we wanted to pay our respects. He was greatly loved.'

'Oh, Von, yes, Peter talked about you very fondly. Thank you, and thanks for your card, it was very kind of you. Poor Barbara always spoke of you highly, too, God rest her soul.'

Von exclaimed quietly. 'Oh, I'm so sorry, you were friends with Barbara. So awful, it doesn't bear thinking about. You poor thing, what you must have been through these past few weeks. There's a dark cloud hanging over the village, one wonders where it will all end.' A thought occurred to her. 'Shall we team up for the search? Would that be alright?'

It was a surreal afternoon, the hundreds of people spreading out, as directed, making their way slowly across fields, heads down, scanning for anything that might strike them as out of the ordinary. Every now and then a hand would go up, a whistle would be blown, and a volunteer in a high vis jacket would make their way to the spot, carefully putting up markers for further examination, of whatever had been found, by a forensics team.

The search continued on, the long hours of daylight allowing them to keep looking. Tessa stoically walked along, head down, repeating her mantra over and over, silently, in her head. *Please don't find her. Please don't find her.*

As the sun slowly lowered in the sky people began to make their way home, disappointment at not having found anything of any help tempered with relief at the failure to find a clue that might lead to bad news for the parents.

Not quite sure what to do, and feeling partly relieved, but equally filled with despair, Tessa, Dave, and Lilith, made their way back to the police station, not wanting to just go home. P. C. Jane Weaver was heading towards them, her face taking on a blank mask when she saw them heading in her direction.

'Nothing? Nothing at all, Jane? Is that good? It is, isn't it? It means they're still out there somewhere? But where? Was anything of any help? We saw people raising their hands here and there? What did you find? Do you have any news at all?' Tessa's voice was becoming loud in her frustration and worry.

Jane glanced warningly at the small gathering of reporters who'd been following the day's events, and were now convening at the police station in the hopes of catching a good photo or two of the parents. 'Let's go inside.' She led them into the station, directing them to a small room with comfortable chairs. 'I'll get some tea sent through and we'll talk through everything. But so far it doesn't seem that anything of any importance has been discovered. I'm sorry. But that's a good thing. It means we've no reason to suspect the worst.'

Jane cursed her mouth as she left the family room. She should learn to keep her mouth shut. She felt for the parents so terribly, and wanted to reassure them. But it wasn't her place to tell them they'd found nothing of concern, she should have waited for a directive from her boss. After all, what if one of the odd items found on the search resulted in evidence of something having happened to the girls? What then? And her having told them they'd found nothing of importance.

A kindly looking older lady brought in a tray of tea, placing it down on the low table in the centre of the room, smiling gently at them, and telling them that P. C. Weaver would be back with them shortly. A slight commotion could be heard outside on the street, loud voices, the sounds of car engines starting up, and they looked up, wondering what was happening.

'Dave?' Tess looked at him fearfully, 'What's happening?'

Dave looked grim. 'I'm going to go and find out, wait here, both of you.'

The crackle of police radios could be heard from the back of the station and P.C. Crossley hurried past, talking rapidly into his radio as Sergeant Denton urgently beckoned him towards him. Jane Weaver, looking harried, was trying to get their attention, attempting to steer them out of Dave's earshot as he appeared in the reception area.

'Jane? What's going on? Did something happen? You've got to tell me! What is it?' Dave was frantic, something had happened, he wasn't stupid. 'This is about my daughter. I need to know. NOW!'

Looking behind her, Jane took his arm, trying to guide him back to his wife and Lilith, where they waited anxiously for news. 'Please, Dave, take a seat for a minute, I'm trying to find out, okay? I don't know what it is, it could be anything, it may not even be related.' Damn, she'd said too much, again.

'What might not even be related?' He allowed himself to be walked back into the family room, feeling dread well up inside. Sitting down, he put his head in his hands. 'They've found something, I know it.'

~

'They're sure, Nick? A girl's body? No doubt? Any idea which one? No, we'll have to wait until they bring her in.' Philip Denton thought rapidly. He'd got the parents in the family room, how to handle this? 'Jane, you need to get back in there, yes, I know. Tell them, well, tell them we may have found something of interest, no, wait. Tell them you don't know anything right now. That's all. On second thoughts, Nick, you go, you've been less involved with them. Keep it simple. Tell them we're busy putting together the day's findings and that we'll update them as soon as we're ready.

And for the love of God, someone go out the front and get those reporters out of here!'

~

Inspector Kavanagh looked grimly around at his officers. 'So we're sure then, we have a girl's body retrieved from the river. Seems she couldn't have moved far from where she was dumped, the water level being so low where she was found snagged on exposed rocks. This was lucky for us, it means she was dumped somewhere close. We need to tread carefully, the less people that know the better, for now. Try to keep the press out of this if at all possible. They're transferring her as soon as the Doc's been and signed off. Nick, Jane, I'm going to need you to advise the parents. We can't keep this from them. It's not going to be pleasant. Nick, you're with Mrs Morton, Jane, you're with the Watsons. You stay with them, you don't leave their sides. And remember, we don't know if it's either of their daughters. Phil, you'll head out and meet Dr Singh at the scene?' Sergeant Philip Denton nodded, already on his way.

P. C Crossley and P. C. Weaver entered the family room, their faces serious. Nick took the lead.

'Please don't be alarmed,' he began.

'Oh God!' Tessa and Lilith both wailed, clutching at each other, as Dave doubled over in both mental and physical agony, his hand reaching for his wife's.

~

Back in London, Cal gently kissed Sasha's forehead as she slept soundly. It was getting late, he'd go and grab something from the hospital cafeteria, then come back and check on her before heading to her flat for the night. Checking both their phones, after switching them on, he was relieved to see that there were no messages. So the search hadn't resulted in anything. He switched Sasha's off, put it in her bedside table and went off in search of food.

PLEASE GOD DON'T LET IT BE MINE

Maureen looked at the letter as it lay on her coffee table. With no Cal, she hadn't known what to do, who to speak to about it. Should she have told the police? It seemed a bit extreme to bother them over a slightly sinister sounding letter. She wondered where Cal and Sasha were, it was odd that they weren't at the search. She tried Cal's phone again, relieved to hear it ringing finally.

Cal chatted to Maureen for a few minutes, explaining what had happened with Sasha, before asking if she knew how the search had gone. Pleased that she'd been a part of it, he finished by asking her how she was and if she was coping alright.

Deciding that now was not the time to bother Cal about some stupid piece of paper that made no sense, Maureen assured him that she was fine and they said goodnight, with Cal promising to send her love to Sasha.

He ate quickly, wanting to check back on Sasha before going to get some sleep, He wanted to be there in the morning, before she went down for her op. Before he switched his phone off again he tried Tessa's number, thinking he ought to update her and ask about the search, but there was no reply and he guessed they probably wanted to be left alone after what must have been a pretty difficult day. ˜

Numb now, and wiped out from all their crying, the parents sat silently in the family room, staring ahead, as dusk fell. Nobody spoke. No-one could voice the thoughts going through their heads. *Don't let it be my daughter.* Who could say those words out loud, when it meant you were asking for it to be the daughter of the woman sitting next to you?

A tray of uneaten sandwiches sat forlornly on the table, the curling triangles giving off an unpleasant smell of warm mayonnaise and souring cheese. All three started in unison every time they heard the slightest sound, so tuned were they to anything that might bring the dreaded news to them.

P.C.s Weaver and Crossley came and went, each taking turns at sitting quietly in the room, while the other one went in search of updates.

It was while P.C. Nick Crossley was checking in with his boss, Inspector Kavanagh, that the call came through from Sergeant Denton to advise them that, following Dr Singh's pronouncement of death, the body had been transferred to the hospital morgue in the neighbouring town of Rentham. The body was in a bad state of decomposition and all the doctor could say was that the female had been dead for at least a week, in his opinion.

Nick stuck his head around the door and caught Jane's attention. With a tilt of his head he indicated she should join him out of earshot of the parents. 'Body's in Rentham at the morgue. Not in a good state. No I.D. yet, we'll need to take the parents through. I'll take Mrs Morton, you take the Watsons. But remember, it might not be either of the girls, although-' he grimaced. 'Well it might be, it might not, let's leave it at that.'

It was like trying to wade through treacle, Tessa thought, as she followed Dave to the car. Each step took all her energy leaving her unable to summon the strength to so much as speak. She'd been able only to look at Lilith with fear, the woman's expression mirroring her own, as both mothers fought the possibility that their daughter was dead. *Please God don't let it be mine.*

Oh, how many times she'd taken the bus on this route to work, Tessa stared numbly out of the window, never imagining that one day she'd be in a police car driving to the hospital to see if it was her daughter lying on a slab.

Jane Weaver led them through a back entrance, thus avoiding the public, even though the hospital was quiet at this time in the evening. Lilith was already waiting, Nick Crossley doing his best to keep her calm as she sobbed and asked repeatedly why she couldn't see the body.

Wilson Mwabila, the mortuary attendant who doubled as the Coroner for Rentham and surrounding villages, and who was also the local funeral director, opened a door and asked the officers to go through.

'We can't let them see her I'm afraid. The body is a suppurating mass, severely decomposed. The only reason we have the whole body, or what we hope is the whole body, is that it's been wrapped and sealed in a number of plastic bags. It's pretty liquified, I'm sure you get the picture. Cause of death is going to be difficult to determine.'

'Anything you can tell us at this stage that might be of interest in our investigation?'

Wilson hesitated. 'Come with me.' As he led the way to the autopsy room behind his office, he paused. 'You might want to put these on,' he said, handing them masks.

'You understand this is just an initial examination? I'll be doing a full autopsy and should know a lot more then. Okay, good. Well, as I said, what we've got is a liquified body which appears to have decomposed rapidly. I put this down to the fact that the weather has been unseasonably hot and the body has been kept somewhere extremely humid, probably for quite some time. From the clothing, we know that this is a female, probably a teenager due to the style of the clothes. She appears to have been kept on, rather than in, plastic bags which were then later wrapped around her body, in other words, her body was left exposed for a period of time. Her body would have ruptured, as gases accumulated, and this is where it gets interesting.' He pulled the bags open and waited, as both Nick and Jane gagged slightly.

'If you look here you'll see there are masses of maggots, flies in various stages of development. Blowflies will have been attracted to her putrefying remains, laying their eggs inside the corpse, and as they hatched the maggots will have begun feeding on the body's tissues. This will have caused the skin to fall off, as well as hair loss. Yes, Nick?'

'So you're saying this is all down to decomposition wherever her body was kept, and not from being in the water?'

'As far as I can tell at this time, yes, there appear to have been more plastic bags used to contain the remains, before disposal in the river. Duct tape is pretty strong and watertight, so I don't think much river water made its way into the bags. This also makes me think she wasn't in the water for very long, possibly only a day or two before you found her. I'll need to confirm that, of course. But what I wanted to show you was this.' He used his long forceps to probe the various maggot masses, demonstrating no signs of life. 'They're all dead, which is unusual, very unusual in fact.'

'So what does that tell us exactly? What does it mean?' Jane was trying to concentrate on the information whilst resisting the urge to throw up.

'Well, my guess is that someone made sure to kill them before wrapping the body in the last of the bags. Maybe to try to disguise the time of death. Most people will know, from TV shows, that we can use the various stages of larval development to aid us in determining such things. But they left the maggots in the body's remains, and all over the plastic, so we can get some idea, apart from the fact that we don't know when the maggots were killed, which does complicate things. I detect a faint smell of household bleach, which would have done the trick, but will check for any other chemicals which might help you with your investigation.'

'Jeez, Wilson, you've got a good nose on you.' Nick was impressed. 'How you can smell bleach above this stench beats me.'

Wilson Mwabila smiled. 'After concluding my studies in the United Kingdom I returned to my native Zambia, working there for many years. At our clinic in Chingola we didn't always have the necessary equipment to conduct our tests. We relied on our sense of smell very often. A habit I've found hard to drop, and one which I still find useful.'

Pointing with his forceps again, Wilson drew their attention to the last item of interest. 'Now this is extremely interesting.' He carefully lifted the length of rope a little, taking care not to change its position, that of loosely encircling the remains of the neck.

'Indication of strangulation?' Jane peered closer, a frown on her face.

Slowly, Wilson shook his head, 'I don't think so although I'll have to confirm that. My first thought is that it was placed there post-mortem. It has the appearance and feel of a prop, to me, as if it was a last minute addition before disposal of the body. Maybe somebody wanted it to look like she was strangled with this rope.' He smiled, 'But that's your job, of course.'

The officers thanked Wilson for his observations before turning to each other to decide on their next course of action.

'I'll note down the clothing details with Wilson, maybe you should-' Jane paused as she looked at the door, hearing footsteps. 'Nick! Stop him!'

Nick rushed to the door, putting his hands out to stop Dave as he tried to enter the room. 'Dave, no, you can't come in here. Sorry mate, no way. Come with me, Jane will be with us in a moment and we can tell you what we know.'

WHAT WAS YOUR DAUGHTER WEARING?

Three sets of eyes looked up as Jane rejoined them, following her movements as she took a chair opposite them.

'You won't be called on to see the body for identification purposes. What we must do is confirm the clothing each of your daughters was wearing on the day they disappeared.' She spoke gently, knowing that they were, in all likeliness, about to receive terrible confirmation for the one, and some measure of relief for the other.

'I have our records here where you, Tessa and Dave, stated that Chantelle was wearing a denim skirt and pink tee shirt, is that correct? And Lilith, Britney was also wearing a denim skirt but her tee shirt was black with a white logo of some kind, is that correct? And Chantelle wore pink trainers with silver stars, right? While Britney wore silver shoes, also trainers, is that correct?'

All three nodded, terrified of what they were about to hear.

With a warning glance at Nick, to be prepared, Jane looked in sympathy towards Lilith. 'I'm so sorry, Lilith, we think we may have found Britney's body.'

Nick lunged just in time, as Lilith, with an animal-like sound, collapsed onto the floor, kicking her feet out at the chairs and tearing at her hair and face. He wrapped his arms around her and held her tightly, preventing her from causing herself harm. Making soothing sounds, he indicated to Jane that she should take Tessa and Dave out of the room.

They stood in the corridor, holding each other, tears flowing down their faces, the sounds of Lilith's keening still loud and painful. Filled with relief, they also felt desperate for Lilith but, knowing there was nothing they could do to help her, and that they were probably the last people she would want to see at the moment, they nodded when Jane said she'd take them home.

'Jane?' Tessa clutched at her arm as they walked to the car. 'How did Britney die? She was murdered wasn't she? What did they do to her? What aren't you telling us, and where's Chantelle? Where's my daughter?'

At times like this Jane wondered why she'd ever wanted to join the police. How did you tell two parents that the same fate had probably befallen their own daughter? Her experience told her that it would only be a matter of time before another body was found. The diving team had already informed them that they would be continuing their search tomorrow, in light of today's discovery.

But she didn't need to tell the parents that. They couldn't be sure, after all. Her job now was to keep them calm and get them home.

'Look, I know this is hard but we have to remain positive about Chantelle. I can't talk about Britney now, we'll need to wait for the autopsy results. There's no reason to think that the same thing's happened to your daughter. You need to be at home supporting each other, and let us do our job.'

It was with relief that she dropped them at their home, promising to check with them the following day.

THE CARING WIFE

It had all been a bit much for him, if he was honest. He'd hardly been able to sleep, so many unpleasant images swirling around in his head. The night had passed in an uncomfortable whirl of flashbacks, nightmares, sweating so much he'd had to keep throwing the bed covers aside, and countless trips to the bathroom.

And now he had a terrible stomach ache, an upset stomach too. His hands shook as he picked up his water glass beside the bed. His pyjamas were drenched from his night sweats, the damp clothing now making him shiver. He wasn't well. He'd have to stay at home, call in to work and explain.

George tried to remember the last time he'd taken a sick day. It must have been years. Mother! He sat up straight, in a panic, he had to see to Mother. And the other thing of course. Bile rose in his throat and he stumbled to the bathroom, making it just in time.

Gingerly making his way back to bed, he paused at Dorothy's door. She sounded like she was talking to someone, whispering and giggling. He shook his head, he couldn't cope with her, not today. He checked his wristwatch, five thirty, he'd try and get some sleep for an hour or two.

Holding her finger to her lips to stop anyone from talking, she waited for his door to close. All clear. She reached under her bed and pulled out her papers, upset with him that she'd had to hide it quickly. Tears filled her eyes. It was ruined. The wet glue had made all her lovely letters slide and crumple on her pretty paper. How could he do that to her?

'How could you do that to me?' she shouted, standing in his bedroom doorway. 'You ruined it! Now I've got to start all over again.' Slamming the door, she stormed off back to her room, feeling better.

Was that Dorothy? Had she just shouted at him? Or had he imagined it? He turned over and looked at the closed door. No, there was no-one there, he must be really ill. He fell back into a fitful sleep.

She hummed as she looked through her collection of paper, which one should she use now? He didn't deserve her prettiest paper, that's why she'd used the one with clocks and books on it, but now she had to throw it away and it was her last piece like that. Birds? Sweet little things, no, that was too nice, and there was no way he was getting flowers. She didn't *love* him. Shut up, she told them as they teased her. Lipsticks and perfume bottles, perfect! He liked his dirty little tarts, all painted up with the devil's powders and potions in their adulterous undergarments.

Excited now, she started to tear new letters and glue them onto the sheet of paper. Why hadn't she thought of writing to her before? She'd written to *him*, to say she was sorry, but, oh, what about *her*. Yes, she should write to her as well. Picking up her notebook she made some notes.

Strange. George was usually up and making tea by now. She wanted to post her letter but the glue wasn't dry yet. Well, she'd make some tea anyway. Humming away happily, Dorothy boiled the kettle and made a pot of tea. Why wasn't he coming? She'd take him a cup, that's what she'd do. The perfect wife caring for her husband, making sure he got off to work on time.

Why? They asked. Why care for him? What does he do for you? He just tells you off all the time, moaning and complaining about everything. You should teach him a lesson. Give him a dose of his own medicine.

Dorothy put her hand over her mouth in amused surprise. They were right. His own medicine, it was perfect! She carried the cup and saucer upstairs and went into her bedroom. Reaching under her bed she retrieved one of the pills. It was a bit fluffy from being in her mouth and getting wet, before accumulating dust from the carpet. Wiping it on her dress, she dropped it into the tea, stirring it until it dissolved.

He drank the tea thirstily, not noticing the bitter taste in his already sour mouth. 'Thank you, Dorothy, I'm not quite myself today, think I'll stay at home and get some rest.' He lay back down, feeling weak. 'Could you call the office for me?'

'I've poisoned my husband, he won't be coming to work today.' She laughed into the phone. No, she couldn't say that, had to be clever, what if she got arrested? What about all her letters? Her friends were quite right. She opened the phone book to find the number, and dialled. 'This is Mrs Newton, George's wife, I'm afraid he's not well and won't be in today. Yes, I'll tell him, thank you.' How proper she sounded. Just like a caring wife.

~

Cal waited anxiously for Sasha to return from surgery. He'd managed to see her for a few minutes, before she was taken down earlier, but she'd been drowsy from her premed.

It was just as he returned with a coffee that he saw the orderlies wheeling Sasha back into her room and he walked quickly, hoping for an update. But no, they couldn't tell him anything, the doctor would be around shortly though.

Wow, it was hard seeing Sasha so helpless. The little tug inside caught him by surprise, his feelings for her were growing. She opened her eyes and smiled at him, catching him gazing at her.

'Hi,' she whispered.

'How are you feeling? Are you in pain? You were gone for hours.' Cal took her hand, stroking it gently. 'I was worried about you.'

'A little bit, I'm probably still drugged up to the nines though. Did you sleep alright? Any news from Tess? Did you find out how the search went?'

'I slept fine, you shouldn't be worrying about me. No news, I couldn't get hold of Tess last night, I expect they were exhausted and just wanted to sleep without any disturbances. I spoke to Maureen, though, she joined the search, teamed with Von who works with your sister. But they didn't find anything, well, as far as Maureen knows. If they found any clues the police weren't telling anyone. But I'll try and get hold of Tessa again this morning. Maybe I should wait until you've seen your doctor?'

Malcolm Bailey breezed into the room, his assistant by his side. 'How's my girl doing? Feeling alright? Pain not too bad?' He stopped, registering Cal's presence. 'Are you Sasha's partner?'

Cal reached out his hand and they shook. 'Cal, Sasha's friend.'

'Good, she needs someone to keep an eye on her for a few days 'til she's back on her feet. Now, if you wouldn't mind stepping out of the room for a minute, I just need to do a quick examination.'

'Hmm, all looks fine, any discomfort here, or here? He palpated her pelvic region, pressing in various places. You're full of surprises, Sasha, we found a nice lot of adhesions in there, little buggers were on your bladder as well as your uterus. Your bladder had become adhered to your uterus but we've separated that nicely. We cleaned out all the adhesions, but your right fallopian tube was severely damaged I'm afraid, no longer fit for the purpose, pretty much glued shut. But the star of the show was your right ovary, a lovely cyst on there, sixteen by eighteen centimetres, which is quite impressive. We had to perform a salpingo-oophorectomy to remove the right tube and ovary, I'm sorry to tell you, but at least you've still got another pair.'

Malcolm Bailey looked at Sasha seriously, 'We already knew that your chances of having children were slim, we've talked about it. With the remaining tube and ovary you might still get pregnant, although your left tube is not particularly healthy and your endometriosis is severe. I certainly didn't expect to have you on my operating table so soon after your last op, which means it isn't giving up any time soon.' He patted her hand, 'We'll see how you get on, you should be fine for at least six months, maybe longer. But in time we may have to consider your quality of life, it might be best to remove everything. You'd feel better, no more pain, and with hormone therapy you'll feel like a new woman.'

Sasha lay in her bed, feeling stunned, she hadn't expected such bad news. It was a lot to take in... *Did he mean-?* 'D'you mean a hysterectomy, Mr Bailey? My womb, ovaries, well, ovary, the lot?'

'Yes, but we're not there yet. And it's not as bad as it sounds, everything will still function as far as sex is concerned. It might even be better. And with hormone therapy you'll have more energy, plus there's a good chance you could feel, and even appear, younger than your years. You'll stay in tonight and if I'm happy with you tomorrow, you can go home. But no heavy lifting, you'll need to take it easy, no driving for about a week. You can remove the dressings in a couple of days as long as there's no bleeding, and you should expect slight vaginal bleeding for a day or two, pads only please, no tampons. You'll need someone to look after you for a couple of days, your friend looks like he'll be happy to do so. And on that note, you should be fine to have sex after about a week, if everything feels fine. I'll see you tomorrow. Try and eat something and tell the nurse once you've passed urine.'

With that, Malcolm Bailey was gone, and Sasha's head reeled from all the information. She looked up as Cal rejoined her. 'It seems I'm less of a woman than I was yesterday. And if this bastard endometriosis keeps on at me, I'll be much less of one before too long. Bloody hell, Cal, I'm so fed-up with it all.' She sniffed, trying not to cry.

'Tell me, Sash, talk to me.' And so she did. She told him everything, grateful for his composure as he absorbed her situation.

FLORENCE NIGHTINGALE

Dorothy was having a lovely day floating around the house, checking on George here and there and feeling like Florence Nightingale. She should have been a nurse! She'd give him some more medicine, that's what nurses did.

She found the two pills stuck together, under her mattress. Perfect. With a fresh cup of tea made, and the pills dissolved, she shook George until he stirred just enough to drink the liquid.

~

Inspector Kavanagh called a meeting to discuss what was known so far about the girl's body they'd found. Chief Inspector Carpenter had informed him that he'd be coming through from Rentham, and it was becoming clear that the case was one for which their small village police station was ill-equipped.

Sergeant Denton stopped Jane Weaver as she was about to leave to check on the Watsons. 'Hold fire on that for now, Jane, we need you and Nick in the meeting, the big boss has just arrived.'

'Stan, good to see you,' Andrew Kavanagh shook hands with his Chief Inspector, before leading him through to his office, where extra chairs had been assembled and were now occupied. 'Okay everyone, you know Chief Inspector Carpenter. Philip, perhaps you can get Stan up to date?'

When Philip Denton had finished his account of the case so far, with additional input from Nick and Jane where appropriate, they waited for their Chief Inspector to speak.

'Where are we with suspects? Have we looked closely enough at the families? It was one thing to keep to basic questions while the girls were missing, but things are different now. I know it's an unpalatable thought, but we have to consider those closest to the girls. And we need to find out if there's a link to the other woman who was killed. And you've still got a girl missing, Andrew, it's not good, not good at all. Small village, popular with tourists, we need to get on top of this.'

Andrew Kavanagh nodded, 'I think it's time to bring the father of the still missing girl in, delve a bit more deeply into things. He knew her friend, Britney, would have had her round at his house often, no doubt. Pretty girl, from her photo, and teenage girls can behave older than their years. What was his relationship with his own daughter? Any problems we don't know about? And did he know Barbara Fenton? Jane, you've been involved closely with the parents, picked up anything odd?'

'Honestly, Sir, I don't think so. They seem genuinely upset, worried stiff. Dave, the father, is out searching for his daughter at all hours, and he and his wife seem very close. I can't believe he had anything to do with it.'

Andrew Kavanagh nodded again. 'Nick, you bring him in. Tell him we need to ask him further questions. I'll sit in with you. Philip, we need a full background check, Jane can do that. Let's examine everything about the family and the dead girl's family, see if we can find any links.'

~

It was with a heavy heart that Nick knocked on the door of number nine, Riverside Gardens.

A red-eyed Tessa opened the door, managing a small smile when she saw P.C. Crossley. 'Nick, come in, Dave's in the kitchen. How's Lilith, is she alright? She's not answering her phone.'

Man, this was difficult. 'Lilith's in hospital, they kept her in under sedation. A sister has come down to be with the boy. Oh, Dave, morning. No, no tea thanks. Look, Tessa, Dave, I'm sorry about this, we're going to need Dave to come down to the station for a chat.'

Their confused faces changed from puzzlement to concern. Both spoke in unison. 'Is it Chantelle? Have you found her?'

Man, he hated this. 'No, no news, look, this is awkward, and it doesn't mean anything, it's just procedure. We just need you to come down so that we can go through a few points in more detail with you, Dave. We always do this with people closely connected to a case, as it progresses.'

'D'you think I had something to do with this?' Dave's voice rose in disbelief and panic. 'My own daughter? How can you? After all we've been through, are still going through! Nick, you can't be serious? To think I'd do something to my own daughter! Wait a minute, you surely don't- not her friend! You think I had something to do with Britney?' He sank to the bottom stair behind him, his legs feeling weak, as his hand felt for Tessa's. A mobile phone rang from somewhere at the back of the house, but went unanswered.

Nick waited for Tessa to wipe her eyes, feeling terrible for the couple. 'Dave, it's like I said, it's just something we have to do. Maybe you can help us with some extra details, that kind of thing, you know, in light of us finding Britney. Look, the sooner you come down, the sooner it's over, mate.'

'Mate? I'm hardly your mate am I? I thought you were on our side, thought you understood. Christ, our daughter's missing, her friend's dead, and you what, you're arresting me?' Dave's wide eyes glared at Nick in a mixture of hopelessness and frustration. 'You should be out there finding Chantelle, not wasting time with me, this is crazy!'

'No-one's under arrest, help me out here, it'll only take an hour or so, I'm sure. And I *am* on your side, I want to find your daughter as much as you do. Come with me now, Dave, let's get it over with, okay?' Nick stood back and indicated that Dave should head out before him.

His shoulders drooped in defeat, Dave turned to Tessa. 'Babes, I won't be long, you'll be okay?' Her nod and worried face remained in his head as he climbed into the back of Nick's vehicle.

~

Sergeant Denton went in search of Jane. 'How are you doing with the background checks? Anything interesting yet?'

Jane looked up from her computer. 'Not sure if it's got anything to do with it, Sir, but it seems Dave, Mr Watson, lost his job and their family home due to some problems. Not sure what yet, but that's why they moved here I'm guessing, new job new start? I've tracked down some of Chantelle's old classmates and there were definitely some problems between father and daughter. She said she hated him, blamed him for ruining her life.'

Philip Denton's eyes sparked with interest. 'Why didn't we know this before? I thought we had them down as the perfect happy family. Good work, Jane, anything else?'

'Again, not sure if it's relevant but Lilith Morton is active on a dating app, she's got a profile showing she's looking for a man for fun nights out, that kind of thing? But I don't think it's connected to Dave, honestly, and even if it was, how would that connect to the two girls?'

Philip's mind raced as he assimilated the information. 'Well you never know, could be that they were having an affair? Maybe one of the girls found out? Threatened to tell the wife? Okay, I tell you what, leave that for now, I want you to go and bring Mrs Watson in. Nick's on his way with the husband, they'll be in the interview room. Let's have her in the family room, see what she has to say, once we've questioned the husband.' He registered Jane's upset expression. 'I know it's unpalatable Jane, but this is what we do. It's been your job to keep in close contact with the family, and I understand that can mean you feel emotionally involved, but it's also your job to find out what happened here.'

Tessa was trying Sasha's number again, having seen a missed call from Cal but preferring to speak to her sister, when the doorbell rang. Relief flooded through her, Dave was back already, he'd forgotten his key in all the upset! She dropped her phone on the kitchen counter and ran to the door. But her relief turned to confusion at the sight of Jane standing on the doorstep. 'Jane? What's going on? I thought it was Dave back already. I don't know why he had to be taken to the station in a police car, what must the neighbours think? Sorry, I'm gabbling, I don't know what to think or say anymore.'

When she got a chance to speak, Jane took a deep breath. 'Tessa, I'm so sorry about all this, I know it's awful for you. We're all just trying to do our jobs and some of it isn't very nice at times. But we really are just trying to find out everything we can. With Britney's body being found well, it's kind of escalated things a bit, you know? We don't know what we're dealing with here, we just have to start again and go through everything. I've been sent to ask you to come down as well.' She put her hands up in the air as if to ward off an attack.

'No-one's saying or thinking that you had anything to do with all this, Tessa, *or* Dave. We just need your help. We need to find Chantelle. We need to find your daughter as soon as possible. I can drive you or you can drive yourself if you prefer, but to be honest? I think it would be safer for me to drive you in your current state. Forget about the neighbours, we all just want the same thing, for Chantelle to be found safely.'

HAPPY FAMILIES

She came to, surprised to find out from Cal that she'd been asleep for three hours. 'You must be so bored, Cal, you don't have to stay with me all the time.'

'I want to, don't worry about me. What do you need? Food? Something to drink? The nurse said you could order food when you were ready, she's left you a menu. Let's see, yoghurt, there's a surprise, oh, scrambled eggs, how about that? I grabbed a bite from the coffee shop while you were asleep but I'll have some tea if you fancy some?'

Back in her freshly made bed after some eggs, tea, and a visit to the bathroom, Sasha asked Cal for her phone. 'It's been switched off for so long, I'd better check if there's anything from Tess. Did you try calling her?'

'I did, I left a message but she hasn't called back.'

Frowning, she looked at the missed calls from her sister. 'Cal, Tessa's been trying to reach me. I need to get hold of her, keep an eye on the door, I'll try to call, tell me if the nurse comes.'

But Tessa's phone went to voicemail, left behind in her panic when she'd left the house for the police station. 'No answer, I'll try Dave.' When Dave's phone also went to voicemail Sasha's concern increased. 'Dammit, Cal, I can't stand it, being stuck in here! We've no idea what's going on.'

~

Dave looked from Andrew Kavanagh to Nick Crossley, in exasperation. 'What d'you want me to tell you? There's nothing more to say, I was out with my wife the night we discovered the girls were missing. She'll confirm it. We were at the pub. I wasn't having an affair with anyone, especially Lilith Morton. I didn't even know the woman, not until all this happened. I work late often, I take extra shifts when I can.

Tessa will tell you, ask her. And yes, I've been out looking for Chantelle at night, what father wouldn't?'

'We'll need your work to confirm the nights you've worked late, Mr Watson. Nick will get the exact dates from you in a moment. Now, how is your relationship with your daughter? Any disagreements, problems of any kind?'

'No! We get on great, we're happy, life was, well, it was good, we've been doing okay. Why, what are you getting at?'

'What about before you moved to Parva Crossing? Any problems that you'd like to tell us about?'

With a groan, Dave held his head in his hands. 'Okay, but that was ages ago, it doesn't mean anything now. What have you been doing? Going back through our lives? I've got nothing to hide. I had some problems, I'll admit it. We lost the house because of me but that's ancient history now, I got a new job here and we settled in, Chantelle's been happy, making new friends.' He looked up. 'What? Yes, she was angry with me, she's just a kid, she was upset to leave her friends, but she's made new ones.' He stopped, thinking about her new friend and what had happened to her. He tried to calm himself. 'Look, I beg of you, you have to believe me when I say we were happy, that I had nothing to do with any of this. Just find my daughter, please, before something happens to her.'

In the family room, Jane read the notes Nick had passed to her. Clearing her throat she spoke gently. 'Tessa, can you tell me where you were the night you realised Chantelle was missing? Okay, that's fine, and you were with Dave? The whole evening? And earlier? Was Dave at work?' Nodding, she carried on.

'Does Dave ever work late, Tessa? Oh, quite often, yes, I understand about the shift work. And he's not been out anywhere else to your knowledge?'

Should she say anything or not? She didn't want to distract the police from finding Chantelle, and telling them her worries about Dave would have them thinking all sorts of terrible things. No, she trusted Dave, if he said he'd been working late then that's what he'd been doing.

'No, nowhere else, just work.'

What seemed like agonising hours later, P.C. Jane Weaver was instructed to take the parents home. As she drove she kept half an ear on their conversation in the rear of the vehicle, not liking it, but knowing it was her job. There was clearly an issue with something to do with Dave's late working hours, but, as Tessa was speaking in a whisper, she found it hard to follow the details. Her rearview mirror told her more than the anxious whispering did. Dave definitely looked guilty about something. He was hiding something, her instincts told her that, but was it relevant to the case?

Hoping to try to glean something, Jane invited herself into their home. 'I'm putting the kettle on, Tessa, no arguments, you need a moment to collect yourself, Dave too. I'll make drinks while you freshen up and calm down. Both Tessa and Dave were too weary to argue, and gratefully left Jane to it while they sank into the sofa. She could hear their whispered conversation continuing as she switched the kettle on.

Waiting for it to boil, Jane's eyes wandered out of the kitchen window, noting what a pretty garden it was. Someone definitely had green fingers, and who'd have thought that these new houses had such a beautiful setting, with a pretty gate at the end of the garden leading to shrubs and, well, what *did* it lead to? She stood up straighter, her mind alert. Quietly opening the back door, she walked down the short path to the gate, opening it and walking through.

Wanting to get back to the station to share her discovery, while at the same time feeling pretty bad about it, Jane took the tray of tea through and informed the Watsons that she had to go.

~

Inspector Kavanagh looked from Sergeant Denton to Jane. 'Good work, P.C. Weaver, but we should have known this before. It's a convenient way to dispose of the girl's body, that's for sure.'

'But, Sir,' Jane's mind was working overtime. 'There's no way the girl's body was in their house all this time, we're talking a week! And we searched the house and garden straightaway, as a matter of course. No, it doesn't make any sense, it must be a coincidence. Oh there's something else, it's probably nothing but Mrs Watson definitely had some kind of problem about Mr Watson's late working hours. I don't know what, but it seemed to me that he was hiding something. That's all I know.'

'Okay thanks, Jane,' Sergeant Denton showed her out before turning back to Inspector Kavanagh. 'Think we should get him back in?'

Inspector Kavanagh shook his head, 'No, we've got nothing solid to charge him with yet, Philip, just information to put in the file for now, although it's not looking good for him. I want to know more about the father's movements in the evenings, find out what he's hiding. Get Nick to make checking with his employer a priority, if it turns out he's been lying we'll bring him back in officially.'

~

With Cal gone back to her place for the night, Sasha clicked on her sister's name, in the hope that they would finally get to catch up. But the nurse, walking in at that moment, had other ideas. 'No phones, Sasha, you know the rules.' And with that, she took the phone from Sasha, switching it off as she walked out. 'Whoever you need to talk to can wait, you need to rest.'

MOTHER

Cal couldn't decide what to do. He knew all about Britney's body being found, about Dave being taken in for questioning, Tessa too. She had finally called Cal's phone and, unable to speak to her sister, she'd poured it all out to Cal. Now he had to go and collect Sasha from the hospital. Should he tell her straightaway or wait until they got back to her place? He made up his mind.

'Sash, there are a few things you need to know. Oh no, not Chantelle!' he hastened to reassure her, before telling her everything he knew.

Sasha sat on the bed, shaking her head in disbelief. 'I can't believe they accused Dave of having something to do with all this. Why? Why would they even think that? We need to get back, I must be with my sister. I'll be fine,' she insisted, in the face of Cal's protestations. 'I'm an old hand at these ops, as long as I'm careful I'll be fine. I've been given the all clear, we can go.'

Concerned but understanding where Sasha was coming from Cal acquiesced, and after a quick stop at the flat the two were on their way back to Parva Crossing.

It was with great relief that Sasha finally got to talk to her sister and, once she'd assured her she was fine, the two went through everything that had happened, while Cal drove as fast as the limit would allow.

~

Chantelle was so weak she just wanted to lie down and give up. How long had it been since he'd been to see her? *And drugged her?* A day? Two days? She had no idea but she guessed it wouldn't be long before he came back. She had to hurry. She worked desperately at the ropes on her ankles, having managed to free her hands and finally remove the eye mask. There was no time to take in her surroundings, she needed to escape. The only thing her mind had registered was that there was no Britney, but she couldn't allow herself to think about that right now. At last her legs were free and she stretched them out, before gingerly trying to stand.

Crying in despair she collapsed back onto the filthy plastic, she was too weak, she'd never make it out of here. Looking around, she noticed a bottle still half full of water, and drank it thirstily, feeling a little better. Trying again, she managed a few steps before doubling over in agony.

It must have taken her an hour, but she had managed to crawl across the room and up the stairs. The closed door loomed in front of her. It might as well have said 'NO EXIT', so sure was she that it was locked. After all, who would risk leaving it unlocked, for anyone to open and find her?

With a trembling hand, she reached for the handle and turned it. The door opened.

~

'No! No more tea, Dorothy! Stop it!' George roughly pushed the cup away from his mouth, as Dorothy was trying to pour it in. She stopped humming abruptly as the cup bounced onto the carpet, tea soaking into the fibres by her feet.

Crying, she ran from the room. 'I was only trying to help!' Why was he so horrid? She huddled on her bed, grabbing at her papers and stickers for comfort, as she asked her friends. But they weren't talking. Picking up her notebook, she started to feel better when she saw who was next on her list. Humming happily, she began tearing up newspaper.

All he could think about was Mother. She'd never forgive him. He'd never left her alone for this long before. A whole day and night! He quavered at the thought of facing her wrath, memories coming back, unbidden, of Mother screaming at him for some minor failing. And now he'd proved her right, he was useless, unreliable, a waste of space.

Groaning, he heaved himself out of bed, desperate now to get moving. With his ablutions over, but still feeling strangely out of sorts, he dressed, and with a quick listen at Dorothy's door, headed down the stairs, fighting his dizziness.

The bread was beginning to mould, but he managed to cut off enough to make two decent slices of toast and, fortified with the addition of a hot coffee, he headed out to his car. No time to stop at the shops, he needed to get to Mother, and *it*... Staggering as he tried to fumble the key into the door lock, he winced at the bright sun in his eyes. His shirt was already wet under his arms and he wiped his brow with a shaking hand. What to do about... *it*? He needed to do something soon, Mother had made that quite clear.

Bumping the kerb, George drove erratically, trying to clear his head. He had to hurry. Blessed sun, right in his eyes, making his headache worse. Almost through the high street, the bridge next, nearly there. His chest was tight, his mouth dry. A car horn startled him and he veered back into his lane as a lorry driver angrily flipped him the finger. A wave of dizziness overcame him and he tried to focus on the road, his squinting eyes almost closed against the sun.

Something was in the road ahead as he turned into the lane. In disbelief, followed by horror, he knew what he had to do. As the apparition in front of him held up its arm pleadingly, he put his foot down and headed straight for it. He passed out as he heard a loud thump and felt the car bump over something solid.

POKER

How much time had passed? Groaning, he lifted his head, expecting to see people milling around. Where was everyone? Where were the police?

Amazingly it seemed no-one had witnessed his crime. Where was she? *It*, he corrected himself, twisting to look out of the car windows, starting to panic. He needed to know, but time was of the essence. A bundle of clothing and limbs caught his eye, lying half hidden under the hedgerow at the side of the lane behind him. Still, and lifeless, he knew then that everything would be alright. Mother would be so proud of him.

Mother. Fear rushed through him at the thought of what she would say at his neglect. But it wasn't his fault. *Oh, stop it George, it's never your fault is it? Always blaming someone else. That's why you never amounted to anything.* Stop it! He covered his ears, blocking out her voice.

With a last glance around, he started the car and drove along the deserted lane, relieved, as he passed the first few cottages further along, that no-one was in their garden to see him. Driving the last lonely stretch of the lane he started to shake with a mix of fear and relief as Mother's isolated cottage came into view.

~

Nick Crossley returned to the station grim-faced and knocked on his Sergeant's door. 'He was lying, Sarge.' Flopping into a chair, he shook his head, 'I trusted him, dammit, I still do, I can't believe he had anything to do with this. But if he wasn't at work, where was he? And why lie about it?'

Sergeant Denton nodded. 'We're here to do a job, Nick, and it's not always easy, especially when you've been closely involved with the family for this length of time. But the odds are beginning to stack up against our Mr Watson, I'm afraid. We've got a guy with a history of problems, he lies about his whereabouts, and we've got two dead females, both of them murdered, in our opinion. We've got easy access to the river, and on top of all that we've still got a missing female, his own daughter no less.

Bring him back in, and this time tell him it's official. Let me know when he's here. We'll need to work him hard, see if we can get enough out of him to charge him, so keep your emotional distance, Nick, remember, he's not your friend, he's a serious suspect. Take P.C. Weaver with you and remember, keep it impersonal, both of you.'

~

'Tess, slow down, what are you talking about? I thought you said they took Dave in and brought him home yesterday?' Sasha grimaced at Cal as she listened to her sister's frantic voice. 'Well, did they say why? Have they found out anything else? Could it be Chantelle? Okay, no I'm not saying it is anything to do with Chantelle, if it was they'd have told you. Look, we're about an hour away, we'll come straight to you. Just wait for me, alright? You can tell me everything and we'll go down to the station and sort it out. I'm sure it's just more questions.'

Sighing, she filled Cal in on the other end of the conversation. He reached across and squeezed her knee. 'How are you holding up, Sash? It's a lot to cope with straight out of hospital, you know?'

'I'm okay,' she gave him a small smile. 'They can't have arrested him or anything, no reason to. It must just be for more details. Although Tess didn't know much, said Dave gave her a quick call from work, he said they were pretty unfriendly, more *official* was the way he put it.' She sighed, 'this is such a nightmare for them, when will it end? And where the hell is poor Chantelle?'

Arriving just over an hour later, Cal stood to one side while the sisters tearfully embraced. Then, having given Tessa a gentle hug, he suggested they sit in the lounge while he made tea, then she could catch them up on the details.

Sasha's mind went into analysis mode as she took in everything. It didn't honestly make sense, why take Dave in for questioning, let him go home, and the very next day take him back in?

'Tess, what exactly did they want to know from Dave yesterday? And from you? Is there anything you can think of that might have given them a reason to want him back?'

'Well, Jane, P.C. Weaver, she wanted to know where I was the night Chantelle went missing, if I was with Dave. And she was asking about his working hours, the extra shifts. Sash, they were asking Dave about before, why we moved, if we were a happy family. What were they implying? That we weren't?' Her voice rose hysterically, 'On no! They think Dave and Chantelle had a problem! They think- oh please no- they think he's done something to her. That means they think he hurt Britney. I should've told them, why didn't I tell them? Stupid. We argued about it when Jane brought us home, I accused him of lying.'

'Tell them what, Tess? What did you argue about?'

After Tessa had tearfully voiced her fears that Dave might be gambling again, instead of always working late, something pinged in Sasha's head. 'Sis, where was P.C. Weaver when you were arguing? She was here? In the kitchen? So she probably heard you. And Dave still insists he was working late on those occasions? Oh, Tess, they'll have checked with his work by now. He's such an idiot. I think I know where Dave was. But he shouldn't have lied to you, and he should have told the police the truth.'

Turning to Cal, she asked him. 'Cal, that room at the back of the pub?'

He nodded immediately. 'Poker nights, might not be strictly legal, depending on the stakes. Not good for poor Jules, too, what a mess.'

'He's playing poker?' Tessa wailed. 'Oh, the stupid twit, I knew it! I should have asked him outright, not just kept on about work and the money. But how do you know if he was there? Did you see him? Did you know, Sash? How could you not tell me, after everything that happened?'

'I wasn't sure, Tess, I promise you I would've told you otherwise. It was just the one night, that bad storm, remember the power went out? I went down to the bar and for a moment I thought I saw Dave, but Jules had only lit a few candles. People were bustling around taking wet jackets off and I thought I glimpsed Dave going into the back room. I knew it was gambling, but I couldn't be sure it was him. And with everything else going on, Chantelle missing, I thought I'd try to find out more once she was safe.'

'But she's not safe, and Dave's been arrested now! What am I going to do?'

'He's not arrested, Tessa,' Cal spoke calmly. 'They won't arrest him unless they think they have enough evidence to charge him. And if they think his lying about where he was at night is evidence then we can sort this out pretty easily. We'll go and speak to Jules, confirm that Dave was gambling. Don't you see? They'll have to let him go.'

'Tessa laughed angrily, 'I don't know whether to be pleased or furious. My husband has been lying to me, losing money gambling, after he promised never to gamble again, and it's the very thing that will clear him with the police. Except if he'd never done it they'd never have questioned where he was at night, he'd have either been genuinely working or here with me.' Shaking her head, she looked at her sister. 'So, what now? Do we go to the pub? I'm coming with you.'

ALIBI

There, now that scarlet woman would have to face the truth! She'd done a bad thing and thought she'd got away with it. But not with me keeping watch, me and my avenging angels. We will cleanse this village of sin. Triumphantly Dorothy pushed the letter into the post box slot and looked around at her friends. Taking their hands she headed back to her house.

~

His head hurt, if only she'd stop screaming at him. 'I've done it, Mother, I've done what you told me. I'm not as useless as you think. Yes, it escaped, but don't you see? It's all worked out for the best, I couldn't have planned it better. Mother, please, I've told you I'm sorry for leaving you all alone, but I was ill, it wasn't my fault. Let me clean you up and we'll get you into a fresh nightdress, you'll feel better then. Yes, yes, we'll have some tea. George will put the kettle on and open a packet of our favourite fig rolls.'

It was a relief to get down to the basement and deal with the clean-up, he thought guiltily, as he left Mother with her tea. But time was running and he needed to show his face at work. With everything bundled and bagged up, he poured the remaining bottles of bleach all over the basement floor, leaving it to soak in.

'Righto, Mother, I'm off for a while, but I'll be back later on this evening. You and your Georgie will have a nice little chat. Maybe we'll be a bit naughty and have a sherry. What's that? Why yes, why not? We can celebrate your George making everything right, yes, it'll be our little treat.'

~

'Are you sure you should be back at work, old boy? You look a bit peaky, at our age we've got to look after ourselves. And what with an employee being arrested, well, I don't mind telling you, I'm feeling a little off colour myself.' Mr Ramsbottom finally stopped talking long enough for George to get a word in. 'Why yes, young Dave Watson. They came in this morning and carted the fellow off. No idea what it's all about of course.'

Oh, the relief! Unbelievable, could they actually think he had something to do with the girl? If they did, and if they found the other one, *not if, when*, he corrected himself, maybe they'd think it had all been him! Father abducts and murders daughter and best friend! He could see the headline, oh, he couldn't wait to tell Mother about this.

~

Unfortunately, being a village, people tend to know too much about other people's business, and tongues start wagging, so it wasn't long before the village grapevine had successfully passed along the news about Dave to all and sundry.

Mrs Pringle, being one of the sundries, was all agog, when Sheila, rather full of herself if Mrs Pringle might say so herself, informed her all about it over tea and custard creams.

'Bold as brass they marched right in and arrested him, so my Brian said. He didn't put up a fight, just walked right out with them. Brian said it'll be about that girl, no doubt about it. When he was servicing the coffee machine at the village deli earlier, he heard a customer talking about the murders. The murders! In our little village, that's what we're known for now! He said to me, you watch this space, girl, reckon we've had a serial killer right under our nose. So anyway, when he saw them arrest him up at the plant he said he just knew. You'll see, he said, it'll turn out he killed 'em all, that Mr Ford, poor Barbara Fenton, the young school girl, Britney wasn't it? Lilith Morton's daughter, well at least she'll see justice now. And then his own daughter? What's he done with her I'd like to know? That's the trouble with these newcomers, he said, you never know what they're hiding.' Sheila paused for breath and a sip of tea, nodding over her cup at Mrs Pringle, her cheeks flushed with excitement. It wasn't often she got the jump on Mrs Pringle.

Rosemary, vaguely searching the shelf for her talcum powder, listened with interest. Who were they talking about? Edging closer to the counter, she was spotted by Mrs Pringle.

'Ah, Mrs Spindlebury, lovely to see you dear.' With a calculating glance at Sheila, who was about to open her mouth, she took action. 'Ah, Sheila, be a love and pop and get us some more custard creams, teabags too, I think we're going to need fortifications today. Yes, *now*, if you don't mind. I'll just see to Mrs Spindlebury.' She wasn't going to let Sheila steal the show.

Rosemary left the chemist with a lighter step, completely forgetting about her talcum powder. She could have kissed Mrs Pringle! She'd cook something nice for Reg's supper tonight, tell him all about it. Not that she'd ever *seriously* thought he'd had anything to do with Barbara's death, of course.

~

Down at the station the little group waited impatiently for P.C. Crossley, who finally appeared, looking a little taken aback at the sight of Cal, Sasha, Tessa, and Jules.

'I really can't talk to you all now, I'm sorry.' Looking at Tessa, his gaze softened. 'Mrs Watson, I'm really sorry about everything, truly, but we have to do our job, I'm sure you understand.'

Cal stood up, holding a piece of paper. 'P.C. Crossley, Nick, can you just hear us out, it'll only take a minute? We can tell you where Dave was on the nights he was supposed to be working late but wasn't. He was at the pub, Jules here has confirmed the dates of the poker nights. She'll assure you that he was there, as will the other players.'

'He didn't tell you because he didn't tell *me*.' Tessa explained. I've only just found out that he's been gambling again. That's why we moved, why we lost our house, and why he and Chantelle had a few problems. She blamed him for everything, and for having to leave her friends behind.'

Taking the piece of paper, Nick rapidly scanned the list of dates. They appeared to match the dates they were querying, but he'd have to check. 'Leave this with me, we'll have to look into it. Look, thanks for coming down, but it's not that simple, we've got to follow up all the facts. But I assure you, if Dave is in the clear we'll let him go straightaway. Go home for now, please, I'll let you know as soon as there's any news.'

'Well, we've done what we can for now, let's get you home, Tessa, and Jules, we'll take you back to the pub. We need to drop off our bags anyway, and I expect Sasha needs a lie down.' Cal looked at Sasha with concern.

'Oh now I feel awful.' Tessa put her hand to her mouth. 'Sash, I didn't even think to ask you how you were. I'm so wrapped up in my own problems, I've got my sister running around straight after an operation. Of course you need to rest, right now. I'll be alright, I'll ring you when there's news.'

MRS PRINGLE HOLDS COURT

Nick and Jane checked the dates against their list, confirming that Dave had definitely been at the poker games on the nights in question. It all made sense, they agreed, a gambling addiction, losing the house, and his wife not knowing, no wonder he'd been less then generous with the truth. Well, lied, of course, when telling them the truth would have prevented so much of this. And now here he was, being questioned over the possible murder of a young girl, and abduction of his own daughter. People could be so stupid, why couldn't they just tell the truth and not keep so many secrets?

Calling Sergeant Denton out of the interview room they took him through everything they knew. Having assigned the job of checking with the names of fellow poker players on the list, to Jane, he told Nick to call Inspector Kavanagh from the interview room too.

'He's not going to turn out to be our guy is he, Andrew?' Philip looked at his Inspector, 'The man's innocent, we're barking up the wrong tree here. And while we do that, someone else is getting away with murder. Let's take a break, wait for Jane to check with the witnesses. I'll get someone to bring the poor man some lunch.'

~

'If you don't mind, I think I'll head back home a little early, still feeling a bit wobbly, you know how it is after a bug.' Mr Ramsbottom nodded, glancing up at George. 'You do that, George, think I might do the same, this whole arrest thing has left me feeling at sixes and sevens. Might get home and put my feet up. You be sure to do the same. Let that wife of yours look after you, be sure to give her my regards.'

My wife look after me? If only you knew. George nodded, and grinned painfully, before gathering his briefcase and setting off. He needed to make a stop at the chemist, but first he'd pop home, see what surprises Dorothy had for him. Then he'd surprise Mother with an earlier than expected visit.

The bell above the chemist's door jangled, as Mrs Pringle held court over her kingdom. Looking up from her little group of rapt listeners, she waved to George. 'Oh, Mr Newton, come on in, have you heard the news?'

He couldn't back out now, but the last thing he needed was to be held up while Mrs Pringle prattled on about the latest gossip. Besides, he knew all about it anyway.

'Sheila dear, let's get the kettle on again shall we?' Mrs Pringle beamed with pleasure, thoroughly enjoying herself. She hadn't had this much excitement in years.

Fuming silently, Sheila re-filled the kettle in the kitchenette, listening to Mrs Pringle begin the whole story again, for George's benefit. By now Dave Watson was a mass serial killer, wanted by the police in his old town, had confessed to all the murders, and was likely behind the disappearance of a woman from Rentham some three years ago. She snorted in derision, didn't she realise she was making a fool of herself? He didn't even live here three years ago. The woman was getting carried away.

George caught Sheila's eye, as Mrs Pringle continued her story, and she went over to him. 'Sheila, I'm in a bit of a hurry, could you help me? I need to collect Mother's perfume, plus purchase some more fly spray, four should do it, I think.' At Sheila's surprised expression, he stopped and explained. 'Well, there's Mother's, of course, then my house as well, I don't know what Dorothy does with the stuff, I really don't. Oh and I'll just-' As Sheila bustled off for the fly spray, he looked around for the air fresheners, picking up two, better not get more, Sheila would think it a bit odd.

'Oh, where did Mr Newton go?' Mrs Pringle looked around in surprise. 'I hadn't finished telling him everything. What did he need?'

'Just the usual, his mother's lavender perfume, more fly spray, that kind of thing.'

'Mm, anyway, so, as I was saying...' Mrs Pringle was off again.

~

The thought struck him as he set off for Mother's, he didn't want to drive past *it* again, couldn't face it, if he was honest. With a bit of luck it would go undiscovered for a while longer, maybe until tomorrow, especially with dusk coming earlier as autumn approached. The cottage dwellers towards the end of the lane were all retired and unlikely to be out and about this late in the afternoon.

So the only way was to drive round and park in Bell's Lane. He could take the footpath across the field, yes, just like he used to as a boy. He could tell Mother, remind her of their walks, she'd like that.

It was a jaunty George who arrived at his mother's a mere half an hour later. 'Only me, Mother! And look what I've got for you, that's right, your Lavender Dreams! Oh, Mother, such good news, everything's going to be just fine. Your George has sorted it all out. I'm going to put the kettle on and just freshen up the place a little, then we'll have one of our nice chats. You'll never guess which way I came here? Oh, spoilsport! You are a one aren't you? No flies on you, Mother. Well, except for these pesky ones still buzzing around. But your George has got just the thing for that.'

These were the best times, thought George happily, as he and Mother sipped their celebratory sherry, talking about the good old days. That reminded him, he had some typing to do, he'd best get that done and get home, he needed a rest. Heaven only knew what state Dorothy would be in though. It would have to be toast again, she'd completely given up on cooking any dinner. He'd have to deal with her soon, the situation couldn't go on much longer.

He gazed at Dorothy's latest offerings sadly. They barely made sense anymore. To begin with he'd been able to understand them fairly easily, but these... He shook his head, he's just have to do the best he could. He'd drop them in the letterbox at the end of the High Street on his way home.

FOUND!

At the station, the general consensus was that Mr Watson should be released with an apology. P.C. Weaver had confirmed his whereabouts, the various witnesses having been rather reluctant to admit to being in regular poker nights, which gave them pause for thought, *just how high were the stakes at these poker games?* But when informed it was connected to a murder enquiry, the information had been given up.

P.C. Crossley was tasked with taking Dave home and, not looking forward to his reception, went to get him. But Dave wasn't as harsh on him as he'd expected, he was truly a broken man.

'You know what the worse thing about all this is? You have absolutely no idea who killed Britney. You can't find my daughter. You've made no progress at all and you've been wasting time on me. Find my daughter, Nick, I beg you. Find her before it's too late. Tess and I can't take any more.'

Feeling useless, Nick could only apologise again, and the two men sat in silence as he drove Dave home, dropping him outside his house.

~

It was as Nick was heading back to the station that his phone rang. 'Nick, are you on your way back? Good. A girl's been found! Yes, by someone walking their dog. Fits the description, yes. Possible hit and run, we're not sure. It could be *her*, Nick, it could be Chantelle! An ambulance is on its way. She's unconscious, but she's alive! I'm on my way with Sergeant Denton, we'll meet you there. In The Lane, about halfway along, past the old St. John's Terrace.

The paramedics were crouched over the body, hands moving frantically as they checked vitals and inserted a catheter for fluids. Looking up, one of them shook his head at P.C. Weaver, 'She's unresponsive, and not in a good way I'm afraid. Severely malnourished, dehydrated, injuries to the head and torso. We need to get her to the hospital right away.' He and his partner secured the head and manoeuvred the unconscious girl onto a stretcher before sliding her into the ambulance. 'We're taking her to Rentham hospital, want to come with us P.C. Weaver?'

Jane hopped in and the ambulance left, lights flashing, as Nick pulled up. 'Is it her, Sir?'

Sergeant Denton nodded, 'Yes, in all likeliness. Clothing looks right, but hard to tell, poor girl's so covered in filth. Lord alone knows what she's been through, and what happened for her to end up here. Jane's with her, I'll follow on now, wait for her confirmation of identity, if possible. Ah, here's the boys from Rentham to set up a cordon. Not much we can do in this half-light, we'll leave them to take their photos. Nick, wait for my call, I'm hoping you'll be going to give the parents the news shortly. Head over to their estate slowly, and if we're pretty sure it's her you can bring them through.'

Trying her best not to get in the medics' way, Jane checked the girl's clothing. Denim skirt; tee shirt, although dirty, was definitely pink; and lastly, the one forlorn pink trainer, its silver star shining bravely, as the other foot lay exposed and shoeless. It was Chantelle. Her hair was greasy and matted, but not so much that Jane couldn't see that it was dark blonde. Come on, Chantelle, stay with us, she willed the unconscious girl as she called her sergeant. 'It's her, Sarge, no doubt about it.'

Nick's training told him to remain calm and collected, but he was excited as well as anxious, terrified he'd get a call at any minute to tell him she hadn't made it. He rushed to the Watson's and pressed the bell while banging loudly on the door.

'We've got her! We've found Chantelle, she's safe! Yes, she's alive, she's got some injuries, look, she's not in a good way, but she's on the way to Rentham, I'm taking you, let's go. I'll tell you what I know on the way.'

Cal put down Sasha's phone and gently woke her. 'Sash, they've found Chantelle! She's not in good shape, but she's alive! Dave was released and Nick's taking them to Rentham, we're to meet them at the hospital.'

~

Pull yourself together, Sash, stop crying. 'I'm sorry, Cal, I don't know what's wrong with me. I don't usually cry like a baby, it must just be everything that's happened, the op, Chantelle, the murders, just, yeah, well, everything.' Wiping her face, she blew her nose noisily, then smiled. 'Let's go! This is the best news we've heard in, like, forever!'

~

'She's here, she's safe. Thank God!' Tessa held Sasha close, laughing and crying at the same time.

'Oh, Tess, I can hardly believe it! It's wonderful! Have you seen her? Has she woken up? Has anyone told you anything yet?'

'No, she's unconscious, we were allowed in for a couple of minutes, but the police are busy now. They have to collect evidence, I don't know what that means? Her clothes? They said a doctor will come and speak to us soon. My poor baby, I just want to hold her, tell her she's going to be alright.'

At that moment, P.C. Weaver exited the hospital room carrying a number of large brown bags. She handed them off to another officer and came over to speak to the group. 'I know this is hard, when all you want is to be with Chantelle. We're working as fast as we can so that you can sit with her. We've had to bag her clothing for possible evidence and that will all go to the lab here in Rentham. I'm so pleased your daughter's safe, Mr and Mrs Watson, we're all rooting for her. Ah, here's the doctor.' She stepped aside with a smile.

Doctor Montgomery was a tall, efficient looking woman, with hair tied back matter-of-factly. She gave a small smile to the group before speaking. 'Mr and Mrs Watson? And you are?' She nodded at Sasha and Cal, before addressing Tessa and Dave. 'Chantelle is unconscious and we want to get her down for a CT scan right away to check for possible swelling on the brain. This may be caused by a small brain bleed, but tests will confirm this. If so we may need to operate to relieve the pressure, but we'll know more following the scan. We also suspect she may have suffered some broken bones during the accident, her left arm and leg, in particular, but again, x-rays will confirm this. Her clothing has been taken by the police. I understand Chantelle has been missing and investigations are underway. I have a nurse cleaning her up a little and popping her into a clean gown, she'll then be taken for scans. After that you'll be able to go in and sit with her. Please don't expect a response, this is quite normal in these situations. Don't be alarmed by the tubes, we have her on fluids, as well as a breathing tube to regulate her breathing. Our neurosurgeon will be along to check her scan results, once we have them, and we can then decide on our course of action.' She looked up as the door opened, nodding at the nurse. 'They'll be along to take Chantelle to x-ray now, you'll be able to sit with her once she's back. I'll check in with you later, once we have further information.' She paused, as she walked away, turning back to them, 'Your daughter's in the very best hands, I assure you we'll take good care of her and do everything we can to bring her back to you.'

Cal offered to go in search of tea and coffee, with Dave getting up to go with him. Sasha held Tessa's hand. 'Oh, Tess, I don't know what to say, it's such a relief that she's here, but we still have so much to worry about. She seems good, the doctor, in control I mean?'

'She does,' Tessa blew her nose again. 'Sash, it's awful, there are terrible marks on her wrists and ankles, they're raw, bleeding, I think she was tied up. I can't bear to think about it, someone had my baby tied up, a prisoner. And she must have escaped somehow. And then what? What happened to her? Someone ran her over? The freak who'd taken her? I just, I just can't understand how any of this could have happened. I can't get my head around it.'

Jane Weaver accompanied the orderlies taking Chantelle to x-ray, stopping them to allow Tessa and Sasha to see her for a moment, before telling the women she'd be back to see them in a little while. Jane had to ensure that blood and urine samples were taken for testing and sent to the lab for fast tracking. She'd had the doctors take samples from both wrist and ankle wounds already, and these were now with the lab. Once this was done she met with Nick and Sergeant Denton in the small conference room.

'What have we got so far, Jane?' Sergeant Denton had a whiteboard set up and was ready to make notes.

'Positive I.D. for Chantelle Watson, Sir. Clothing and both parents confirm this. Evidence of restraints being used on both wrists and ankles, samples are at the lab. Blood and urine samples have been taken and are also at the lab. Hair and nail samples same. It appears victim was held captive in a confined area, evidence of repeated soiling of clothing and underwear, with small black, possibly plastic, particles adhering to her legs in particular. Samples of these have been taken to the lab as well. No evidence of sexual assault, which is unusual, although a relief of course. She was given little food and water, resulting in severe malnourishment, and is currently unconscious. The guess is that she escaped somehow, and was then run over, possibly by her abductor, and left for dead. She sustained possible broken bones in her left arm and leg, as well as suspected brain injury. I'm hoping for preliminary lab results later this evening, they've put a priority on them, although they couldn't make any promises. That's it, Sir.'

'Well, good for her for escaping,' Nick spoke grimly. 'Pity her friend wasn't so lucky. Looking pretty sure that they were both held in the same place, don't you think, Sir? Tied up and kept on black plastic sheeting or something? If so, something happened to keep our abductor away long enough for her to escape. Reckon it was him who ran her over? Must have been. Must've thought she was dead, but weird he just left her lying there to be found. Wonder why he didn't move her?'

'All good questions, Nick, and good work, Jane, thanks. I want you both here tonight, wait for the results from all the samples, see what you can come up with. The SOCOS will be updating me tonight with what they've got so far, so hopefully we'll know something about what type of car hit her. I'm heading back to update the Inspector and will be back later.

Parents holding up alright? Good. Let's hope the girl wakes up, save us all a lot of trouble, she could lead us straight to the bastard.'

PERFECT TIMING

Chantelle lay motionless in her bed, the only sounds the gentle pop and rush of the ventilator, and the gentle beeps of her heart monitor. Doctor Montgomery had, true to her word, returned to give them an update, and the patient was scheduled to have her broken bones set first thing in the morning. The brain swelling was minimal and her hope was that it would subside on its own, negating the need for surgery.

P.C. Jane Weaver had popped back in a couple of times to chat to them, before leaving them for the night. She hoped they would know more during the course of the next day but the lab results could take some time.

Tessa and Dave would be staying the night, and would not be leaving their daughter's side for any reason whatsoever. Sasha and Cal left them there with promises to bring toiletries and clean clothing the next day.

As Cal drove them to the pub, Sasha allowed herself to relax for what seemed like the first time in nine days. Nine days, was that all it had been? 'Nine days, Cal, can you believe it? So much has happened! And now Chantelle's safe, I only hope she pulls through. If only she'd wake up, she could tell us everything, otherwise it's up to the cops to work it all out. They should be able to shouldn't they? There must be loads of evidence on her clothes, surely they can work out where she was held?'

Grinning, Cal reached across and squeezed her leg, something he'd done once or twice recently, much to her pleasure. 'Let's take the night off, Sash, let the cops do their thing. Don't forget you had an operation during those nine days as well, and you're still supposed to be taking it easy.'

'I know, you're right, but I actually feel pretty great, maybe it's just a massive euphoria rush, but at this moment I feel fantastic. I could murder a large glass of wine. And yes, I am allowed, before you ask,' she laughed, as Cal opened his mouth and closed it again.

Checking the clock on the dashboard, Cal laughed too. 'I wasn't going to ask that, I was going to agree with you, a cold beer sounds perfect to me, and some food, I'm starving! I reckon we'll just make it before Jules closes the kitchen.'

It felt weird to be sitting together out by the river again, just as they had a little over a week earlier when they'd first met. The evening air had cooled during that time, in direct contrast to their relationship, which had heated up slowly but surely. She felt as if she knew Cal so well, but realised that she actually knew so little about him. With a sinking heart she acknowledged that, if, no *once*, Chantelle recovered, she must stay positive, she'd have to head back home. Back to her lonely flat and her attempts at earning a living.

'Penny for them.' Cal was gazing at her, his eyes twinkling in the half light.

Sasha groaned, putting her head in her hands. 'I was thinking how little I actually know about you. And I was thinking that I'd have to leave here soon, once Chantelle's okay, and that I don't really want to.'

'Then stay.' He reached over and held her hand. 'Forget London, come and stay here, at least for a while. Then we'll have all the time in the world to get to know each other properly.'

Her stomach somersaulted, just as it had the first time she'd set eyes on him. 'I, I couldn't, what would I do? Where would I live? I have my business there, well, what's left of it, I have kind of neglected it recently. Besides, you don't want me hanging around all the time do you?'

'I can think of worse things.' He grinned. 'Sash, don't stress it, you'll work it out, *we'll work it out*. You and I, we can do whatever we want, we're both free spirits so let's see what happens.'

While Cal went to get them more drinks, Sasha wandered over to the river bank and watched the twinkling movements of the water. It all seemed like déjà vu. Well, up until this moment at least. Cal's arms circled her from behind as he gently kissed her neck. She turned to him and her body melded into his as their lips met.

A very pleasant while later they pulled apart slightly and smiled at each other. 'I wish we could take this further tonight,' Cal's eyes were dark with desire. 'But I know we can't...'

Groaning, she leant against his chest, 'I wish we could too... but my stupid body, you know? I have to heal... perfect timing as always, Sash.'

YOU ARE THE SINNER

'Where are we, people?' Inspector Kavanagh was impatient to get started, wanting updates on everything; what, if any, lab results were back; what had the clothing told them; who was liaising with the SOCOS; had Chantelle woken up? He looked around at the assembled group.

Sergeant Denton was working with the scene of crime guys and so far they had found out little of any help. The dirt lane, where the girl had been found, was hard and dry and offered up little in the way of tyre tracks. Those they had been able to identify were now photographed and cast, where possible. 'I have P.C. Crossley compiling a list of all vehicles that regularly use The Lane. Once we have that he'll check with the owners of the vehicles, for elimination purposes.'

Chantelle Watson was in surgery, having her broken bones set. The swelling of her brain was being monitored but showed signs of reducing. She remained unconscious. Fibrous particles had been identified from the wounds on her wrists and ankles and were definitely from a rope of some kind, not nylon. Maybe it was the same rope as had been found around Britney's neck, the lab would check. The lab had been able to advise that her urine showed evidence of some kind of nonbenzodiazepine hypnotic, in other words, some kind of strong sleeping pill. Further testing would identify exactly which one, but it was likely a drug which required a doctor's prescription. P.C. Jane Weaver sat back down.

'Good work. Jane, you can start by checking with all local pharmacies, see who's taking sleeping pills, look for any unusual quantities. We have to face the fact that the girl may not wake up, if so it's down to us to find out what she's unable to tell us herself. We haven't just got a kidnapper to catch but Britney Morton's murderer too.'

~

The soft thud on the door mat alerted Maureen to the arrival of the post. Taking it through to the lounge, she sat down with her coffee and looked through the few envelopes. Nothing of interest except, oh, now what was this? With a feeling of foreboding, she tore open the envelope, pulling out the single sheet of paper. She read the typed words in disbelief.

YOU SHOULD HAVE BEEN PUNISHED NOT HIM.
YOU ARE THE SINNER.

Gasping, she dropped it onto the coffee table. The sinner? Who would say this? What did it mean? She rushed through to the kitchen and retrieved the first letter from behind the fruit bowl. Her hands trembled as she compared them but, apart from their tone, they were nothing alike. She needed to get hold of Cal and Sasha.

~

She woke up and realised that she felt fine, no, better than fine. She'd never taken long to recover from her operations and, she had to admit, that little interlude with Cal last night had probably helped... It was going to be a good day! She showered and dressed, her growling stomach spurring her on for some of Jules's breakfast.

Cal joined her just as she was finishing a bowl of yoghurt and fruit. 'I got your text. How are you feeling? You look good, mmm, and you smell good too.' His lips brushed her cheek as he sat down. 'Maureen called, wondering if we can visit. She's received two odd letters and wants to show us, one came today, the other one a few days ago. She was going to ask us about it but there was the search, and we were in London, so I think she kind of forgot about it. Oh and she's chuffed about Chantelle, horrified of course, but said to tell you she's so pleased she's safe.'

Sasha gasped. 'The letters- I'd half forgotten about them. We need to see them, it must all be connected in some way mustn't it? Maybe we can call at Maureen's first, before going on to the hospital? That's if you're okay to drive me to

Rentham? There's no change, I spoke to Tessa, but I'll need to call at their house and get them some bits.'

'Sash, I'll drive you anywhere,' he smiled at her before turning to greet Jules and place his breakfast order.

~

The letters were laid out on the table, together with their envelopes. Cal picked up the first letter and looked at it in puzzlement. 'What the hell is this? Looks like a nutter made it, or a kid. Flowery paper, glitter, letters torn from newspaper headlines by the looks of it, and hearts everywhere. And the message, if we can make sense of it, says it shouldn't have been you but her. So, who is *her*? Well, whoever sent this was saying sorry for something. Which envelope did it come in? Oh, this is interesting, different handwriting for the address, see that?' He handed it to Sasha.

'Not just the address,' Sasha's eyes sparkled, 'look at the name, it's written really badly, and in a different pen. Maureen, this letter wasn't meant for you. Whoever wrote the address added the letter 's' to 'Mr'. I think this letter was written to your husband.'

The three of them looked at the envelope in silence for a moment. Sasha was right.

Maureen's voice wobbled slightly. 'Someone was apologising to Peter for his death and saying it should have been me. I should have died, not Peter.'

'And then this second letter: *You should have been punished not him. You are the sinner.* This is meant for you. But this time it's typed on plain paper and the name and address is typed. It's like two completely different people did this. Or three, if you count the other handwriting.' Sasha thought for a moment. 'The other letters were typed, the one my sister received, Lilith's too. We're sure poor Barbara received a typed letter as well. And Von thought your husband received a typed letter the day he- oh, Maureen, I'm sorry, this is so awful for you.'

'It's horrible,' Maureen's voice was a whisper. 'But if this is going to help in some way, if it's got anything to do with your niece being taken, with all the deaths,' her voice was stronger now. 'Then I'm glad I received them. Will you take them to the police?'

'We will,' Cal was grim. 'We're going on to Rentham hospital so we'll hand these over to Nick, I'm sure he'll be there.'

Just as Maureen was showing them out she put her hand to her mouth. 'I've just remembered something. It was the last time I spoke to Barbara, she started to tell me something. Oh, why didn't I think of this before, she said something about the two girls from the new estate following someone. Him, she definitely said *him*, I'm sure. She must have been talking about your niece and her friend, Sasha. But she was laughing like it was funny, as if she knew him. I didn't think anything of it, and what with Peter of course, and then Barbara was killed soon after. I feel dreadful, do you think whoever Barbara saw them following, abducted them? And then killed that poor girl? I could have stopped it.'

'Maureen,' Sasha put her arm around her shoulders. 'It was a passing comment, how could you have known? And you had enough to cope with, please don't feel bad, it helps us, it gives us more information. And if Barbara knew him, then whoever took Chantelle and killed Britney is a local. The question is, did he kill Barbara too? We've got to look within this village.'

~

P.C. Jane Weaver began her pharmacy checks at Pringles Chemist in the village, deciding to finish off back in Rentham so that she could go straight to the hospital and report her findings, if any, to the team.

'Oh, hello dear, and what can we do for you on this fine morning?' Mrs Pringle smiled, all ready for a chat with the nice police woman. 'Sheila, kettle, there's a dear. Well, you must be pleased with yourself, catching the killer in our midst? I always say, don't I, Sheila, our police are a Godsend, especially in these dark days of missing girls and serial killers. And who'd have thought it was the father? Would you believe it? And thank the Lord that you found his daughter in time, of course we don't know the details yet, just what we heard from the postman, who heard all about it from the McGregors in

The Lane. What put you onto him, if you don't mind my asking? I shan't breathe a word of course, not one for gossip.'

Jane Weaver fixed a small smile on her face. 'Good morning, Mrs Pringle. I'm pleased to hear you're not a one for gossip, especially when people can get their facts so wrong. I'm not sure where you got the idea about the father, but it won't do to be saying things like that, it really won't. We have no reason to believe that poor Mr Watson was involved and it would be quite awful if anyone was spreading stories about him, after all he and his wife have gone through. They and their daughter need all the support they can get at this time.'

Mrs Pringle bristled, feeling embarrassed. Honestly, anyone would think she was being accused of spreading gossip. She tried to think of all the people she'd been talking to yesterday. It was Sheila's fault, she'd come in all full of the story, and she could wipe that smirk off her face, standing there waiting for the kettle to boil.

'Mrs Pringle? Do you have the names for me? A list maybe, or a file where you keep filled prescriptions?'

'Prescriptions? Names? I'm not quite sure what you-?'

P.C. Weaver repeated the question. 'We'd like to know the names of all customers who have filled prescriptions for nonbenzodiazepine hypnotics, sleeping pills, anything like that. Anything that you can tell us that struck you as out of the ordinary, any large amounts maybe, that kind of thing.'

Mrs Pringle tried to concentrate. There'd been the young couple who'd just taken over the hardware store, and old Mrs Tomlinson, oh, and the waitress from the tea shop, now what was her name, Nadia, was it? And of course, Mr Hobson had been there, had two cups of tea he had, and who knows how many biscuits, any excuse to take a break from his deliveries. 'Sleeping pills, you say? Well certainly we can give you a list. Sheila, leave that kettle, there's no time for tea, really. Can you show P.C. Weaver the prescription file?'

Jane Weaver left with a list of names and prescription drugs, but as far as she could tell nothing looked out of the ordinary. She'd head on to Rentham.

Mrs Pringle was still running through names in her head and trying to ignore Sheila. That's right, Mrs Winter had been there for a while, she'd been telling them about her new season's line in at Madame Couture, and had stayed for the tea and chat, now who else... Something was niggling her in the back of her mind, to do with sleeping pills, whatever was it? Oh, there'd been the butcher's wife, Mrs Alison, she'd been in to buy face powder, and she was always one for a gossip, not that they'd been gossiping...

SOMEONE LOCAL

They decided they'd quickly pop in on Tessa, Dave, and Chantelle, before going to find the police in the conference room at the hospital. By mutual consent they'd agreed not to mention anything about Maureen's letters, or her memory of Barbara's comment about the girls following a man, figuring that Tessa and Dave had enough to cope with.

Back from surgery now, Chantelle appeared to be sleeping peacefully. 'Maybe she'll wake up after the anaesthetic wears off?' Tess's face looked hopefully at them all. 'You never know, right?'

Dave held her hand, smiling sadly, 'You never know love, anything's possible they said. We'll just keep on talking to her, maybe she can hear us.'

Sasha and Cal made a quiet exit, leaving the worried parents talking to their daughter, and went to find P.C. Crossley.

Jane Weaver had just reported back her findings from the pharmacy checks, such as they were. It gave them a list of names but nothing that rang any alarm bells, other than the fact that an astonishing number of people appeared to be in need of sleeping pills.

With Nick still out on his vehicle checks, it was Jane who spoke to Sasha and Cal when they knocked on the door of the conference room at the hospital.

'Hi, Cal, Sasha, good to see you both. I'm not really going to be able to give you updates, you understand? We're pretty tied up with our investigations right now. Oh, I see, well come in then, I'll get Sergeant Denton to join us.'

Sergeant Denton shook his head in frustration. 'I can't work out what the hell all these letters, and rumours of letters, are all about. One thing's for sure, we've got a definite case of good old poison pen letters here. Last time I heard about something like this I was watching a Miss Marple on TV with the wife. And I agree with you, it does look like these two letters are from different people entirely, and that one was intended for the husband. The question remains, do they have a bearing on the deaths or the missing girls?'

It was Jane's turn to speak. 'Peter Ford's death has been confirmed an accident, Sir, although there could be an argument that the letter induced stress which resulted in his death? But it's only supposition that he received a letter, we found nothing in his office. We do know that Barbara Fenton was murdered as, we believe, was Britney Morton, although we await the inquest for full details. We believe Mrs Fenton received a letter before her death and, as previously stated, possibly Mr Ford too, whereas Mrs Ford is alive and her letters seem to be more about accusation and blame. The letters received by both Mrs Morton, Britney's mother, and Mrs Watson, were received at different times. Mrs Morton received hers after her daughter went missing, and Mrs Watson received hers before Chantelle disappeared. Both the women are, obviously, still alive, so it doesn't seem that the act of receiving a letter necessarily results in the recipient's death. Unfortunately we don't have all the letters, only Mrs Morton's, as well as these two now. But from what we can gather all the letters, apart from the strange one with cuttings and stickers, were typed. Someone's stirring things up in the village, Sir, but who, why, and if they're related to our abductor and killer, remains a mystery.'

Sasha and Cal had been waiting patiently while Jane summarised the situation, but now Sasha spoke. 'There's one more thing which we think you need to hear. Maureen, Mrs Ford, has remembered something that Barbara Fenton started to mention to her on the phone. She didn't finish, there was a distraction or something, and it was the last time they spoke before Barbara was killed. She told Maureen that she'd seen the two girls from the new estate following someone. She definitely used the word 'him' so it was a man, without doubt. Maureen said it sounded like she knew him, like she thought it was funny, so it sounds like they were following someone local?'

Sergeant Denton nodded, thanking them both for coming to them with the information. 'I have to ask you both to keep this information strictly private, tell absolutely no-one. I'm sure you realise how important this could be? We'll definitely look into it, and Jane, you need to pay a visit to Mrs Ford to confirm everything.'

~

The local paper was full of dramatic headlines and information from 'this confidential source' and 'that unnamed source', which, most locals knew, meant that Des Barnsley, who was getting a bit old for reporting the news, and therefore took the easy road whenever possible, had probably picked up most of his titbits from either one of the two local watering holes, or Mrs Pringle at the pharmacy.

Nonetheless, headlines such as 'LOCAL MAN FREED!', 'SERIAL KILLER STILL AT LARGE!' and 'MISSING GIRL FOUND ALIVE!' caused much excitement, and discussion, all over the village.

One household experienced no such excitement. Rosemary Spindlebury replaced the phone handset, feeling aggrieved. She'd given the chap a piece of her mind, but he was adamant his boy had delivered their paper this morning, same as every morning. Now that she thought about it, she had heard the letterbox rattle while she was getting dressed, but had only found a flyer lying on the hall table. Reg had told her not to bother about the missing paper, it was filled with useless gossip anyway, and had insisted on them visiting the golf course in Carringham, a four-hour round-trip away. His suggestion that they stay overnight was a pleasant surprise, and while he'd been getting himself ready she'd been unable to resist phoning to complain. But she wouldn't bother Reg about it, no need to mar the trip, now to decide what to pack for dinner that evening...

~

George was in a flat spin. Dorothy was becoming too much for him to cope with, on top of everything else. She'd barricaded herself in the living room and spent the night apparently having some kind of party. Their old record player had been playing Abba repeatedly and from her talking and laughter you'd have thought she'd had about ten people in there.

He knew he was going to have to do something but didn't want to draw attention to himself at the moment. Especially not after reading the headlines of this morning's paper. He'd actually thought he was having a heart attack. *Not that it would be the worst thing to happen.* But then he'd thought of poor Mother. She needed him. And he needed to go to work, to try and act normal. But the girl was alive! How could she be? She'd been lying beside the road, dead, he'd been sure of it. He should have gone and checked, but there'd been no time. What did it mean? Had she told the police about him? They'd be coming to arrest him at any moment. Why hadn't they? What game were they playing? She must have told them everything, why else would they have let the father go?

Somehow he survived the day, flinching every time someone knocked on his office door. He needed to find out what was happening, and there was only one place to go for that. Maybe he could say he'd dropped the perfume, that the bottle had broken.

AN INNOCENT OVERSIGHT

Mrs Pringle wasn't quite her usual chatty self when George visited the chemist. Dying though she was to discuss the local newspaper's headlines and stories, she was still feeling somewhat chastened from P.C. Weaver's earlier visit.

This frustrated George no end for you couldn't usually stop Mrs Pringle from talking, and he could hardly raise the subject himself. Explaining to Sheila that he'd unfortunately dropped Mother's perfume and could he buy another bottle, he hovered by the counter while Sheila went to the back, in the hopes of tempting Mrs Pringle to gossip by his presence alone. But she wasn't going to be tempted that easily and neither, it seemed, was Sheila, with both women remaining unusually quiet.

Did they know something? Why weren't they talking to him like they always did? What had happened to the girl and how could he find out? Starting to sweat, he paid for the perfume and hurried from the store with a mumbled goodbye. He needed Mother, she was the only one who could help him.

~

Oh, what a miserable day it had turned out to be. A day filled with news and events and she couldn't breathe a word for fear of being a gossip and reprimanded by the police. And it didn't help that Sheila had worn a slight smirk on her face all day. 'Just the perfume for Mr Newton was it, Sheila? That's odd, didn't he just buy a bottle yesterday? We'll have to put in an order for him. Oh, dropped it did he? Well, accidents will happen.'

Accidents will happen... why did that ring some kind of a bell? Something else had been dropped or broken... now what was it? To do with Mr Newton, she was sure. She racked her brain for the answer. It was Mrs Newton! That's right, the younger, not the older. Poor Dorothy had dropped her pot of pills in the bath, if she recalled correctly, and George had asked her to replace them. Well of course, he was going through a terrible time with her at the moment, on top of coping with his mother. Not wanting to attract Sheila's attention to a possible oversight, she sent her out on an errand, before checking back in the drugs book.

Oh dear Lord, she hadn't written it in the book. Now what was she going to do? And poor Mr Newton, such a nice man, a *good* man. The last thing he needed was the police banging on his front door because Mrs Pringle told them about one simple mistake. He certainly wasn't the kind of man to go around drugging and killing people, he was a pillar of society and you didn't get too many of those these days. She wasn't trying to hide anything, well, not really, it had been an innocent oversight on her part... And the way that young policewoman had looked at her this morning, no, she really thought it would be best all round to keep it to herself.

~

P.C. Nick Crossley was seriously bored. A police check set up on a busy road was one thing, but on The Lane? He'd already identified all the car owners, having visited most of the cottages, declining invitations in for tea and cake by elderly occupants who were lonely and welcomed the opportunity for company. They'd all told him virtually the same thing, there were only six car owners in the whole lane, most residents being either housebound or making use of a taxi or the bus service, the bus stop being conveniently located at the top of the lane. He'd checked on all six cars and was pretty certain that none of them were likely to be an abductor or killer, nonetheless, they were all detailed in his report. There remained only to try and identify any other regular users of The Lane, delivery men, visiting relatives, etc.

He put his hand up as the lone car approached. 'Afternoon Sir, mind if I just ask you a quick couple of questions? Oh it's you, Mr Newton, how are you?'

Nick watched him drive off. Poor frail old guy, and on his way to look after his mother. She must be really ancient, looking at him. Some people really had a time of it. He sighed, looking at his watch. He'd head off soon.

~

George cowered on his knees in front of his mother. 'I didn't tell him anything, Mother! I'll fix this, I will. I just need to think. No, I don't know about the girl!' Sobbing, he listened to Mother's angry screams telling him how incompetent he was.

~

'It's not often you get any post, Cal.' Jules looked quite mystified as she handed Cal the envelope.

Turning it over in his hands, Cal looked at the typed address, before holding it out to Sasha.

'You've got one! You've got a letter, Cal! What does it say? Wait, maybe there are prints. 'Jules, have you got any plastic food gloves?'

They stared at the sheet of paper, reading the words in disbelief.

FORNICATOR! WAS SCREWING HER WORTH IT?
LOOK WHAT YOU DID.

'What the-?' Cal looked at Sasha in horror. 'Who the hell's writing this stuff? And what the crap are they talking about?' He thumped the bar table angrily.

'Are they talking about me?' Sasha's face was horrified. 'And why would anyone care what we're doing? Not that we're doing anything. And not that it's anyone's business. Cal? Has there been someone? You can tell me.'

'No-one Sash, there's been no-one, only you, and we're not even- this is just evil. And what do they mean *look what you did*? I didn't do anything. Whoever's sending this filth is seriously deranged. I mean, what do they even hope to gain from crap like this?'

'We'll give it to the police tomorrow morning, see what they make of it. Maybe they can get some fingerprints or something. What we need to work out is who they're referring to, is it me or someone else, and why. Let's get a drink, you look like you need one.'

'I need about ten.' Cal grinned, 'Sorry, I lost my cool for a moment there. Let's go outside, I need a smoke.'

~

Records and their covers were strewn across the floor, Simon and Garfunkel now quiet, the needle clicking softly on the still-revolving vinyl. Dorothy woke up, surprised to find herself on the couch in the living room. It was getting dark and she was hungry. Hurry up, they told her, he'll be back soon. Giggling, she moved the table from the door before rushing upstairs to use the toilet and gather her writing materials. The bread was going green, but she broke off the bad bits and made herself a jam sandwich. Did she have time to make tea? Only if you're quick! Forget the milk, it's probably gone bad!

Back in the living room, she moved the table across the door, locking it with the key again for good measure. She'd play some more music, have another party with her friends. Humming along as she took everything out of her writing box, she stopped, confused. No, no, no, why was it still here? She hadn't posted it, how could she have forgotten? It was probably George's fault, spoiling her plans as usual. All this time she'd thought she knew. You're right, I can make it prettier, more stickers, more glitter. Smiling fondly around at her friends, she sorted through her stickers. Flowers, flowers for a funeral! She danced around gleefully, she was a dancing queen! Oh, she loved this song. Hugging her letter to her chest, she swayed to the music, imagining Rosemary Spindlebury's face when she received her letter.

A CREAM SLICE FOR LUNCH

Oh, the relief. George read the headline of the daily newspaper again as he drank his morning coffee. *Girl still in coma!* Thank you, Lord. He was safe, at least for now, and hopefully she'd never wake up, it certainly didn't sound promising for her. He paused at the door to the living room, hearing Dorothy's gentle snores, no, he'd leave her alone.

~

P.C.s Weaver and Crossley didn't expect to hear anything new at the inquest into the death of Britney Morton, having been furnished with Wilson Mwabila's full report the night before. However, their presence was requested by the Coroner and both of them would be required to give evidence.

Reporting back to Inspector Kavanagh and their sergeant, at the hospital, they filled them in on all the details. The most notable points were the traces of permethrin found on the body and plastic, a common ingredient of household fly spray. This explained the dead maggots in varying stages of development. It was Wilson Mwabila's best estimate that Britney had been dead for seven days when her body was found. The poor girl had been killed the day she went missing. The rope found around what remained of her neck tissue had definitely been placed there posthumously, possibly to imply that she'd been strangled with it. It was old rope, friable from previous use, with traces of oil and dirt. In other words, just like any old rope found in someone's garage or shed. Death was not caused by strangulation, with rope or otherwise, but by a blow to the head, or a fall, resulting in the same.

'Her killer wanted us to think she'd been strangled with rope for some reason, maybe to try and tie her death in with Barbara Fenton's.'

'But Britney's body was wrapped in plastic, let's not forget that, which is a difference between the two murders. And clearly the killer held onto her body for some reason, sick freak.' Nick's frustration was evident. 'Does any of this actually help us?'

'It will in time, slowly does it, Nick.' Sergeant Denton was calm. 'We can check on purchases of fly spray. Whoever killed Britney must have had a huge fly problem, they'll have been buying fly spray in sizeable quantities. Someone must have noticed. Check the sales in local stores, see if anything stands out.'

'I dunno, Sarge, there's been a massive fly problem this summer, it won't be easy to narrow it down. But we'll give it a shot.'

'Keep at it, everyone, we've got a young girl counting on us, in this very hospital. She may never wake up, but whether she does or doesn't, someone took her and her friend. And then he killed her friend. We'll get him in the end. Keep up the good work.' Inspector Kavanagh took his leave.

~

All was quiet. He's gone, wake up. She tiptoed upstairs, making sure he wasn't hiding anywhere, before going into her bedroom. She'd go shopping she decided, get some groceries. She'd first post her letter, then pop along to the supermarket. It was a lovely day for a walk. Oh, she was already dressed. She smiled at her reflection in surprise, she did love her yellow dress. Frowning, she pulled at her hair, she needed more hairclips. Finally, happy with her appearance, she sprayed on some perfume before heading out.

~

He'd call home first, make sure she wasn't doing anything stupid, before going on to Mother's. There'd be just enough time to make Mother some tea and, oh that was a nice idea, he'd take her a cake from the bakery. Maybe she wouldn't start on at him again he thought, feeling disloyal. Mother was right, of course, he *was* useless, but he'd find a way to make her pleased with him again.

The living room door was open and he looked inside, sighing at the muddle. What had Dorothy been doing now? His eyes lighted on her writing materials. Strange, she didn't usually leave her precious papers out for him to see. But she was nowhere in the house. Surely she hadn't gone out? Now what? Should he go looking for her? He didn't have much time, he needed to get to Mother and back to work. Coming back in to the kitchen from the garden, he decided to set off. Time enough to worry about Dorothy later.

'I thought we'd share a cream slice for lunch, Mother! What a treat! And your George is a clever boy, he's found a solution to everything!'

George was finishing up his story to Mother. 'And so it doesn't sound like the girl will wake up! And it's so perfect, the police will think he killed her as well, they'll arrest him for both murders! And your Georgie will have sorted everything out, just like he promised! Ah, there we are, there's that smile your George loves!' He patted his mother's arm affectionately but froze when she began shouting at him. 'No, Mother, I told you, she probably won't wake from her coma! Well, I don't know what will happen if she does, maybe she won't remember anything. Mother please, I'm trying so hard to make this right. And I brought your favourite cake, too. Please don't shout, Mother, I'm trying my best.'

Upset and shaking, he cleaned up the broken china where his mother had thrown her tea cup across the room, before going upstairs to the little attic room and his typewriter. He sat, hunched and miserable, and began typing, finding it hard to concentrate, upset as he was. Quickly addressing the envelope, he went back downstairs, relieved to find Mother sleeping. He had just enough time to post the letter on his way back to work.

~

Sasha woke up dreamily, she didn't want to move, the feel of Cal's arms around her was too good. Carefully reaching for her watch on the night stand, she checked the time, surprised to find it was so late. Smiling, as Cal gently kissed her bare shoulder, she sank back into his warm body before turning to him. 'We have to get up, I wish we didn't but it's lunchtime already and we have to show the police your letter.'

With a grin, Cal twisted himself on top of her, holding his body carefully so as not to put his whole weight on her. He kissed her longingly, his lips gently moving from her face to her body, as Sasha squirmed hungrily. His tongue twirled around her navel piercing, before flicking over the dragonfly tattoo on her belly. Lifting himself, he grinned at Sasha. 'What's the story with the piercing and the tattoo? I love them, very sexy.'

'Oh, thanks,' Sasha giggled, pleased. 'Well, I got the piercing after about my eighth laparoscopy, thought it might hide some of the scarring, and then the dragonfly came after about my twelfth lap, to hide more scars. It kind of works, I think, plus I love them anyway.

'Me too.' With a last lustful gaze, Cal groaned and lifted himself up. With one movement he was out of the bed, giving Sasha a perfect view of his naked body.

Filled with desire, she cursed her own body for its shortcomings. 'Cal, I wish we could have, you know, gone further last night. A couple more days and I'll be fine, but I can't risk it, I'm sorry I'm such a pain in the ass.'

He lifted her out of the bed so that she was standing in front of him and, holding her hands, gazed into her eyes. 'Sash, don't apologise, I've been with you right through this, it's not your fault. I can wait, it'll be worth it. His eyes roamed over her body with desire, as his hands cupped her buttocks. 'And this is the best-looking pain in the ass I've ever seen.' She giggled, leaning into him happily. 'Is your shower big enough for two, d'you think?' he asked.

'We're going to take this crazy letter to the cops at the hospital, check on your niece, and then I'm taking you for lunch. Sound like a plan? I'll just get some clean clothes from my room. Reckon I can streak across the landing without running into Jules or the cleaner?'

Sasha laughed as Cal made a run for it. She felt guilty that she felt so happy, but at least Chantelle was safe, even if her future was uncertain at this time. She gave her wet hair another rub with the towel before getting dressed.

Sergeant Denton was alone in the conference room at the hospital, both Jane and Nick being out following up on the latest findings from the inquest. He looked at Cal's letter with interest. 'And you have no idea who or what this letter is referring to?'

Cal shook his head, 'There's been no-one in my life for a while, well, not until Sash.' He smiled at her. 'And not that it's anyone's business, but we haven't, well, it's been purely platonic so far, but like I said, it's no-one's business. The letter makes no sense at all, not that any of them do, to be honest.'

Sergeant Denton thanked them for bringing it in. 'We'll run some tests, see if we can get any fingerprints or anything. In the meantime, if anything occurs to you, let me know, okay? And for now, let's not tell anyone else about this.'

Tessa and Dave were exhausted, and Sasha, refusing to take no for an answer, sent them both home for a shower and a change of clothing. 'Sorry,' she whispered to Cal. 'Can we make the lunch an extra late one?'

'No problem, Sash, you sit here with Chantelle, I'll go get us some drinks and something to eat for now.'

Returning with tea and bacon rolls, he paused at the door to Chantelle's room, smiling as he heard Sasha talking to her niece. 'I wish you'd wake up, Chants, I'd really like you to meet him. He's so hot, he's kind and funny, kind of perfect, you know? You'd like him.' Aware of someone behind her, Sasha stopped and looked round, embarrassed when she realised Cal had probably heard what she'd been saying.

'Keep going, don't mind me.' Cal grinned, before passing Sasha the bacon roll.

'Oh wow, this smells good, thanks, I'm starving! And don't let what I said go to your head, okay?' She laughed, before taking a bite of her roll.

Tessa and Dave returned a couple of hours later looking fresher, although still tired. With hugs and promises to call them if there was any news, they sent Sasha and Cal off.

'Now for that late lunch, there's a great pub out on the road back to the village, they do a mean lasagne, sound good?'

DOROTHY GOES SHOPPING

'If I keep eating like this I'll end up the size of a house by the time I return to London.' Sasha groaned, holding her belly. 'But damn, that was good, and that garlic bread, so buttery and delicious.'

'Yeah, about that,' Cal's hand reached across the table. 'London, I mean, not the garlic bread. I'm not sure I want you to be so far away. I know we're still getting to know each other, but we have something, don't we, Sash? Tell me you feel it too?'

'Oh, Cal, of course I do, and I'm loving what's happening between us, but we haven't exactly been able to get to know each other under normal circumstances. I mean, think about it, my niece disappears, it turns out she's been abducted, together with her friend, who is then murdered, as is your friend Barbara. So we have a killer on the loose, not to mention the poison pen letters, and to top it all off, I go and have a damn operation to remove bits of my insides. Bits I kind of wanted to hang onto, if I'm honest, seeing as they are a big part of what makes me feel like a woman, stupid though that is. So yes, we have something, but we haven't even had the chance to explore that, to take it further, and it's just so frustrating.'

'Are you done? Honestly, Sash? If we can feel what we feel, even amidst all the crap that's been happening, don't you think that's a good sign? Doesn't it mean we have more than just some basic physical attraction? Believe me, I want to take you to bed and do all sorts of things to you, and I hope I get to do that pretty soon. But I'll take whatever I can get of you, until your body's ready, and if that means just being with you, kissing you and holding you in bed at night, then that'll work for me. But if you go back to London, well, I don't want to lose you, that's all.'

'I don't want to lose you either, Cal, and if I'm honest, I'm not exactly excited about going back to London. But my flat's there, and my work, well, what's left of it, seeing as I've kind of neglected it completely. I can't just never go back, life doesn't work like that. Look, I'm not going yet, am I? Let's not worry about things that haven't happened yet, yeah?'

'You're right, we should enjoy the time we have now, and worry about things as they happen. But I still don't want you to go, I kind of like having you around.' Cal's grin was meant to reassure her, but she couldn't help but notice that it didn't quite reach his eyes as it usually did.

~

Dorothy waltzed through the supermarket, smiling at the other shoppers faces as they turned to her. Why weren't they smiling? What was wrong with them? Some of them looked ill, oh, she mustn't get sick, don't get too close to them. We don't want Dr Singe coming to see me again. She burst out laughing. Oh, she loved this song, she was so glad she'd gone out, she hadn't had this much fun in ages. She sang along, putting items in her basket until it was full.

Oh yes, her friends nodded, see how important you are? Everyone makes way for you. They don't want to make you wait in a queue. She placed her basket on the counter, smiling at the cashier, as she carried on singing.

George put the phone down rather too forcefully, attracting the attention of Sylvia, the office's ancient secretary, who didn't miss a thing. 'Everything alright, Mr Newton? Anything I can help you with?'

'Thank you, Sylvia, I'm fine.' The last thing he needed was Sylvia knowing about this and telling the whole office. Although, knowing this damned village, everyone would know before too long anyway. Just when he thought he'd got one part of his life under control another piece started falling apart. 'I have to go out for a while, Sylvia, it shouldn't take long.'

Bracing himself, he entered the supermarket and was immediately confronted by a hovering youth with red hair and acne.

'Mr Newton? Ah, good, I'm Lewis, the assistant manager, thanks for coming down so quickly. Your wife's fine, well, she's unharmed, not that she should have been harmed, I mean, well, look, let's put it this way, she doesn't seem quite well in herself, but we've sat her down out the back of the store. We thought the fresh air might help her. I've got Doris, our accountant, sitting with her, thought a woman's touch might be good. Let me take you through. What happened exactly? Oh right, well, your wife was shopping, but she was behaving rather oddly. Look, I'm sorry, this is awkward, she was singing loudly as she went round the store, and not only that, Sir, but some of the customers were complaining that she was a little... unfresh? And then, unfortunately, she didn't appear to have any means of paying for her shopping. At that point she got rather upset. Luckily Doris recognised her, so we knew who to call. And here you are!' Lewis finished off, triumphantly, relieved that his part in this whole saga was nearly over. Honestly, if he had to spend any more time near that woman he might gag. 'Ah, Doris, here's Mr Newton. Thanks again, Sir, I'll leave you to it, shall I? Call me if you need me, anything at all.' And with that, he extricated himself smoothly from the whole thing.

'Good God, Dorothy, what on earth have you been up to?' Red-faced, George thanked Doris for her assistance. 'It will have just been one of her turns, we'll get the doctor in once we're home. I'll take her around to my car, get her settled, then pop back in and settle up for the groceries.'

He stared at the assortment of goods displayed on the counter, in confusion. A hairbrush, a packet of pasta, two potatoes, rooibos teabags, *what?* two tins of dog food, *why on earth?* a packet of plastic dinosaurs - his mind had gone blank - a can of peach slices, a bag of frozen fish portions, and a cellophane-wrapped bunch of flowers. Hurriedly paying for the items, and too embarrassed to question Dorothy's selection, he took the shopping bags, deftly packed by the cashier, and escaped with a murmured word of thanks.

With the car windows fully open, he drove home, not quite feeling up to the task of asking Dorothy what she'd been thinking, as she chattered away happily beside him. At least he'd be able to make them some kind of normal meal tonight, fish and mashed potatoes, followed by peaches.

~

Jane and Nick had reported back their limited findings regarding sales of fly spray. Yes, there had been some purchases of two or three cans at a time, but it would take a while to find out who the customers were. Plus, as Jane pointed out, she herself had sometimes bought two cans at a time. She'd also hoped for more information from Mrs Pringle of Pringle's Chemist, but after their last interaction Mrs Pringle had given her a somewhat frosty reception. She supposed she'd asked for it, having previously made the point about the dangers of gossip in the community.

~

Doctor Montgomery had been in to update them on Chantelle, but, although her brain swelling continued to go down, they still couldn't be sure if or when she would regain consciousness.

She was remaining positive, Tessa told Sasha, when they spoke on the phone that evening. Her and Dave were fine, no need for her to come through. Spend the evening with Cal, relaxing. He was nice, they were a good match.

'I've been given my orders,' Sasha informed Cal. 'I'm to spend the evening with you, relaxing.'

'Sounds perfect,' he grinned. 'Let's get a bottle of wine from Jules and sit out by the river.'

Three bottles of wine later, they lay in bed together, drowsy but content. *Four days down, I just need to resist him for a couple more days, and then...* Sasha drifted off to sleep, imagining what she and Cal would do once she was recovered.

A LITTLE PIGGY THIEF

Tom Bridger was feeling his age this morning. He set off from the post office, looking up at the grey sky as it began to drizzle. He'd finish his round as quickly as possible, be nice to get back home in good time and put his feet up. Heading along Wisteria Terrace, he double checked the address on the envelope in his hand. The drizzle had turned to a steady light rain, and the ink on the envelope had smudged. Now, what was the name, all but washed away, it was definitely Mrs, but was that Spinsburg? Was he sure? He thought of all the times Mrs Spindlebury had complained about him delivering Mrs Spinsburg's mail to her by mistake. Of course it wasn't always his fault, people were always getting confused between Wisteria Close and Wisteria Terrace. Throw in the similar names and no wonder things got muddled at times. But no, he was sure, this was addressed to 15 Wisteria Terrace, definitely not Wisteria Close, so it must be Mrs Spinsburg. He pushed it through the letterbox and hurried on along the road.

'What's that girl? Who's there? Is that a letter for Mummy?' Iris Spinsburg leant down and stroked her elderly Jack Russell, who murmured contentedly, before padding along with her owner to retrieve the post from the doormat.

'Oh look, it's all wet, good job we didn't go for our walkies yet isn't it?' Topsy looked up hopefully as Iris sank back into her armchair. 'No, it's raining, my little precious, we'll go out later.' She opened the envelope and removed its contents, reading the one line slowly, mystified.

I KNOW ALL YOUR SECRETS YOU DUMB BITCH.
YOUR HUSBAND'S A MURDERER.
I WATCHED HIM KILL HER.

Oh goodness, how awful. Her hand went to her breast, her heart beating rapidly. Was this to do with those terrible murders in the village? Well unless her husband had risen from the dead, they certainly weren't referring to her Derek, may he rest in peace, so it must have come to the wrong address. And no wonder, she thought, peering myopically at the smudged envelope, no-one could make sense of that. She popped one of her angina pills under her tongue, trying to stay calm. 'We'll ask our Deborah, she'll know what to do, won't she? She's coming to see us tomorrow, I expect she'll bring you some of those nice treats you like, yes, that's what we'll do.' She picked Topsy up and settled her on her lap, relieved to have found a temporary solution to a worrying problem.

~

What did it mean? Rosemary pondered Reg's behaviour over the newspapers. He'd picked up the paper from the doormat, upon their late evening return from their mini-break, saying he'd read it later and she'd not seen it since. Anxiety began to creep in, what was he hiding from her? She daren't ask him, but if she was to have a coffee at the Village Deli after her shopping today, she'd probably find the last day or two's papers there. Pleased with her plan she began making her shopping list in the kitchen.

~

Her tummy hurt. It was *his* fault, he'd made her eat all that food last night. She'd write one of her letters, her friends were right, that would make her feel better. Laying all her papers out on the bed, she contentedly tore out letters and glued them to the sheet of paper printed with farm animals. You're right, she laughed with them, she is a pig! A little piggy thief, stealing my baby like that.

Once all the glue had dried, she carefully addressed the envelope. Then she had an idea. What did they think? Yes, they said, do it. She would, she'd take it right to her. Pleased with her plan, Dorothy brushed her hair, clipped it with her flower clips, and sprayed on some Lavender Dreams. There, she was ready to face the pig thief.

~

George was feeling on edge, a feeling he supposed he should be used to by now. When would he hear something?

Surely the woman would run to the police? She wouldn't shield him, would she? He'd addressed it correctly hadn't he? Yes, he must have, but he did have a lot on his mind... With a sinking feeling in his stomach, he allowed himself to think about Dorothy. He should have called Dr Singh last night, he couldn't put off the inevitable. His wife was ill and needed help, more help than he was able to give. He couldn't continue trying to hide her condition from everyone, and who knew what stunt she might pull next time? He made his mind up, he'd go and talk to Doctor Singh.

~

Tessa and Dave were having a heated discussion, keeping their voices low, as they sat beside their daughter. 'Dave, you have to get help, you promised it would never happen again. You let me down and you let Chantelle down. What were you thinking?'

'I know, Tess, and I'm sorry. I will, I'll get help. I'll give it up, I don't know what happened. It was difficult, new town, new job, trying to start over, and then I heard about the poker nights, and well, it was just too tempting. I hated that you had to go back to work because of me, seeing you take in ironing for people as well, it broke me. I thought if I can just have a few wins, make a bit of extra money... I had this idea that we'd take a nice holiday, somewhere exotic, Chantelle would love it, it would be good for all of us.' He hunched over, holding his stomach, 'And now she might never go on holiday again.'

'Don't say that!' Tessa's eyes flashed. 'Never say that! She's going to wake up, she's going to be fine. But I'm serious, Dave, this is your last chance, if you ever gamble again it's over between us, I swear. We've been through enough.'

~

Mrs Pringle was alone in the chemist, when the bell jangled, signalling a customer. She fixed a smile on her face, looking up to see who it was. 'Oh it's you, Mrs Newton, how are you, Dorothy, are you alright?' Oh dear, her nose wrinkled as the unpleasant odour of unwashed body and clothes, mixed with, *was that Lavender Dreams?* reached her.

'You're a thief!' Dorothy shouted, looking around and laughing as if she had an audience 'You stole my baby, I hate you!' She thrust an envelope at Mrs Pringle, before turning and skipping back out of the store.

Not sure what to do first, Mrs Pringle looked at the envelope in her hand, before deciding to spray some air freshener. It wouldn't do for customers to come in and be subjected to such an unpleasant odour. Dorothy had been in the same dress, she was sure, as she'd been wearing that day she'd called in to check on her. Should she speak to Mr Newton about her? But surely the man knew something was wrong? And she certainly didn't want to be accused of meddling, she thought, still feeling vulnerable since the constable's visit.

Her name had been written, barely legibly, on the envelope, reminding her of the letter she'd taken from Dorothy, to post. Opening it, she pulled out the crackly sheet of paper and looked at the mess of torn letters and stickers decorating a sheet of farm animal stationery. Pig. It definitely spelled pig. Well that was unkind. And thief, yes, well, technically it said theif, but still... and then, baby? My baby? Sorry he's dead. Did it say that? It was no good, she couldn't make sense of it. It was a mad woman's ramblings. Clearly Dorothy was in need of help, Mrs Pringle would have to do her duty as the village pharmacist. She was, she felt, responsible for the well-being of the community. She'd have to take action. She needn't mention Dorothy's strange letter, there were enough other issues to raise. The next question was whether she should speak to Mr Newton, or to Doctor Singh?

MY WIFE HAS GONE COMPLETELY MAD

'Oh, Mum, why ever didn't you call me yesterday about this?' Deborah's face crinkled in concern. 'We have to take this to the police, I don't like the look of it at all, or its tone. I think it was meant for the murderer. No, now don't you go getting upset now, there's no way anyone would know it came to you by mistake. I wonder who it was meant for? Oh my goodness, Mum, d'you realise we may be about to help the police solve a murder? Or more than one? We mustn't tell anyone else about this. I'm going to call the police right now, I'll speak to Jane, that'll be best, she'll tell me what to do.'

Relieved, Deborah returned to her mother in the lounge. 'There, that's all sorted. Jane's at the hospital in Rentham, they've set up their incident room there or something. I said I'd take it to her there as it's on my way home. Right, let's have a quick cup of tea, to settle our nerves, then I'd best get going.'

~

'Sarge!' Jane Weaver was excited. 'I've just had a very interesting phone call from an old school friend of mine. Her mother's received an extremely strange letter, it's typed, like the others! It's from someone saying they saw a murder! She's bringing it to us now. This could be our break!'

~

Mrs Pringle had made up her mind. She'd go and speak to Dr Singh, he'd know what to do about poor Mrs Newton. And here was Sheila back now, no time like the present. She told Sheila she had business to attend to, and left for the doctor's.

~

Thanking her again, P.C. Jane Weaver said goodbye to her old school friend, and carefully laid the letter out on the table, as the others gathered round eagerly.

I KNOW ALL YOUR SECRETS YOU DUMB BITCH.

YOUR HUSBAND'S A MURDERER.
I WATCHED HIM KILL HER.

'What d'you think, Sarge? It's definitely not referring to Debbie's dad, he's been dead for a couple of years.'

'And where does her mother live again? Do we know the address?' Sergeant Denton was heading for the village street map fixed up on the wall.

'Er, that would be Wisteria Terrace, number fifteen, I used to go and play there as a kid. Her mother's name? Spinsburg, Iris Spinsburg.'

Nick Crossley circled the address on the map in red marker pen. 'What about the neighbours? Can you tell us anything about them, Jane? Maybe it was meant for one of them?'

'Bloody typical!' Sergeant Denton fumed. 'We get a letter directly referring to a woman's murder and we can't read the address on the envelope. Nick, keep trying to decipher it if you can, and call forensics, see if they can help. So, Jane? What about the neighbours?'

'To be honest, Sarge, I haven't been round there in a long time, couldn't tell you who lives next door even. Should I go and check them out?'

'Yes, but not in person, let's do our research first. I want details on everyone in Wisteria Terrace, as well as any other similar sounding surnames in the village, oh, and any other streets with similar names. What's that, Nick?'

'There's a Wisteria Close, as well as a Wisteria Avenue. Blimey, someone had a severe lack of imagination when they named the roads in the village, that's for sure.'

'Okay, then let's get started. Get me the surnames of everyone living in all three roads, and then we'll see what jumps out at us. We're getting close now, I'm sure of it.'

~

Dr Singh stood up, signalling the end of the meeting. 'Thank you for coming to me with your concerns, Mrs Pringle, I appreciate it. I cannot, of course, discuss Mrs Newton's medical conditions with you, although you will be aware of some situations due to the nature of your work. But please be assured that I will take everything you've told me very seriously, very seriously indeed.'

As Mrs Pringle was being shown out of the door to his office the outer surgery door opened. George Newton walked in, nodding at Mrs Pringle and greeting her distractedly. She hovered, trying to eavesdrop, not that she'd ever call it that, but the doctor closed his door behind George, with a polite smile at her.

'It's such a relief to talk to you, Doctor Singh, it really is.' George sat back, feeling as if a weight had been lifted from his shoulders just by telling the doctor his concerns for Dorothy's well-being. He'd told him everything, right down to the supermarket incident, putting his embarrassment aside when he informed the doctor about her lack of hygiene. No need to mention her letter writing though, that was just her private little hobby of course. With a deep breath, he finished with a final statement. 'I honestly think my wife has gone completely mad.'

Doctor Singh excused himself for a moment to order tea for them both from his receptionist. A cup of tea was always reassuring and calming, and he wanted Mr Newton to relax a little as they discussed their next move. He made a call from the front desk, nodding and thanking the person on the other end of the line.

With their tea served, Dr Singh spoke. 'I'm going to visit your wife later this morning, Mr Newton, if you can be there? Good. I'd like to assess her, but in light of what you've told me, I do feel that it might be an idea for Dorothy to spend some time in a place where she can receive the care she needs. It's clearly too much for you on your own, and there are places where she can receive round the clock care. It needn't be permanent, we can see how she gets on. You'll be able to visit of course. Here's a leaflet for Meadowvale. It's a lovely place, very comfortable, nice gardens, she'll have her own room of course. I've spoken to Mrs Goodwin, who runs Meadowvale, and she has a room available. Dorothy will be able to stay there for as long as she needs to.'

With a time confirmed for Dr Singh's visit, George left, filled with relief.

~

'Got it, Sarge! Mr and Mrs Spindlebury, fifteen Wisteria Avenue!' Nick Crossley practically danced around the tables in his excitement.

'Well, I'll be damned, that's Reg and Rosemary.' Sergeant Denton's brow creased in confusion, his mind trying to make sense of it all. This was a couple he'd enjoyed a drink with, here and there, he'd even played the odd round of golf with Reg. 'Now, no jumping to any conclusions everyone, let's keep an open mind until we've had a chat with them. There might be a simple explanation for all this.'

Nick and Jane shared a look. 'Sarge, with all due respect, the most likely simple explanation is that he did kill someone, isn't it? I mean, isn't that what all these letters are about? It's someone telling the truth, or their perception of the truth. Trouble is they're telling it to the wrong people. They should be telling us.'

Jane picked up the thread. 'Yes, why is that? It reeks of the old poison pen letters in murder mysteries, except those were sent to all and sundry to stir up trouble. These seem to go direct to the person or family concerned, or am I missing something? And, most important of all, who is actually writing the damn letters?'

It was Sergeant Denton's turn. 'You're not missing anything, Jane, although we have to assume there are two people involved somehow, judging by the two letter styles. As to who they are, we still have no idea. But I have to correct you on one point, I'm pretty sure these letters are still designed to stir things up.'

'So,' Nick spoke slowly, 'Who did he kill then? Who's the her in the letter? Is it the girl, Britney Morton? Is it Barbara Fenton? Or is it someone else?'

'Or is it all of them? Have we found a serial killer in our midst?' They all swivelled round to look at Inspector Kavanagh, who had quietly entered the room a minute or two earlier. 'Did Reg Spindlebury take the lives of Peter Ford,

Barbara Fenton, and Britney Morton? And if so, do we assume that he also kidnapped Chantelle Watson with a view to taking her life also?'

'Well, one stroke of luck is that this letter went to the wrong address, so he's unaware that someone saw him kill someone. And he's also unaware that we have the letter. What should we do, Sir, bring him in straightaway?'

Inspector Kavanagh nodded at P.C. Weaver. 'Let's get him to the station and have a chat with him. No need to alarm him, we just have a few questions to ask him regarding recent events. Nick, you go with Jane. Sergeant Denton and I'll meet you back at the station.'

MOTHER ALWAYS KNEW BEST

About to tell Reg that she was off shopping, and having delayed telling him until the last second, Rosemary stopped in her tracks as the doorbell rang. She could just about make out two darkly dressed figures through the mottled glass of the front door, and a knot formed in her stomach.

'Mrs Spindlebury? I'm P.C. Weaver and this is P.C. Crossley, is your husband around?' Jane Weaver's eyes searched the hallway behind Rosemary for signs of movement. 'We'd like to ask him a few questions.'

Reg appeared from the living room, a big smile on his face. 'Nothing to worry about, girl, expect I've forgotten to pay a parking ticket or something. What can I do you for, Officers?'

'Morning, Mr Spindlebury, we'd like you to come with us to the station, if you don't mind, we just have a few questions to ask you.' Jane returned his smile with her own, noting his wife's anxious expression.

'Oh, no need for that, come in, come in, Ro'll put the kettle on.'

It was Nick's turn. 'I'm afraid not, Sir, we'd like you to accompany us to the station, now, please, it's for the best.'

'Oh, Reg,' Rosemary's face crumpled as tears formed in her eyes, 'What's it about? What have you done?'

His grip on his wife's arm was tight, both officers noticed, as he turned her away from the door. 'Quiet, girl, you hear me? It's nothing. Now, you stay here like a good girl, alright? Nice and quiet does it.' His slightly threatening tone was instantly replaced with a pleasant one, once more, as he turned back to them. 'I'm all yours, I'm sure we can clear up whatever it is, in a jiffy, it'll just be a misunderstanding of some sort.'

Rosemary watched them get into the police car, filled with dread. What did they know? Was it ancient history, or more recent? It must be the former, they'd arrested that chap for the killings, so they must have found out something about her and Reg's past. But why did they only want to speak to Reg then? Bile rose in her throat, and she ran to the cloakroom, lifting the lid of the toilet just in time.

~

Dorothy was humming happily, rocking back and forth in her chair, when George showed Dr Singh into the living room. 'Dorothy dear, here's the nice doctor, he's going to have a little chat with you.'

She loved staying in hotels! Always such fun! What a pity George was too busy to be able to come with her. Dear Dr Singe, she'd misjudged him, he was so sweet, wanting to help her, understanding how hard it was for her to do everything at home all on her own. And George was being so nice, packing a bag for her, asking her what she wanted to take with her. Her writing box! She had to have her special things with her, she might need to write some letters while she was on holiday. George had nodded, of course, and she'd watched her precious box being placed safely into her bag.

~

Mrs Goodwin greeted Dorothy kindly, making a big fuss of her, and showed her to her room, telling her she'd be back in a few minutes to settle her in. 'You won't want to make a big fuss when you say goodbye, Mr Newton, no need to upset her. Visit whenever you wish, but trust me, your wife's in good hands, I'm sure she'll be very happy here.'

Oh it was delightful! And such a lovely view of the garden! Silly old George, getting all tearful on her, it wasn't her fault he was too busy to stay with her. And such a nice manageress, the personal touch, that was what was missing at so many hotels these days. Dorothy nodded to herself, yes, this was a good choice. She unpacked her bag, placing her special box on the desk and lining up all her dolls on the shelf, smiling happily at Mrs Goodwin as they discussed what she'd like for her lunch. The suggestion of a nice spa bath was made, best to enjoy that before lunch, didn't she think? And Dorothy was having such fun that she'd agreed. She wouldn't even have to lift a finger! Mrs Goodwin would send along Janet to give her a special pampering session. She was beginning to feel like a very special little girl indeed.

~

Having drunk some water and washed her face, Rosemary shakily sat down at the kitchen table. Maybe this was it. Maybe the law had caught up with them. Unless it was, oh, she could hardly bear to think of it, but what if it was about Barbara Fenton? Which meant that the police didn't think the other man had done it. But why would they think of Reg? And why had Reg been hiding the papers from her anyway? Taking her out, the overnight stay? She'd known something was up, she always had done, with Reg, she just tried to bury it, generally, life was easier that way.

Pulling on her rubber gloves she made up her mind, opening the back door and lifting the tied-up rubbish bag from the dustbin. Screwing up her nose distastefully, Rosemary sifted through the contents until she found what she was looking for. Nodding grimly, she unfolded the two papers, and laid them out on the ground. Never mind the tea stains and potato peelings, the headlines on both papers were clearly legible.

'LOCAL MAN FREED!'
'SERIAL KILLER STILL AT LARGE!'
'MISSING GIRL FOUND ALIVE!'
'GIRL STILL IN COMA!'

Forcing herself to remain calm, she carefully placed the papers back into the bottom of the rubbish bag, tied it up and put it back into the dustbin. Back inside, Rosemary slumped into the nearest chair. Well, that was that, then. Reg *had* killed Barbara, after all, and the Police would be arresting him for it. But he couldn't have had anything to do with the girls, surely? Reg never did anything without a reason. No, but the Police might think otherwise, unless they knew his reason for killing Barbara. But that would mean confessing... about everything... Her head was spinning. Enough, stop thinking about it all. She'd make some tea and ponder her options.

~

The news of Reg Spindlebury's alleged arrest spread like wildfire. In fact, it was one of the rare occasions when Mrs Pringle was almost the last to hear the news. It was Mr Newton who'd told her, and him never one for a good gossip generally. But he'd been in fine fettle, positively jaunty, when he'd all but waltzed into the chemist shop.

Oh well, of course, the man was obviously relieved about his wife, that's what it would be, Dr Singh must have taken action. Yes, yes, he'd said, she was fine, thank you, but Dorothy would be spending some time at Meadowvale, in fact he'd taken her there a little earlier. Just for a little rest, he'd been careful to point out, help ease her stress, she'd had a lot to cope with lately.

Mrs Pringle had nodded sagely, murmured the right words of encouragement and understanding, and then her sharpened senses had honed in on his agitated manner, his barely contained excitement. She was an expert at drawing gossip from people, years of practice had made her so, and it was like taking candy from a baby as she gently extracted every piece of information about Reg Spindlebury from a helpless Mr Newton.

Sheila looked on, trying to hide her admiration. She had to hand it to the woman, she could smell a story a mile away, and no-one could withstand her powers of interrogation.

'Well, well!' Breathed Mrs Pringle, exhaling satisfyingly as she tried to keep her excitement in check. 'Reginald Spindlebury, as I live and die! A serial killer, and with a wife too, don't tell me she didn't know anything about his goings on? And who knows how many he's killed? And there we were, murdered too, but for the love of God, every night we slept in our beds thinking we were safe.'

Mr Newton was off to his mother to tell her the good news, he'd informed them, as he'd fluffed around at the selection of ladies' scarves, albeit rather old, having sat there since the year before. He would take her a gift, a little treat, she did love neck scarves. Seeing the expression on both Mrs Pringle's and Sheila's faces, he'd stammered slightly, explaining that he meant the good news about dear Dorothy, of course. 'Terrible news about Reg, of course, very upsetting, very unpleasant.'

Oh yes, they'd both nodded in agreement, terrible, but at least they could all feel safe now, with him behind bars. And that poor girl in hospital, Sheila had pointed out, she'd be able to give them all the evidence they needed, wouldn't she, once she woke up? *If* she ever woke up, Mrs Pringle had added, in a sinister tone, after all, every day that passed things looked less promising there.

~

'Ta Da!' George trilled around with the scarf he'd bought Mother, waving it around her shoulders, until they'd both collapsed in fits of giggles. He loved it when he made her laugh, it was the best feeling in the world. 'Gifts, Mother! Gifts for my special girl, look what else I've got you, some chocolate digestives, yes, I know, naughty, and some coconut ice, to have later, you know how much you like it. I know, I remember everything, Mother,' he beamed, as he lovingly draped the scarf around her neck.

He basked in Mother's approval when he told her about Dorothy, agreeing that she was in the best place, and of course, she'd never been able to look after him as he deserved, as Mother had done. There was a tricky moment when George mentioned that Dorothy had taken her writing box with her. He'd quickly placated Mother, seeing her worried expression. Dorothy could play around with her stickers and her letters to her heart's content he'd laughed, they wouldn't mean anything to anyone, no-one had ever seen one. They'd had a good chuckle over that, which felt wonderful.

It was a fabulous evening, everything had gone so well, Mother had been proud, had said some really sweet things to him, made him feel on top of the world. He'd felt like a real man, a man who takes care of things, who deals with problems. His mistake had been in saying that to Mother.

Who takes care of things? She'd screamed at him, suddenly. *Who deals with problems? There's a problem sitting right there in the hospital in Rentham and what are you doing about it? Nothing, that's what!* He'd sat down on the rug, clasping her bony knees, pleading for her to stop. It wasn't a problem, not really, she probably wouldn't wake up, he'd whined, hoping desperately that she would agree with him. But Mother always knew best, yes, he'd nodded, yes, of course, he'd deal with it. Soon.

YOU ALWAYS THINK YOU'LL KNOW

Sasha and Cal arrived at the hospital to find the incident room locked up, the cleaner informing them that they'd all rushed off yesterday, amidst great excitement. 'You'll have heard about the arrest of course,' she said, nodding her head. 'My aunt phoned me earlier, she cleans up at one of the posh houses in Parva Crossing, said they took him with them in the car. Looked regular guilty, she reckoned. And them living the life of riley in their flash house, throwing their money around, and him a real-life serial killer. Oh,' she put her hand to her mouth. 'Apologies, your poor niece, what a narrow escape.'

'Who the hell are you talking about?' Cal's confusion was written all over his face.

'Oh, you didn't know? Why, it's that Mr Spindlebury, that one with the wife always dolled up to the nines, her with her airs and graces. Full of herself she was, when I was over there at the pub one time with my aunt. This'll bring her down a peg or two, that's for sure.'

Cal took Sasha's hand as they hurried up to Chantelle's room to see if Tessa and Dave were there. 'D'you think Tess and Dave know?'

Not having heard a thing, Dave cursed and thumped the wall in frustration. 'Why haven't they told us? We're the flaming parents. And who is he, this Spindlebury? I swear, if he did this to Chantelle I'll kill him.'

'Dave, for goodness' sake, calm down, if they knew something they'd tell us,' Tess pleaded.' We don't even know if it's anything to do with Chantelle.'

'Calm down? How the hell can I? When is this going to end? It's a bloody nightmare and there's nothing I can do, I've got no control over anything. I feel like I'm going mad.'

Reading the situation, Sasha looked at Cal, who suggested he and Dave go and get a coffee.

'Tess, listen to me, darling, you and Dave have spent virtually every minute here since Chants was found, no wonder things have got snappy between you. Yes, I know, I understand about his problem, but you have to put that aside for now, at least until we know where things stand with Chants. I honestly think you both need a little time out, a break from the hospital, and give each other a bit of space for a day or two. Spend some time at home, catch up on things, Dave needs to get back to work too. You can't live at the hospital, just pop in for an hour each day for now, they'll call you immediately if there's any change, you know that. Cal and I will pop in and check on her each day too. Go and get Dave from the cafeteria and go home. I'm sure the police will let you know straightaway if they have anything new, otherwise we'll try to find out, okay?'

Tessa finally agreed to her sister's suggestions, and, with Sasha having promised to check back on Chantelle later, headed home with Dave.

'So what do we do now? Do we call at the station, see if we can speak to someone?'

'I'll try to speak to Nick, see if he'll tell us what's going on.' But Nick was unavailable, as were all the officers, he was informed.

'The Spindleburys, that's the couple you pointed out to me in the coffee shop isn't it?' At Cal's nod, Sasha carried on, 'So they must think he's connected to something in all this, the question is, which part? Some of it, all of it? Barbara? Even Peter? The girls? I just can't get my head around it all. What do we do? How do we find out?'

'We can't, not really, not until we can speak to Nick. You're holding your stomach, are you alright?' Cal glanced at Sasha in concern.

'I'm fine, just a bit sore, I've run out of pain killers, I meant to say I need to call at the chemist to get some more, is that okay?'

~

Mrs Pringle tried to hide her excitement as her customers entered the shop, knowing she'd have to tread carefully. 'Well, hello to you two dears. How's your dear sister and her husband taking the news? What a shock, I must say, none of us could ever have imagined it was Reg Spindlebury, not that I was ever fond of the man, but you always think you'll know, don't you, when someone's bad? And I'm just so relieved now, you know, I could have said the wrong thing, the police asking so many questions, get you all confused don't they? And there was me nearly telling them about the extra sleeping pills and all that fly spray, when it would have sent them down the wrong path good and proper. And that poor man, he's got enough on his plate, no, thank the Lord that I kept my counsel and didn't go jabbering away about other people's business. His poor wife's in the best place now, of course, getting the help she needs, yes.' Pausing for breath, Mrs Pringle realised her customers hadn't said one word, and, feeling embarrassed, hurriedly asked them if she could help with anything.

With business conducted, Cal enquired as to the actual facts surrounding Reg Spindlebury's arrest, to which Mrs Pringle confessed, as Sheila looked on, that they didn't actually have any, other than the fact that he was taken to the police station. So yes, that was true, it could be to do with anything at all, although surely, when all was said and done... Looking a little shifty, Mrs Pringle asked them if they could give her a moment, and there followed a whispered discussion with Sheila, who then took her purse and left the shop.

Clearing her throat, Mrs Pringle asked them if she could just run something by them, as she knew they'd been trying to help with the whole situation in the village, a bit like private detectives perhaps, and they'd know about the rumours of those letters? Giving a little embarrassed laugh, she began. 'Look, I'm sure it's nothing, and she's getting help now but, well, the poor lamb, it was the other day you see, I just popped round to check on her, and she was in such a tizz.'

Totally confused by now, Cal and Sasha looked at Mrs Pringle in wonder. 'Who, exactly, Mrs Pringle?'

'Oh yes, poor Dorothy, Mrs Newton, she's been having some issues, all under control now, but I said I'd post it for her, then I realised she hadn't addressed it properly, just his name, and of course, she meant it for the wife, so I corrected it and wrote the address on, you see. And then, when she rolled in here, all in a state, well, she said some things I won't repeat, of course I don't hold it against her, but then she gave me a letter, well, not a letter really, more like something a child would make, you know, letters torn out and such like. She said something about me taking her baby, called me a thief! Me! And of course she doesn't have a baby, well I'm sure you know that. And I just know she wouldn't be behind any kind of poison pen letters, so I didn't want to stir things up...'

'Mrs Pringle, hold on.' Sasha's head was reeling. 'Do you still have the letter?'

Pursing her lips and looking a little embarrassed, Mrs Pringle fetched her handbag from the little kitchenette area behind the counter. She removed a rather crumpled envelope from one of its many pockets. 'Like I said, she wasn't herself, not making any sense at all really, doesn't know what she's saying, poor thing. All a load of nonsense, but well, when I came to think about it, what with the letter for poor Mr Ford, well, his dear widow, of course, well, here it is.'

Sasha took the paper out of the envelope and opened it up on the counter, where all three gazed at it. 'Yes, I see what you mean, Mrs Pringle, it certainly doesn't make any sense at all.'

'Is that? Does that spell out *pig*?' Cal squinted at the jumble of paper cuttings glued to the page. 'I definitely think she's saying you stole something, Mrs Pringle.' Cal was feeling quite amused. 'But yes, she's sorry, or wanted to say sorry, about something. A he, or him, for being dead.'

'Look, like you said, this lady's obviously not quite well, Mrs Pringle,' Sasha placated. 'But, I tell you what, why don't Cal and I take this, if you don't mind? We can check it out a little further, see if we can put your mind at rest, how's that?'

'Oh, would you, dears?' Mrs Pringle's relieved smile told them that she was glad to offload this strange item onto someone else. 'She's at Meadowvale, by the way, if it helps.'

And with goodbyes said, as the bell signalled the arrival of a customer, Sasha and Cal left the chemist.

'I don't know, Cal, this is so freaking weird, don't you think? I mean, it can't actually *mean* anything, can it, it's just some sad old lady who's lost her marbles? So, she wrote, or tried to write, to Maureen, or Peter, if what Mrs Pringle is saying is right, which is what we also thought, and Mrs Pringle interfered, *no surprises there*, and she got upset with her, hence this little work of art.'

'Yeah, it can't be connected to the other letters, just one of those weird coincidences, but still, what d'you reckon? Should we show it to the cops? Or would we just look crazy ourselves?'

'Well, we did take them the one Maureen received, but maybe we should find out a little more first? We could go and visit her, what's Meadowvale, a care home I'm guessing? Oh hell, I promised Tess I'd check on Chantelle, told her to take some time out.'

Agreeing to head through to the hospital after having some lunch, they found a table at a rather quaint touristy spot overlooking the river, and proceeded to enjoy some delicious quiche and salad, the lunch of the day.

ORDER AND METHOD

George had passed a sleepless night, not least because Mother's words played in his mind in a loop, but also because it was the first night he'd spent alone in the house. His wife might have lost her marbles, and been a huge problem, but still, the house felt dreadfully quiet without her. He'd have to get used to it of course, at least for the foreseeable future. But more importantly, he'd worried about just what Mother expected him to do.

Talk had buzzed around the offices all morning, Reg Spindlebury's arrest was the hottest topic, it seemed. The general consensus appeared to be that he was singlehandedly responsible for everything that had blighted the village in recent weeks. And it had to stay that way, decided George. He'd have to do it in his lunch hour, Ramsbottom might not take too kindly to him taking yet more time off. Do what though? Well, he'd have to see about that once he was there, assuming he could access the girl.

It wasn't as difficult as he'd feared, finding out which room the girl was in. Visiting hours being between midday and two o'clock meant that the corridors were peppered with friends and family wandering around looking for their loved ones, bunches of flowers in hand. A handy board opposite the nurses' station on each floor listed the patients' names and room numbers.

George blended in easily, and was able to locate Chantelle's room with ease, peering through the window in the door, to make sure there was no-one else in there. He figured if no visitors were with her now they would be unlikely to come until the evening. A curtain partially obscured the bed and he could see blankets covering the bottom part of it. Quietly opening the door, he slipped inside, hearing the gentle beep of monitors. And there she was, lying there motionless. Looking around, his eyes settled on the spare pillow on the chair next to the bed. Perfect.

~

She'd decided she'd have to face up to whatever was going on with Reg. The police officer had graciously called her to say that Reg would be staying with them overnight but couldn't tell her anything further, and she'd ended up spending a strangely pleasant evening on her own. A bottle of wine added to the experience and she wondered if this was how her life would be, if they found Reg guilty of Barbara's murder. She pushed the other darker thoughts away, there was no reason to suspect they knew anything about Reg's past history. She was beginning to see it as Reg's past, not hers, she was innocent in it all really, at least, that's what she'd tell them if they asked. So, to the police station she would go.

~

'I've told you a million times, I don't know anything about those girls, or anyone, for that matter.' Reg was tired and irritated, not to mention furious at being detained overnight, and his head was throbbing, which didn't help. He tried to think, as he'd been doing the best part of his uncomfortable night. They hadn't asked him one question about the cash job. So, he could relax about that, if they knew anything they'd have mentioned it by now. No, this was about Barbara Fenton, had to be, that blasted woman who started all the trouble, that's if you didn't count his stupid wife with her great big gob. But then why hadn't they just come out with it and asked him straight? Unless they didn't have any evidence, were just poking around in the dark...

'Tell us again about Peter Ford, Reg. We know you played golf with him on occasion. Have a falling out did you? What happened, did he catch you watching the young girls? Who caught your eye first? Was it Britney Morton? Hot little bit was she? You like them young don't you, Reg? Maybe your own wife doesn't do it for you anymore, too old to get you going. Or was it his wife who caught your eye? She's not young, but she's an attractive woman. Peter got upset with you when he saw you checking out his wife, did he? So you had to shut him up? We know the girls were seen following you when we found his body, did that make you angry? Is that what made you snap and take them captive, Reg?' Sergeant Denton sat back, glancing at P.C. Crossley to continue.

'What we don't get is how Barbara fits into it all, Reg, help us out here. What was the story, was she jealous? Had her sights on you did she? Maybe you rejected her and she wouldn't leave you alone? She'd been friends with your wife hadn't she? And Peter's wife? Cosy little set-up by the sounds of it, all friends together. Or did she catch you looking at the schoolgirls and get upset about it? Or are we barking up the wrong tree here, Reg? Maybe you and Barbara were having an affair and you wanted it to end, but she became a bit of a bunny boiler? Is that how it all played out? Is that why you strangled her? Going to tell your wife, was she? Come on, Reg, give us something, let's get this over with.'

Reg shook his head back and forth, slowly, gritting his teeth in frustration. 'What. The. Fuck?'

Sergeant Denton spoke again. 'Now, come on, Reg, no need for that talk. Where did you keep the young girls, Reg? Let's start there.'

'For the last bloody time, I never took the girls, I never kept them anywhere, and I never killed them!' A vein pulsed in Reg's temple, his red face angry as he spluttered in exasperation.

'Whoah, steady on, Reg, one of them's still alive. Of course, once she wakes up she'll tell us everything, but you could make things easier on yourself by coming clean now.' Nick sat back, a smile on his face. 'I tell you what, why don't we take a break, get some tea, give you a few minutes to think about everything.'

Reg sat in the interview room, watching the steam drifting up from the white mug. It was beginning to dawn on him that the police had pretty much decided that he'd killed Peter Ford, Barbara Fenton, and Britney Morton, and that he'd abducted Chantelle Watson. But why? That's what he couldn't get his head around. Why would they even connect him to Barbara's murder, there was no evidence, he'd been careful not to touch anything while he was there. What the hell did they have that was making them go on and on about it?

Inspector Andrew Kavanagh sat looking from one to the other as Philip Denton and Nick Crossley filled him in on the latest questioning session with Reg. When they'd finished, he glanced at Jane, who'd been standing quietly just inside his office. 'Yes, Jane, what's up?'

'Mrs Spindlebury's here, Sir, wants to know what's going on with her husband. What should I tell her?'

'Well, I reckon poor Mrs Spindlebury could benefit from some tea and sympathy, don't you, Jane? How about taking her into the family room, more comfy there, and see if you can get her talking. Give her little bits of information, just enough to get a response, see where it goes. All informal, of course, but if anything rings an alarm, call a stop to it and come talk to me, okay? Right, back to Mr Spindlebury.'

'What do we think? Overall gut feeling? Are we on the right tracks here, gentlemen?' Andrew Kavanagh again looked from one to the other.

'To be honest, Sir, unless we can tie him to any of these deaths forensically, we need him to give us something. Right now he's just fuming, he's angry, stubborn, and refusing to say anything, pretty much, other than denials.'

Nick picked up the thread. 'One thing I did notice, for what it's worth. He seemed more anxious and wound up to begin with, before we started questioning him. As we started asking him about the different victims he seemed to become more confident. Not sure what that means, but something changed slightly. Maybe we need to separate the victims out, stop grouping them together. Concentrate on the females, one at a time.'

'And show him the letter. I'd say it's time, see what his reaction to that is.'

Sergeant Denton was nodding. 'Right, Sir, we'll get back to it if that's all. Nick?'

~

'I don't know what it is about this place, but the food just tastes so damn good everywhere.' Sasha rubbed her belly, feeling full, as Cal drove them towards Rentham hospital. 'The trouble is I keep feeling guilty, like I shouldn't be enjoying all these pleasures when so much awful stuff has happened. D'you know what I mean?'

Cal grinned, 'Yes, I know, but we have to eat, and it can't be helped if the food's so good. The joys of living in a touristy area I suppose, everyone has to stay on top of their game. Anyway, nothing wrong with enjoying pleasures... There's another one I'm looking forward to enjoying with you, very soon, I hope...' His wink gave her the usual little flutter inside, and she laughed, squeezing his firm thigh affectionately.

~

George stiffened, the pillow in his hand. The voices were suddenly louder, as the door swung open, the two nurses chatting animatedly about something. He rushed into the bathroom, still holding the pillow, and stood there silently, trying to hold his breath.

'Anyway, I told him he could go and run, no way was I going to do that, thank you very much.' The other nurse laughed out loud. 'I don't blame you, what a weirdo! Next he'll be asking if he can borrow your nurse's uniform. Oh, what are we like? We clean forgot to stop next door, too busy chatting, that's us. Poor Mrs Tomlinson's dressing won't change itself will it? We'd better do that first, before matron ticks us off, it'll only take a minute, then come and see to our poor little girl here.' The voices faded as the door swung closed again.

Trembling, George, peered out of the bathroom. What on earth would he have said if they'd caught him in Chantelle's room? He had no justifiable reason for being there, not one. He'd be looked at with great suspicion. He returned the pillow to the chair and quickly exited the room. He'd wait just along the corridor on one of the visitors' chairs, and go back in once the nurses had done whatever it was they had been about to do.

~

Sasha waited by the lift while Cal bought them some water, feeling sad that they weren't bringing Chantelle a gift. How wonderful it would be if they were visiting her with a gift that she would open with a smile, chatting away about how much better she felt. Stay positive, Sash, she told herself, any day now...

~

Watching the nurses unobtrusively, as they left Chantelle's room, George tried to muster his failing courage. He could hear Mother's voice haranguing him, *Get on with it you useless boy, do it, do it now!* Checking his watch he realised he only had minutes to spare before he needed to head back to work. He stood up too quickly and felt a rush of dizziness but, trying to ignore it, he stumbled along the corridor towards the room. A couple coming in the other direction were in his way and as he was about to reach for the door handle he registered their slowing pace, watching with horror as the man reached for the door and opened it. The woman looked at him quizzically as he muttered apologies and shuffled past, knocking her arm as his continuing dizziness disorientated him.

'Are you alright?' Sasha asked him, feeling concern for the elderly, frail looking man. He ignored her, and she watched him put out his arm to steady himself against the wall. Poor thing, maybe he'd just had bad news. She watched him for a few seconds more, relieved to see him straighten up and walk off with a steadier gait. Entering Chantelle's room she went to the bed and gave her niece a gentle kiss on her forehead. 'Hi Chants, it's Sash, how are you my love?'

~

What was he going to tell Mother? She'd be furious, he could hear her already, her cruel, cold, laugh when she told him how useless he was. He wondered why he'd never told her what he'd done for her, all those years ago. Of course, he knew why really, could still remember his shock at how quickly she'd changed. All he'd really done was exchange one problem for a new one. And all these years later, here he still was, still seeking her approval, and still trying to make things right. For once, he was quite relieved to be going back to work, even if he had failed in his mission. He needed a little order and method to calm him. That made him smile. How often they'd shared a conspiratorial grin as their favourite Belgian detective had admonished his friend with those very words. He'd loved their reading evenings, their shared pleasure as each mystery unfolded. 'This woman is the Queen of crime,' Mother would say, in thrall to the beloved author. 'But you're my queen, Mummy,' he'd always reply, and they'd laugh and collapse in cuddles on the couch.

A loud prolonged hoot from the van behind him snapped him out of his reverie, and George quickly turned at the traffic lights, making it back to work just a couple of minutes late.

~

With a message sent to Tess, letting her know that Chantelle was stable, although no change, Sasha and Cal went on their way to Meadowvale. 'Is it just me or do you also feel that we're getting close to finding something out?' Sasha looked at Cal, feeling excited, but not sure why.

'Finding out that some poor old dear is a basket case, maybe, not sure what else we'll find out.' Cal grinned at her. 'But I must say, I'm intrigued enough to see if we can get any sense out of her.'

'Well, me too, and I just keep getting this feeling that it's a strange coincidence that two letters found their way to Maureen's house, one typed, for Maureen, and one from this poor old thing, meant for Peter. I keep feeling like there's a link there somewhere, only I'm not seeing it. Oh well, here we are, let's see what we find out.'

Mrs Goodwin walked towards them, as they waited at reception, a welcoming smile on her face. 'How lovely, friends of Dorothy's I understand? She'll be delighted to have visitors, I'm sure.' Not waiting for them to correct her assumption, she called over a passing staff member and instructed him to take them to see Dorothy.

'Well, that was easy,' Cal murmured out of the side of his mouth, as they followed the care assistant, whose name badge declared him to be Greg. 'I just hope we can work out which one's her.'

STRUMPET WHORE

Dorothy was sitting in the residents' lounge and, as the other three occupants were fast asleep, and thanks to Greg's announcement, 'Yoohoo, Dorothy, how are you today, my darling? Who's a lucky girl and gone and got herself some visitors then? That's right, you, my precious.' It was made abundantly obvious who Dorothy was, therefore nullifying Cal's fear.

Dorothy smiled happily, rocking back and forth rapidly in her chair, allowing Greg to take her hand and pretend to bend over and kiss it. 'Love you,' she gurgled, simpering, before looking away coyly.

'And I love you too, darling,' Greg was nothing if not an enthusiastic carer, in every way it seemed. I'll bring you all some tea, how's that?' Their thanks were hardly noticed as Greg was already off towards the door marked 'kitchen', with a wave.

Sasha smiled at Dorothy, not quite sure where to begin. 'Er, Dorothy, you don't know us but I'm Sasha and this is Cal.' Dorothy's eyes kept glancing at Cal, making him slightly uncomfortable. 'We came to visit you because we saw your beautiful letter you made for Mrs Pringle.' At this, Dorothy's eyes gave a tiny spark of something, which urged Sasha on. 'You remember Mrs Pringle don't you, from the chemist?'

'Thief!' Dorothy spluttered, rocking faster, 'Little piggy, she took my baby.' She looked upset, and Sasha, concerned about the imminent arrival of the tea, tried to soothe her. 'Yes, how unkind, but she's very sorry, she didn't mean to upset you. She told us.'

'She is?' Dorothy looked up, in a rare moment of lucidity. 'Well good, she shouldn't have taken it from me in the first place, I always post my own letters.'

They waited quietly while a girl in an apron placed the tea tray down, before thanking her and turning their attention back to Dorothy.

Cal took a turn. 'Dorothy, do you remember Mrs Ford, Mr Ford's wife?'

The reaction was surprising. Dorothy's voice was harsh and spiteful as she spat words out. 'Whore! Slut! Poor man, I told him. I told everyone. So many bad things.' She suddenly stared at Cal, 'You!' Her finger pointed at him as her eyes glared, but then she leant back, turning her head to the side, as if listening to someone. A crafty smile played on her lips as she nodded and made whispering sounds. She suddenly clapped her hands in delight and laughed, before getting out of her chair and making for the tea tray.

Sasha quickly intervened. 'Here, let me pour the tea, why don't you sit down and relax, Dorothy?' She glanced at Cal in confusion, wondering how to proceed.

But Dorothy dictated the next move by stamping her feet and stubbornly saying, 'No, not with him. Bad.'

'Shush, shush, don't worry, he's leaving now. It's just you and me, that's better.' Sasha placated Dorothy, sitting her back down as Cal quietly edged away and made his way to the corridor. 'Why is he bad, Dorothy? D'you want to tell me? And Maureen? Mrs Ford? Did she do something wrong? Is that why you wrote to Mr Ford?' Sasha felt as though she were on the brink of understanding something, but it eluded her, as she strained to understand Dorothy's mutterings, her lucid interval now over.

'Booted you has she?' Greg waltzed over to Cal, as he spotted him in the corridor. 'She can be a real little whatsit at times but you've got to love her haven't you?' Cal agreed, hoping that Greg wouldn't start asking awkward questions about their connection to Dorothy. But Greg was on his own mission. 'Poor thing spends most of the time tearing up bits of paper and sticking them on other bits of paper, keeps her happy though, hums away she does, gets all secretive on us, thinks we don't notice, so we pretend not to see.'

Cal tried to compute the information, 'Er, don't notice what exactly? What do you pretend not to see?'

'Oh well, firstly we pretend we don't see where she hides her wooden box that she seems to find very important. She gets very worried if the cleaners get too close to it. We've checked it of course, made sure there's nothing harmful in it, but it's just packed full of bits of newspaper, glue, flowery paper, that kind of stuff. Hey, if it makes her happy that's fine with us. And then off she goes, down the garden somewhere all important like, clutching her latest envelope like she's off to the post office or something! Bless her heart. That reminds me, I must ask the gardener where she's putting them, must be quite a pile of them stashed somewhere by now.' With a laugh, Greg took his leave of Cal, 'Things to do, people to see. Coming, Mary,' he called out, as a harassed carer's face appeared from a doorway further along the corridor.

Sasha was feeling pretty nonplussed. Dorothy's tears were running down her face as she sobbed quietly, rocking back and forth, her arms wrapped around her body. 'I said I was sorry. It should have been her, not him. He was a good man.'

'There, there,' Sasha frantically tried to placate Dorothy, sure that she was going to be asked to leave by a staff member at any moment. Dorothy's words ignited a memory. She'd heard them before hadn't she? Where though? And then it came to her, Maureen!

'Strumpet whore!' Dorothy spat the words out. 'With him! Scarlet woman, I saw them hanging there, red and black lace. I had to tell him.' Nodding, Dorothy leant back, a sly smile on her face.

With a jolt of shock Sasha realised she was talking about Cal. She remembered Cal showing her his preliminary work on Maureen's painting. Maureen was wearing scarlet panties with black lace. Was this how it all started? A simple misunderstanding by an elderly woman? She needed to talk to Cal, see if they could come up with anything useful from this.

'Dorothy, I have to go. Thank you for seeing me, maybe I'll come and visit you again. Would that be alright?' But Dorothy had returned to her humming, smiling at various of the empty chairs nearby.

She found Cal outside and they both rolled their eyes. 'Anything useful?' Cal asked, getting the car keys out of his pocket.

'Well a couple of things actually. Firstly, I think we can be pretty sure that she sent Maureen, or rather, Peter, that little piece of art. She just repeated the words almost verbatim. And secondly, you're going to need to brace yourself, Cal, this isn't so great. She saw you visiting Maureen, at least I'm almost certain that's what she was trying to tell me. I think she thought you were having an affair.'

'What?' Cal's face paled in horror. 'This is awful, what do we tell Maureen? So hold on, if she wrote to Peter to tell him she was sorry, it should have been Maureen, was that it or had she sent something to Peter before?'

'And who sent Maureen the other letter, the typed one? Telling her she was the sinner or whatever?' Sasha got into the passenger seat as Cal started the engine. 'Definitely not Dorothy, she's not in a fit state to type letters that's for sure. And we're pretty sure, thanks to Von, that Peter received a typed letter right at the beginning of all this.'

As they headed down the long driveway contemplating the different origins of the letters, Cal suddenly remembered what he'd meant to tell Sasha.

'Oh I nearly forgot, I was chatting to that carer, Greg, was it? Yeah, well, he was laughing about Dorothy, they're all obviously pretty fond of her or find her amusing at least. So anyway, she's been writing letters, sticking bits of paper on other bits of paper, you know. Does it all in secret, although they keep their eye on her. Says she's got this special box she keeps hidden with all her papers inside. Oh and then, get this, she goes off down the garden to post them. At least that's what he reckons is in her head. He said he was going to ask the gardener where she's been putting them.'

Something pinged in Sasha's brain. A tiny ping, already fading as she tried to grasp at it, before it eluded her completely. Something to do with the garden.

'What's that about the garden?' Cal looked at her enquiringly.

'Oh sorry, I must have been thinking out loud. Cal, something's bugging me, but I can't remember what it's about. Something to do with gardens, the village, damn, what was it? Is there some weird history in Parva Crossing, something in the gardens, like, I dunno, old milestones from Roman times or something, but not actually milestones? Old post boxes! Victorian post boxes, that's it! I read it somewhere, I'm trying to think where, must have been at the pub. Cal, we need to go back! Turn round! We need to speak to Dorothy again!'

Cal was trying to keep up with Sasha as she hurried towards the entrance of Meadowvale again. 'Sash, you gonna explain? What's going on?' He stopped as Sasha explained to the receptionist that they'd forgotten to tell Dorothy something very important and could they just visit her again for a few minutes?

Sasha's face was flushed with excitement as she pulled Cal by the hand. 'Bear with me, it'll be quicker to ask Dorothy to show us, if she'll co-operate. Actually, maybe you should keep out of sight, let me deal with her.

Cal hung back and watched Sasha bend down to speak to Dorothy. Whatever she'd said must have worked because Dorothy all but bounced out of her chair and, taking Sasha's hand, led her out of the lounge and through the open doors to the garden. Keeping his distance he watched Dorothy lead Sasha to the bottom of the garden where the gardener's shed sat, next to an old coal bunker.

'Is this the letter box, Dorothy?' Sasha kept a friendly smile on her face, trying to hide her excitement as her suspicions were confirmed. 'Shall we see if the postman's taken them yet?' At Dorothy's nod, Sasha lifted the metal lid on the top of the coal bunker and peered inside. There they were! Dorothy's latest missives, lying in a heap amidst ancient coal dust. She'd ask Cal to get them out, best to have a look at them, but it had confirmed something important. 'Dorothy,' she asked gently, 'Did you post your letters in a letter box in your garden at home?'

Dorothy's sly smile and knowing look gave Sasha the feeling that she was definitely on the right track. 'He was always watching us, out of the window.'

Signalling to Cal, as Dorothy chattered away happily, enjoying showing off to her new friend, Sasha allowed Dorothy to lead her back towards the lounge. But this time Dorothy continued to her room, looking back and smiling shyly at Sasha. She placed a finger to her lips and giggled. 'It's a secret,' she whispered.

She was such a lovely new friend, not telling her what to do or not do. She was so nice to her! She hoped she'd stay, and not leave her. Perhaps if she showed her all her special things, she'd stay.

Sasha pinned an expression of delighted interest onto her face as Dorothy silently removed a wooden box from behind the cushion on the armchair. Placing her finger to her lips again, Dorothy placed the box on her bed and opened the lid. She looked at Sasha proudly, waiting for her reaction.

'Wow, this is amazing, Dorothy!' Sasha whispered, as she took in the contents. 'Can I touch?' At Dorothy's nod of the head, Sasha gently rifled through the sheets of stationery, the stickers, and bits of old newspaper. It was what she'd been expecting, not much to learn from it. But at least it meant they knew who'd sent some of the letters. Presumably there were many more that had never made it to their intended recipients. Getting up to go, Dorothy put her hand out, holding Sasha's arm.

As Sasha waited, not sure what Dorothy wanted, Cal peered around the doorway, showing her a bundle of dirty envelopes. She gave him the thumbs up, indicated that she was almost ready to leave, and then turned back to Dorothy, who was holding an old piece of newspaper out to her as she bent almost double with laughter. At Sasha's raised eyebrows, Dorothy nodded, handing the yellowed paper to her before spluttering with laughter.

She gasped in shock as she looked at the old photo in the newspaper article. 'Dorothy, could I borrow this do you think? I promise I'll give it back.'

'No!' Dorothy grabbed the fragile paper back from Sasha, holding it to her chest. 'It's mine.'

'Well,' thinking quickly, Sasha took her phone out of her pocket. 'That's okay, what else have you got here?' Dorothy placed the paper on the small side table as she busied herself looking for something else to impress her newfound friend with. Surreptitiously taking photos of the clipping, Sasha smiled and enthused about the sheets of stickers Dorothy proffered, before saying that she had to go, but would see Dorothy again real soon. 'And Dorothy, keep that paper safe won't you? It's very special.'

About to leave, her attention was caught by the assortment of dolls lined up on the shelf, reminding her of her own collection, from when she was a young girl. 'Wow, these are amazing, Dorothy, you must have dolls from all over the world here!' She reached out a hand to touch an exotic black doll in a brightly-coloured gown.

'No!' Dorothy pushed her away, standing in front of the dolls protectively. 'You can't talk to them, they look after my secrets but they'll never tell.'

Sasha left the room as Dorothy hummed to herself, straightening the dolls' dresses and appearing to whisper to them.

Barely able to contain her excitement, Sasha thrust her phone at Cal, once they were back in the car. 'Who does he remind you of? Imagine him with a beard. And her? Obviously they're both much older now.' She watched Cal's expression change from curious to incredulous.

'I don't believe it, that's Reg Spindlebury! And the blonde on his arm, it's Rosemary! How old is this?' Cal expanded the image to squint at the date. 'Looks like - nineteen eighty-nine is that? What the hell? And Dorothy's got this?'

'Yep!' Sasha was grinning, 'She wouldn't let me borrow it so I took some photos without her knowing. Cal, we've got to show this to the police as soon as possible, I think we've just found ourselves a couple of runaway criminals! Well, one, and an accessory at the very least. They've been hiding in plain sight all these years!'

'We'll go straight to the police station.' Cal started the car. 'Nick Crossley's not going to believe this! But, Sash, where does this fit in to everything that's been happening? It doesn't, does it?'

'I don't know to be honest.' Sasha mulled it over. 'It seems like so many bad things have happened in such a short space of time and I can't work out what's connected to what, or if anything is at all. But one thing that occurred to me is this, if Dorothy's had this old newspaper clipping, maybe she wrote a letter to the Spindleburys? But even if she did it's not getting us anywhere further.

'I'm going to open these letters that you retrieved from the coal bunker. I feel kind of bad but we need to see what else she might have been saying to people. Oh look, this one's for Greg. Very flowery paper. Listen to this – *I saw you* – hold on, something about *other men, Richard*, I think that's supposed to say, and *kissing*. Well no surprises there. Here's another one – *Mary, Mary, from the dairy*, lots of stickers of food, *took the money box*, more stickers, and *thief*. Hmm, that's not so nice. Okay, this one is very simple – *You're a cheap whore*. Charming, not sure who that was for, looks like it might be someone called Bobby? No that can't be right, Barby? Oh, whatever. Seems our Dorothy enjoyed writing pretty unkind things about people, the question is, did any of them ever receive them? We only really know of the two, Maureen and Mrs Pringle.'

Cal,' she laid a hand on his arm. 'Do you happen to know where Dorothy's house is?'

'No idea, but your brother-in-law works with her husband at the paper plant doesn't he? So he might know. Why?'

'It's a hunch, well, more than a hunch, but we need to go and check something in the garden.' Sasha texted her sister, then explained about the whole post box thing. 'I remember where I read it now, it was a tourist leaflet in my room at the pub. It talked about the old Victorian post boxes, how some were still around, had even been incorporated into the back gardens of some of the older houses. Cal, I think there's one in Dorothy's back garden, and she's been posting her letters in it. If I'm right, they could just be sitting there. I don't know what it'll prove but what if someone knew about it? And they read Dorothy's letters maybe? Oh,' she shook her head. 'It sounds stupid when I say it out loud. But we might as well check don't you think?'

Her phone pinged with a text from Tessa. 'Dave's finding out the address for us and will text me, but we don't have a lot of time, we need to get there before the husband, George, gets home from work.'

They drove slowly past the house to the end of the road, counting the house numbers and then, turning left, looked for the dirt lane that was supposed to run along the back of the row of terraced cottages, according to the map on her phone. Counting the houses in reverse, Cal pulled up outside a little garden gate leading into the back garden belonging to the Newtons.

'It's not locked, but we could have stepped over it anyway, I guess security isn't a big concern in a village, although, thinking about what's happened lately, maybe it should be. Here it is!' Sasha looked at Cal excitedly.

The ancient post box sat comfortably just inside the back garden, nestled against the fence and surrounded by shrubs, some of which were quite overgrown. Tentatively, Sasha felt the edges of the little door used by postmen years ago to collect the mail. But the gap was too small. 'Dammit, we need something to pry it open.'

'It might be locked, Sash, might have sat here locked up all these years.' Cal looked around for something to use. 'Be right back.' He fetched a painter's knife from the boot of his car. 'Never thought the tools of my trade would come in useful for something like this,' he shrugged, slipping the edge of the blade into the gap. With a slight twist, the door eased outwards a little and Cal took hold of it, pulling it fully open.

They gazed at the pile of letters sitting inside the box. 'Jackpot,' breathed Cal.

Sasha scooped them up, making sure to leave none behind. 'I suppose, technically, we're breaking the law. But anyway, we'll just borrow them, if there's nothing of interest we can always put them back.' She looked at her watch. 'We'd better go.'

'So where now? Cops? Or pub? Shall we have a look at these letters first, over a drink? Might as well go through them, then we've checked out everything we can, before we hand them over to the professionals.'

POISONOUS LITTLE WORKS OF ART

Rosemary Spindlebury left the station feeling quite confused. The female police officer had been very kind to her, but had clearly been trying to pry information from her. But she hadn't asked anything about the cash job so it had to be about something else. She shuddered. Please don't let it be Barbara, she couldn't bear it, to think of Reg doing that. No, P.C. Weaver had more seemed to concentrate on things like whether Reg had ever had an affair, had he been seeing anyone, wanting to know what they did in the evenings, if they spent all their time together. If only Reg could have told her what to say. She'd tried her best, but had got herself in a muddle in the end, so she wasn't sure which nights she'd said they'd been together and which ones not. One thing she knew for sure, her Reg would never have an affair. If he went out in the evening it was always to do with business, what kind of business he never elaborated on. But an affair? Definitely not.

~

Reg looked at the piece of paper, reading the typed words slowly, trying to look unconcerned but seething inwardly. Who the hell had written this? And how had the cops got hold of it? Rosemary! His useless dumb wife, that stupid bitch, they'd got that bit right. She must have opened it and given it to the cops instead of showing it to him. He'd kill her.

'No idea.' He looked up at Sergeant Denton and P.C. Crossley, shaking his head. 'No. Fucking. Idea.'

'Again with the language, Reg. Now, come on, you can do better than that. This letter was meant for your wife. It's talking about *you*, for crying out loud. Who'd you kill, Reg? Who was she? Was it the young girl? Or was it Barbara Fenton? Who saw you? Reg, at the moment you're going down for all these deaths as well as the abduction, don't you get it?

Every single one. Now's your chance, if there's anything to tell us you need to do it now.'

Frantically he tried to think. They were bluffing of course, they couldn't seriously think he'd killed, what, some young girl, as well as a grown man, for no reason whatsoever, oh, and abducted another girl, don't forget that, when all he'd ever wanted to do was shut that drunk cow up. And there was no way they could ever link him to that, it was impossible. But who the hell had seen him? He needed to find out and deal with it. He looked up. 'There's nothing to tell you. I haven't done anything. Whoever wrote this?' His hand flicked at the letter, 'Nut job. Now let me go or I'll be getting my lawyer involved, I've had enough of this.'

~

Sasha sipped her glass of wine, trying to decipher the jumble of letters stuck onto the page. 'Cal, I think this was meant for Barbara! Listen to this, here's what I can make out – *You are a drunk. Fat. Ugly. No friends*. Remember the scraps of burnt paper we found? Drunk and ugly, those were the words! Cal, Dorothy wrote this to Barbara and posted it in the post box in her garden. But someone else saw it, typed it up and sent it to Barbara. But who? And why?'

'What the-' Cal looked gobsmacked. 'This is *my* letter! *Sinner. Fornicator. You had sex together. Bad. Look what happened*. I don't believe it, that mad little old lady we saw today wrote this. To me!'

'Er, yeah, Cal, and then someone else fine-tuned it. That is so creepy, or sinister, or something.' Sasha busied herself with her phone. 'What's Maureen's address again?' She tapped a few times, nodding, and then asked, 'And Barbara's?' Holding her phone out to Cal, she pointed on the screen. 'This is Dorothy's house, and look which street she'd have been able to see from the back windows if she looked to the left, and more to the point, which house.'

'Maureen's. She was watching. When I went there to work on my preliminary sketches, she was watching us. The sick old cow.'

'And now look, here's Barbara's, well the back of her house and her garden, she'll have seen that straight across the dirt lane. I wonder who else she spied on?'

Picking up another piece of paper, Sasha frowned. 'I'm not sure what this is about? It looks like it's saying she saw someone's husband kill someone. And then, *I know your secrets.* This is dangerous, Cal. It's a pity there are no envelopes, there's no way of knowing who this was for.' She grinned suddenly. 'Listen to this one, no mystery here. *Reg Spindlebury likes to touch the blonde's bottom. I saw you together at the club. Whispering your little secrets. Does your stuck-up wife know?*'

Cal was quiet, holding another of the letters in his hand.

'What is it, Cal?'

'You were right all along, Sash. This was written to Maureen's husband Peter. *Slut. Your slutty wife. Doing dirty sex with him, that artist.* He *did* get a letter. Whatever Von glimpsed on his desk was a typed version of this. Oh man, I feel terrible, that poor bloke, he was sitting there in the pub, I actually saw him looking at me. And he thought Maureen and I were- that we were sleeping together. I was just painting her portrait as her gift for him. Why didn't he just ask her? Or me, for that matter?'

'That's so sad. And so cruel. It means his death probably was an accident then,' Sasha squeezed his hand gently. 'Although it was caused by him being upset because of the letter, so whoever sent it is indirectly responsible for his death, at least in my mind. Cal, we can't wait around with this, we need to go and show Nick or Jane, right now.'

Reaching to bundle the pages together, one of them caught her eye. 'Oh no. Cal, I think this was meant for Tess. *Good for nothing daughter. Little thief.* Poor Tess, she didn't deserve this. *Your husband sleeps with whores.*' Sasha was furious. 'Where the hell does she get off writing evil stuff like this? It's so totally untrue. Look what damage she's caused. And who else has she accused of lies she just made up in her mad frigging head?' Throwing the paper down onto the table she took a deep breath to calm herself. 'Sorry.'

'Hey, no need to apologise, I'm with you on this, all the way, babe. But remember, Dorothy's letters are all here, well most of them, as far as we know. Which means she never sent them to people, Sash. She's mad, she's lost her marbles. I mean, look at this one, *I know why you all sleep all day. Devil's work at night. Bright light.* Totally nuts, right? Whatever she thought she was doing, I doubt we'll ever know, but once she'd made her poisonous little works of art, she popped them into that letter box, and there they would have stayed if someone hadn't got their mitts on them and decided to cause major trouble.'

Babe, he called her babe. She liked that.

Cal was still speaking. 'So what d'you think? Could be him, couldn't it? I mean, I'm not sure why, unless he's as mad as his wife, but...'

'Oh,' she put the warm fuzzy feeling aside. 'Her husband, yes, what's his name again? And what's he like?'

Cal considered this, his head tilted. 'His name's George. As to what he's like, difficult to say, Dave might know more, from seeing him at work maybe. But from the odd times I've seen him I'd say he's someone who you don't really notice. Does that make sense?'

'Yes I think I know what you mean, like he's overlooked, maybe always has been. Sort of diminished, those types of people, well, they're almost invisible really. Maybe that could be a reason, if he's the one who's been typing out Dorothy's letters and sending them? Could have given him quite the sense of power.'

Cal shrugged. 'Makes sense I suppose, if you're crazy anyway. But look, Sash, anyone could get into their back garden.'

'But they'd have to know about Dorothy's malicious little pastime wouldn't they?'

'True. Anyway, time for us to take this little lot to the cops. See what they make of it all, don't you think?' Cal stood up.

SUCH A NICE MAN

It was late afternoon, and quiet at the chemist, where Mrs Pringle found herself alone, Sheila having taken a rare afternoon off.

With a fresh cup of tea, and a glance towards the door, Mrs Pringle eased her feet up onto the little stool below the counter, sinking back into the more comfortable chair she'd wheeled through from the kitchenette. The community newsletter lay in her lap where she'd been glancing through it, she always enjoyed seeing the photos of people she knew.

As she felt herself drifting off, thoughts played through her mind. She supposed it was because of the couple wanting to go and visit poor dear Dorothy. Yes, she'd done the right thing in speaking to Doctor Singh. Now why did that make her think of something else? Pills. That was it. Doctor Singh had prescribed the first supply of zopiclone. But Dorothy had dropped them all in the bath. She could remember Mr Newton telling her, no doubt as he was buying more perfume for his mother, and fly spray. Always fly spray. Why did the man need to buy so much? The police woman's face appeared in her mind, her mouth moving, a slightly patronising expression on her face, if you don't mind. Pills and fly spray. That's what she'd asked about wasn't it?

Trying to come to, Mrs Pringle's foot slipped off the stool spilling her tea into its saucer. Distractedly she poured the liquid from the saucer back into her cup before taking a large mouthful. And then she made her decision. She couldn't stay on the side lines not saying anything because of a sense of loyalty. She'd been asked about the hypnotics and she'd given the officer a list, but she'd omitted to tell her about the replacement pills. She'd also forgotten to write it in the book, to her shame. And when asked about purchases of fly spray well, she'd had one of her strange feelings about the amount of spray Mr Newton had been buying, but for one, she'd been put off by the young woman's reprimand plus, well really, it was Mr Newton! She'd known him all his life, his mother too.

No, she had to do what was right, wasn't that what she was on God's earth for? That's what her mother had always told her when she'd found herself faced with a difficult decision. *'It doesn't matter if they're your friends or not, Dolly, you do what's right. You tell the truth. You stick to the facts. You're not the one passing judgement you're just the vessel passing on the information.'* Her mother, God rest her soul, had been right of course, but she'd always felt sad that she'd lost her friend's companionship that day. Well here she was again, about to speak out about a friend. And what would be would be.

Mrs Pringle began the process of closing the shop early for the day, her mind on whether she needed to take a cardigan with her for the short walk along to the police station.

~

Inspector Andrew Kavanagh had assembled everyone in his office. Jane had something of interest for them to consider, following her friendly chat with Rosemary Spindlebury.

'I know it doesn't really give us anything concrete, Sir, but she let slip about her friend Barbara Fenton. She was sobbing and none of it really made sense. Something about the night they had drinks while they watched a show on television. It sounded like she felt it was all her fault, if she'd never told him, and I'm guessing she meant Reg, it would never have happened. I tried to get her to tell me more but she changed the subject, laughing it off saying she was just upset, that having Reg here had got her in a state. She kept asking me why he was here, wanted to know if it was something to do with what's been happening in the village. I did ask her what else she thought it could be about but she wouldn't be drawn. But I think the letter must have been right, Sir, someone saw him kill her and Rosemary knew about it.'

P.C. Crossley excused himself to answer the desk bell and found Sasha and Cal anxiously awaiting him. 'What can I do for you guys? We're a little tied up right now to be honest.'

'We're hoping we have some information that might help you.' Cal was serious. 'You're going to want to see this, Nick, trust me, some of it's pretty heavy stuff.'

With Dorothy's letters spread across the table in the small conference room, together with the phone images of the newspaper clipping, Sasha and Cal took turns in bringing Nick up to speed on what they'd discovered and how. Asking them to wait, he returned to his Inspector's office. 'Apologies for interrupting, Sir, but I think you should all come and take a look at this.'

Half an hour later and everyone was up to speed and in a state of disbelief about the huge impact of the tiny newspaper clipping. Nick had been tasked with going through to Meadowvale and appropriating Dorothy Newton's stationery box, which he'd just returned with. It was Jane's turn to excuse herself as the desk bell sounded again, and she went to attend to Mrs Pringle. Returning to the group her flushed face told them that she had something important to add to the mix.

Before she could speak Sergeant Denton regretfully told Sasha and Cal that they'd have to leave. He thanked them profusely for the information but advised them that they would have to leave it to the police now.

~

He couldn't face Mother's disappointment in him, he really couldn't. Looking at the clock on the wall of his office he willed the minute hand to reach the hour. He'd go back to the hospital straight from work and finish it. Whatever it took. And then he'd go to Mother and everything would be alright.

~

Jane finished explaining about Mrs Pringle's rather garbled story. 'She was terribly embarrassed, said she was sure it was nothing but felt it was her duty to tell us. Seems she's known him all her life, him and the family, and she's obviously very fond of them all. But, Sir,' she addressed her Inspector. 'The pills were nonbenzodiazepine, also known as

Zopiclone or Zimovane. That's what Chantelle Watson had in her system! That, together with his purchases of large amounts of fly spray, well, unlikely as it seems…' She looked around, seeing agreement on all three faces looking at her.

'Good work, you might have just found our killer for us. Maybe we've been barking up the wrong tree with Spindlebury, although that remains to be seen.' Inspector Kavanagh spoke approvingly. 'Jane and Nick, find him and bring him in. Let's see what he's got to say about it all. Philip, you and I are going to go and have a nice chat with our Mr Spindlebury just as soon as I've updated C.I. Carpenter.'

~

Cal turned to Sasha as they left the police station. 'Well we've done our bit. All seems a bit of an anti-climax doesn't it?' But Sasha was distracted.

'Mrs Pringle, are you alright?' The older woman was sitting on the bench outside, looking as if the world had ended. 'Can we help with anything?'

'Oh dear, it's very kind of you. Just doing my duty you see, but there, I'd hate to be doing an injustice to anyone, especially a friend. Such a nice man, and with his wife just settled in at Meadowvale, well he's all alone, except for his poor mother of course. Oh dear what have I done?' She looked up at them with downturned mouth, the picture of dejection.

With a quick glance at Cal, Sasha sat down next to her. 'Are you talking about Mr Newton?' she asked gently.

'How did you know?' Mrs Pringle was surprised. 'Oh of course, you'll have been to see Dorothy. How was she?'

'She was fine, very happy, settled in well, but obviously she's very confused which I'm sure explains her odd letter to you.' Sasha took a chance. 'But there are concerns for Mr Newton's wellbeing as you probably know, perhaps that's why you came to the station?'

'Oh you understand, what a relief. I kept wondering about all that fly spray, and then the pills, a whole month's supply gone just like that. I was happy to give him a replacement of course, but I had to clear my conscience. Maybe Dorothy did drop them in the bath, but what with the lady police officer asking about them, and that poor girl being held captive and no doubt drugged, why, she's your niece isn't she?'

Cal interrupted. 'Mrs Pringle, the pills were a sedative of some kind weren't they? What was the name again?' Mrs Pringle obligingly gave him the name. 'Oh, that's right, Zopiclone.'

A chill went through Sasha. But Mrs Pringle was fumbling in her bag, drawing out a folded newsletter. 'Here he is, such a nice man, you see? That's the paper plant's annual raffle, they do such a lot of good for the needy.'

Sasha's chill turned icy as she looked at the man in the photo and she turned to Cal in horror.

'Mrs Pringle, I'm really sorry but I forgot something at the station, we have to go. Cal, we *really* have to go.'

Cal didn't hesitate, Sasha's expression filling him with foreboding. As they rushed back into the police station he asked her what was going on.

'I saw him. He was at the hospital earlier, Cal. He almost bumped into me right outside Chantelle's room! We need to tell someone now!'

Jane and Nick were rushing through the back office, heading out of the rear door to their vehicle, but Cal called out to stop them.

'Cal, mate, whatever it is can it wait? We're in a rush to be honest.'

'George Newton was at the hospital earlier today.' Sasha was breathless with panic. 'He was right outside Chantelle's room. I, I think he was going to go in, do something to her, but we were coming in the opposite direction. I asked him if he was okay as he looked a little shaky but he ignored me, kept on going. He's connected to this with the girls isn't he? He drugged Chantelle and kept her somewhere. Which means poor Britney-' She sobbed in her panic and looked at Nick in desperation. 'What if he goes back? Oh God, he could be there now and there's no-one with Chantelle!'

'Right, don't worry, we'll head straight there and call the hospital and local police on the way.'

Jane Weaver placed a reassuring hand on Sasha's arm. Leave it to us, Sasha, we've got this okay?'

They watched the police officers rush out speaking into their radios, and then Sasha collapsed against Cal's chest.

~

'Can I help you, Sir?' The nurse's enquiry brought George out of his reverie in an instant. 'No thank you I'm fine.' Fixing a smile on his face he walked on along the corridor. It was no good thinking about how he'd tell Mother that everything was fine now, that he'd dealt with the problem, and pleasurably anticipating her praise. He first had to actually do it. He pressed the lift button for the fifth floor.

Sasha's phone rang, 'Oh it's Tess, what do I tell her?' She looked at Cal in anguish.

'Nothing about all this stuff we've discovered, or about the police going to the hospital. No need to panic her and Dave. Why don't you just say that we're on our way to check on Chantelle again?'

Nodding, Sasha answered her phone, putting on a bright tone. 'Tess, hi, darling! We're actually just on our way to Chantelle now, we- what? What's that, Tess? She's woken up? Oh Tess, that's wonderful news!' She turned and grinned at Cal. 'How is she? We're on our way! Has she spoken?' A few more nods and brief responses and the call was finished. 'Tess and Dave are at the hospital. The doctor called them about half an hour ago. Chantelle's awake! Can you believe it? She hasn't said much yet, but they say she's showing no signs for concern, although they're busy running some tests right now.'

Cal's face broke into a grin, and he bear-hugged Sasha. 'That's fantastic, babe! Let's go!' He grabbed her hand and pulled her along the road towards the car.

There it was again, babe. And tonight was *the* night, too. Her stomach flipped at the thought. Much as she'd wanted them to finally be together *in every way*, she'd not said anything to Cal about tonight and her being healed enough inside. She knew why, it was because it just felt wrong somehow with her niece lying unconscious in hospital and with Tess and Dave in a constant state of high anxiety. But all that had changed in an instant with the news about Chantelle.

~

Meanwhile back at the station, C.I. Stanley Carpenter and Sergeant Philip Denton were taking enormous pleasure in the myriad changing expressions passing across Reg Spindlebury's face. In the space of approximately thirty seconds his face had displayed disinterest, bemusement, puzzlement, shock, horror, denial, horror again, defeat, and finally fear. *This* was what he'd been worried about, maybe they *had* been on the wrong track all along, accusing him of murder, although both men privately felt sure that he was Barbara's killer.

Reg slumped in his chair. 'Ro was never involved in this. She had nothing to do with the job.'

'By Ro you mean Rochelle do you Reg?'

His eyes flicked towards Sergeant Denton. 'Yes she was always Ro, so Rosemary made sense, it meant that I couldn't slip up when I shortened it. She never knew about the job at the time or for a long while afterwards. It's just me you want, keep her out of it.'

'Very gallant of you, Reg, I'm sure, but the thing is she did know about the job in the end didn't she? She knew where all the money came from. She knew you were on the run. That's why you both changed your names. She didn't turn you in, Reg, and that means she's an accessory I'm afraid. Hell, maybe we'll even make her an accessory to the murder of Barbara Fenton, just for fun, because you're going down for that without a doubt.'

Reg scowled at the chief inspector, knowing that he was right, and that there was nothing he could do to protect Ro. He couldn't even warn her they'd be coming for her. And they did. Sergeant Denton collected Rosemary from her house half an hour later.

~

George peered through the door's window making sure there was no-one else in the room. He could make out the shape of the girl's lower half underneath the blanket, her upper half being obscured by the partially drawn curtain beside the bed. Quietly, he entered the room, picked up a pillow from the chair and drew the curtain aside to expose the girl in the bed.

Only it wasn't the girl in the bed. George's brain was still trying to compute this fact as P.C. Crossley took hold of his arm. 'Mr Newton? You're coming with us. Hands behind your back please.' Nick roughly pulled George's arms behind him, cuffing his wrists, not in the slightest bit bothered by George's yelps of pain at his manhandling. He deserved a lot worse in his opinion.

P.C. Weaver looked at George in disgust. 'And just what exactly do you think you were doing in this patient's room, Mr Newton? And what was the pillow for?'

In shock, George struggled to get the words out. 'I, er, well, I wondered how she was doing. I'd read about it in the paper, and-' inspiration hit. 'Her poor father works at the paper plant with me, I thought I'd visit on his behalf.'

A roar erupted directly behind George and he was jerked backwards. 'You fucking monster! Don't even talk about my daughter, you sick bastard! What did you do to her? What were you going to do now? Try and finish the job you started?' Dave was stopped in his tracks by Nick, who pulled him off telling him now was not the time. 'We've got him, Dave, it's over. She's safe. Chantelle's safe and this bastard is going to pay for what he's done don't you worry.'

Tessa, looking on in horror, as were the few visitors and staff in the corridor, was relieved at the sight of Sasha and Cal. 'Thank God, Sash, they've got him! He was going to kill her, he was going to kill my Chantelle!' They huddled in a kind of group hug, Dave joining them now that he'd released his rage. The four of them watched George Newton being half led, half pulled, along the corridor. Tessa spoke for all of them when she said, 'He's just an old man. Why did he do all this?'

Sasha shook her head slowly. 'At this moment I'm not sure what the reasons were for anything that's happened. Nothing makes sense, not properly, some bits do, but oh, I don't know, it's more like a whole lot of different issues collided to create the nightmare from hell in the most unsuspecting of places, a quaint English village. We will get answers to everything though.' A thought struck her. 'Where is Chants?' Did they finish running the tests?'

As if on cue two nurses wheeled Chantelle into her room. Dave explained. 'The cops called the hospital, while Chantelle was having her tests, telling them to keep her in a different room until they gave the all clear. They told us to keep out of sight, when they got here, and then they set themselves up in wait for him.'

The next few minutes were filled with laughter and tears as they squeezed around Chantelle's bed, everyone talking at once. But Chantelle's pale face alerted them to the fact that she needed to rest, and the stern face of, albeit a very happy, Doctor Montgomery, appeared around the door asking them to please leave and give her patient time to rest. They had all avoided raising the subject of what had happened to Chantelle, wanting to give her time.

Jane Weaver arrived back as they were hovering outside Chantelle's room. 'I'll be asking Chantelle a few questions as soon as she's up to it. The sooner we can find out what happened to her the better.'

A WEE DRAM OF ARRAN WHISKY

Chief Inspector Carpenter and Inspector Kavanagh were in their shirt sleeves. It had been a long day. 'I think this warrants a wee dram of Arran whisky don't you, Andrew?' He opened his briefcase and retrieved the bottle of twenty-one-year-old single malt. 'Had this delivered today, don't think the wife will mind if I open it now. Best whisky I've ever tasted this is. The wife and I have been holidaying on Arran for years, best thing they ever did opening a distillery there. 'D'you know, the actor Ewan McGregor opened their first cask of single malt? Late nineties that must have been, wife swears we were there at the time. Tell you what, call Philip in, Nick and Jane too, I'd say we've all earned a whisky, and get them to bring us some glasses.'

Nick was just finishing off a call with the Essex police division, finalising arrangements for Reg's transfer the following day, and Jane had just finished writing up her report, filling Sergeant Denton in on the results of her visit to Chantelle at the same time. 'She's still a bit fuzzy, Sir, obviously she's tiring easily and she's still trying to come to turns with everything. Poor girl, it's been a huge shock for her. But there's no doubt about it, she and Britney were following George Newton the day we found Peter Ford's body. She didn't say where they followed him to though, she got too distressed to continue, so I'm going back first thing in the morning to see if she can carry on.'

They gathered in the inspector's office and watched the chief open the bottle with great care before pouring five measures into the glasses. 'Cheers, everyone,' he said, raising his glass as they followed suit. 'We've solved a thirty-year-old cash heist, apprehended the villians, caught our local murderer, and prevented another murder. There's still work to do, still a grey area around Spindlebury's involvement in Barbara's death, but I'd say it's been an unbelievably good day's work. Take a moment to savour it, everyone. Tomorrow's another day.'

~

Mrs Pringle was beginning to feel that she was losing her touch. Usually the first to know everything that was going on, it was Sheila, *again*, who informed her of George's arrest. She'd called her with the news, excitedly recounting the events surrounding the drama at the hospital. 'Like something out of a TV show, it was, my sister-in-law said. They set him right up, let him go into the room. Into the very room! He was about to smother her! Well he would have been, if they hadn't moved her to safety. She, Janice my sister-in-law, saw the whole thing, she was right there in the corridor. I had to give her a sherry to calm herself, well we both had to have one. What a to do. George Newton, who'd ever have thought it? A serial killer, people are saying, on account of he must have killed Barbara Fenton too.' Sheila's pause for breath had given Mrs Pringle the opportunity to proffer her own contribution to George's arrest, but for once in her life she'd not felt like sharing the information. She felt quite sad about it all. She'd known the family for so many years, it was still hard to come to terms with the awful truth about everything. And poor Mrs Newton would be devastated. She'd raised that boy all alone, ever since that rotten husband of hers had upped and left without a by your leave all those years ago. Just a short note to say he was leaving her and then never a word from him since.

~

The newly opened French restaurant, La Petite Souris, was pumping. It had been Tessa's suggestion that they go out to celebrate and with a quick glance and a squeeze of Cal's hand, Sasha had said yes what a wonderful idea. Back at the pub, before they went to shower and change, she'd apologised, checking with Cal if he minded. 'We've got all night, Sash, and all the time in the world ahead of us. I think your sister and Dave deserve to let off some steam. Let's go, it'll be fun.'

She hadn't told him that tonight was the night. That she was fully recovered from her operation and that she didn't want to wait a moment longer before taking their relationship to the final level. She'd save that treat for later, keep it as a nice surprise for when they got back to the pub. She'd showered, slipped on the sexiest underwear she had with her, beneath her jeans and shirt, and was now on her second glass of wine. Cal had been right, it was fun. And it was fabulous to see Tess and Dave looking so happy.

Between them they'd polished off about four bottles of wine together with the most divine onion soup and baked camembert, followed by, for the girls, cheese soufflé as light as air, and for the guys, the coq au vin. Flaming crêpes with fruit and cream had filled any space they had left and, after everything that had happened, it felt like the best night of their lives. No-one wanted the evening to end, and Dave's suggestion of cognacs to finish off, was met with great approval.

Sasha took a few photos of the evening, including the beautifully presented food, and smiled as she posted a couple of them to her Graffic account. The red notification alert caught her eye. Woah, that was a lot of notifications. She'd have to catch up with them all at some point, but not now.

~

Mrs Pringle's evening was no such fun. She felt downright miserable about everything, doubting her judgement of people's character, something she'd always felt she excelled at. As she ate her dinner for one from the supermarket she mulled over what had happened. How on earth could Mr Newton have taken those girls? Why would he have done that? And to have killed one of them? And Barbara Fenton too? She felt quite ill at the thought. He'd seemed such a good man, caring for his mother and then for his wife too. Her hand stilled, the fork loaded with lasagne halfway to her mouth. His mother! What about his mother? All alone in her cottage.

~

She peered through the windscreen, squinting her eyes to see the dirt road. Night driving was not something that she did very often. But she wasn't one to shirk from her duties and right now poor Mrs Newton senior needed her. She couldn't bear the thought of the poor woman all alone in her cottage with no-one having visited to care for her. Switching off her engine, she got out of the car, locking the door as a habit. The silence and darkness engulfed her. Oh dear she should have brought a torch, what had she been thinking?

A chilling thought struck her. George might have kept the young girls here. No, she shook her head, don't be ridiculous, Dolly, his mother would have known. No it must have been somewhere else. The gate to the front garden was locked but she knew there was a gap between the wall and the fence around the back of the cottage where it bordered the field. She'd visited old Mrs Newton often, back before George had become so possessive of his mother, and knew where the spare key was kept. Even George didn't know about it. 'He'd say it was an invitation to criminals if he knew,' Mrs Newton had scoffed. 'Criminals in our little village? Silly boy, I don't know where he gets his ideas from.'

Treading carefully, it certainly wouldn't do for her to fall and hurt herself all alone out here, she made her way to the gap and slipped through. Her eyes were becoming accustomed to the dark and she could make out shapes at the back of the cottage. Now, where was the stone cat? Stooping, she carefully felt the smaller shapes, identifying the cat and lifting it, hoping there weren't too many cheesy bugs writhing underneath it. She picked up the key.

'Mrs Newton?' Tiptoeing along the corridor Mrs Pringle switched on the light. 'Hello? Mrs Newton, it's me, Dolly.' All was quiet. Maybe she was asleep. She'd check the lounge before checking upstairs. The door opened quietly, the strong scent of lavender filling her nostrils, and she switched on the light. Ah, there she was, she could see the top of her head above the back of the armchair. 'Oh, you poor dear, all alone in the dark.' A thought occurred to her, Mrs Newton wouldn't yet know about George. Well she wouldn't distress her, not tonight. She flapped a fly away as it buzzed in her face. 'Now don't be alarmed, it's me, Dolly, I've come to look after you, help you to bed.'

But it was Mrs Pringle who was to be alarmed. Not Mrs Newton, who'd lost the ability for alarm, or anything else, quite some time ago.

She didn't scream, it was more of a whimper, as her hand clutched her chest, trying to calm her racing heart. The petrified remains of what had been Mrs Newton grinned at her ghoulishly, her mummified features frozen into place. Stepping back, Mrs Pringle bumped into the little side table, knocking it over and spilling its contents. She clutched at the chair beside her and regained her balance. Gasping and still in shock she backed out of the room.

If ever she'd wished for one of those mobile phones it was now. But she'd have to use the landline and her heart sank as she remembered where it was. Mustering her courage Mrs Pringle re-entered the lounge, refusing to look at the cause of her horror. She dialled the number from memory and prayed for someone to answer it quickly.

~

Jane Weaver was still at the station. She'd intended going home but couldn't shake the feeling that she was missing something. Once they'd placed the cash heist firmly in the court of Reg and Rosemary Spindlebury, it had seemed that George Newton was assumed accountable for the deaths of both Britney Morton and Barbara Fenton. But Jane could think of no earthly reason why he would kill Barbara. Plus, someone had written to Mrs Spindlebury, laying her murder squarely at his feet. No, it didn't make sense. To be honest, him kidnapping two girls and killing one of them didn't make sense either. And since when did murder ever make sense anyway? She was tired. She closed her notepad filled with her jumbled thoughts. They'd get to the bottom of it all she knew that. She'd go home and make herself a huge plate of buttered toast, slathered in peanut butter, and a pot of tea.

She was just locking the door of the station when she heard the phone start to ring. Tempted to leave it, after all, Nick was on call tonight and it would re-direct to him eventually, she changed her mind. She was here, she might as well answer it.

'Oh, someone's there. Oh, thank the Lord.' The woman's panicked voice and heavy breathing pricked up the hairs on the back of Jane's neck.

'This is P.C. Weaver, who's calling?' She waited, hearing ragged breathing sounds in her ear. 'Hello? Who's calling?'

'Oh, P.C. Weaver, it's Mrs Pringle. Come quickly, please come. Oh it's awful, I've never seen anything like it. She's, well, she's dead.'

'Who's dead, Mrs Pringle? Where are you?' Jane's tiredness and hunger had evaporated in a split second, her senses now fully alert. 'Are you sure the person is dead?' She fetched up Sergeant Denton's number on her mobile phone in readiness. 'Mrs Pringle?'

'Oh dear. I can't stay in here with her. It's Mrs Newton.' Jane's puzzlement lasted only a moment. 'I'm at her cottage in The Lane. Please hurry, I'm going outside.' The phone line went dead.

'Go, Jane, I'll call Nick, and an ambulance. We'll meet you there. And be careful, we don't know what we're dealing with here.' Sergeant Denton rang off and Jane galvanised into action.

A shaking Mrs Pringle emerged from her car and fell into Jane's arms when she arrived. 'Mrs Pringle, I'll need to go in alone. More people are on the way and they'll look after you, just sit back in your car for now. Is there anyone else in there aside from Mrs Newton? How did you get in?'

Grabbing her torch, Jane made her way around to the back of the cottage and cautiously entered the kitchen, switching on all the lights that she could find. Following Mrs Pringle's garbled information, she took the few steps along the passage and entered the lounge. She wasn't one to be easily shocked but the sight in front of her succeeded in doing just that. No need to check for signs of life here. The sounds of sirens and the flicker of flashing lights told her that the others had arrived and she left the room, opening up the front door. 'This way, Sarge, Nick.'

The three officers stood looking at the mummified remains of the elderly woman. Nick whistled. 'Looks like George Newton's got even more explaining to do. What a twisted freak. And I thought I'd seen it all, I really did.'

'You can send the ambulance away, Jane, we won't be needing their services that's for sure. And no need to pull Dr Singh from his bed tonight, we'll get him here in the morning, together with forensics. Let's have a look around shall we?'

Nick took the basement, Sergeant Denton the ground floor, and Jane the upstairs.

Nick pulled the door to the basement open, switching on the light to see his way down the stairs. The strong smell of bleach assailed his nostrils, together with another chemical type smell which, though familiar, he couldn't put his finger on. The basement area was pristine, neat and tidy, with no signs of dust or dirt. Which decided Nick was, in its own way, suspicious. Especially with the mummified corpse of an elderly woman sitting up there in the living room.

Why would George Newton keep the basement so clean and spotless? He poked around at the boxes on a couple of shelf units lining the walls, deciding to check everything in detail. Nothing seemed out of the ordinary, boxes of old ornaments, an old suitcase filled with men's clothing, another with what had once been a woman's fur coat. But still, why did the space feel, and smell, like it had been so thoroughly cleaned? He could think of one reason...

Philip Denton examined the living room first, followed by the small dining room at the back of the cottage, and finally the kitchen. Apart from the fact that the cottage was occupied by a mummy everything felt quite normal. The sight of a tea tray set with two cups and saucers gave him a chill. He wondered when it had last been used. Looking in the fridge he noticed an opened carton of fresh milk as well as a small jug containing some of the milk. So somebody had been here having tea. But tea for two? His face creased in revolt at the thought, his imagination providing bizarre images of the tea party. He pressed his foot on the pedal of the bin and leant down to look at the contents. The outer wrapper of a packet of fig rolls, a can of fly spray... Frowning, he delved deeper, finding at least two more empty cans of fly spray. His gloved hand picked up the fig roll wrapper and he looked for the expiry date. It was a long way off. Yes, someone had been eating and drinking here very recently, and whoever it was had felt the need to use plenty of fly spray.

Jane walked quietly around the upstairs of the cottage, finding it all pretty eerie. It *felt* like a dead person's house. A line of empty Lavender Dreams perfume bottles filled the window ledge in the bathroom and she noticed a talcum powder of the same scent on the dust-covered shelf. Gingerly she pulled back the plastic shower curtain above the bath, hoping for no surprises. She exhaled, surprised to find she'd been holding her breath. The bath was empty but dusty.

The small back bedroom, or box room, held nothing of interest as far as she could tell. But the main front bedroom, with its double bed, made her shiver. A nightdress was laid out on the bed as if in readiness for someone's bedtime. The indentation in the bed was clear. A woman's blouse and skirt, together with a cardigan and undergarments, draped the small velvet covered chair in the corner. She checked the dust-covered contents of the old-fashioned dressing table, before opening the large wardrobe. Nothing out of the ordinary. Her gaze fell on a folded yellow scarf and man's tweed cap on the shelf, before travelling over the old-fashioned dresses hanging on the rail. Closing the door she left the room.

The handle of the cupboard door on the landing turned easily, the door swinging open to reveal stairs. Surprised, Jane kicked herself for not having realised that the cottage had an attic room. With the light on, she ascended the narrow stairs and found herself in a small room, bare but for an old desk and chair. The typewriter sat proudly, dead centre, a neat pile of paper and envelopes beside it. Excitedly she headed back down the two flights of stairs.

'Sarge, I've found a typewriter in the attic! I think Sasha and Cal were right, it was George Newton who was typing the letters, using his wife's creations to give him the information.'

She turned and led him back up the stairs, where they stood looking at the scene before them.

'We'll get forensics on it in the morning, but I think you're right, Jane, it's the only thing that makes sense, if you can call it that. Anything else of interest?' Sergeant Denton looked at Jane questioningly.

She led him into the main bedroom where he looked, with disquiet, at the bed and clothing arrangements before commenting, 'It looks like our Mr Newton has been refusing to accept that Mummy's dead.' A call from Nick distracted them and they returned down the stairs to the ground floor. 'What have you got, Nick?'

'I'm not sure, but the basement's interesting, come and have a look.' Nick led them down. 'It's been scrubbed clean, no doubt about it, the smell of bleach alone tells us that. And there's another smell, not sure what.'

'Fly spray.' Philip Denton spoke. 'There are empty cans in the kitchen bin. Too many to make sense.'

'And look here, Sarge, I shifted the boxes off the shelves, look at all the dead flies. Hundreds of them, dropped behind the boxes on the floor. Why would there be so many flies in a basement? Unless...'

'Unless there'd been a dead body down here!' Jane voiced their thoughts. 'He must have kept the girls here. We know they were following him. They could easily have followed him here.'

'It doesn't matter how much bleach he used, forensics will find traces. And, Jane, you're back with Chantelle Watson in the morning, you have to get the information from her. The sooner we have more of the story the better.' Sergeant Denton shook his head. 'Such a diminutive man, you wouldn't notice him. I still can't imagine him overpowering the girls, or killing Britney, or Barbara, for that matter.'

Sergeant Denton's musings were cut short by a call from one of the officers sent through from Rentham station, by Chief Inspector Carpenter, to help man the fort in such extenuating circumstances. 'Sarge, Mrs Spindlebury wants to talk, seems she wants to look after number one and distance herself from her husband as much as possible. Says she's got information about a murder. What d'you want me to do? Oh, and Mr Newton's in a terrible state about his mother. Says he needs to go to her. Says she's all he's got and he has to go and take care of her.'

'I'm on my way back now, Steve.' He turned to the others. 'Well this will be interesting, our Mrs Spindlebury wants to spill the beans about a murder. Now which one's that, d'you think? Maybe it wasn't all Mr Newton after all. And talking of Mr Newton, it seems he's extremely worried about his mother all alone in her cottage. I'll bet he is...'

WE WERE SO HAPPY

Fuelled by the wine and cognacs the party of four was in high spirits and wanted to keep going, but the restaurant was closing. 'We could go to the pub, Jules would let us have a couple of drinks in the bar I'm sure.' Cal winked at Sasha, trying to convey both his desire to have her all to himself, as well as his understanding that Tessa and Dave needed this.

'Or back to ours? We've got a bottle of whisky gathering dust, we could put it out of its misery?' Tessa and Dave looked hopefully at the other two.

Sasha grinned, squeezing Cal's hand and announced what a great idea it was, to much cheering. Her night with Cal was beginning to look more like a drunken party than a romantic coming together of the two of them under the sheets. But his answering squeeze told her that he understood. Hanging back, as Tessa and Dave went ahead, with Dave calling a cab, Sasha whispered to Cal. 'Sorry, I wanted tonight to be special for us, you know?' His arm snaking around her waist and pulling her against him told her he did know, as did his hungry kisses on her neck.

'It still will be, babe, we'll have a couple of drinks back at theirs and then I'm taking you back to the pub to have my evil way with you.' He pulled away and looked at her mischievously, 'If that's what you meant, if you're okay now?'

'That's exactly what I meant.' Sasha kissed him on the mouth hungrily. 'And I'm definitely okay now.'

They piled into the cab and headed for nine Riverside Gardens.

~

With Nick left at the Newton cottage, Jane accompanied Philip Denton back to the station. 'Let's go and see what Mrs Spindlebury's got for us shall we? I think we'll start with the letter Dorothy made about her cheating husband, that might get us a result.'

Rosemary Spindlebury read the offending mess of torn letters, their message clear. Her Reg had been cheating on her after all. And with the slutty blonde from the club. How could she have been so stupid? Any vestige of loyalty she'd felt towards him was gone in an instant. 'Where did you get this?' Surely Barbara hadn't concocted such a strange letter? 'Did someone send this to Reg?'

'Never mind about that, Mrs Spindlebury, the main thing is that it's clearly referring to your husband. Now why don't you just tell us everything from the beginning?' Sergeant Denton waited expectantly.

Rosemary spilled everything, the words tumbling out in a rush, and finally sat back, looking from one to the other of the officers. 'I'm telling you the truth, I wasn't involved in the heist, I only guessed about it later. Reg was my boyfriend, I knew he was involved with some dodgy people but he never talked about it. I was a young girl, it didn't matter to me where he got his money from as long as he had it. I only found out about the money after he asked me to go away with him. It was all very sudden, he didn't want me to tell anyone. You've got to understand, although I loved him, Reg could be, well, he could be quite scary if he wanted to be. He said if I went away with him I could never talk to any of my old friends or my family, but he promised me he'd give me a good life. And he did, we never wanted for anything. He said we should hide in plain sight, he's clever like that, Reg is, and he said we'd change our names just enough so we wouldn't make any mistakes. I got used to our new life, and by the time we moved here we were seen as a well-off couple, people treated us with respect, like they do when you've got money. Of course, I never knew the bastard was cheating on me, and with such a piece of trash. But anyway, then, out of the blue, the letters arrived.'

Philip and Jane looked at each other, knowingly. 'Letters, Mrs Spindlebury? Can you elaborate?'

Nodding, Rosemary Spindlebury blew her nose before continuing. 'We each got one. Mine said something horrible about my past, what I used to do. But it was cruel, vindictive, it called me a whore. It called me a vile stripper whore.' She looked at them pleadingly, 'But I never did that, I wasn't a prostitute. I did dance and, well, I was young, we all were, we danced and we took our clothes off.' Embarrassed, she couldn't look the officers in the eye.

'And the other letter, Rosemary?' Jane spoke gently, sensing the woman's discomfort at talking about her past.

'Well that really set Reg off. He was convinced I'd been talking, saying things I shouldn't to someone. I told him I hadn't but he didn't believe me. Someone knew about what he'd done. It said they knew what he'd done and he couldn't escape the law forever. Or something like that.'

'And what happened next, Rosemary? What did Reg do about it? Who did he think had sent the letters?'

'Well Barbara of course, Barbara Fenton, who else could it have been?' Rosemary's surprised expression caught them off guard.

Jane's puzzlement was evident. 'But why did Reg think it was Barbara Fenton who sent the letters?'

'Oh God, it wasn't was it? Oh what have I done? He'll kill me. But he said it must have been her, that's why he said he'd deal with it. It wasn't Barbara was it? I can tell by your faces, it was someone else. Oh poor Barbara, he killed her for nothing. Who was it? Who sent the letters? Who would do that?'

'Mrs Spindlebury, slow down. You're telling us that your husband killed Barbara Fenton because he thought she'd sent the letters?'

'He said I must have told her something. Barbara and I used to spend time together. We were friends, we used to have a girl's night together, watching TV, drinking wine, chatting, it was nice. Reg made me go through every time we'd ever been together, trying to work out what I'd said. There was this one night, we'd had a fair bit to drink and there was a show on the television about a group of youngsters in Essex. Well, I recalled saying something about how I used to work there, in the club. It was in Basildon you see, and they all went to the club, it's still there, different name and all that, but I recognised it straightaway. I remembered exclaiming that I used to work there. And then I realised what I'd said and I changed the subject. But Barbara was sloshed, we both were, and I doubt she remembered anything about it the next day. But Reg was convinced that was it. He said she knew about us, had probably found out all about what happened and knew who we really were. He said she'd blackmail us. Want money. He went out that night, told me to go to bed-' She paused, looking sad. 'But she didn't do it, did she? It wasn't her. Oh, Barbara.' Rosemary's voice was a whisper. 'That bastard killed her and she was my friend.'

Jane was actually feeling sorry for the woman. 'We can't give you any details, Mrs Spindlebury, we're still busy putting everything together. Can you tell us what happened next, after he said he'd deal with her?'

Rosemary Spindlebury continued with her story, describing her fear at what she'd thought Reg had done, and her horror at the discovery of Barbara's body.

'Poor Barbara Fenton,' Jane and Philip were back in the office, having returned Rosemary to holding. 'He killed her for no reason. She didn't know anything about their past. Such a cold-hearted act of cruelty. We've got him haven't we Sarge? We've got him for her murder?'

'It looks like it, Jane. We're beginning to make sense of it all finally. Reg Spindlebury murdered Barbara Fenton, George Newton abducted the girls somehow, and killed Britney Morton. We're still left with Peter Fenton's death, but it doesn't look like there was any foul play, just a terrible tragedy. Caused, of course, by the letter he received. And that brings us back to Mr Newton. And his wife of course, although I'm not sure how accountable she'll be given her current mental state. But indirectly they're both responsible for his distressed state on receiving the anonymous letter, and subsequently for the events that led to his death. Let's go and have a chat with Mr Newton about his mother now, shall we?'

~

Cal's phone rang from inside the kitchen, and Tessa brought it out to the patio, where they were enjoying the mild evening temperature. Thanking her, Cal frowned, looking at the caller's name. 'It's Jules, wonder why she's calling so late?' Answering the phone, he got up and walked to the end of the garden, looking out at the river.

Sasha watched him, hearing the murmur of his voice and noticing his hunched posture. He glanced back towards her a couple of times, his expression difficult to read. She thanked Tessa for the refill of whisky, sipping it while wondering what was going on with Cal. His voice was louder now, his hand movements angry, and suddenly he'd finished his conversation and was walking quickly back towards them. 'I'm really sorry, babe, I have to go and sort something out. Tess, Dave, thanks for a great evening. Sash, I'll explain everything later, but I really have to go. Trust me, okay? Everything's going to be fine, I just need to deal with something.'

'Well, I'll come with you.' Sasha was concerned. 'Whatever it is, Cal, let me come with you, it's late anyway.'

'No!' Cal's tone was harsh and abrupt. I need to get to the pub now and I need to go on my own. I'll explain everything in the morning, okay?' He softened, pulling Sasha towards him for a hug. 'I'm sorry, something's come up, something that I have to attend to. Look, why don't you stay here tonight? Would you do that? Stay with Tess and Dave, have another drink, enjoy the time together. I'll see you in the morning.' He kissed her, pulling away to call for a cab, and headed through the house to the front door.

Upset, Sasha wasn't sure what to do. Clearly Cal didn't want her with him. Her head swam slightly, the whisky going to her head. Maybe it was best if she did stay here. Whatever it was, Cal would sort it out, and she'd see him in the morning, find out all about it then.

'Yay, stay here, sis, you can sleep in Chantelle's room, the bed's all made up. It means we can stay up late, 'til we drop, like the old days. Let Cal deal with whatever it is. Let's finish this bottle!' Tessa was so happy, Sasha agreed with a grin. Why not? It had been a long time since she and her sister had enjoyed a sleepover. Tonight wouldn't have been the best night for her and Cal's first time anyway, she'd had far too much to drink. She put her concerns over Cal aside, whatever it was he was dealing with it.

'Okay, I'm staying! Dave, more whisky please!' She lit a cigarette, putting her worries aside and deciding to just go with the flow. 'But I warn you now, I'll need toast and tea later. Something's got to soak up all this booze if I'm ever going to sleep!'

~

It was hard to believe that this shrunken excuse for a man was responsible for abduction and murder. George Newton sat before them, shaking in his anxiety to impress upon them the importance of his mother's situation.

'Please, you've got to let me go to her. I'm all she has. She's all alone, she'll be wondering where I am.'

Neither Jane nor Philip were quite sure how to proceed. At Sergeant Denton's nod, Jane spoke. 'Mr Newton, P.C. Crossley is at your mother's cottage right now. Sergeant Denton and I were there earlier as well.' She spoke gently. 'Mr Newton, your mother doesn't need your help, or anyone's.' She looked at Philip for confirmation, before continuing. 'We found your mother's body, Mr Newton. Your mother's dead.'

'No, that can't be.' George looked confused. 'Mother's not dead. I was with her last night. She was fine. What have you done to her? Mother was fine...' His voice trailed off in confusion.

Trying again, Philip Denton spoke. 'Mr Newton, your mother's been dead for some time. A long time, by the looks of it. We've found the typewriter, George, the one you used to type your letters on.'

At this, George's eyes narrowed, a slyness creeping into his expression. 'Well I had to type the letters, Dorothy couldn't put the words together, just like Mother when he'd upset her. Don't you see? I was controlling *everything*! It was *my* words that people believed, *I* made things happen. I was planning on telling Mother about *him*, how I'd protected her from him, and eventually freed her from him. We were going to have sherry and cake, her favourite probably- she loves a cream slice, does Mother. My whole life I had to try to make things better, to *do* better, she- Mother would make me keep trying until I got it right, and then – oh, the joy... So that's all I ever did for Mother, tried to make things better. Everything I did was for Mother. I've always wanted her to be proud of me.' He sobbed quietly. 'But she never was, not really. Even after I got rid of him, she still wasn't happy. I did everything right. I just wanted her to be happy. But she wouldn't stop complaining. She blamed me, it was always my fault. Shouting. Always shouting. I couldn't bear her disappointment. I thought if I could just sort it out today she'd be proud of me.'

'What did you try to sort out today, George?'

'Why, the girl. Mother said I had to sort it out. She was right, of course. If I could just sort out the girl, once and for all, then everything would be alright. Mother and I could be happy together, just the two of us. But she wouldn't stop shouting, you see. I had to stop her, I had to stop her shouting at me. I couldn't stand it any longer. And she did stop. And then we were so happy. Everything was fine. Until those girls messed everything up. It wasn't my fault, you see? I didn't mean it to happen.' George stopped talking, lost in his thoughts, his eyes vacant.

'Alright, George, why don't you get some sleep? We'll talk again in the morning.' Sergeant Denton had had enough. This was beyond his pay grade. They needed a psychiatrist for this. It was all beginning to sound like a lot of mumbo jumbo to him- Mother this, and Mother that, and protecting Mother from some man, and Mother telling him to kill girls- not forgetting that Mother was dead herself-. He shook his head, no, definitely a job for a psychiatrist- let them have the pleasure of George Newton. A few minutes later he and Jane headed for their beds. Tomorrow was another day and they'd tie all the pieces together once and for all.

~

Nick Crossley heaved the shelf away from the wall, the basement now a jumble of boxes. He knew he should have waited until the morning, for the forensics team, but something was niggling at him. The amount of dead flies behind all the boxes made sense, if a girls' dead body had lain here slowly putrefying, but there were literally piles of them. Piles of crusted, dried out flies, some of them mere fragile crusts, as if they'd been here for years.

He looked at the rag stuffed hole he'd uncovered. Before he touched it he'd check what was the other side. With his torch in his hand, Nick followed the wall outside, trying to calculate the spot where he'd been inside, down in the basement. Shrubbery had grown over the old coal bunker, but he pulled it away, revealing its crumbled remains. Clearly it hadn't been used for years, probably decades, and, his suspicions confirmed, he returned to the basement.

He supposed he was just beyond getting freaked out by anything after all they'd uncovered at the cottage. Gazing at the exposed skeletal remains, Nick wondered who it had once been. He had a sneaking idea, but would wait until morning to alert the team, and then he'd make his enquiries. Right now he was knackered, and in need of coffee. Grimacing, he wondered if he could stomach anything from the kitchen.

Passing the open door to the sitting room, he swatted at a fly before pulling the door closed, and headed into the small kitchen. A cursory search revealed a lack of coffee but a fresh box of tea bags, that would have to do. He made himself a drink and sat down, yawning, to await daylight and the activity that would commence.

BORING PEOPLE LEADING BORING LIVES

Wilson Mwabila arrived first, with forensics right behind him. Sergeant Denton was at the cottage a few minutes later, P.C. Weaver having gone to the hospital to speak to Chantelle, and P.C. Crossley was instructed to go home and have a rest.

'No way, Sarge, I'm fine. I had a bit of a nap in the kitchen. And there's something I want to show you.'

Wilson examined the body in the sitting room with interest. 'Well, this is fascinating. We've got a case of partial mummification here. Not complete of course, the temperatures would not have remained consistent enough, but the relatively mild indoor temperatures, and the closed area, have allowed this body to become quite well preserved.' Gently he eased the upper part of the body forward, examining the head. 'The back of the head has sustained an injury of some kind. We can clearly see the damage to the skull. This was probably the cause of death, and would likely have occurred approximately six to twelve months ago, although it's not an exact science. The clothing is interesting. The deceased could not have been wearing these clothes when she was killed. Her clothes would have been destroyed by the body's fluids over time. It looks like someone's been playing dress-up with our corpse, Sergeant. I must say, the cases from Parva Crossing are certainly proving interesting, if you'll excuse my slight flippancy, but I do find it helps one to cope with the unpleasant nature of this business.'

Wilson Mwabila began organising the movement of the body to his mortuary in Rentham, with his team, and forensics wanted to know where they should start. Sergeant Denton was about to send them to the basement when Nick stopped him. 'Sarge, if they can hold off from the basement for a moment, there's something I need to show you.'

'I don't believe this, I honestly don't.' Philip Denton was grim as he looked at Nick's discovery. 'What the exact hell? I mean, this is turning into something out of a horror film. Death Cottage would make a good title.' He phoned Inspector Kavanagh with the news, before turning back to Nick. 'Nick, call Wilson, he's about to leave, tell him we need him down here.'

'I'll have to charge you double, Sergeant.' Wilson Mwabila's eyes were alight with interest. 'What have we here?' He bent down, inspecting the skeleton. 'Any ideas on who this might be at all?'

'I've got an idea, Wilson, tell me if I'm wrong, but I reckon it's a male and I'd say he's been here for about fifty or sixty years.' Nick looked at the others, feeling quite proud of his discovery.

'You might not be wrong, P.C. Crossley. Hmm yes, looks like a male. See here? This is the pelvis, it's quite narrow, a female's would be wider. And the skull, here it's nice and clear, see how the forehead slopes backwards? That's the case with males, a female's would be more rounded, and smaller. The teeth don't look too worn, which means he was fairly young when he died. Now, I wonder why this fellow died.' Wilson Mwabila continued his careful examination.

'Nick, what are you thinking?' Sergeant Denton was impressed.

'I reckon it's the husband, Sarge. Either the mummy upstairs did it, killed her husband, or George Newton did. Course, he'd have to have been a kid at the time, but nothing about him would surprise me.'

'*Even after I got rid of him.*' Sergeant Denton nodded, quoting the words George Newton had spoken the day before.

'Not much clothing remaining,' Wilson was murmuring as he worked. 'Of course, synthetic fabric lasts longer. We've got remains of what looks like a waistband here. The bones have some fine vertical cracks in them. Yes, that would make sense, probably got freezing down here each winter. I'll get him moved to my mortuary and do further examinations. Hard to say what caused his death, possibly hit his head, there's some skull damage here, and here. Ah, and here at the back of the skull, yes, this could easily have been caused by a blow to the back of the head. Very interesting, gentlemen. It looks like I've got a busy day ahead.'

The officers thanked Wilson Mwabila and left him to organise the removal of the skeleton.

Once Philip Denton had advised forensics, he and Nick walked outside, breathing in the fresh air. 'Every time we think we're at the end of this crazy nightmare something else happens, another body crops up. Let's hope this is the last one. I don't know about you, Nick, but I've just about had a bellyful of this.' He kicked the old cast iron door stop on the front step, in irritation. 'Damn that hurt, that thing's stronger than it looks.'

'Me too, Sarge, but I think we're done. Think about it, George Newton's got some major obsession with Mummy, poor sick little man, and we've got her dead in there-' he indicated the cottage behind them with a tilt of his head, '-and a bloke dead in the basement who I'm convinced will turn out to be Daddy. Pretty much everything about all this revolves around George Newton. He held the girls here, killed one of them, and was obviously trying to kill the other one. Still don't know why or how that all happened, hopefully Jane's getting some more info from the Watson girl. Reginald Spindlebury might have killed Barbara Fenton, but it was George's letters that set him off. Same thing with Peter Ford, a letter from George upset him, the rest is history. Course, if you want to go back even further, then both those deaths are the fault of his mad wife, I mean, she started the whole letter thing with her little works of art didn't she?' Nick stopped talking, shaking his head.

Philip Denton looked at him proudly. 'You know, Nick, I couldn't have summarised it all any better myself. Nicely put, I reckon you'll make a good detective some time soon, son.'

Pleased, Nick grinned. 'Thanks, Sarge, but to be fair, a lot of the credit goes to Sasha, she and Cal found out a lot of stuff that's helped us.'

~

Jane Weaver and Chantelle had hit it off immediately, which had helped enormously with Jane's questioning. Chantelle was feeling so much better and with the promise that she'd be able to go home, if Doctor Montgomery signed off on it, she was feeling full of spirits. 'Go on, Chantelle, you were going to tell me about following Mr Newton.'

Chantelle's expression darkened. 'Yeah, well, we didn't know his name, we'd just followed him a few times before. He wasn't the only one, we followed people all the time. It was Brit's idea, she thought it'd be a laugh, see what people were up to, if they had secrets. Course, no-one did, it got a bit boring, to be honest, everyone was just going about their boring lives in this boring village, and just being, well, boring.' Jane nodded, indicating she should get back on track. 'Well anyway, the one time we'd followed him, we'd gone all the way to the, to that-' she stopped, anxiety filling her eyes.

'It's okay, Chantelle, you're safe. Tell me what happened.'

'Well, okay, so we followed him to that place, the cottage. First we thought he lived there, but then we realised he only stayed a short while. We could hear him talking to someone, laughing and going on. Brit reckoned he was having an affair. She said just 'cause he was old didn't mean he wasn't doing it. I remember us thinking it was so funny, and we tried to see more through the window, see who the woman was. So we saw him holding her arm out, spraying perfume on it, and that's when we saw that something wasn't right. It wasn't a woman. It was more like some kind of doll or something. Anyway, suddenly he looked up, right at us, it seemed, and we panicked, we ran and hid in the bushes. He even came right outside, checking, but we waited for ages then legged it home.'

'You're doing really well, Chantelle,' Jane was encouraging. 'How about I get us a coke from the vending machine?' She returned with the drinks and encouraged Chantelle to carry on. 'So you and Britney went back again? Did you follow him? Can you remember when it was?'

Chantelle shook her head. 'I'm not sure, might have been the next day, or the one after. To be honest I wasn't that keen. I mean, the guy was clearly a freak, but Brit said we had to solve the mystery, and I suppose I was kind of intrigued. I mean, he had something in there, sitting in a chair, that he talked to and kind of played with. Gross. So yeah, we followed him, and this time he left the front door open a bit. Brit said she was going to try and have a look inside. I said she wouldn't dare.'

Chantelle's lip trembled, her eyes watering. 'I hid and watched her sneak in the door. It was dead quiet, then I heard him shout and he grabbed something off the doorstep. The next thing was there was a kind of thud, and then it was quiet. I think it was Brit. I think he hit her or something. I didn't know what to do, but she was in there. I thought if I went and shouted at him he'd let her go.' Chantelle's eyes were misty with tears as she clenched her hands on the bed covers.

'Is that what you did? Did you go in? Did you see Britney?'

'No, that's the thing. I mean, I did go in, even though I was terrified. But it was all quiet and there was no sign of him or Britney. I could see the thing in the lounge, in the chair, it was like it was grinning. There was a door open, I could see steps going down, so I thought maybe Brit was down there hiding from him or something. I remember standing there and calling her quietly. And then- and then I saw him behind me, and then I was just in pain, for a split second, and then I don't remember anything.'

Jane had to lean forward, Chantelle was speaking so softly.

'The next thing I remember is being in the pitch black. And being in pain. My head was killing me and my whole body hurt. I was tied up and he'd put something over my eyes. Oh, Jane, it was so awful. And I needed the loo, but I couldn't move. I tried to call Britney quietly, I was so scared that he was there. But she didn't reply, she never made a sound. And then he was there, making me drink some water. And then it was just darkness, all the time, sometimes I could hear him talking upstairs, and laughing, and then he'd give me more water. Sometimes he'd give me something to eat, like a sandwich or some crackers, but most of the time I just felt sick and kind of woozy like I couldn't stay awake. And it was so hot and stuffy. And I messed myself.' Chantelle cried softly, not able to meet Jane's eyes.

Jane reached out a hand and rested it comfortingly on Chantelle's fluttering hand, trying to soothe her.

'He had me on plastic, and sometimes he put fresh plastic under me. The smell was awful. My clothes were all wet and soiled. And then the smell got worse and there were flies. There were hundreds of flies buzzing around all the time. I still tried to call Brit but I think I kind of knew. I knew she was dead. I knew that's what the bad smell was. He kept spraying stuff to kill flies but more kept coming. But then one time I woke up and I remember, I was really thirsty and hungry, but he never came. It just seemed like days that he didn't come, I don't know how long it was. I think he'd been drugging me, that's why I'd been so woozy before and sleeping all the time. But then I thought, well he hasn't come so maybe I can try to get out, and for the first time I was with it enough to be able to work on the knots and stuff, and I got them untied.' Chantelle stopped and drank some coke before continuing.

'I remember feeling so scared. I thought he was going to come back and tie me up again. Britney wasn't there. And it stank of bleach.' She stopped suddenly. 'He killed her didn't he, Jane? Tell me. Is Britney dead?' Her wide eyes looked beseechingly at Jane, who nodded slowly.

'I'm afraid so, Chantelle. We found her body. We think she'd been dead for some time, probably from not long after she went inside the cottage. He disposed of her body in the river. From what you've told me it sounds like something happened to her straightaway. She probably didn't know anything about it.'

Nodding, Chantelle gritted her teeth and carried on, holding back the tears for now. 'I remember feeling so weak I didn't think I'd make it up the stairs. I drank some water from a bottle on the floor. That was stupid. But I wasn't thinking straight. But I got out and I managed to walk along the road. I was just praying for someone to come, but no-one did, and I could feel myself getting all woozy again. I was dizzy and I remember thinking you stupid girl, you just drugged yourself and you're trying to escape and now he'll just take you back, and no-one will ever know. And then a car came. I was so relieved. I tried to wave for help but I couldn't stand up properly, and then I recognised the car and I knew it was him. He drove straight at me. I don't remember anything else.'

Jane hugged Chantelle, 'You've been fabulous, my love, and really brave. You have a rest now, and I'm really hoping the doc lets you go home today. I'll see you soon, okay?'

Chantelle nodded, smiling, and feeling better for having told her story. All she wanted to do now was forget all about it, if she ever could.

~

Smiling, Sasha pressed herself against Cal's firm body, wrapping her arms around him as she pulled him into her. Disturbed, someone was calling her, she opened her eyes.

'Sash, wake up! How's the head? Mine's not too good, that flippin' whisky! Listen, here's some tea, Dave and I are off to the hospital, we're hoping Chants can come home today. Make yourself some toast if you want. I'll see you later, sis.' Tessa planted a kiss on her sister's head and was gone, leaving Sasha to come to, groaning as her head pounded painfully. Dammit, it had been a nice dream... Looking at her watch, she gasped, it was almost lunchtime.

~

With the team back at the police station, it was almost time for Reg Spindlebury's transfer. Rosemary would be released for now, but had asked to see her husband. Inspector Kavanagh had approved it, but wanted them to observe on camera.

'Well, girl, I reckon this is it. We've had a good time over the years, but I don't think I'll wriggle myself out of this one.' Reg smiled at his wife ruefully.

'Oh, Reg,' Rosemary's eyes filled with angry tears. 'You're a bloody fool. Barbara never wrote those letters. It was someone else. She didn't know anything and you killed her. I'll never forgive you for that, Reg.' Rosemary stood up to leave. 'And another thing, you shouldn't have cheated on me, and with that blonde slapper from the club. How could you, Reg? You deserve everything you get, you bastard.'

'What's that? I never cheated on you, Ro, I swear. And who did write the damn letters then? Alright, I admit it, I went to Barbara's that night, I wanted her dead, but I'm telling you Ro, she- Ro? Come back here, Ro, don't you walk away from me! I'm telling you, she was-' Reg was still roaring after Rosemary left the room.

Sargeant Denton nodded, 'That'll do nicely,' and switched off the camera.

'She was already dead.' Reg finished his sentence, but there was no-one to hear it. 'Someone else killed her,' he started to laugh. He'd wanted her dead, had gone there to do the job, but someone else had beaten him to it. And now he was going down for her murder anyway.

Jane Weaver was impatient to update them on her chat with Chantelle. 'Sarge, loads of interesting stuff from Chantelle. But most importantly for now, it sounds like he hit Britney Morton with something when she went into the cottage. The girls had followed him a few times and had seen his mother in the chair. They wanted to find out more and Britney went in, I'm thinking he hit her and she fell down the basement stairs and that's what killed her. Chantelle went into the cottage to look for her and it sounds like he hit her too. She said that after Britney went in he picked something up from the front doorstep, just before she heard a thud.'

'The door stop!' Nick's eyes gleamed. 'Sarge, remember you kicked it? You said it was stronger than it looked? You hurt your foot.'

'Yes, great lump of a cast iron heart-shaped thing. Call forensics, they'll still be there. Tell them to bag it- tell them it's probably the murder weapon.'

Nick looked at Sergeant Denton. 'D'you know what I'm thinking, Sarge?'

'The father? He could have used it on his father, bit heavy for a lad but it's possible.' Philip nodded as Jane looked confused.

'Someone want to tell me what's going on?'

'Sorry, Jane, forgot to tell you the latest from Death Cottage. We found another body. Yeah I know, crazy right? Squashed into the old coal bunker down in the basement. Just a pile of bones really, it's been there that long. Long enough for George Newton to grow up and become an old man.' Nick shook his head, 'Old Georgie boy probably killed both his parents.'

Jane was suitable shocked. 'Have you asked him about it yet? And what about his wife? What about Dorothy? D'you think she knew about all this? That she was married to a murderer?'

'Haven't the foggiest. We're going to have to try and interview her, although I'm not sure what help she'll be to us. Nick, you and Jane go and have a further chat with Mr Newton. Ask him about the body in the basement. Let's see what he has to say about that.'

George sat looking at the officers, a look of resignation on his face. 'He was a bully. He hit Mother, you see. I couldn't bear to see her crying. I just wanted to take care of her, we were so happy together when he wasn't around. And then he'd come in and spoil everything. There was so much shouting.' He leant forward, his head in his hands. 'I tried to help. I took Mother's letters, all ruined from the drinks spilling on them, and I typed him better ones. Mother was always so proud of me when I typed nicely. I thought I could get him to go away. If it was just the two of us everything would be alright. I woke up one night and there was so much shouting, Mother had been drinking and was crying. And then he hit her really hard. She wouldn't wake up, she just lay there. I thought he'd killed her.' He looked up at them calmly. 'I wanted to kill him. I got the heavy door stop from the front step and told him there was a noise in the basement, and then I hit him on the head.' He looked surprised. 'It was that easy. He just crumpled, and then fell down the stairs.'

'So you admit that you killed your father, George?'

'Oh yes.' Sitting up straight in his chair, George was calm and matter of fact. 'It took me ages to roll and pull his body to the coal bunker. It was never used so I knew no-one would ever look there. It was all broken outside, the bricks had fallen in. I managed to get him inside and then I covered him up with old sacks and things. I put the door stop back and went to check on Mother. She was breathing and making the odd groan. I remember feeling so happy. She was alive! It would be just the two of us. That's when I had the idea of the letter.' He beamed at then proudly. 'I went up to the attic and typed a letter from him, telling her that he was leaving her. I put it on the side table by the front door. And then I packed a suitcase with some of his clothes and put it down in the basement. Mother never went down there. I helped Mother to bed that night and crawled in beside her. I remember thinking that this was how it would be now, and it was wonderful. I laid there breathing her beautiful lavender scent. I can honestly say I'd never felt happier in my life.'

'And then it was just you and your mother?' Nick encouraged him to keep talking, his mouth twisted slightly in distaste.

'It was just Mother and me. We were so very happy. She didn't seem that upset about his letter, or his leaving. Eventually we forgot all about him, everyone did. It was like he'd never existed.'

'But one day you left your mother and married Dorothy?' It was Jane's turn to keep George talking.

Sighing, George spoke again. 'I was faithful to Mother as long as I could be. But Mother wanted me to be the best man that I could be. She was quite right to tell me of my shortcomings. Dear Mother, she had my best interests at heart. But sometimes it hurt. As long as I could make her happy again then I didn't mind though. I knew what she wanted me to do when she invited Dorothy to tea.' He looked up in surprise. 'Dorothy and I were very happy together. No children, of course. And Dorothy was very understanding about my relationship with Mother. She never interfered. And the years went by...' George's voice faded off, his eyes glazing over, lost in memories.

The officers looked at each other in surprise. George was crying, his voice like a young boy's. 'But Mother kept criticising me, saying I wasn't doing well enough. One day it was my job, another my house. Nothing I did was ever good enough for her. I just wanted everything to be like it used to be. I wanted us to have fun, to laugh about things, share our day with each other. But she wouldn't stop. She said I'd never amounted to anything. I wanted to stop the hateful things she was saying. It was easy of course. I just took the door stop and hit her. I sat her down in her chair, cleaned her up, and made us some tea. And after that it was just like the old days again. Everything was fine.' His face darkened. 'Until those girls spoiled everything. They ruined it all. And then Mother started complaining again, telling me I had to sort it all out. But I did, I sorted it all out, I had my plan. Mother was going to be so pleased with me. And now it's all gone wrong. And she's all on her own.'

'Alright, George, I think we all need a break. We'll get you a cup of tea brought through.' P.C.s Weaver and Crossley left the room. 'Amazing,' Nick whistled. 'One murder weapon for three murders, spanning back over half a century, and it's just been sitting there on the doorstep for anyone to find.'

'Except no-one was looking. Until now.' Jane switched the kettle on, in need of tea.

WE NEED A NICE CUP OF TEA

Sasha thanked the cab driver and hurried into the pub, anxious to find out what the problem had been with Cal the night before.

'Sash.' Jules's voice held a warning in it, her expression sympathetic.

'Jules, what is it? Have you seen Cal?' She followed the direction of Jules's eyes towards the door through to the rooms. A woman was emerging, carrying a bag. Sasha's first thought was how beautiful she was. Her second thought was how heavily pregnant she was. Her third thought being why was Cal following the woman, carrying suitcases?

'Cal? What's going on? Is everything alright?' She couldn't read Cal's expression, his eyes guarded, not wanting to meet hers.

He looked at Sasha, putting the cases down by the entrance to the pub before walking towards her. 'Sash, I'm really sorry, I was going to tell you.'

'Tell me what?' she looked in confusion as the woman walked up beside Cal and put her hand proprietorially on his arm.

'Cal? Tell me what, Cal? Who's this?'

'I'm his wife.' The woman smiled at Sasha smugly. 'Cal, we really need to go.'

Cal nodded. 'Wait for me outside. *Please*.' He waited for the woman to leave before turning back to Sasha. 'Sash, I can explain, I-'

But Sasha didn't want to hear whatever Cal had to say. 'It doesn't matter, Cal, I get it.' She turned and walked through the door, climbing the stairs to her room.

Her phone pinged with a message, waking her up. Not sure how long she'd been asleep, she checked her watch, surprised to find that it was already late afternoon. *Chants is home! Celebration tonight at ours! Just like the old days! Bring Cal, we're getting pizza! Tess xx*

Her eyes were crusty from her earlier tears, and she rubbed them, trying to make sense of what had happened with Cal. He'd lied to her. All along, he'd been lying, he had a wife. And not only that, he was going to be a father. She'd really thought they had something special. And to think that last night she'd been planning on sleeping with him. She shook her head. What a complete bastard. She didn't want to hear what he had to say. She didn't ever want to hear from him again. Angrily she brought up his number, blocking it and deleting it from her phone. *Another bad choice in men bites the dust.* And then she replied to Tessa. *Great news! I'll see you later, just me! xx*

~

With Reg Spindlebury transferred to Essex, and George Newton awaiting transfer to the larger holding cells in Rentham, it was suddenly quite calm and peaceful at the station. Jane decided to tidy up some of the papers strewn across the table in their task room. She placed Dorothy's letters, *or works of art*, one of top of another, smiling at the childlike arrangement of stickers, and the letters forming their jumbled words. What problems the woman had caused with her spying. She supposed the letters would have stayed undiscovered in the old post box for years, if it hadn't been for her husband using them to cause trouble, and all borne from a childhood desire to *make things better*. Jane shook her head at the craziness of it all. Placing the last letter on top of the pile, she glanced at it. *I know why you all sleep all day. Devil's work at night. Bright lights.*

Something about the words struck Jane as interesting. Of course, they could just be made up rubbish, like many of Dorothy's ramblings, pure figments of her wild imagination. But Jane wasn't a police officer for nothing. People who sleep all day... and bright lights at night... She had an idea and looked around for the street map, shoving the other papers and items aside so that she could spread it out on the table. There were twelve other houses easily visible from the Newton house, excluding Maureen Ford's and the deceased Barbara Fenton's. No harm in going to take a quick look. She'd change out of her uniform first though.

Ten minutes later and Jane was parked in an adjoining road. She strolled along, casually checking out the houses of interest. Kids played in gardens, doors were hooked open, windows too, so that sounds from indoors drifted out to join the late-afternoon laughter of the children. This was true of all but one of the houses. Four, Hill View was silent, its curtains closed fast against the sun's weakening rays. Keeping her walk casual, Jane turned and wandered down the road that would lead her, by turning right again, into the road with properties backing onto the house in question. Looking down the open driveway of the house behind Four, Hill View, Jane could clearly see past the end of its garden. The back of the sleeping house was as closed up as the front. Not one curtain was open. She retraced her steps and returned to the station.

Nick was on his way down to storage with the boxes of papers and other objects which Jane had begun tidying earlier. 'Nick, hold on, there's something interesting I want to show you.' She indicated that they should go into their back office. 'There's a map in here somewhere,' she said, rummaging through the box's contents.

'This is easier.' Nick turfed everything onto the desk in one go, receiving an aggrieved look from Jane. 'What are we looking for?'

'The map, and one of Dorothy's letters. And then we need to find out who lives at Four, Hill View. Maybe you could look it up quickly?' She glanced up at Nick, but he was flicking through a notebook.

'I think I can tell you that. It may well be someone called Burton. Look at this, Dorothy's notes, all her little reminders of who was doing what. She's written it all down, the minutiae of everyday life in a village, or her perception of everyday life, anyway, which was clearly somewhat twisted.'

Grabbing the notebook, Jane's eyes scanned the entry regarding the Burton household at Four, Hill View. *Curtains closed all day. No-one goes out. Lights always on. Bad people come at night.* 'Nick, I've just been there, the curtains are all closed tight, windows heavily condensed, no sign of life. If Dorothy's notes are correct we could have a weed house right here under our noses. We need to tell the Sarge. Maybe our Dorothy's self-imposed surveillance operations will help us catch some more bad guys.'

Sergeant Denton returned to the station a few minutes later, accompanied by Inspector Kavanagh, both replete from their golf club lunch. They looked at Jane and Nick's eager expressions. 'Don't tell me,' said Andrew Kavanagh, 'What've we got, another ten dead bodies turned up in the vicar's garden this time? Tell me the worst, Officers.'

With explanations given, it was decided that Jane and Nick would carry out further investigations once it was dark.

~

Sasha showered and dressed, before making her way downstairs to be met by a concerned looking Jules. 'Sash, are you okay? I didn't know, I had no idea, she just pitched up. If it's any consolation, I don't think Cal was-' Sasha stopped her.

'It's okay, Jules, really. I'm fine. Everything's fine. Cal's married. He's going to be a father. I've been a fool. But I've got a niece fresh out of hospital and a pizza night to get to at my sister's. I'm going to spend some precious time with my family, we've got some celebrating to do.' On impulse, she hugged Jules tightly. 'Thanks, Jules, for everything. I'll be fine. I'll be back later.'

Tessa was concerned. 'But why no Cal, Sash? What's going on? Did you two have a fight? Talk to me.'

But Sasha was firm. 'Tonight's Chantelle's night. It's your night. We never knew if we'd see this day, let's enjoy it.' She looked at the three of them. 'I love you guys. Let's open some wine and eat this pizza, it smells divine and I'm starving.'

It was a good evening in the end, hard not to have fun when everyone was so happy. Sasha entered into the spirit of it, taking pictures on her phone of them all, for posterity. She left them amid much hugging and kissing, promising to see them again tomorrow. Falling into bed a while later she scrolled through the photos, smiling at their happy expressions. She'd put some of these on Graffic, but not now. Right now she needed to sleep. And not think about Cal.

~

Chief Inspector Carpenter, having been informed of the suspicions surrounding the possible weed house, had insisted on sending through a team from Rentham. They would take over the operation once Jane and Nick had briefed them. The two officers were informed of this just as they parked, ready to begin their observations of the property. Both were disappointed, but aware that these situations could be dangerous, depending on who was inside. 'Let's go and take a gander anyway, just a stroll around.' Nick was keen to check out the property himself.

Jane put a hand on his arm, stilling him, as they approached the house. The gentle breeze was blowing in their direction bringing with it an unpleasant smell. 'Smell that, Nick?'

He nodded. 'Yep, nasty, and listen.' They stood still, adjusting their hearing to the night, picking up the soft whir of machinery. 'Fans?'

Jane nodded as they retraced their steps to wait for the team.

~

Mrs Pringle was in fine fettle when she opened up the chemist in the morning. She'd recovered from her shock at her discovery at Mrs Newton's cottage, and was eager to welcome customers and hopefully indulge in some pleasant conversation. Not that she'd gossip of course. But so much had happened, and to top it all, the village was abuzz with the story of a huge drugs bust in the village during the night.

'Really, Sheila, I just don't know what's become of our little village, I really don't.' The two women leant on the counter, studying the newspaper. Des Barnsley had done himself proud, it seemed.

DEATH COTTAGE!
SERIAL MURDERER UNDER ARREST!
MISSING LOCAL MAN'S REMAINS FOUND!
CHANTELLE WATSON, LOCAL HERO, OUT OF HOSPITAL!
GETAWAY DRIVER FROM FORTY-YEAR-OLD CASH HEIST CAUGHT!

DEAD MUMMY FOUND MUMMIFIED IN LOCAL COTTAGE! *(He'd been particularly proud of that one.)*
POISON PEN LETTERS!

The newspaper was a veritable treasure trove of grisly stories and the two women lapped up every word.

~

Dorothy Newton hummed to herself as she listened to the staff chatting amongst themselves. The talk was all about the house in Hill View and the discovery of the cannabis farm. She smiled and nodded at her friends as they praised her. Yes, she'd been right, she'd known something was wrong at the Burton house.

In an increasingly rare moment of lucidity, she turned her attention to the newspaper and started to laugh. George had been a busy boy it seemed. Of course she'd known what he'd done to his father, he'd talked about it in his sleep enough times, but his mother was a pleasant surprise. Turning the page she studied the colour photo of Reg Spindlebury, chuckling at his stupid yellow cravat and his tweed cap. That had been a clever move of George's, to rope her in like that. It hadn't quite worked out as he'd hoped of course, he was still going to spend the rest of his life in jail for three murders, but he had managed to send Reg down for Barbara's murder.

Had she known it was really George that night? Maybe, but Reg Spindlebury deserved everything he got. He really shouldn't have been cruel to George that night at the club. That wasn't nice, George hadn't deserved that.

The fog drifted back into Dorothy's brain, and her thoughts were wiped away, never to be remembered. She began to hum, rocking back and forth in her chair.

~

'Well I knew those Spindleburys had something to hide. Where did they get their money from I always said. Didn't I always say that, Sheila? And him not only a thief but a killer too, what a world we live in. And I always had my suspicions about George Newton, always thought there was something off about him. Right from a boy, if I think about it, the way he and his mother were so close. It isn't healthy, I used to say. But of course no-one listened, they never do. And all that perfume he was always buying for her, and to think she was in that cottage dead as a dodo this past year or more. Well I don't need to tell you what a shock it was, Sheila, to find her sitting there like a doll out of a horror film. I nearly died myself from the shock. I had a feeling he'd done something to the father, years ago I had my suspicions, but it doesn't do to gossip out of turn does it? I'm not one for that. And as for those nasty letters, pure venom, goodness only knows the trouble they caused. Well that poor Mr Ford's a shining example, may his soul rest in peace. Of course Dorothy didn't know what she was saying, but George really ought to have known better. Those poor girls, now that's another story altogether.' Mrs Pringle racked her brains, trying to find an angle, something she'd been suspicious about, but before she could come up with anything, the door chimed. They had customers. *Oh, there was Des Barnsley.* She straightened up, adjusting her blouse. Today was going to be a wonderful day. 'Let's get the kettle on, Sheila, I think we need a nice cup of tea.'

Sheila did as she was bade, before returning to the counter while she waited for the kettle to boil. She sighed, shaking her head. 'So much harm done from a few senseless lies, and innocent village lives ruined by cruel village lies.'

'Well said, Sheila, mind if I quote you on that?' Des Barnsley was already taking out his notebook.

Mrs Pringle glared at her. *Why hadn't she thought of that?* 'Sheila, the tea, if you don't mind.'

The End

EPILOGUE

Sasha hit the road, blasting her music as the village of Parva Crossing receded in her rearview mirror, her voice singing along tunelessly with Gloria Gaynor until she stopped at a service station for a drink.

Idly she flicked through her phone as she sipped her tea, smiling at some of the photos in her gallery and skipping quickly past the ones of her and Cal. She clicked onto her Graffic account, remembering she had a ton of notifications, and frowned at the unfamiliar name. Someone had tagged her repeatedly. Odd. Clicking on the account, she viewed the array of photographs in which she was tagged.

A female appeared in a number of the photos, a hood covering her head, thus hiding her identity, her arms and legs bound. The caption was the same for each photograph.

@sashablue So you think you're a detective now.
Let's see how good you are. #sashablue #findthegirl
#beautifulart #cansashasaveher #livingart

She was going to need a strong drink when she got home, Sasha Blue had a new mystery to solve.

AFTERWORD & A FEW INSIDER SECRETS!

I had great fun writing this book, and slipped in many fond anecdotes, as well as memories, one such memory being that of Dartford, in Kent. I grew up in this town and any comments are made in the spirit of fondness, as a former 'Dartford girl'.

Sasha Blue needed a social media account to post photos to, and this is how Graffic came about. Graffic features heavily in my next book – Graphic Lies – coming soon. It will all make sense to you then!

Is Sasha Blue modelled on the author, you may ask? Well, I definitely drink too much, and probably smoke too much, but I've made a great man choice in my wonderful husband, so Sasha and I don't share that in common! We do, however, share the painful experience of living with severe endometriosis, something with which fellow sufferers will sympathise.

Oh, and that piercing and dragonfly tattoo of Sasha's? Come on, did you seriously think I'd tell you if we share that in common as well? Some things will just have to remain a mystery! But I'll share this snippet with you instead - we both love the same pizza - I guess we both have excellent taste!

Why does Chief Inspector Stanley Carpenter love Arran whisky so much? Well, here's one of those sneaky little 'author privileges' we get to indulge in as writers. Stanley Carpenter was my grandad and I loved him very much. I also love the Isle of Arran very much (if you've visited this special island off the west coast of Scotland you'll understand why), as well as its Arran Whisky, so it seemed the perfect fit to have C.I. Carpenter passing out drams of Arran Whisky to his team.

Aren't poison pen letters a little passé you may ask? Well, perhaps, although I believe they still exist, maybe just in their modern form, via social media. However, as I grew up with an enduring love for works by greats such as Dame Agatha Christie and Ruth Rendell (Baroness Rendell, CBE), I had a desire to write something with a hint of nostalgia. I think it works! But you, my readers, will be the judge of that. I hope you found the same pleasure in reading this book as I enjoyed in writing it.

DON'T MISS THE NEXT SASHA BLUE MYSTERY!

Graphic Lies – Available on all Amazon stores.

Someone's been tagging Sasha Blue on her Graffic account. The mystery person has been posting photos of a female, bound and hooded, with the caption:

@sashablue So you think you're a detective now. Let's see how good you are. #sashablue #findthegirl #beautifulart #cansashasaveher #livingart.

The scary thing is that some of the photos were taken in Sasha's own flat in Shepherd's Bush...

Her stalker builds up a following, with girls copying the poses in the photos, and Sasha knows she needs to put a stop to it, fast, and find the girl.

As she investigates, Sasha becomes increasingly sure that she knows who the woman in the photos is, and that she herself is a target...

Her friend's ex-boyfriend, Miles, helps Sasha, and she's not complaining. Miles is hot, kind, and *very* attractive. Maybe she's finally found a decent guy...

Rage, tragedy, past secrets, romantic hopes, and some skilful detective work are thrown into the mix in Graphic Lies, the second, darker, book in the Sasha Blue Mystery Series.

ABOUT THE AUTHOR

Linzi Carlisle grew up in Dartford, Kent, in the UK, before moving to Africa, where she met her husband. She spent thirteen memorable years in Chingola, Zambia, and five years enjoying the wines in the Winelands of the Western Cape, before settling in the Garden Route in South Africa. She and her husband live in the beautiful town of George, nestled between the Outeniqua Mountains and the Indian Ocean. They have been the proud parents of many beloved children of the four-legged variety over the years, these being, at the time of publication, two beautiful rescue cats.

A MESSAGE FROM LINZI…

Enormous thanks for choosing to read Village Lies!

If you enjoyed it and want to stay in touch and keep up to date with new releases, you can follow me in a number of ways, as well as visiting my blog page, or following my Amazon author page, for updates on my books.

I love social media interaction and am active on many platforms, so I'd love to hear from you!

How about a photo of you with your copy of Village Lies? Or a creative Instagram post!

Please also feel free to review Village Lies on Amazon, Instagram, Goodreads, or any other e-store, as well as on your own blog or social media account.

Nothing beats word of mouth! Sharing book recommendations is one of the ways I've been able to enjoy many great books over the years, and have hopefully returned the favour time and again. Chat to your friends and family- it's a great way to help readers find out about my books!

Thank you! Here's that list!

Blogger: www.linzicarlisle.blogspot.com
Instagram: @linzicarlisleauthor
Facebook: @linzicarlisleauthor
Amazon: amazon.com/author/linzicarlisle
Goodreads: goodreads.com/linzicarlisle
Twitter: @linzicauthor

Printed in Great Britain
by Amazon